"I'm not strange, weird, off, nor crazy, my reality is just different than yours."

— LEWIS CARROLL

MAD WORLD

Lost Souls

BRANDON T BERNARD

MAD WORLD: Lost Souls

First Edition 2021

Any reference to historical events, real people, or real places are used fictitiously. Names, characters, images, and places are products of the author's imagination.

ISBN: 979-8-9851510-0-8

To Mom & Dad
for not always understanding,
but always encouraging my curiosity.

MAD WORLD

·LOST SOULS·

BRANDON T. BERNARD

THE PAST

PAT & BILL

The light from the runes of the four pillars flared and faded like an unnatural, angry heartbeat. Each throb dimmer than the last. This was the only source of light in the cavernous throne room. Pat and Bill had to rely on the pulses of light to maneuver through the tangled bodies and shattered stone as they raced for the massive doors rumbling closed. Bill lost his footing in a pool of blood, but Pat grabbed his wrist and yanked him back in stride. As the glow faded, so did the woman's screams in the distance. The anguish, rage, and fear in her voice clawed at their bones. The dwindling screams, the dimming glow, and the closing doors all heralded their approaching death. When one ended, so would they all.

Every breath Pat took scraped against her dry throat like stone on stone. She pushed her already worn muscles past the point of failure, pulling Bill with her as they sprinted towards the shrinking exit. The light of the pillars is almost out. Her grip tightened on him, and with both arms she flung him through the narrow passage, using his momentum to catapult herself through after him. Bill collapsed to the floor alone. But the doors had Pat. She clenched her eyes shut as the first crack rang through her body, ready to lose a limb or her life to the throne room. After all she and Bill had done, this was the least she deserved. Her body relaxed, surrendering to her fate.

Crack.

But there was no pain. The doors had caught the head of the large wooden hammer she carried on her back, instead of her. Its tight leather strap across her chest, dug into her already battered body.

The cracks continued loud as thunder, with black lightning traveling through the wood until the hammer shattered into dust. Pat finally collapsed to the ground as the doors sealed with a deep and final rumble, like a giant's last breath.

Bill pressed his ear against the stone door. Nothing. The screams and lights died together. Once again everything was still and silent. His fingertips searched for the thin spaces between stones to pull himself towards the sound of Pat's gasps. He tried to swallow, hoping his spit would grant some relief to the burn in his throat, but only viscid mucus remained, choking him.

Pat's legs buckled more than once as she struggled to her feet. She dug her fingertips into her thighs and commanded her exhausted muscles to obey and rise. Once she regained an unsteady control of her legs, she pulled Bill to his feet, and they leaned against each other to stay upright. She took the long handle of what used to be her hammer from its leather holster to use as a cane for them both. The pain in their bodies would not subside, but they had to push on. The danger was not over. It would never be over.

An unnatural silence filled the corridors and extended to the night air as they left the castle. Not even the wind's howl was present. It was as if the entire city was a graveyard, each building top a headstone, and the castle at its center a looming mausoleum. Not a soul stirred. Person, beast, or insect. Pat and Bill wished someone else knew what transpired that night, but no one would. It was their job to make sure of it.

The night grew ever darker as the pair descended through the Crest into Stonehaven and across the bridge to the main gate of the city. Below, the old wood and dark stone of the Boroughs soaked up what little moonlight penetrated the castle's shadow. The destitute starved even for light. They exited the short side door next to the gates and helped each other descend the stone stairs which led underneath the portion of the bridge outside the city walls. The guards ignored them. But even still they waited until they were out of sight to release every wail and moan they held within their bodies. Bill vomited bile down to the stones and river below. Once they were able to catch their breath, they grasped the rails of the thin wooden stairway which ran down the steep cliff side. Pat huffed with each step, her thighs exploding with pain. Bill used the rail to take the burden of their weight the rest of the way down.

The night's labors ended at the small wooden cabin perched halfway down the cliff. Long ago, Pat and Bill decided they would not live with the other servants in the castle. Instead, they built their home far beyond the castle's gaze. They stumbled the last few steps and collapsed just outside the front door. Bill ran his fingers down its intricate wood carvings. He thought he would never again see his own craftsmanship. Something they created, not because someone commanded them to, but because they willed it.

Pat grunted as she tugged on one of two hanging cords beside the door. A small spigot opened in the awning above them, and water piped from the city's reservoir rained down upon them. They suffered the cold stinging shards of water against their bruised skin, and peeled the bloody leather clothes from each other, reopening clotted wounds. Belts, boots, aprons, and trousers all squished into an unrecognizable wet mound. Unable to stand again, they remained on the wooden planks and let the water take the dirt and blood from their bodies and send it through the planks into the darkness below. With trembling hands, they rubbed the thicker layers of filth from each other's chests, arms, necks, and faces until their pale skin and green hair were visible again.

They should stay on the floor for the rest of the night, or at least inside the cabin and rest for the weeks it would take for their injuries to heal. But their absence in the castle would be noticed.

After her body was numb and could no longer feel the water, Pat pulled on the second cord to stopper the spigot. Their bed was just inside the cabin, but neither could make the distance. With the last strength in their bodies, they wrapped around each other for warmth through the night. The distant babbling of the river beneath them and the soft yawns of the cabin's wood lulled them both to the edge of sleep.

Before they faded away, Bill said in a whisper, "Can you still hear the Queen's screams?"

Pat's eyes shifted out of focus, looking to the sky beyond the awning. And as her eyes fluttered shut, she answered, "They will haunt me into the next life."

PART I

CHAPTER 1

CHESHIRE

Deep within the Rookwood, Cheshire combs through the study of the Rookridge magistrate as the rest of the village slumbers. The moon smiles from outside, and her beauty peers through the solitary shuttered window, illuminating a small part of the room in dim shades of blue and peaking over his shoulder. He crouches at the foot of a wide oak bookcase. His hood up and his long, tattered cloak, which he wears underneath his vest spread across the floor behind him on a thick woven rug, too fancy for the likes of Rookridge.

Cheshire enjoys the soft rub of the leather-bound ledgers against each other as he pulls one after another from the bookcase. The spine creaks open and the pages *thwip* as he thumbs through them, page after page of nearly three hundred books, which chronicle the village's history, shop openings, land purchases, arrests, large commissions from the forge, curious incidents in town, changes in town statutes, births, and deaths. His fingers dance upon the pages as he reviews every line and date in search of any useful bit of information since his previous visits years ago.

After he has inspected each ledger and returned them to their original spot and angle with a soft muffled thud, Cheshire turns his attention to the magistrate's gaudy desk, inlaid with small golden accents to match the wood's curves. It must be a recent acquisition by the new magistrate. Numerous stacks of accounting papers and a sizable velvet purse of spilled gold coins cover its surface.

Cheshire uses a ring of silver keys he took from the nightstand beside the sleeping magistrate earlier in the night and unlocks each drawer. All the smaller drawers are either empty or filled with blank parchments, more records of money and various transactions, and metal tipped quills. But the largest bottom drawer holds a plain iron chest, the size of a large loaf of bread, wrapped with thick plate metal banding. He pulls it from its hiding spot and places it on the desk. Its heft is too light for gold, but something shifts inside and thumps against the metal, and Cheshire will know what it is. But no key fits this particular hole. He runs his fingertips across every inch of its surface, seams, and edges, feeling for an indentation of a secret release or hidden latch, but finds none. He grabs two quills and tries to pick the lock, but before he can manage it, the magistrate shuffles into the room in his long, striped nightshirt, stretching the sleep from his eyes.

"Excuse me." The lanky magistrate points a brass

candlestick holder and a flint stock pistol at Cheshire, both with equally shaky aim. The small flame casts wobbling shadows on his gaunt, wrinkled face.

Cheshire prefers the paunchy bearded predecessor who could sleep through a thunderstorm by the power of his open-mouth snores. In Cheshire's memory, this new magistrate must be the seventh since his search began.

"You should be asleep," says Cheshire.

"I beg your pardon." The magistrate scoffs and scratches his gray side whiskers against his boney shoulder.

The hammer of the pistol sits forward, so Cheshire indulges the magistrate. "Return to your bed, old man."

"What in all nine hells are you doing in here? Remove your hood at once and face me," the magistrate demands. "I've caught you in the act, villain."

"Villain?" Cheshire chuckles. "I've been called worse." Cheshire climbs and perches atop the desk and rests his forearms on his thighs. He keeps his head lowered and the edge of his hood's shadow at the tip of his nose.

"Why are you here? Who are you? What do you want?" The magistrate slides a step closer. "Gold? Take it. You've found the purse, no doubt. But you'll never have a chance to spend one coin."

"This gold?" Cheshire picks up a handful of pieces and flicks them across the room at the magistrate, bouncing coin after coin off the pistol, candleholder, and his chest. "Not interested."

"What then?" The magistrate flinches to catch them, but

keeps the pistol aimed at Cheshire. "Why have you come? Speak before I call the authorities."

"By all means. Your sheriff and guards sleep comfortably with their wives at the southern end of the village," says Cheshire. "I've already paid them a visit. And there's not been need of a night watch for some time. Not since last autumn."

Even if he had not found this information as he read through every copious volume in the study, Cheshire would have come to the same conclusion. On the two previous nights, Cheshire made sure to find a way into every home and shop within the limits of Rookridge, careful not to wake any villager or sleeping mongrel or cat they kept. He opened every locked door to see what they hid and why, but found nothing other than personal effects and inventories. Even the meager jail on the south end sits unattended and on the verge of becoming derelict. The dirt covered floors within the cells showed no sign of recent delinquents or offenders, and the small walkways between barely any traffic at all. And during the days, he watched travelers, peasants, and farmers enter and leave the village from the western and southern roads. All is as it should be. Or rather, it is as it was when Cheshire last came to the village.

The magistrate's face stiffens in the soft orange glow. "How do you know these things?"

"It's my business to know," is all Cheshire says.

"What do you want, then? I'm tired of these unanswered questions." Both hands steady, and his face distorts as he tries to pull the details of Cheshire's face from the shadows into the flickering light.

"Secrets," Cheshire says through a wide grin. "Now, if you'll kindly hand over the key to this chest, I'll conclude my work here and leave with the night breeze."

"I'll do no such thing." The magistrate pulls his hand with the candleholder to his chest, and the brass clinks softly against concealed metal beneath his nightshirt.

"Ah." Cheshire smiles. "There we are."

The bones in the magistrate's back pop as he straightens his posture and rolls his shoulders back in a useless attempt at intimidation. "Leave. Now."

"This is your last warning." Cheshire's tone drops. "Return to bed."

"You little shit." The magistrate steps closer. "You dare order me? Thief."

"Yet another moniker bestowed upon me." Cheshire rolls one last gold piece in his fingers. "Thief. Murderer. Killer. They're not wrong."

The magistrate's eyes widen and his face falls slack as the candlelight catches the purple of Cheshire's eyes. "Killer," he whispers. "By the gods. You're him. You're the Queen Slayer. Come to Rookridge."

Cheshire loses his smile and pushes against the inner part of his cheek with his tongue.

"I expected someone older. How could someone your age have committed such atrocities?" The magistrate steps back, tapping his foot behind him, searching for the edge of the staircase.

"You'd be surprised. All I wanted was information, and I would have finished collecting it shortly and then been on my way. I had no intention of killing you this night. But you have complicated matters." Cheshire lowers his hood to his shoulders, knowing now there will only be one outcome to this encounter. "But if you truly believe I am who you speak of, you're not nearly terrified enough."

The magistrate shudders and realizes his pistol is not cocked. He fumbles for the hammer, but the candleholder limits the reach of his bony fingers. Cheshire takes the gold piece in hand and flicks it through the air, harder than before, and slices through the tip of the candle's wick, returning the room to darkness. The magistrate only has time to gasp once. Cheshire whips around the room, silent as a ghost, and pulls the pistol from the magistrate's hand as he thrusts his heel into his hip, sending him down the stairs behind him.

The shock smothers his screams. He flails and claws at the banister and wall to stop himself, and lets out a sharp, raspy whimper when three of his fingernails pull back and completely off of his fingers. His frail arms and legs snap as he tumbles down the stairs in a series of muffled thumps until his body crumples lifelessly to the floor below.

Cheshire walks down and flips the magistrate's body in a more plausible position, so those who find him in the days to come will believe his feeble legs gave out, or he became disoriented and fell to his untimely but expected death. He unhooks the chain from around the magistrate's neck, pulls the small iron key from within the collar of his nightshirt, and returns to the chest in the study.

The small click the lock makes when it opens sends a shiver of excitement down Cheshire's back. Inside sits a small leather-bound journal with the unmistakable diamond shaped crest of the capital. His blood boils at the sight of it. He would rip it from the cover if he was not worried about leaving evidence behind.

He takes it from the chest and flips through each page, his finger tips worn and numb from the night, and looks for any word or phrase to call out to him, to fill in one of the missing puzzle pieces in his mind. But only numbers, and transactions the magistrate wanted to keep off the city ledgers, stare back at him from the pages. There are several entries of payments from the capital treasury, which would account for the rug, desk, and other ostentatious decorations around the study. The mounted boars' heads, the tall silver candelabras, among other things.

From the crest upon the cover, Cheshire believed there would undoubtedly be something worthwhile in the journal. But he finds nothing useful. He sits on the floor and hits the journal against the desk leg, fighting the urge to tear the room apart, rip every page from each ledger, and topple the bookshelf and desk.

He grows tired of one fruitless venture after another, but will not allow his frustration to ruin years of searching. He places the journal back into the chest, locks it, places it back within the desk drawer, and picks up the gold coins he threw earlier and drops them back in the pouch on the desk, before returning to the magistrate's body. Cheshire hooks the chain back around his neck and pulls the pistol from his loose grip and replaces it with the key ring. And last, he returns the pistol to the small drawer left ajar in the nightstand beside the magistrate's bed.

Once sure everything is as it was before he arrived, he climbs out of the study window to the roof and leaps from eave to chimney, east across the village, and into the Rookwood as the blue world around him shifts to gray before the approaching dawn.

CHAPTER 2

JONATHAN

The table sits beneath the sprawling oak on Jonathan's land, and could easily sit twenty or even thirty visitors. Each chair surrounding it is as unique as the corner of Wonderland it originated. On the table, beautiful porcelain and metal teapots of all shapes and colors adorn its length, along with a variety of cups, creamers, and candles.

Jonathan woke before the dawn to begin his inspection and preparation. The distant chirps of crickets and crunch of morning grass beneath his feet keep him company as he straightens and polishes each cup, saucer, spoon, fork, and butter knife on the table, assuring each is equally spaced and brilliant. His turquoise eyes shine clear in their reflection. The slight tinkling of silverware and the gentle scrape of cup on saucer creates a soothing melody to his ears.

He sits in each chair to make sure every teapot is visible

from each seat and returns the chair to its aligned position when finished. Jonathan straightens the candles in the cascades of wax draped from the candelabras and lets the fallen leaves stay on the table to add character.

Inside the watermill Jonathan calls home, he pulls pristine silver trays from the long silent gears which once powered and whirred life into its wooden and stone walls. The wooden giants now serve as shelves for folded tablecloths, blankets, tea services, plants, and March's books and swords. The spaces between are fitted with the finest comforts: A sitting area with a plush couch and chairs, an elaborate kitchen converted from what were the adjoining stables, a small study on the second floor landing, and the bedroom he shares with March on the third level. It is small but has a breathtaking view of the entire hollow and valley. In the kitchen, he loads the trays with tarts, jams, muffins, biscuits, and small cakes, and hooks baskets of bread on his forearms, and carries them out to the table. And after all are displayed and positioned, he stands back to admire the idyllic vision before him. Goose flesh covers his bare chest and arms.

"Almost complete."

Back inside, he sets a large iron cauldron to boil over his hearth stove, then stands before the centerpiece of his home—a towering apothecary cabinet spanning the length of an entire wall from the ground to the ceiling of the third level of the mill, carved by his own hands. Thirty columns wide and forty-five rows tall. One thousand three hundred and fifty unique teas from across Wonderland and beyond, each with its own tiny drawer to call home. Jonathan selects precisely thirty-five, making sure to include those from the bottom and topmost rows so none feel neglected, and ferries each individually to its designated teapot.

The morning slips away, and the sun casts dabble shadows down through the oak onto his table. Jonathan, unsure of the last time he has blinked, presses his eyes shut to watch the soothing dance of shapeless colors and forms against the cool darkness of his eyelids. Once he opens them, and the brightness shrinks away and his table comes into focus, he is once more enamored with his work. With all prepared and scrutinized to his taste, he allows himself to relax in the tall wingback chair at the head of the table. A small black and red ladybird crawls from the white Jacquard upholstery onto Jonathan's shoulder, travels across his chest without a care in the world, and flies away to parts and adventures unknown. Jonathan's eyes follow it until the speck disappears in the movement of the undulating leaves at the east end of the Hollow.

He checks the time on his timepiece, treating it with the care a father would show his newborn son. His thumb traces the edges of its crystalline face three times and he realizes he knows better than to keep her waiting. He sets down his timepiece at the edge of the table and curls its chain into a perfect circle around it.

In the Hollow's clearing, March waits with a sword sheathed at her hip. Only one of her extensive collection. Her short olive tunic ripples in the breeze and her bright pink eyes blaze in the sun. Braids, with silver, rune-etched beads woven in their lengths, run through her pink hair from her temples to the backs of her ears, and hang loosely down her back.

Jonathan approaches and pulls his broadsword from the earth, where it has slept since yesterday's match. It's dull and partially rusted from the elements, but it will suffice. His claymores rest carefully among March's collection on the second level of the mill and have not seen the sunlight for many years.

March unsheathes her sword, a shimmering blue steel blade with a basket hilt. She swirls it through the air, raises it between her eyes, and their dance begins. A cautious circle introduction for near ten minutes, eyes locked and faces stone. A new record by Jonathan's count, as March waits for him to break, to smile, and signal the start of their match. He can never conceal it for long. He cannot help himself when he looks upon her.

March spins and thrusts her sword at Jonathan, which, had he not deflected, would surely have pierced his shoulder.

"I did not smile," says Jonathan, ready for her next attack.

"Your eyes betrayed you."

March delivers barrage after barrage with no quarter, aiming for his heart, neck, head, and thighs. Their blades clang and ring out through the afternoon air, frightening birds in the tree line and those who roost atop of the mill. Jonathan stands over a head taller than March, possesses the arms and chest of a smith or stonemason, and should easily be able to overpower her in a fight, but her skill is unmatched with a single blade, and legendary when she wields two. She is an artist of the highest caliber, and her mediums of choice are the sharpest iron and steel. Jonathan fights with every bit of his strength and stamina to keep March at bay, and he is able to do so because she is his tutor. When Jonathan leaves an obvious opening, she points it out to him with the heel of her boot or the flat of her blade.

Their duel travels the entire breadth of the clearing in the Hollow, around the mill, to the brook beyond the northern tree line, and back to the table. When the match carries on longer than March cares for, she makes quick work to end it, with a spin, flourish, and sweep of Jonathan's leg, leaving him disarmed and on his back.

"I win." March sheaths her sword and stands over Jonathan's legs.

"No, I win." Jonathan sits up and glides his lips across March's thighs.

She unbuckles her belt, drops her scabbard to the grass, and unclips the single clasp on her hip keeping her tunic secured. The breeze reveals the full beauty of her body, except for what her boots cover, and Jonathan refuses to hide his smile any longer. Even though they spend the majority of every day without a shred of clothing, it doesn't matter. Every time he looks upon her, Jonathan cannot help but marvel at the strength and beauty of this woman who is a piece of his soul.

He kisses up her body as she lowers herself onto his lap. With every kiss, he nuzzles his face and glides his bottom lip against the warmth between her thighs, the taut muscles of her stomach, the curve of each breast, her neck, and finally her waiting lips. The salt of her sweat is sweet on his tongue. His kisses start gentle at first and grow rougher as he climbs. March wraps one hand in the back of his hair and claws at the muscles of his shoulders with the other.

As they kiss, her deep sighs and exhalations in his mouth reach into Jonathan's core and ignite every desire he has held at bay all morning. He shuffles his trousers down to his boots. Before he can kick his boots off, March pulls back, playfully lays him back on the soft grass, and shakes her head. There are times, this being one of them, where she prefers them not to be fully undressed. And Jonathan is more than willing to oblige.

March stares into his soul, her eyes sparkling in the sun. Wisps of her hair hang down over Jonathan's face like the branches of a willow. Her hands explore and massage his flexed chest muscles, then slide up to his neck, and then down to his stomach, unintentionally tickling him. He runs his fingers up her arms, to her tense shoulders. March cups his right hand in both of hers and takes control. She folds his fingers and runs his thumb across her bottom lip, then down to her breasts to circle her nipples. She leans down to kiss him and at the same time pushes her hips lower, welcoming him. Jonathan sits up and holds her tight. Both their bodies quiver as one. They need not hold back their moans, laughs, and cries of ecstasy this deep in the Rookwood. They treat this moment as if it is their first and last time together.

The afternoon is lost, the sun beginning its slow arc toward the horizon, as they fulfill every pleasure the other thinks of without needing to say a word. They leave a trail of clothing to the oak and continue their worship in its speckled shade. The sunlight and shadows wrap and undulate around their glistening bodies. Finally, exhausted and satisfied, they end in Jonathan's wingback chair. She sits in his lap and reclines against him. His arms hold her close as the sunlight sways between the leaves of the oak, at first white, then purples and ambers.

Perfection, he thinks to himself.

Jonathan closes his eyes to take in every lingering sensation —the heat of his body still pulsing against hers, the cool breeze running over their warm skin, the small beads of sweat running between them, the scent of lavender from March's hair. Jonathan runs his fingers along March's hips, making her laugh and squirm.

She turns to straddle him and wraps her arms around his neck, unable to hide her smile this time. But the chime of Jonathan's timepiece interrupts their tender moment. With a huff, March carefully picks it up from the table by its chain and hands it to Jonathan.

"Come darling," he says to her, nose to nose, inhaling her sweet breath. "Time to dress for tea."

"I thought I already was." She lowers herself, taking him in once more and squeezing her muscles. Jonathan's eyes lose focus, his warm breath filling the space between her breasts.

Instinctually, he wraps his arms around her again and holds her against him while her hips continue to rise and fall, kissing her breasts and neck between each word. "Under normal circumstances, yes, oh, yes, but dusk is almost upon us and Dormy will arrive at any moment and you know she only visits every six months."

March ignores his words and presses and circles her hips against his. She teases her lips against his, never kissing, but making him speak against their touch.

"Darling." Jonathan can feel every one of her muscles as it

tenses and relaxes and has difficulty finding his words. "I would like nothing more than to ravage your body for the rest of the day and well into the night, but tea time is tea time. We are not savages. Time is a precious commodity."

"One I do not intend to waste."

He concedes and stands with March, her legs hooked over his forearms, and they stay joined, exchanging breaths until back inside the mill. By the time they reach their bedroom, both their breaths become quick and shallow. She squeezes her legs and arms around Jonathan as he embraces her tight, holding her against him, both shaking from pure bliss. Jonathan will not be late for tea, but he will never leave her wanting.

While March dresses upstairs, Jonathan tends to the boiling water in the kitchen. Small droplets fling themselves out and hiss and smoke upon the burning wood. He presses a lever with his boot on a pipe running from the bottom of the cauldron, through the wall, and outside. Jonathan grabs a plain black iron kettle and follows the path of the black pipe, almost grown over by the short grass, all the way to its spout cleverly disguised at the base of the oak. He fills the kettle several times to fill each of the teapots on the table. The resulting aromatic amalgamation excites Jonathan to the point where he realizes he should take his own advice and dress for tea, at least this night while they have company. But before returning inside, he gathers his timepiece from the table, and then the trail of clothing, boots, belts, and swords they left scattered throughout the grass. His smile grows wider as he collects each, thinking of what it took to lose them.

In their bedroom, Jonathan laces a fresh pair of leather

trousers and dons his favorite frock from their wardrobe—a long patchwork robe he and March created many years ago, faded and fraying in many places, but Jonathan refuses to repair it. He turns to collect his scarf from its peg on the wall but finds it waiting in March's hands.

She stands before him in her favorite teal linen dress, cut deep to below her navel, sides completely open, and held closed by a thin strip of linen tied around her waist. She wraps the scarf around his neck as they both stand together in the looking glass. March's expression gentle and pensive. As much as the warrior in her inspires him and the vixen exhilarates him, these private calm moments with March he adores most of all. A chance to glimpse the true delicate rose behind the valley of thorns.

"You are the very vision of my heart personified," he whispers to her as he runs his fingers down the curve of her bare hips.

"I do not need your affirmation," she says, almost embarrassed.

"I give it freely, because you deserve it." He turns her and lifts her chin with a curved forefinger. Her eyes shimmer in the sunlight spilling through the open balcony door. "After all these years, you doubt?"

"I doubt myself, not you. Never you. You are my constant, which keeps my mind, body, and soul tethered to this horrid world. But there is a lingering sensation which creeps its way from the back of my mind and poisons my thoughts telling me I do not deserve your words or your love at times."

Jonathan laughs. "The same thoughts run through my mind

every time I look upon you, but your sweet smile reassures me and I stay anchored. You are the sole reason I function."

She rests her head on his chest, and his chin gently on the top of her head. To Jonathan, she is much more than his anchor. Her light and strength fill the cracks in his past and in his mind, keeping him whole.

CHAPTER 3

CHESHIRE

Cheshire hangs upside down, from an ancient oak, his feet wedged tight in the fork of a large moss-covered bough overhanging the eastern road out of Rookridge, looking up at the world below him.

The world makes more sense this way.

His long cloak pulls his vest down and they barely cling to his shoulders by the spread of his arms, leaving his bare torso exposed to the dewy morning air. A soft breeze rustles the leaves of the lush canopy in waves and sways his body as the branches groan and creak. He runs his fingers through his tousled purple hair, shakes loose a thin leaf from an ash tree from the other side of the mountains, and watches it spin through the air, rising to the forest floor. It's unlike the wide oak leaves with the round knobs dancing below his feet. It stands to reason it's clung there for a week's time, at least.

Despite its reverent beauty and vibrant colors, the

Rookwood proves perilous to travelers unaccustomed to its inhabitants and dense primal terrain. The safest ways through the Rookwood are the three major roads branching out of the village of Rookridge like a compass rose, missing its southern point, created by the gods before Time himself could remember. Only bandits, the brave, and the dimwitted dare travel the small byways carved through the tangle of trees stretching out for miles in every direction.

It is not uncommon for bandits to leave a fresh or even rotten corpse strung up on the main road as evidence they are near and still an ever-present threat. It is where Cheshire first got the idea to gather information from those who travel to and from Rookridge. People reveal who they really are when they think no one is watching, and what better disguise than a corpse?

With each breath, Cheshire lets the weight of his body stretch towards the ground, and the tips of his fingers spark and pulse with heat while his chest and back tingle from the cool air. Thin shafts of sunlight pierce through the canopy at sharp angles and appear and disappear as bits of dust pass and insects drift through them. The ballad of rustling leaves and the conversations of sparrows and thrushes lull him into tranquility. His hanging cloak obscures most of his face, and he has learned to keep a soft gaze as if staring a hundred miles away and blink every few minutes. Those who pass will think him dead while he is able to gather the information he needs, with them being none the wiser.

First to pass is a farmer hauling a modest cart overflowing with carrots, squash, and cabbages fresh from the ground on his way to the market in Rookridge. His boots and woollen trousers still half covered in dried soil from his fields, as if plucked from the ground like his vegetables. From beneath his wide-brimmed hat, he hums a simple tune to match the rhythm of the long uneven road. When he spots Cheshire, he removes his hat and says a prayer in an old tongue, used by those who live far from the great cities of Wonderland, before continuing on his way.

Other merchants and farmers pass by without raising their eyes to Cheshire. It is not until the sun casts shadows from overhead, that the next set of travelers on their way to Rookridge notice him. Three women, sisters, from one of the outlying farms far beyond Rookwood's eastern border drive under Cheshire in their wagon while they lust after his body. The mint-haired girl riding in the back tugs at the strings of her already loose bodice and describes at length how she would share him with her sisters behind the oak if he was still alive, as they do with their stable hands. Her sister, with a darker shade of green hair, jests while she steers the wagon about how they should bring him down and see if there's any life left in him. The third sister stares off into the wood as her sisters laugh and they drive towards the village.

After a long stretch without any travelers, and over the novelty of impersonating a corpse, Cheshire sits high in the same twisted oak, feet dangling below him, out of sight of any passerby this time. As the sun descends, her bright shafts of light return below the canopy, but this time in warm oranges and deep purples. Birds still chatter with each other in melodic songs high in the treetops.

The next to pass under him is a woman on her way out of Rookridge. One hand holds her tawny dress and beige apron up to avoid the dirt, though the backside collects more than its fair share, while the other holds a woven basket against her hip full of fruits, breads, and wrapped salted meats. Her pace is cautious, and she looks into the brush for unseen dangers. She hugs her basket tight, weighing the decision to proceed or find another path, but she is aware this is the only eastern road out of Rookridge. She gathers her resolve and hastens her steps past Cheshire.

"What an utter waste of a day," Cheshire says to himself.

There are, however, benefits to being in the Rookwood, which he's put off long enough. Jonathan and March wait for him, at their home twenty miles farther in the wood, isolated from the rest of the world, though they do not know he is near. Cheshire stretches, legs and arms shaking, and is about to jump for another tree to journey to Jonathan and March, when a loud thump followed by several smaller thuds draws his attention behind him.

The woman is on her knees, fallen, basket snapped, and scrambles to collect the fruits and breads as they spill and roll away in every direction, unsure of what to grab first, and ends up grasping as much dirt as food. But no matter how hard she tries to gather her food back into her basket, everything spills again and again through the crack in its side, until she resigns to her frustration and slumps to her knees. Helplessness overtakes her honey-colored eyes.

"Damn it."

He surprises the woman when he lands next to her, and she

draws a short kitchen knife concealed within the waistband of her apron ready for her would be assailant. The lines of her weathered face draw into her wry grimace, but once her eyes measure Cheshire, her concern eases to reveal the gentler but firm features of her face. Cheshire gathers the farthest outlying food, wipes off the dust from the apples off on his cloak, picks a pebble out of the indentation of a loaf of bread, and rolls two heads of lettuce to her with his foot.

"I can manage," she says.

"Ungrateful. I was minding my own nearby for a bit of relaxation when your accident disturbed my thoughts, broke me out of a peaceful state, but yet here I am helping you, regardless."

"Are you always this full of shit?" she says, stone faced, studying Cheshire with a mother's gaze, from his shining purple eyes to his ragged appearance.

He smiles and tosses her several apples, which rolled into the short grass at the road's edge.

She shoves the smaller fruits between loaves of bread to keep them in place and bundles them together in a makeshift sack made from her apron.

Cheshire helps her tie a knot to keep the bundle secured. Despite his help, her eyes swirl with mistrust, and her fingers rub the rough grain of the knife handle.

"You're a curious one, ain't you?" she asks dryly. "What are you?"

"I beg your pardon."

"Well look at you. Isn't a cloak supposed to be worn outside? Not under a vest, which is clearly too small for you.

And you're too young and pretty to be a brigand or bandit. Or perhaps you are a bandit. That fancy sash round your waist is not cheap, I wager. You must've nicked it from someone important. And surely those muscles you're showing off would be of better use in the fields, earning a wage, or at least helping your family. But your body isn't built from farm work, is it?"

"I'm older than my appearance, I assure you." Cheshire has always looked younger than his years, and perhaps at one point he could have grown into a man, but he gave up such a possibility long ago. And she has a keen eye. Cheshire's never done a day of farm work in his life. Farm hands are strong indeed, but bulky and slow, and Cheshire cannot afford to be either. His body is the result of years of fighting and survival.

"I'm sure I've not seen your face in the market, but it's familiar. Can't place it though."

Thankfully for Cheshire, but more so for her, the peasants who frequent Rookridge are too preoccupied with their harvest, homes, and feeding their families to pay attention to the country's minutia within the village. She has probably seen his face on one of the parchments delivered from the capital and nailed to the board outside the magistrate's office.

"What're you doing out here?" True concern fills her tone.

"I will answer your question if you answer one of mine." Cheshire sits cross-legged next to her.

"I don't see the harm." Her knees pop as she settles on the ground with him. "What would you like to know?"

"Have you seen anything out of the ordinary in Rookridge, or Rookwood for that matter? Strange goings on? Peculiar, unsavory people?"

She breathes deep, looks west towards Rookridge, and massages her forehead with two fingers and her thumb. "Nothing. As far as I can tell. All the village folk I know are always where they should be."

"And you are familiar with everyone in the village?"

"Not everyone, I don't think, but I can call the majority by name."

"You would recognize strangers in the village?"

"Strangers?" She laughs. "Travelers from all over the Queendom pass through Rookridge. It's the only bloody place to stop through the damned Rookwood. But then again, I come to the village every third day for food for me and my children, but in all my years, I've seen nothing out of the ordinary. Truth be told, you're the most peculiar sight I've seen in some time."

Cheshire raps his fingers against his knees. Her eyes are honest and her answer logical, which is the worst kind, especially when it is not what he wants to hear.

"Now I've answered your question. Questions. Now answer mine, from before. What're you doing out here?"

"Minding my own, observing the ambiance."

"And searching for peculiar people. Your business is your own, so I'll not pry." The woman takes firm hold of her bundle and stands with a slight pop of a knee. "But it's late now. I have little to offer, but you're welcome to rest at our cottage overnight if you have need. You can bunk with my boys in the hayloft."

"In truth, I do have somewhere to be, far from here, and I have kept them waiting long enough."

She shakes her head and begins her journey home once

again. "You remind me of my eldest, a little older, but the same spirit."

"And what spirit is that?"

"Trouble." She turns back once to say, "Thank you." But Cheshire is already up the tree and out of sight.

"Thank you," he replies with a mouth full of apple. The sweet juices flood his mouth and ignite a twinge in the very back of his jaw, sending shivers down his neck and throughout the rest of his body. Its tart juices trickle down his chin, onto his chest, and he watches the drops slowly race down his stomach before they disappear into the edge of his grey trousers.

But as he rolls the mush of chewed apple from one cheek to the other, he notices the distinct absence of the Rookwood's hum. The birds' conversations have fallen silent, or they've fled from a harbinger Cheshire is altogether familiar with. His heart races and tingles crawl from the nape of his neck, down his back to his groin.

Snap.

He glances back to the road with the expectation of a new traveler, but it remains deserted on both ends.

Snap.

This time from above, in the canopy ablaze with the twinkle of the rich oranges of dusk.

Snap.

Cheshire widens his eyes to the canopy until he spots a shadow out of place, too dark to be natural in the already fading light of the foreboding wood. This dark figure waits five trees away, obscured by the spread of two gnarled branches as if the forest's hands try to conceal this evil from the world.

"I wondered when you would catch up. Come along now, dawdling is not appreciated."

There is no response, but his unblinking eyes stay trained on the speck of darkness, no larger than the width of his hand.

"Fine. On with the game."

He lowers his gaze, and in a half second's time, his voyeur obliterates the tangle of branches between them and slices through the branch Cheshire stands on with his ax blade, as easily as a hand would cut through water. Cheshire hardly has time to flip to the neighboring tree.

"Have you missed me?" Cheshire chuckles. "What am I saying, of course you missed me. You always *miss* me."

His fearsome stalker waits poised on the splintered remains of the branch where Cheshire once stood. He's known by many names across the country. The Butcher of Wonderland to the cities, the Nightmare or the Reaper to the countryside and villages, the Bodach in the far corners of the map, and many others long forgotten by most.

Ages ago, Cheshire dubbed him the Ace of Spades, not only because he is the symbol of death incarnate but also more simply, his black hood and cowl reminds Cheshire of the card suit. The unnaturally pale ivory skin of his body stands out against the black iron forged skull he wears low around his waist as a codpiece holding together the shredded remains of what were once trousers, covering little of his body. In his hands, a beast of an ax with a sweeping onyx blade, which stands at least eight feet in height, a head taller than the Ace.

But despite the muscles, height, skull, and ax, his most threatening attribute is his face, or lack thereof, for no matter the amount of light that shines upon him, be it flame, moon, or sun, it is never visible from beneath his dark hood. Two tiny glints shine where eyes should be.

The Ace's sinewy muscles bulge and constrict with every silent breath as he wrings the ax's handle as he would Cheshire's neck. He holds his stance, but slowly shifts his weight to his right foot. The movement is so slight, it would go unnoticed by the average person, but Cheshire has studied the Ace for countless years and knows his tendencies and tactics well. With one push from his massive legs, the Ace leaps for Cheshire, ax cocked back, ready to split the entire tree in half.

Cheshire scarcely has time to land on a new branch and fling himself to the next before it's reduced to splinters. The Ace does not possess the grace of Cheshire, and smashes through limbs with every leap, sending shards of wood and full branches raining down to the road below. Cheshire scrambles higher into the canopy where the branches are smaller and cannot support the Ace's weight. But the sweep of the ax at full extension cuts wide swathes through the top of the canopy.

Severed branches clatter and clack as they hit each other on the way down and block the Ace's sight for the briefest moment before he bats it away. It is enough for Cheshire to bolt further down the road where he can use his knowledge of the Rookwood's geography to his advantage. After a few moments of searching, Cheshire finds his destination. A massive oak with a split trunk, each half as thick as the trees around it. The branches of nearby trees and saplings form a tight web across the gap except for a single small opening, just large enough for Cheshire's body. As he takes position on an adjacent branch, splintered wood from a branch the Ace crashes through less than ten feet away, pelts the back of his back and head. Cheshire whirls his body around and jumps for the hole, arms stretched forward as if to plunge from a cliff into deep water.

The wind from the Ace's grasp hits the bottom of Cheshire's feet. He threads his body through the hole and lands on another tree in time to see the Ace hit the wall of branches full force. The resounding thunder crack shakes the entire forest, and the Ace falls to the ground with such force all the leaves near him shoot out in a near perfect circle.

"I have missed you." Cheshire's grin beams down on the Ace lying motionless, but his joy is short lived. He looks back to the path of destruction they tore through the trees and the debris on the road below. Spilled apples sit in a growing pool of blood, and the woman's limp and broken arm protrudes from between the felled branches.

Fuck.

He's not allowed any more time to process what they've done, nor does he wish for it, because the Ace is on his feet again and takes aim at the trunk of the oak in which Cheshire kneels. With one swing of his ax, the tree explodes as if hit with a twenty-four-pound cannonball, bringing the entire tree crashing to the ground.

The Ace mounts the trunk and slices branches like blades of grass as he stalks its length. His swings become wild, fueled by hatred, rendering every part of the fallen tree to less than kindling.

Cheshire applauds while he leans against another tree farther off. An unwise attempt at mockery, because by the third time his hands meet, the Ace closes the distance and swings again. This time so close Cheshire can see the reflection of his face in the blade as he ducks beneath it. Taking advantage of the time it takes for the Ace to recover from his swing, Cheshire flees south, deeper into the Rookwood.

A fog creeps in from the north like a sluggish eerie tide distorting the entirety of the forest. Even though he has lost sight of the Ace, the distant muffled snaps of roots echo between the trees and bite at the back of Cheshire's neck. He has enjoyed three months of peace without any sign of the Ace, though Cheshire must be ever vigilant. He knows his only recourse is to return underground to the catacombs through one of the many hidden doors scattered throughout the country, concealed in plain sight in rocks, beneath waterfalls, and in the trunks of large trees. One stands in a circle of old oaks on the far southern side of Jonathan's home. The Ace will never relent in his pursuit nor will he ever tire, unlike Cheshire, who pushes himself the twenty miles without stopping.

His muscles burn and his movements slow, but he cannot stop. Every shadow he passes in the fog he fears is the Ace lying in wait, and then the game will truly be over. As Cheshire does not want to involve Jonathan and March in this fight, though it would not be the first, if he wants the game to continue, he will need to enlist their help.

The trees end abruptly and Cheshire stares into the small meadow of the Hollow. The fog swirls in front of his face with each heavy breath. The soft glow of distant candles burns through the fog and mark Jonathan's table, the single oak about it, and the edge of the mill.

For the past five miles, he has heard no sign of the Ace. He has heard nothing at all. The Rookwood bates its breath, waiting to see the outcome. But there is strength in his arms and legs yet, and he decides to circle around the perimeter of the Hollow, find the door, and wait in the catacombs until the Ace's search leads him far from here.

But his plan shatters like the tree inches from his neck as the Ace slashes uncontrollably, violently, without any sign of slowing. But when Ace twists and arches back for a death blow, Cheshire, out of breath, leaps over the Ace, grabs the ax's metal handle between the Ace's own hands, and uses it to bring the butcher down by his neck. The Ace's back and head crack against exposed hard roots. Cheshire sprints in the direction of the candles taking advantage of the few seconds the foolish gambit provided.

He bursts through the orange haze, leaps over the back of Jonathan's wingback chair, and jumps to the table.

"Cheshire!" Jonathan exclaims from behind.

"Draughts!" he yells to Jonathan, March, and Dormy, as he runs down the length of the table, careful not to displace a single dish or teacup. "Draughts!"

A small warning, but it is enough for them to understand. Cheshire dives from the table and enters the tree line on the far side of the meadow as he hears the crash of wood, porcelain, and metal. Jonathan will be distraught, but March will console him, and Cheshire will make amends if and when he is able to return. Less than half a mile past the tree line, Cheshire reaches the oak circle and digs his heels into the damp soil in order to stop.

Twelve gnarled oaks in all, each at least the width of five grown men shoulder to shoulder, stand as if they mark the hours on a clock face, the door hidden in three if Cheshire stands at twelve. Unmistakable to his eyes, but kept from the rest of the world. All he must do is close the door behind him, climb down the rickety wooden ladder, and he'll be able to rest his weary body in the catacombs.

But yet again, his plans are dashed as an unexpected and unfamiliar young woman with hair black as charred wood and eyes a deep blue emerges from behind the sixth oak of the circle. His lips bottle the frustration and scream meant for her. Cheshire has heard whispers and rumors of women from the other world who somehow cross into Wonderland, with their dull or mismatched eyes and hair, but has no time to give her a second thought. She is in his way.

"Hello," she says, on the edge of tears. "Can you help me, please? I think I am lost."

Cheshire can feel the Ace's approach, but cannot risk revealing the door now in front of this woman. He's killed others who have come close to discovering an entrance to the catacombs, and this strange woman is no different. If it's a choice of his life or hers, Cheshire will sacrifice her without a second thought in order to escape. But the image of the woman's hand on the road to Rookridge flashes in his mind, mangled and bloody.

"I fucking hate this day."

He grabs the woman by the wrist and leads her out of the

circle between the sixth and seventh oaks and through the underbrush.

"Wait!" She tries to plant her feet, but Cheshire pulls her into stride.

She'll be the death of me, he thinks. He has outrun the Ace for years and now jeopardizes everything he has accomplished for this woman from the other world. It would have been easier if he would have left for Jonathan's earlier in the day, then the woman on the path would still be alive, the Ace might have strayed and never found him, and he would have never encountered this woman.

"Please, stop," she says again. "Can you tell me where I am?"

Cheshire ignores her words, because no answers he gives would make sense in her fragile state.

"Please, I need answers." Tears flow from her wide eyes as she guards her face with her hands from the small branches whipping against her.

"Don't we all."

"Will you please tell me where I am!" She tries to pull her hand from his grasp.

They reach the edge of a gully and Cheshire lets her momentum lead her past the edge and tumble down the incline, head over foot until she comes to rest in a bank of dried leaves. He stays long enough to see her move and make certain she isn't dead.

"If you wish to stay alive, do not move, stay there, and shut up," Cheshire commands, before he races back to the circle, and hides behind one of the oaks. It's too late. The Ace's sinister dark figure, distorted by the fog, stalks within, arm and ax outstretched, a deadly clock hand added to the circle's face.

Cheshire attempts to tame his lungs to slow his breath and keep any sound at bay, but fears the loud thumps of his heart can be heard by the Ace. If the Ace swung at Cheshire now, the ax would cleave through his body and the oak he hides behind, before he ever knew. He wonders if he would be able to watch his legs stand as his severed upper body fell to the ground, before everything slipped into darkness.

If he ran the opposite direction, the Ace would give chase, and Cheshire nears exhaustion. Instead, he waits for the Ace to turn his back and search another part of the oak circle before darting to the next tree, and the next, and a third time, but the Ace begins to suspect and slows his search. But an opportunity presents itself from the unlikeliest of places.

"Excuse me," the woman calls as she returns from the gully meant to save her life. "Young man, I said I needed help."

The Ace spins towards her voice, where Cheshire stood mere moments ago, and had he hesitated a few seconds longer, he would have been at the mercy of the Ace.

Cheshire tried to save her, and will not squander this chance, regardless of what happens to the woman. The Ace steps to the edge of the oak circle, closer to her and away from him.

"Help," she cries, as the full horror or the Ace bears down upon her.

Cheshire holds his breath, steps into the circle, grabs the oblong knot in the third trunk and pulls as his toes find the release lever tucked far between two giant roots and steps down.

"Help, someone, please," she screams as she presses her back against an oak rather than fleeing.

The woman's scream masks the creak of the door. Cheshire opens it wide enough to slip inside, and the last image he sees before the door shuts on the outside world is the terror in the woman's eyes as the Ace blocks her from view.

Once the door seals, the thump of Cheshire's heart and a high-pitched ring overpowers his ears. Everything on the other side of the door is silence. He descends the ladder to the catacombs below, but his sore thighs give out and he collapses to the stone floor below before he can reach the third rung. The darkness welcomes him back, and the cold beneath Wonderland laps against his overheated body like waves on the night sea. He will wait until morning, and hopefully the Ace will have moved on to continue his never-ending hunt, and Cheshire can return to the mill and Jonathan and March.

CHAPTER 4

JONATHAN

By the time Jonathan and March reemerge from the mill, they find Dormy, head back and mouth agape, asleep in her favorite worn leather chair. She slumbers in the shadow of her pony-drawn wagon secured to a nearby post. In actuality, it is less of a wagon and more of a cottage smashed together and placed on wheels, complete with two levels, shingled roof, windows, deck on the second level, and planters. It is a wonder the vehicle does not topple over from its weight, and the assortment of barrels, crates, and nets full of other wares hanging from every available hook and corner. Besides the hours she works, the trek through the Rookwood to arrive at the mill would drain any grown man, let alone a petite girl. She traveled the hidden path off the eastern road which leads to the Hollow and had to move and replace seventeen branches meant to obscure the path.

"The poor thing works so hard she could fall asleep while driving her wagon." Jonathan smirks.

"She has," says March. "More than once, with us aboard."

A few of Dormy's unkempt marmalade hairs dangle in front of her face until her breath sucks one into her mouth, and she snaps awake, nudging the silver teaspoon in front of her with her little finger. She catches sight of Jonathan's eyes, which are the size of tea saucers themselves, and the beads of sweat immediately forming on his forehead. She straightens the teaspoon and the surrounding utensils in case she accidentally nudged them as well.

"Forgive me, Jonathan."

"Quite unnecessary," says Jonathan as he pulls out an ornately carved wooden chair for March and tucks her in on the right side of the table next to his chair. Dormy stands for Jonathan to tuck her in as well, on his left. He won't be able to enjoy his tea otherwise. After making sure both are comfortable, he sits in his wingback chair at the head of the table. Dormy hands Jonathan a striking stone from one of the many pockets concealed within her oversized jacket. He lights the tallest candle, and the others along the table ignite in succession. A beautiful carpet of candlelight rolls out before them. Jonathan attempts to count them at the speed at which they light, but never can.

"Shall we begin?"

The soft evening fog embraces the table, forming halos around each candle and a dome of light around them, as if only they existed, floating in the sea of darkness around them.

Jonathan serves March and Dormy tea from different pots. He takes a circular, metal flask from within his robe and adds the smallest drop to his cup. Their conversation remains entertaining and their tea hot.

Dormy lists the new wares she added to her collection with great excitement. A trunk half eaten away by saltwater, a pair of pincers for hauling large blocks of ice, the skull of a crocodile she discovered in the Wetlands, and thin bottles of blue and green glass with years of soil yet to be cleaned out among them. March recounts a past adventure in Adamas, the gilded city of the northwest, where she skewered three men's arms with one sword, pinning them all to the post of a tavern, all to save Dormy after they accused her of stealing a small bag from their saddles.

After an hour's time, there is a lull in the conversation and Jonathan decides to entertain his guests. He takes a long drink of his tea, holds his teaspoon in front of his lips, and exhales a small cloud as if the temperature outside were in deep winter. Tiny ice crystals form and crawl around the curve of the spoon.

"Winter Frost tea from the mountains to the north." Jonathan smiles. "Intriguing, is it not?"

"Intriguing indeed." March humors Jonathan with a gracious smile.

"Which do you have?" Jonathan asks.

"Emerald Needle," March replies without hesitation. "From the Highland forests."

Dormy rubs her fingertips together as if to light kindling, knowing Jonathan will ask her next. "Candy Long Grass," she says with an unsure scrunched nose.

"Well done. Exceptionally well done," says Jonathan.

In her newfound confidence, Dormy reaches for a silver teapot to test Jonathan, but March stops her.

"Don't even try," March says. "The game is rigged. Jonathan can recall every tea he's ever tasted by taste, aroma, sight, and texture."

Jonathan, proud of the compliment, hides his smile behind his cup as he continues to drink. They all continue to enjoy their cups and company in silence thereafter, while the moon's hazy visage smiles down from above. Dormy walks round the table, sampling from every tray, and stuffing her pockets with chocolate-covered muffins, blackberry tarts, and shortbread biscuits. Jonathan watches the dark bits of leaves swirl around the bottom of his cup and attempts to create shapes and lines. March leans to him and runs her fingers through his hair.

Jonathan takes her hand and holds it to his lips. *Are you happy?* he asks without words, and a furrowed brow.

March joins the silent conversation. Her scrunched nose says, *Why would you ask such a question?*

The sparkle in Jonathan's eye says, *I will always ask. And that was not an answer.*

I don't answer stupid questions, March says with her smirk.

Jonathan smiles, saying, *Thank you, for being here.*

Always, March says, her smile matching his.

Dormy, back in her chair, plate and pockets full of pastries, keeps up with the conversation as if watching a decisive match of badminton. She is perceptive, which makes Jonathan question why he and March still engage in their silent banter.

But old habits stick with them both, like the fragrances of his teas within their drawers.

March gives Jonathan a clearer answer to his question and gently bites his earlobe, causing him to choke on his tea and cough out a burst of Winter Frost, freezing the rest of the tea in his cup. Satisfied, she reclines back in her chair and pops a small cake in her mouth.

A distant crack echoes behind them in the night and catches their attention, and then another.

"Tree fall?" Jonathan asks.

"Yes," says March, her eyes peering into the fog. "But not of nature." She pulls a crude iron sword she always keeps beneath the table.

A third crack louder than the previous makes them all wince, and before Jonathan can say another word, silent or otherwise, he and his chair flip backward.

"Cheshire!" Jonathan would know his form anywhere, even as it passes over him in a blur. Emptiness and yearning fill his chest. For as much as March is a part of his soul, Cheshire completes the set, three sides of the same coin. And he has not seen Cheshire for many years, and to have a glimpse is cruel. But a second is better than not at all.

"Draughts!" Cheshire yells.

Jonathan scrambles back to his feet, prepared to witness the destruction of his beautiful table. But besides his chair, and the slightest tinkling of the cups and saucers, Cheshire disturbs nothing as he runs along the table.

"Draughts!" he yells again and bounds from the table and disappears into the fog.

Cheshire's words pull a memory from within the cockles of Jonathan's mind to the surface.

Years ago, March accompanied Jonathan to the Draughts, the thin ravines snaking through the large Casissan mountains to the north. Carved stone effigies of castles, kings, horses, knights, warriors, and other mysterious figures protrude from both sides of the steep cliff faces. On a clear day, their figures blend with the other rocks. But on a day when the mists creep down the mountains, those who risk the climb to the Draughts, can look up from the bottom of the ravines and make out every shadowed figure wrapped in the white haze engaging in a fierce battle frozen in time.

At the time, Jonathan sought the cones of the Grey Pines which peppered the cliffs and fall to the ravine floor, to experiment with a new tea concoction, one of his many original brews. On their second day, while breaking camp in a ravine, Cheshire sprinted past them. It was not common, but also not unheard of for Cheshire to run into them while out venturing the country. But this time, the Ace was on his heels, closer than Jonathan had ever witnessed. March kicked Jonathan to the ground, and both he and she rolled to the corners of the narrow ravine to escape the speeding shadow above them.

Before Jonathan has time to react, March's boot plants firmly in his side and kicks him to the grass as she pulls Dormy down with her. He clenches his eyes and rolls away in the grass, but looks up in time to see the Ace charge after Cheshire with the force of the Great Wonderland Express, flipping his table, and hurling chairs and his delicate tea services in all directions. Jonathan's eyes, unable to comprehend the devastation before

49

him, try to account for every saucer, spoon, napkin, teapot, cup, candle, sugar and honey bowl. He crawls along the grass, ignoring the Ace entirely, and piles every piece he can in his trembling arms.

The wheels in Jonathan's mind spin uncontrollably and block out all else. He mutters the names of each teapot, his fallen friends bleeding in the grass as he searches for them. "Periwinkle porcelain gourd, eggshell flower bottle gourd, white double spout round pearl, silver rainbow, flint nail top, dandelion stone box..."

He would have listed and repeated into infinity if not for March. She grabs his face with both hands and forces his head to still and his eyes to lock with hers, but they still jump erratically around the grass.

"Jonathan!" she pleads. "Go after Cheshire. Dormy and I will handle the table." She pulls him closer, forcing him to look at her, and says softly, "Go."

His eyes finally fix on March's and he stops trembling. She knows the look in her eye and the tone in her voice will pull him from any pit he dares spiral down. He kisses her and races into the fog without hesitation, trusting March and Dormy to attend to the devastation behind him.

The Ace is fast but Cheshire more so, giving them a substantial lead ahead of him. Fortunately, the Ace's footsteps are deep and easy to follow. Jonathan, however, does not possess the grace of Cheshire maneuvering through the wood, but he keeps his footing through the bramble and tangle of moss-covered roots spreading beneath the moist soil. He tracks them as best he can until there is no trail to follow.

"They could not have both disappeared," he says to himself. "Where, oh where, oh where are you? Give me a sign, a signal."

"Help!" a voice cries in the not-too-distant wood.

"That will work," he says.

"Help, someone, please!"

The voice buckles Jonathan's legs. It is a woman's voice he has never heard. In all the years he and March have lived in the Rookwood, no one has ever found their home, except for a stray bandit whom she quickly dispatched and disposed of, but never a woman, never here. An odd mixture of worry and gratitude battle for dominance within Jonathan's gut. He fears her shrieks herald a grim future for them, but they will guide him to where he needs to be. He has to save her, whoever she is, and resumes his chase with newfound speed and urgency, his stride sure footed.

He reaches a circle of oaks and finds a dark-haired, blue-eyed woman not of his world pressed against one of them, and the Ace with his ax tilted towards her.

"Not out here. Please, no," he says to himself, his arms and face cold.

Instinct, instead of sound judgement, takes over Jonathan as he throws himself between the two and shields the woman. The Ace's ax tickles the small hairs on Jonathan's throat. He holds his breath and lengthens his neck to get it further away from the edge of the blade, but realizes he provides a bigger target.

The incident in the Draughts was not Jonathan's first encounter with the Ace, but this is the first time he has been close enough to peer into the dark faceless void, and his veins may as well have Winter Frost in them.

"What brings you this far into the Rookwood, Ace, sir?" A stupid question, for he knows full well the Ace seeks Cheshire. Jonathan can also feel the woman behind him grab tighter onto his robe and bury her face in his back. Her breaths quick inhalations.

The Ace ignores Jonathan's words and tilts his head to look upon the woman, and tightens the grip on the ax. The striations of his dense chest and shoulders tense and flex as if breathing heavily, but no sound escapes the darkness within the hood.

Jonathan attempts to put a finger on the head of the ax to lower it, and the Ace's head snaps back to Jonathan with unnerving speed. "Right, terrible idea. Don't touch the ax. Got it." It's all he can do to stop his own lips from trembling as hard as the woman behind him.

"There is no reason for you to linger, sir. Your quarry has fled, and the longer you stay, the more substantial the lead he gains over you."

The Ace slowly slips the blade in between Jonathan and the woman, forcing her hands from his back. With a jerk of his arms, he sends Jonathan skidding across the clearing to the opposite side of the circle.

"Wait!" Jonathan cries as he raises himself to hands and knees. "There's no need to hurt this woman. I know you know this to be true. She is not the one you hunt. Why not be a good chap and run along?"

In less than a heartbeat, Jonathan is face to face with the dark sockets of the black skull around the Ace's waist. Death moves quick and towers over him. Jonathan looks up and the emptiness within the hood pulls on his soul. The ax hangs overhead, ready to split him in twain. But with no warning or reason, the Ace rests the ax over his shoulder and fades into the fog like a specter with no quarrel to begin with, in whatever direction he believes he will find Cheshire.

Cheshire, he thinks, as the looming shadow of the Ace distorts and disappears into the night fog. *Please, run.*

Quiet fills the circle, the true calm before the storm. A bead of sweat runs down Jonathan's face, counting the seconds until he must take action. It dangles on the tip of his nose before letting go. He looks down and watches it fall towards the ground, a part of him growing smaller and more distant, and once he loses sight of it, turns his attention back to the young woman.

She huddles against the same oak, holding her knees to her chest. Her night dress shows signs of a quick, if not long, run through the wood. Small twigs hang from loose strands of lace at the bottom hem, fresh soil stains her knees from where she's fallen, and it's with rips and snags from every angle.

Jonathan approaches her again, cautiously, his fear matching her own. She winces with every step he takes.

"You are safe now," he assures her. "I will not harm you."

The young woman does not respond, but raises her head. Her bright blue eyes pierce through her tangled black hair. His nerves coil in his stomach like a serpent. He hoped the fog played some trick upon his senses, and he would find the woman's hair a dark blueberry or deep indigo, along with her eyes, but her hair is indeed black as coal and her eyes blue as the spring sky.

"Are you unharmed?" he finally brings himself to ask.

The woman sits catatonic, the blacks of her eyes the size of poppy seeds.

Jonathan tries not to think of the scene he would have happened upon if he arrived any later than he did. He does, however, think of Cheshire and wants to follow the Ace at a distance in case Cheshire finds himself in need of help. The few times they fended off the Ace together, whether it be skill or dumb luck, Cheshire always prevails and disappears like the fog, sometimes for years. And although Jonathan knows it is to keep the butcher away from him and March, he hopes it is not the case this time.

But for now, this woman from the other world needs his attention.

"Your face is smudged." Jonathan kneels and holds out a handkerchief from his pocket.

She accepts it with a simple, "Thank you." Her voice quivers with the rest of her body.

"He gave you a right scare. The Ace has that effect on, well, everyone."

Before Jonathan can ask another question, the woman explodes with her own, trying to catch her breath at the same time.

"Where am I? Where is my home? I know where I am. That is, I know where I ought to be, but I am not sure anymore. Where am I? Who are you?"

Jonathan offers her a hand and helps her to her feet. "My manners are absolutely atrocious. Please, forgive me. I am Jonathan Carter, and to answer your question both simply and not, you are in Wonderland."

Her eyes beg to ask many more questions, but as her lips form the first syllable, her eyes roll into her lids, and she faints straight away, falling back to the ground.

"Shit."

CHAPTER 5

CHESHIRE

Several stones lay on the cobblestone floor of the catacombs, pushed from the wall by the thick roots of the oaks above. Cheshire yanks one of the smaller exposed roots free and lobs it down the tunnel, screaming curses at the woman and Ace. The root shatters a cracked vase on a broken side table. The impact and drizzle of porcelain on stone echo through the abandoned subterranean corridors. He grabs a loose stone from the ground, ready to hurl it at a looking glass farther in the darkness, but places it back into the wall instead, causing several more to crumble to the floor. Cheshire sits and rests his muscles on the dusty stones. He takes time to repair the wall as best he can, pulling out the rest of the roots and turning each fallen stone in hand to find the correct fit within the wall.

He wonders how long the Ace will linger and prowl about the oak circle, waiting for him to resurface. Long ago, in the grasslands to the west, outside the city of Clava, the Ace waited for over twelve hours while Cheshire watched from another hatch half a mile away. Yet, other times the Ace abandoned the area immediately once Cheshire disappeared, knowing their paths will always converge in a bloody conflict. Cheshire will take no chances this night, not with Jonathan and March, and Dormy near. Although the Ace will never stop in his singularly minded purpose to remove Cheshire from this world, wipe him from the board, no matter who or what else crosses his path, he will not harm Jonathan, March, or Dormy as long as Cheshire is not in the vicinity. A hard lesson learned at a young age with constant reminders, such as the woman earlier on the road to Rookridge.

Cheshire walks miles through the endless network of catacombs, thankful for the cold stones beneath his tender bare feet, their soft pats upon the stones the only sound in the long tunnels. The consuming darkness, thick as the night sea, would cause the strongest of wills to lose their senses and reduce them to lunacy, but over the years Cheshire's eyes and mind overcame and adjusted to the dark as well as the light, if not better. If not for his search, and Jonathan and March, he would prefer to live out his life in the depths below Wonderland and forget the world above all together.

The catacombs spread throughout the entire country like veins beneath its skin. They are a relic of a bygone age, the Age of Kings, when war ravaged the land and travel by any means above ground became dangerous. During those years, the roads and woods were fraught with tribes of brigands, and invaders from foreign countries bent on toppling the monarchy and destroying the Wonderland way of life, or so the stories say. In response, the catacombs were constructed for the wealthy and nobles to travel across the country without risk to their persons or property. But their use and even the knowledge of them fell into obscurity over a millennium ago after the first crowned Queen ended the Line of Kings and the wars as well. Fortunately for Cheshire, he is the last who remembers they exist, and therefore has an entire world unto himself.

He picks up loose pebbles between his toes and flicks them at the keystone of every support arch he passes, and also takes aim at the discarded paintings, clocks, books, and other antiquities littered throughout the tunnels. Some were decorations at the height of the catacombs service meant to soften the harsh gray interior, while others were left by travelers too busy to remember they forgot something. He imagines himself in the belly of a great leviathan frozen in time. The curved ceiling arches its ribs, and the surrounding trinkets—the remains of ships the beast consumed. It would make sense. Over the years, Cheshire has come across the remnants of the odd skull or leg bone.

The tunnel Cheshire walks ends at a tall wood plank door with a curved top to match the curve of the catacombs ceiling. It takes more effort than Cheshire expected to crack the rust off its wide iron hinges and push the door open. On the other side, a waypoint chamber links nine other tunnels, each with a door as unique as their destination. The tall copper door with carved filigree heads to the north mountains, the thin wooden door made from old ship parts leads to the coastal villages to the east, the shortest faded blue door with a tarnish golden knob starts the journey to the garden to the east, hundreds of miles away, and the others connect to other waypoints with their own set of doors and destinations. And Cheshire knows where every door leads and each path ends.

There are words etched in each door by his hand when he was a child to help him navigate before he had the tunnels committed to memory. *Water* on one, *There, Over There, Cold, Flower, Far, Too Far, Wall,* and the door leading back to mill, Jonathan, and March, says *Them* scratched deep into the wood.

He takes a striking stone from his cloak and lights the candles on the glass pedestal table at the center of the room. The candlelight reveals the waypoint's forgotten beauty. Thin stone columns frame each door, black and white tiles shrink as they spiral to the center point of the room, and a large chandelier with hundreds of crystal adornments hangs from the center of the vaulted ceiling.

Cheshire pulls another apple from within his cloak and stares at his dull and distorted reflection in its skin. Or it could be the face of the woman from the road looking back at him, who is still there, crushed dead, leaving orphaned children to discover her body and fend for themselves. In the countless battles with the Ace, there has been more collateral damage and deaths than Cheshire cares to recall, so he chooses not to. He wants to feel something, anything for them, but he denies himself. Feeling sorry for the dead will only stall him, and he must keep moving, keep searching.

He sets the apple on the table for morning, undresses, and stretches his weary body, massages his shoulders and thighs, and arches his back in all directions to relieve the muscles running along his backbone.

Several loose seams in the remnants of his trousers need his attention and care. They are more stitches than fabric and barely reach his knees now. His vest, which was once a jacket, but now sleeveless and cropped high on his body, needs some minor care as well, tightening the threads to keep the few remaining buttons secured. What little he has from his past, he cherishes and preserves the best he can. Jonathan and March once sewed a pair of trousers and persuaded him to try them on, but their experiment lasted all of a minute. It felt perverse, as if slipping into someone else's skin. He will wear his rags until they are beyond patches and stitches, and then go on wearing nothing at all.

When finished with his repairs, he bundles his clothing into a pillow and curls himself on the floor, hugging his knees to his chest. He wraps his sash around his neck and rubs the thin fabric between his fingers under his nose, inhaling deep in search of a memory. The fragrance has long since faded, but Cheshire can always find the hint of vanilla and bergamot left within its threads, or perhaps just in his mind.

Shadows cast by the chandelier dance back and forth on the ceiling, bringing life once again to this dark room. A memory sparks to life in front of him, of a beautiful young woman with short purple hair. His mother. The glow of her soft smile is brighter than any candle lighting up the dark, and her eyes wide with wonder and love, dance in its radiance. Her ivory lace dress and brilliant purple shawl drift slowly, as if on the surface of a gentle stream. She kneels by the smallest door in the room, not this particular door, but one similar and far away.

A small boy, Cheshire, no more than five years old, opens the door and crawls out, his clothing covered with dust from knee to ankle and wrist to elbow. She surprises him, picks him up in her arms, and tickles him. His little arms keep a tight hold around her neck as they twirl about the room, while his tiny robust laugh fills the tunnels. Eventually, he curls up and lays his head in the mother's lap.

He looks up into her deep purple eyes as she strokes his purple hair and sings him off to sleep. "'Will you walk a little faster?' said a whiting to a snail. 'There's a porpoise close behind us, and he's treading on my tail. See how eagerly the lobsters and the turtles all advance. They are waiting on the shingle – will you come and join the dance? Will you, won't you, will you, won't you, will you join the dance? Will you, won't you, will you, won't you, won't you join the dance?'"

The memory fades when Cheshire realizes the voice singing is his own and no longer the memory of his mother. His breath quivers and a tear trickles down the side of his face into his ear. The candles flicker out and all is still and silent, except for the thin tendrils of smoke climbing to the ceiling.

He thinks of the forsaken trinkets in the catacombs and how they were perhaps once someone's cherished and beloved memories, but now they are forgotten, or could have been meaningless and easily forgotten, forever. Cheshire hopes his memories one day will also fade into oblivion, but such a thing is not possible. He is Wonderland's memory.

CHAPTER 6

MARY ANNE

Mary Anne's head rests on her forearms, on what she believes is the desk in her study, a normal spot for her to fall asleep after a long night with her ledgers. The gentle amber glow on the other side of closed eyes either her fireplace or the dawn through the window. Her consortium meeting in London ran two hours longer than expected, and the train back home to Lyndhurst felt especially long this evening. And after cooking her mother supper, preparing for bed, and hours of reviewing shipping schedules and receipts, an early night in the study is deserved.

But as she shifts her arms, the long sleeves of her nightgown rub against fabric, not papers or the mahogany wood of her desk. She lifts her head and opens her eyes to a bright haze, and once they come to focus, she finds herself seated at the side of the longest table she has ever seen filled with tea services and multilayered trays of small pastries bathed in the golden light of what must be one hundred candles at the least. Every piece upon the table, from the smallest spoon to the glaze on miniature muffins, sparkles like sunlight through crystal. She believes the sight before her a beautiful dream, for nothing so breathtaking could exist in her drab town of Lyndhurst or the whole of London.

On the other side of the table by a large solitary oak out of the candles' warmth, two figures, a broad-shouldered man in a long robe and a significantly smaller woman engage in a rather heated but hushed conversation, their arm motions small but jerky.

Mary Anne closes her hands as she stretches and winces at the unexpected flash of pain. She opens them again to discover fresh scrapes and bruises dressed with linen bandages and treated with camphor. She presses her thumb into the meaty part of her palm and the immediate sting bites at her hand and up her arm.

Oh, God. These marks are from the unfamiliar trees she ran into and pushed against while frantically searching for her way home. The spacious birchwood groves on the outskirts of Lyndhurst somehow transformed to dark, twisted oaks covered with ivy and moss, their roots cresting above the dank earth like a tangle of serpents. At most, she was half a mile from her home, but she ran for hours with no sign of anything familiar. *This must be a dream.* But she has never felt pain in dreams. *I ran, then there was the younger boy, the wicked hooded figure, and the man who saved me.* She turns back to the conversation in the shadows, unable to make out his face, and pulls his name out of the fog. *Jonathan.*

The hot pulses of her heartbeat pour down to her fingertips and toes, as they did earlier in the forest. Whether a dream or not, Mary Anne suppresses the urge to speak or call out to release the incessant timpani in her chest and head. She watches the conversation of the shadowed figures calm and slow, until they embrace and remain still for quite some time.

Who are these people? she wonders. But she is distracted by the table, the elegant but worn wingback chair at its head far to her right, and the peculiar teapots running its length. Some tall and slender, others short and squat, and even some with more than one spout. As she follows the curiosities to her left, she notices a young girl, with eyes and hair as orange as the candlelight, seated next to her.

She cautiously bites into a small cake with a speck of grass stuck in its icing. They stare at each other through an awkward silence, unsure of who should speak first.

"Hello," Mary Anne finally says, wondering if this young girl has been there the entire time.

"If you don't mind my saying, I think you're quite pretty, miss," the young girl says.

"Thank you. As are you." Regardless of this is a dream or not, Mary Anne's upbringing insists she repay a compliment. "Curious." The word slips through Mary Anne's lips before she can catch it.

"What is, miss?" the young girl asks.

"Everything." Mary Anne stops herself, not to be rude and comment on the girl's appearance. But she cannot keep herself from investigating this unique girl further. Besides her strange hair, she wears a long, oversized coat half corduroy and half leather, several leather belts with at least ten pockets in each, slung over her shoulder and around her waist, and tiny round spectacles no bigger than shillings, which rest like eggs in her nest of hair.

The man and woman finish with their conversation and approach the table and enter the candlelight. The appearance of the orange haired girl to her left could not prepare Mary Anne for these two. The woman stares at Mary Anne, unblinking, with pink eyes, the color of pulled taffy, and hair to match. Her clothing, merely long scraps of fabric draped down tied around her waist exposing her skin on the side of her body from shoulder to foot, exceeds the indecent. But as for the man, Jonathan, if this truly is his name, he possesses a gentle half smile permanently displayed upon his face and a twinkle in his piercing blue, almost teal, eyes. The only shirtless men Mary Anne has seen before now are the burly, stocky, and often hairy dock workers on the Thames when she visits London on business, and her neighbor who looks quite the opposite. Jonathan's body, however, appears carved from marble, with the curvature of muscles she has seen in works of art. With his frock open, the muscles upon his chest and torso shimmer, while the shadows between cut deep in the candlelight.

The man pulls out the chair diagonally across the table from Mary Anne for the woman accompanying him to sit, but she ignores his chivalry and sits directly across from her. He does a poor job of suppressing his smile as he sits in the chair intended for her.

Mary Anne averts her eyes to follow modesty and decorum, even if they will not. But the temptation to glance back at this man wins over her etiquette, at his smile, eyes, and body. Twice, and a third time, and by the fourth he takes notice and wraps his thick robe closed around himself, with a playful grin. The man and woman across the table from here appear to be her age, in their mid-twenties, twenty-six at the most, while the shorter girl to her left seems younger, perhaps only twenty.

"I believe introductions are in order," he says, the same gentleman as earlier. "Jonathan Carter, at your service. We met before in the oak circle, if you recall, and I do apologize for the traumatic experience you endured, but you are welcome and safe here, I assure you. To my left, allow me to present Audrianna March."

"You may call me March, if you must," the pink haired woman says as she smears what appears to be strawberry jam on a biscuit without breaking her gaze to watch Mary Anne as if she were the danger among them.

"Doris Mayfield, Dormy for short," the orange haired girl says through the pastry lodged in her mouth. "Pleasure to meet you, miss. It's not often we have guests, and come to think of it, we never have guests, so you're a pleasant treat this evening."

"May we inquire as to your name, so we may address you properly?" Jonathan prompts Mary Anne.

Dormy shoves another pastry in her mouth, Jonathan's middle finger circles the rim of a teapot, and March twirls a small butter knife between two fingers, as they all wait for an answer.

Their names mean little to her. She questions her mind again, unsure if this is a dream or not. The soft dirt beneath her feet, the smell of candles and pastries in her nose, and the pain in her hands is real. If this is no dream, she must believe these people are tragedians set up to perform some unheard of theatrical production, but in her heart, somehow she knows this not to be true.

"Mary Anne Elizabeth," she says, seeing no harm in a simple introduction.

"Wonderful. Welcome, Mary Anne Elizabeth. You have arrived in time for our second attempt at evening tea and conversation." Jonathan takes the teapot from beside him and fills the cups in front of Mary Anne, March, Dormy, and ends with himself. To Mary Anne's astonishment, the tea changes color with each pour—hers deep red, Jonathan's purple, March's a light blue, and Dormy's yellow.

The confused look on Mary Anne's face draws Jonathan's attention.

"The tea?" he says with a smile. "It's called Prism Cascade, a draft of my own creation. It's one of the rarer in my collection and is one of the few teas still available this evening after an unfortunate incident earlier. Oh, and an official thank you is in order to Dormy and March for your diligent work to assure we still have tea this evening. Mary Anne, would you care for—"

"Please," Mary Anne interrupts. "Can someone please tell me how I arrived at this place?"

"What a silly question," says March, pointing to Jonathan with the butter knife. "He carried you."

"Not to the table. Here, this land, all of you, none of you or this should be here, you can't. I mean, how did I arrive in this place?" Mary Anne asks. "Is this a dream or hallucination? It all seems absurd."

"Absurd," scoffs March. "Who is the one of us running through the wood unaccompanied in their night dress?"

"March," says Jonathan in a meager attempt to chastise.

"You suggested conversation. I'm obliging." March finishes her cup and stabs a small cake with the knife. "Pray tell, Mary Anne Elizabeth, to aid in answering your own question, precisely how you stumbled upon our gathering this evening."

Mary Anne thinks of the events which led to her sprint through the forest outside of town, and does not want to disclose any more information than she has to. She answers simply, "I ran."

"Fascinating, spellbinding, really I can hardly believe the tale," March says dryly, slicing through her cake. "Since now you have answered your own question, we can move on to less intriguing conversation."

"I ran into the forest on the outskirts of my town, and... I do not know. I suppose I got lost. But I know the surrounding countryside and forests as well as I know the inside of my home. I knew exactly where I was, I should know exactly where I am, and I should be exactly where I know, but I am not." Mary Anne wrings her dress, ignoring the pain clawing at her palms. "This should not be here, none of you should be here."

"But we are," says March. "To us, you are the anomaly, the figment, the stranger, yet you treat us as if we trespass on your land."

"I got lost once," Dormy says to cut the tension. Jonathan and March look to her to continue. "Just once."

"Perhaps Mary Anne would prefer to discuss topics of a more lighthearted nature," says Jonathan.

"Forgive me, but no. I require answers," Mary Anne demands. "I must return home. If someone at this table would please tell me how I arrived here, I will gladly depart and find my way back."

"Are you always so impertinent?" The venom weighs thick in March's voice. "I do not fancy myself a gentlewoman in the slightest, but at least I possess the courtesy to allow someone to finish speaking, especially if I intruded on a party to which I was not invited."

Mary Anne, at a loss for words, wants to reprimand this woman who would dare question her manners, and the others for being obtuse, but to get the information she wants, she needs to be civil and keep a level head.

"My apologies," she tells everyone. "I truly am sorry. I meant no disrespect, but I must know where I am, how I got here, and how I return home."

"Wonderland," says Jonathan, "to answer the *where* portion in your string of questions. I made mention earlier, but perhaps your thoughts were understandably preoccupied. In the Rookwood to be precise. And for your other inquiries, we do not have a clue, actually. Dormy spoke true earlier. We are miles from the closest village and travelers do not venture this far into the Rookwood. Our meeting was as unexpected to myself as to you."

Mary Anne sinks back in the chair and tries to believe the answers given. Their answers are preposterous, vague, and not helpful in the least. Her heartbeat intensifies again and throbs from her temples to the scratches on her palms. She sits and listens to the drums within her while the trio sips their tea and moves on to other conversations about the cakes and teas on the table, ignoring her.

"Please," says Mary Anne in a small lull in their conversation when the others finish their cups, ready to ask firmly for more answers, but apparently too quiet for the others to hear.

"Clean cup?" Jonathan addresses the group as he sets his cup down on its saucer with two hands.

"Clean cup," March and Dormy respond together, and the three of them move down the side of the table to new empty chairs. They all stare at Mary Anne in silence and wait for her to move to the empty chair next to Dormy. She does so, but cannot comprehend the reason behind this custom. They each select a new teapot and serve themselves normal colored tea, and Dormy pours Mary Anne a fresh cup and adds milk.

"Why not refill your original cups?" Mary Anne cannot help but ask.

"Because we are not barbarians," says March, as though Mary Anne should be privy to this information.

"One should never cross contaminate tea," says Jonathan. "Each individual flavor must be savored independently, with time in between to let the palate rest. Mixing simply is not done."

Ridiculous, Mary Anne thinks. *Is this a ploy to distract me? But why?* Her heart continues to pound. She wants to tell them all how disrespectful their actions are, but Jonathan interrupts her. "You—"

"I'm thinking of words beginning with the letter '*u*'." A sly grin crosses Jonathan's face.

"Mixing is *unheard* of," Dormy says, slowly putting down her tea.

"Unacceptable," March counters, leaning forward in her chair.

"Uncommon," Dormy matches her every movement.

"Unwise," adds Jonathan.

Mary Anne can hardly process everything happening around her. She looks to Jonathan for some hope of an explanation, but he smiles and sips his tea in silence, pleased with the argument he has incited. No, not an argument, a game. The three battle back and forth, transforming the respectable tea service into a unruly tavern.

"Unappreciated," says March.

Wonderland, Mary Anne thinks to herself. *No such city exists in England, I am sure.* Her impatience grows with each word batted back and forth across the table as though she is not even there. Her heartbeat pounds in her head and overtakes the sound of their words, but she can still make them out from the shape of their mouths.

"Uncouth," Jonathan adds.

"I would very much..." Mary Anne tries to speak, barely audible over the shouting and laughter.

"Undesirable," says March.

"I would very much like to go home," Mary Anne says, this time with more resolve.

"Uncanny," shouts Dormy.

"I MUST RETURN HOME, NOW!" Mary Anne brings the game and their party to an abrupt halt. "I did not mean to raise my voice, but you have not answered the questions I need answered most. I just want to go back home."

"But you've only just arrived," says Dormy.

"I do not want to be here." Mary Anne cannot hold her tongue any longer. "I do not know where here is. I want to return home, to my home, to my mother who by now is overcome with worry, and all you three can do is laugh and make jokes at my expense."

"Apologies." Jonathan puts his cup down for the first time since sitting back at the table and looks her in the eyes. "In truth, we did not know how to handle the situation, which is what March and I discussed earlier away from the table. We thought perhaps a bit of levity would help your disposition, all things considered, and we went about our evening as planned, hoping we could lift your spirits even slightly."

"Well, if we are destined to journey down this rabbit hole, where are you from?" March asks.

"England," says Mary Anne. "Lyndhurst to be specific, and my business is in Southampton." She cannot make out the exchange between the three of them, but they look at each other queerly as if England is a figment of her imagination.

Jonathan presses his lips together before he begins. "Mary Anne, we wish to help, we do, but we have no knowledge of where you speak or how you arrived here, and do not know how to direct you back home."

"I do not understand. I was just there," says Mary Anne. "Now you have me speaking as if this is all true. I should not be more than a mile outside Lyndhurst. The lights from Southampton, less than ten miles from here, should be visible in the sky even through the fog." She points to a direction she believes is south, even though she has no bearing of where she is.

Jonathan's face distorts, the thoughts too much for him to convey, which unsettles Mary Anne. "To return to your home," he continues, "that is, to return you to where you are from, is not as simple as walking back down the road. I am unsure how to put this gently?"

"Not gently," says March. "You are not in this England anymore. You are quite a long way from home, actually. So far in fact, I dare say you could not reach it no matter how hard you searched or how far you walked. But I do encourage you to try."

Mary Anne can feel the tingle of her lower eyelids heralding her tears, not of sadness, but anger, but she will not give this lot the satisfaction of seeing them. She pushes away from the table and puts distance between her and it. "You are cruel, cruel people. I will not be mocked or ridiculed. If you will not help me, point me in the direction of Lyndhurst, Southampton, or anyone else besides you lot and I will be on my way."

March swiftly points in an arbitrary direction.

"You do not understand." Jonathan's attempt to comfort her falls flat. "Wonderland is a different realm, or world, I am not sure which description is correct, but you could search for the rest of your days and not find England, Lyndhurst, or your home, because they simply do not exist here."

"You lie," Mary Anne seethes at Jonathan.

"How dare you," says March, rising from the table. Jonathan gently takes hold of her wrist to keep her from reaching for something beneath the table.

"This is another game you're playing, like the previous one with the words." Mary Anne's face hardens, wondering how these three could be so heartless. But Jonathan's words strike a chord. "A different world? How am I to believe this? What makes you believe you're in a different world than my own?"

Dormy holds up a lock of her hair for Mary Anne to see, and then glances to Jonathan and March. Jonathan lifts his brows to make more of the sharp blue of his eyes visible. And the glare from March means for Mary Anne to contrast them to her own eyes and hair, as if these outlandish hair and eye colors are a signifier and commonplace in this other world.

"You mean to tell me," Mary Anne says cautiously, "no one in this...world has dark hair?" She looks into Jonathan's eyes, and Dormy's, and even March's, and can see no falsehood behind them.

They wait in a tense silence for her to seat herself again. March follows soon after, her gaze more intense than ever.

"If I am to believe you," says Mary Anne, "I am not in England, nor my world. So, I can never return home."

"We do not know," says Jonathan. "There are whispers of people from another world who enter Wonderland, but those are old wives' tales. We at this table do not possess the wherewithal or knowledge to accomplish such a feat, if at all possible."

"Who then?" Mary Anne asks, determined to find her own path. "If you do not, there must be someone who knows a way out of this forsaken place."

After a long, thoughtful pause and a sip of tea, Jonathan

says, "There may be one person, maybe, who might be able to help."

"Who?" Mary Anne asks, her fingertips pressing into the table, starved for information.

Jonathan pauses again long enough to make Mary Anne uncomfortable, as if she expects someone to pull the chair out from under her, but he finally turns to address March and Dormy. "We take her to Mirus."

"Absolutely out of the question." The daggers behind March's eyes turn to Jonathan.

"Yes," shouts Dormy.

"Can she not take herself?" March blurts out. "She was willing to walk to whatever the bloody hells Lyndhurst is moments ago, and fine with us pointing her in a direction, is that not what she said?"

"Who is Mirus?" Mary Anne asks.

"Mirus is the capital city of Wonderland," Jonathan smiles. "But the *who* we seek would be the Duchess. At this moment, I do not know anyone else to ask, but there is a chance even she may not know the answers to your questions, but if anyone would, it would be her, I would wager."

"You speak as if you can simply waltz into Mirus, through soldiers and guards, and ask for an audience with the Duchess," says March.

"Please," Mary Anne says weakly. "I must return home."

Jonathan inhales a deep breath and lets it escape as a brief sigh. "March is correct. An audience with the Duchess is not easily obtained, but we will help you. It takes several days to reach Mirus from here, and we do not expect you, nor would we allow you, to go on your own."

"Days?" Mary Anne asks, with no fight left. Before the sun set, she stood in the study with her mother, and now, somehow, she is days away from returning. She wants to believe this entire conversation, the run through the wood, the boy, the murderous fellow with the ax, all a hallucination. It would ease her mind and nerves if it were. Then she could wake up in her bed tomorrow morning, or from her desk possibly, and these figures would fade from her mind like any other dream. She also wishes the argument with her mother, which began this entire ordeal, would disappear with the dawn as well.

"I am sorry," says Jonathan. "I know the importance of home, and I too would be overwrought if I was told I could not return to mine. You have no reason to trust us, but I promise you, I will see you return home."

"It would be our honor to see you to the capital safely," says Dormy.

"If it is my only recourse," says Mary Anne, with a feigned smile. "I believe seeing the Duchess would be the best option. When shall we leave?"

"On the morrow. It is far too late to travel this night," says March. "Or if you would rather start now, Mirus is that direction." She locks eyes with Mary Anne and points off in a different direction than before.

Mary Anne wishes she could retract her statements from earlier, but gives thought to the idea of walking. But she was already lost once, and during the day. If she were to wander off during the night, she would certainly become lost again, and might end up in a place less hospitable.

"We will begin our journey tomorrow," says Jonathan. "I believe all present could use a good night's rest."

Mary Anne realizes Jonathan's insinuation. "Out of the question. A woman should never stay the night with a strange man, no matter the circumstances," she says, blushing.

"No need for concern." Jonathan smiles again. "Your honor and reputation will remain intact. You will stay inside the mill with March and Dormy, and I will sleep in Dormy's wagon."

Reluctant at first, Mary Anne sees no other option besides sleeping here at the table, and agrees.

"It's settled then," he says, rising from the table. Dormy races inside without a word, while March waits for Mary Anne to pass in front of her.

At the end of the table, Jonathan cups his hand around the tallest candle and blows it out. The other candles go out one by one like dominoes down the table until they all give off the faintest trail of smoke. Mary Anne tries to think of any possible way the candles could have plausibly extinguished in such a manner. She wonders if she conjured this fantasia to live out the wild adventures denied to her in England, and if she has squandered her time with complaints and tears instead of embracing the fantasy.

Mary Anne tries to stay on the crudely spaced stone path from the table to Jonathan's home. The moonlight outlines the tall, imposing structure they approach, more shadow than wood and stone, but gives little guidance towards it. Without their conversation, the empty night intensifies the volume of Mary

Anne's breaths, the squish of her swallows in her ears, the footsteps on grass and stone of Jonathan in front and March behind, and the sharp noises of mysterious creatures or insects. She scans what she believes to be the horizon for lights from a city or town, but all is darkness other than the moon's watchful face above her.

Jonathan holds open the door for the women, but does not enter. "Goodnight, Mary Anne," he says before walking to the oddly shaped wagon in the distance.

"Good night," she replies.

Inside, Dormy has already lit a candle and placed it on a small table beside a plain looking couch along with a patchwork quilt and a grey down pillow. After Mary Anne settles onto the couch, she watches the shadows of enormous wooden gears, as large as the factories in London, vibrate ominously overhead from the single flame. The height of the room and the odd scent mixture of spices, fruits, and earth almost overload her senses. She pulls the quilt over her nose, but the odors seep through or already have permanently infused themselves into the fabric.

With March upstairs and Jonathan outside, Mary Anne turns to Dormy to thank her, but finds she is already curled up and fast asleep in the armchair next to the couch. The blanket's warmth pulls the anxious feelings from her body, and for the first time, she relaxes and will give no more power to her thoughts tonight. In the morning, she will awake in one place or another and confront whichever reality is true.

But before Mary Anne can let her heavy eyelids rest, March walks down the stairs, nude from head to toe. The clothing she wore previously did little to cover her body to begin with, and she did not have the manners of Jonathan to cover herself. As she walks through with unyielding confidence, Mary Anne cannot help but study the definition of the muscles on her arms, thighs, and stomach. Nowhere near as pronounced as Jonathan's, but still noticeable. She is still a slender, almost petite woman, and if she wore normal modest clothing, Mary Anne would never have guessed her physique. There is an air about this woman, infinitely stronger than Mary Anne ever thought she, herself, could be. She saw it in her eyes at the table, heard it in the words she spoke, and now feels it as she walks out the front door to join Jonathan, paying Mary Anne no attention at all.

When the door creaks shut and the metal latch clicks, a feeling stirs within Mary Anne. She is unsure if it is curiosity, envy, or perhaps her body telling her it must sleep. And before she dares let her mind wander to the possibilities to take place in the wagon between Jonathan and March, she blows out the candle and hides her face within the blanket. She has no choice but to see this charade play out and wake tomorrow morning in her bed, or go with them and see if there is in fact a way out of this world, if it is indeed real.

CHAPTER 7

JONATHAN

The first rays of dawn find their way through the myriad of stacked and hanging wares in the wagon to Jonathan's face. He wakes with March wrapped around his body, her legs intertwined with his, and her face nestled in his neck. Jonathan brushes his lips and cheek across her forehead and softly draws filigree with his fingertips from her hips to her breasts through her hair, and back again as if he traces the surface of a still pond, wanting to feel the water but not disturb its peace. He cannot see her face, but can hear the smile in her gentle sigh.

Careful not to disturb any of the hanging pots, birdcages, and nets, and without waking her, Jonathan lifts and carries March through the morning fog to the Mill. They are not halfway up the stairs to their bedroom when Dormy's dry snores draw Jonathan's attention back downstairs. She lies upside down in an armchair, legs folded over its back, hair dragging the floor, and mouth agape once again. Jonathan cocks his head to see through the spindles of the largest gear in the mill which runs along the stairs, to discover Mary Anne bundled on his couch, and a shiver runs down his bare body, not from the morning air. This day started like many others, and he almost forgot their visitor. Jonathan does not want to think of the events of the day before or the journey ahead of him.

Once upstairs, he lays March in their bed, drapes their cotton sheet over her, and steps out on the balcony where the cool morning air rushes over him. Their highest floor of the mill pokes out over the low fog this morning. An ocean of soft pinks, oranges, and blues fills the Hollow and rushes beneath him, breaking around the mill. He grips the rail and imagines himself at the bow of a great ship to uncharted lands, far beyond the Rookwood and mountains surrounding his home, some place where they have never heard of Wonderland. March barks orders, her voice booming the crash of waves against the hull and the bellowing canvas overhead, Dormy naps in a hammock in the hold below in the middle of her inventory, and Cheshire stands at the tip of the bowsprit to guide them forward. But as the sun rises between the mountains, the blanket of fog disappears as does Jonathan's vision.

He thinks of Mary Anne curled on the couch downstairs in her ripped nightdress.

It would be most inappropriate to present Mary Anne to the Duchess in her current state, and he doubts she would want to spend the next several days without a change of clothing. However, Dormy's trousers and shirts are far too small, and presenting any of March's wardrobe to Mary Anne is out of the question, except for a green hooded cloak and an old pair of boots. They will suffice for now, but Jonathan knows a visit to Rookridge is in order before they depart. He fastens his watch to his trousers and checks the time. He plans to set out with Mary Anne on foot, and by the time they make their purchases, Dormy and March will have packed for the journey and arrive shortly thereafter.

Jonathan selects another pair of leather trousers, since the pair from yesterday still hang over a stack of books in Dormy's wagon, a loose linen shirt without ties, and a blue longcoat with heavily frayed silver thread embellishments, and his top hat, covered with the same patchwork as his robe, with a length of orange fabric wrapping around its crown and hanging off its back.

In the kitchen, he packs a small satchel with the essentials: a small block of cheese wrapped in cloth, bread, a pair of tangerines, a glass bottle of water, few silver coins, tea service for two, and a small jar with Scale Petal tea—a cold brew from the bulbs of Snake's Head flowers and lemongrass. Lastly, he grabs a new flask from the cupboard and takes a morning sip before he tucks it into his coat pocket.

In his study, he scribbles a quick note on parchment with his plan and instructions to meet them in the village. He places it on the pillow next to March, moves the hair from her face, and kisses her lips once more. She takes his hand and tucks it under her head, knowing even in sleep he has to leave. He would spend hours like this, for no other reason than to be near her until she awakes and he could see her smile.

"Every step away is a step back to you," he whispers, slipping his arm free.

Jonathan did not hear Dormy rise, but by the time he returns downstairs, he finds the chair beside Mary Anne empty and the door ajar. He peeks out and chuckles as Dormy fights against the weight of sleep and tries with all her might to walk a straight path to her wagon. Jonathan has seen drunkards accomplish better, but she reaches the rear of the wagon before she falls flat on her face into the back door, feet hanging out, followed by a loud clatter.

The racket is enough to stir Mary Anne for the first time this morning. She sits up and stretches with a smile of a peaceful night's sleep, but once she sees Jonathan, her face loses all expression and color. She expected to see someone else, somewhere else.

"I hoped it all to be a dream," she says, hanging her head. "Why could it not be a dream?"

"I am sorry it is not," Jonathan says from the door. There are no words he can say which will lift her spirits at the moment. He lays the cloak and boots on the chair next to her and makes them both a hot cup of Juniper Apple tea. He tells her of the morning plans before leaving her to her thoughts. Jonathan slings the satchel over his shoulder and takes his tea outside. His body craves to sit at his chair, at his table, but he knows if he approaches, he will lose the rest of the day. Instead, he collects his boots from Dormy's wagon and sits by the rear door next to Dormy's feet to finish his cup. Mesmerized by the remaining specks of tea leaves floating at the bottom of his cup, Jonathan does not hear Mary Anne approach until she stands next to him, hood drawn to hide her eyes. Jonathan puts his cup down on a small pickle barrel and stands to join her.

"This way, m'lady."

As he leads her across the meadow, Jonathan glances over his shoulder again and again, each time his home growing smaller. The last time he turns, March's eyes catch his. She leans against the doorpost, holding their sheet closed with one hand and his note in the other by her side. His lips tighten and he fights to keep his breath.

If she would have slept a few seconds longer, Jonathan and Mary Anne would have cleared the tree line, so he would not have to see the fear and disappointment on her face. But he is grateful for one more glimpse of his love.

They travel through the thickest part of the wood for ten miles, through the tangle of roots and vines beautifully woven throughout the Rookwood's damp soil, over large outcrops of boulders of the same gray stones of the surrounding mountains, down and up steep gullies, and across the dried riverbed which once powered the water mill. All the while, Mary Anne spends her time investigating the canopy and the far-off spaces between distant trees. She jumps and stumbles over a large root as a fox darts past them without a care.

"You say this isn't England," she asks, "but another world entirely?"

"Yes," says Jonathan. He pauses to help her, but keeps his distance to not shock her again. "Do you doubt your senses?"

"That's the problem. I would expect a different world to be more fanciful, like the story books I read as a child, full of dragons, or talking animals, and other such nonsense running about. Everything here appears different, but not out of the ordinary except for the candles, tea, wardrobe, and your hair and eyes." Mary Anne trails off, not intending to make her observation personal.

"You noticed." Jonathan smirks.

"These could all be elements of an elaborate charade to make a fool of me, to have me believe in the fantastic and be ridiculed for it, or to keep me from my responsibilities."

"To what purpose? Are there such people who would do this in your world?" It takes Mary Anne a moment to respond, but in the silence, Jonathan can see in her face—her worries have cause and history.

"I don't know," she huffs. "This all seems impossible."

"Tell me what that word means."

"Do you not have that word here?"

"Of course we have the word impossible here. It just doesn't mean much. I want to know what you think it means, because you speak it as if nothing impossible happens in your world whatsoever." She bites her lip and her thoughts sink inward. "You've been told certain things are impossible, yes?"

"Quite often in fact," says Mary Anne.

"And do you believe them?"

"I cannot afford to believe them."

"So you have experience making the impossible possible."

"Yes." Mary Anne resurfaces from her thoughts a more confident woman. "But in England, candles do not act of their own accord, tea does not change color, and people wear clothing. Every person I have encountered since my arrival has been half naked, if not more, except for Doris. And although she dresses in men's clothing, at least she has the sense to cover her body, unlike others."

Jonathan wonders what Mary Anne's reaction would have been if she arrived anywhere else besides the Rookwood. Should she have found herself in Rookridge or any other village or town, she would have found women in full length tunics, dresses, aprons, bonnets, and gowns depending on where she arrived, and men in their trousers, breeches, doublets, and frock coats. She would have an entirely different opinion of Wonderland and its people, as far as modesty is concerned, and felt more comfortable from the look of the attire her people wear to sleep in her world, covered from neck to wrist to ankle.

"You contradict yourself, you know?" says Jonathan. "If you can believe in the impossible and have overcome it yourself, why do you deny its existence here?"

"It's a much simpler explanation than believing I'm in a fictitious world outside my own." Her breath grows quicker. The corners of her mouth twitch. "I need to return home. I've much to do."

"Mary Anne." Jonathan stops and removes his hat and scratches the top of his head. "In order for you to return home, you will need to start believing in the impossible. Here we may use the word, but we do not believe in it. You have only seen the Hollow, but this world is vast and beyond even our comprehension. Accept where you are, so you can move forward. Because the more you fight against what is real, no matter how different, the harder your journey will be."

Jonathan can see the wheels tick away through her eyes, much the same way as he stares at the gears of his timepiece.

She takes deep breaths through her nose—each time her shoulders relax and lower—nods, and they continue on their journey.

During the silence between conversations, Jonathan's own mind races with thoughts of Cheshire's fate, the possibility of another outburst from Mary Anne, their path to Mirus and the Duchess, and the expression on March's face as she leaned against their door, watching him leave.

After another stretch, Mary Anne breaks the silence again. "The trees, they seem to go on forever."

"It does seem so, but not forever," Jonathan replies, optimistic at the chance of conversation. "The Rookwood is the largest forest in the country, stretching out for hundreds of miles in all directions. From the valley we walk, all the way to the eastern and northern coasts. One could wander for days or even weeks before finding their way out, or another person. But that is nothing compared if you would have appeared in the Wilds."

Mary Anne's eyes narrow, curious.

"It's another forest far from here. Be thankful you did not arrive there. It is far more neglected and overgrown, darker some would say, with trees which twist and grow in such a way, each appears to have a gnarled face, or so I've heard. And house creatures like borogoves and snarks. These are just stories, of course. I have met no one who has stepped foot there. In actuality, no one has lived there for thousands of years. The forest is untouched by human hands, and allowed to grow wild without interference, with only the coast as its boundary."

"It sounds awful," says Mary Anne.

"I imagine it would be rather beautiful," says Jonathan.

"I do enjoy the occasional walk through nature, but I much prefer the city," says Mary Anne. "Would it not have been wiser for us to stay on a path or road?"

"For our purposes, no. There are a few roads, but they twist and turn through the wood and it could have taken us significantly longer to get where we need to be if we followed them."

He tells her a half truth. They take the most direct route to Rookridge and stay off the roads for Mary Anne's safety. Though Jonathan has many allies in Wonderland, there are those who would do Mary Anne harm. Rarely does a woman cross over from the other world, but when they do, their arrival sets all manner of events into motion. Most people would consider her curious and exciting, but there are others who revile strangers from the other world and see them as evil, maybe even demons. Regardless, since her mismatched eyes and hair will stand out in any crowd, she must remain concealed until they reach the Duchess.

Their conversation is cut short by a bandit who emerges from his hiding place behind a wide oak. He picks the dirt from beneath his fingernails with a dagger and sucks a lodged piece of food from his teeth. His prolonged nose hangs over the scarf meant to conceal his identity, or perhaps the scar running down his right cheek. A secondary bandit, this one bald with a milky film over his left eye, approaches from the rear, cursing as his foot gets caught on the underside of a root. Both men's coats scrape the ground, their hems all but worn away and caked with dried mud.

"Not again," says Mary Anne and grabs Jonathan's arm, her fingertips digging into his skin.

"Gentleman, and I use the term loosely," Jonathan says, tipping his hat. "How may we help you this afternoon? You are far from the roads, are you not?"

The scarf muffles the scarred man's words. "What can we say? Times are hard all over." He pockets his dagger and unsheathes a rusty, ill-treated sword. He flicks it upward as a signal for Jonathan to throw over his satchel.

"Sorry?" Jonathan knows what this means, but feigns ignorance to have fun at their expense, causing the scarred man to repeat his motion again and again, frustrated by Jonathan's confusion.

"Just fucking give us the bag," the scarred man finally says. "It's not that bloody difficult to understand. Me, sword, you, bag. Give me the fucking bag or we'll run you through and leave you to the worms."

"Listen," says Jonathan. "Frank, Ralph, you two are horrible at this. Perhaps a little more rehearsal before your next attack would increase your ferocity."

"Those aren't our fucking names!" the scarred one snaps.

"Well, I have to call you something." Jonathan smiles. "Ruffian one and two seems silly, but if you would prefer something different, how about Clarice and Margaret?"

"Shut it!" the bald one shouts behind them. "Hand over the purse, you little twat."

Mary Anne's grip tightens on Jonathan's arm. This feeling is all too familiar, but these two do not hold a candle to the ferocity of the Ace, or March. Though not as skilled as her, she has trained Jonathan well over the years. Inexperienced bandits like these men will pose no actual threat.

"Everything will be fine," Jonathan tells her, and pulls away from her grip.

"And we'll be taking the girl as well," the bald man demands, closing the distance between them.

"Absolutely not, Geoffrey," says Jonathan.

It all happens in a matter of seconds. The scarred man reaches out for them, but Jonathan swings his satchel around his body, knocking away the sword and throwing the scarred man off balance. The bald man reaches for Mary Anne, but Jonathan turns and kicks deep into the man's chest, knocking him to the ground. All the air the bald man thought he possessed escapes in one hoarse exhalation. He pulls the scarf from his face and forces air back into his lungs. Jonathan spins to avoid the scarred man's sword several times, and flings the satchel into the back of the man's head each time.

Jonathan's fear becomes reality in front of his eyes as the bald man grabs Mary Anne by her neck and yanks her backward, causing her hood to fall around her shoulders. He pulls a flintlock pistol from his coat and aims at Jonathan's back.

"Jonathan!" Mary Anne screams and struggles against her capture, but to no avail.

"Son of a bitch." The scarred man stops swinging and looks past Jonathan to Mary Anne. "Stop!" He pulls his scarf down to be clear. "I said stop, you buffoon."

The sight of Mary Anne's hair spooks the bald man, unable to see her at first through his left eye.

"Change of plans." The scarred man stumbles over tree roots as he circles around Jonathan to join his partner.

"You will not lay another hand on her." Jonathan takes the satchel from his shoulder and spins it like a flail.

"That's enough heroics for today," the bald man says as he points the barrel at Mary Anne's ribs, but has a tough time keeping the pistol and his hand from shaking.

The scarred man takes the dagger from his belt and cuts a small lock of Mary Anne's hair before pushing her into Jonathan's arms and disappearing into the wood with his partner.

Jonathan steps away to examine Mary Anne from head to foot. "I seem to ask this too often of you, but are you unharmed?" Whatever the intention of these two men will bode ill for Jonathan and Mary Anne, and he hopes they will not see them again until they reach Rookridge, or at least the eastern road. They will meet with March and Dormy, and speed to the capital as quickly as her ponies will take them.

"I am, thank you," she says, shaken but confident, at least outwardly. She looks off in the direction the two men disappeared. "I do not understand."

"Neither do I, but let's consider ourselves fortunate." He pulls Mary Anne's hood over her head once more. "But until I say contrary, I must insist you make sure your hood remains on."

CHAPTER 8

CHESHIRE

C heshire sits at the door of the hollowed oak in the circle while he finishes his apple for breakfast. His tongue plays with its stem and moves it from one side of his mouth to the other. This morning, there are no screams to mask the door's creak this time. If the Ace prowls anywhere near the circle, the groan of the iron hinges will certainly draw his attention. Cheshire wraps his cloak and sash tightly around his waist. When he jumps from the pitch black of the catacombs to the bright morning light blind, he cannot afford for his cloak or sash to catch in the door or snag a branch. He knows, or at least hopes, the Ace is unaware of the door, and therefore there is no chance of the ax falling upon him once he leaves his safe confines. But, on the off chance the Ace waits with his ax at the ready, Cheshire will need to bolt and close the door behind him. If the Ace ever had knowledge or, dare he think it, access to the catacombs, Cheshire would never be safe again.

He places both hands on the curve of the door and breathes deep to calm his racing heart. He steps down on the interior release lever, and the moment the lock clicks free, Cheshire whirls through the door into the bright morning light, slams the door behind him, and scrambles up the neighboring tree ready for the first attack. Cheshire waits and watches for any sign or sound of the Ace, but only the hum of life within the Rookwood fills his ears. The sparrows sing to their children in their nests above, and the crickets chirp and flit through the air below. He climbs through the large branches of the oaks, searching every direction until he has completed the circle.

After deciding the Ace has indeed moved on, Cheshire drops back to the ground and discovers deep gouges in the dirt and signs of a scuffle, but no blood or dismembered body parts. But there is another set of boot prints easily distinguishable from the Ace's deep impressions and the woman's bare feet.

"Jonathan."

Cheshire intended for Jonathan and March to hold the Ace at bay or delay him, but of course, Jonathan would give chase without thought to his own wellbeing. Cheshire unwinds his sash and cloak while he dances through the footprints, following their path and piecing together the fray. It appears Jonathan may have talked his way out of the debacle. When March would jest Jonathan could move mountains with his words, Cheshire would correct her, and say Jonathan's words do not move mountains. His words get others to move them for him. But despite his silver tongue, Cheshire wonders if the Ace would listen? But then again, Jonathan is not the target.

The Ace's footprints lead off to the west, and Jonathan's head south, back in the mill's direction.

"Curious," says Cheshire. "Where are the woman's?"

Cheshire follows Jonathan's footprints back to the Hollow, through the meadow and to the table, and finds a fourth set heading to the front door of the mill. Jonathan, March, Dormy, and the woman.

"Damn it all," he says. "This woman is an unwelcome nuisance."

But as he approaches the mill, he finds two pairs of fresh boot prints continuing south through the meadow. The imprints suggest Jonathan and March, but the stride of her boots appears timid and cautious. Furthermore, they would never leave without Dormy, and her wagon and ponies still sit in front of the mill, and half her body hangs out the back. Cheshire turns Dormy over and shoves her legs inside the wagon and latches the door before she can fall out again.

He scales the outside of the mill, climbing the stone walls of the lower half and jumping to the wooden beams of the higher floors until he reaches the balcony of their bedroom. Inside, Jonathan and March's garments and boots lay carelessly flung across the bed and floor. A sign Jonathan has left, because he could never handle an utter mess such as this. March, however, is downstairs in the midst of a heated rant about the woman.

Cheshire sneaks down to the study and finds several of March's rapiers and short swords wrapped in cloth and laid on the table, ready to be packed. He looks over the railing, and on the bottom floor are several open trunks, half packed with clothing, swords, and small boxes of tea.

March emerges from the kitchen wearing one of Jonathan's linen shirts, untied and with the sleeves rolled to her elbows. It flows behind her, like her hair, as if the fire within her creates her own wind. She carries enough boxes of tea to finish filling the trunk to its rim, treating them with more care than she did the clothing in the bedroom. She uses several colorful words to describe the woman. Rake fire, cow sack, whiffle, sow's ass, among many others, but amidst the menagerie, Cheshire plucks out the woman's name. *Mary Anne Elizabeth.*

Before he dives headlong into the tempest, he cannot help but explore and fiddle with the new long feather quills on Jonathan's desk, the new wax seal with a crest of Jonathan's design, a small hand carved stone raven, and an assortment of leather work and sketches on parchment. When he has had his fill, he sits atop a bookcase and waits for March's return, listening to her rant.

"I should have done it and let it be over with," she says, climbing the stairs. "We could be out in the meadow right now, instead of this shit."

"Rough morning?" asks Cheshire. "Or a rough night? Considering the condition of the bedroom. Sorry I missed it."

"Dormy and I wagered on when you would reappear." His presence does not surprise her in the least. "She said within the fortnight, while I bet we would not see you again for neigh another year. Guess I owe her a silver. And do not act as though you have not been skulking in the rafters for however long and are not already aware of the reason."

"Not the rafters," says Cheshire, lying on his back atop the bookcase with his head hanging off its edge. "You seem perturbed."

"And thank you, by the by, for bringing the Ace to our doorstep. I know you are aware that in the entire span of time we have lived here, the Ace has never, never once, crossed into the Hollow. Ass."

"I also know there is more to your troubles than him," he says with a sly gravel in his voice.

Rather than answer, March wraps three more swords in thick linen and binds them with thin leather strips.

"Indulge me," says Cheshire. "If nothing else, it will be therapeutic to express your frustrations with words rather than throwing things about."

"She has the nerve to come here and disrupt our lives," March explodes, sheathing long daggers into a black leather belt. "And how did she find her way here? How did Jonathan happen upon her? Hmm?"

Cheshire decides not to divulge his participation, especially while March has weapons in her hands. "Do you really think it was her choice?"

"Are you going to let me rant or not?"

"Proceed."

March continues, but her tone softens. "Of all places, here, why here? You bring the Ace and Jonathan brings this otherworld woman to our home. This is not how the evening or morning should have gone, especially with you here with us."

Cheshire knows March at her core is a gentle but guarded soul, like Jonathan and himself. This is how they survive the harsh hand Wonderland has dealt them. Each of their lives is much like Wonderland and the catacombs. The beauty and majesty of the land is a facade, and the true wonder lies beneath.

"And now he is off yet again, and so are we," March says, tossing the belt of daggers into a trunk below.

They share the same mixture of sadness and longing. He drops to the desk and crouches face to face with her, his nose full of both her and Jonathan's intoxicating scents. He fights the temptation to reach out and pull her close, no matter how badly his body wants to feel her pressed against his. After all, Jonathan must be here to join them. He removes the apple stem with his tongue from his check to his lips and points it toward March with a grin. She leans in, slowly bites the stem with her teeth, taking it from Cheshire, and spits it over the edge of the study.

"And to where, pray tell, has this woman absconded with our Jonathan?" Cheshire laughs.

"Rookridge, to buy her a traveling dress for the road," says March.

"Jonathan has a good heart, and if he did not want to help everyone, you and I would not love him the way we do," says Cheshire.

The words ring true to March's ears. She huffs and runs her fingers roughly through his hair. "Dormy and I will depart soon. You are welcome to join us."

"Thank you, but no. I do not care to wait," Cheshire says. Jonathan and Mary Anne have a sizable lead on him, and to catch up, he must be fleet footed, still all the while keeping a watchful eye for the Ace. "You still have a few hours left before you depart, especially since your driver still sleeps."

"The more she sleeps now, the safer I will be on the road later, so leave her be." March trails off as she walks downstairs to continue packing. "Will I see you in Rookridge?"

"Depends on how soon you arrive."

Cheshire slips out without another word and races through the meadow after Jonathan's footprints.

He is surprised March allowed Jonathan to leave with this strange woman. Of course, from Cheshire's interaction with her the previous night, she seems as much a threat as a wisp of cloud or puddle after a rainstorm. But it is still curious, because March is protective of Jonathan more than anyone. Cheshire appreciates her tenacity since he travels for so long between visits.

An epiphany strikes Cheshire as he bounds from tree to tree. In his haste, he neglected to ask March about the trunks. They are packed for a much further journey than Rookridge, but rather than doubling back, he will collect the answers from Jonathan. But the thought of this woman walking with Jonathan through the wood makes the hair on the back of his neck bristle, matching March's contempt. Mary Anne survived, which Cheshire regrets having a hand in, and now dares intrude on their time, his time. She is a mystery, and Cheshire will not let this abide.

He reaches the eastern road leading to Rookridge and perches high in a tree a mile from the village to hear any news of the magistrate's untimely death or anything else of use to him. Well aware three miles behind him is the spot the woman died by his and the Ace's carelessness, he chooses to stare toward Rookridge.

Two traveling textile peddlers, a tall man with gaunt features and bulging eyes, and a squat man with faded orange whiskers stabbing out of his chin and misshapen patches on his cheeks, both in leather jerkins and skull caps, return from business in Rookridge. Their stacks of rolled fabrics, assorted damasks, jacquards, silks, and linens cause their backs to hunch so they resemble snails rather than men.

"I tell you, houses of recently deceased nobles and gentry are the ideal places to collect fabric." The shorter of the two imparts wisdom to his companion, who has obviously heard this at length multiple times. "Linens hidden away in closets, tablecloths, bed curtains and sheets fetch a handsome sum, if they're not soiled, and even if they are, I make sure that piece is hidden well within the roll. So, by the time they become awares, my purse is full and I'm off to the next village."

"Look there," the tall man says, dismissing the squat man's advice when he sees Cheshire's cloak waving high above them, as if caught on a branch and not worn by Cheshire. "Nice weave, long, too long for his short frame, unique ombre, triple panel hood construction. Seen better days, but you can tell it used to be a fine garment."

"Not worth the trouble to climb up there and get it." The shorter man points with a stubby finger. "The bottom hem is horribly frayed and ripped, plus I'm not sure if that's a dye ombre or just dirt, and the little ass cut armholes."

"Who said anything about climbing?" The taller says, "We

kill him and take it. Stitch it up, cut off the frayed bits. The ombre alone would fetch ten silver."

Cheshire tries to listen to their irksome banter, but the thought of the woman on the road lingers in his mind.

The squat peddler cannot argue with the prospect of more coin filling their purse, so they both let the weight of their bundles topple them to their backs on the side of the road. Their arms and legs flail like overturned beetles, trying to rock themselves upright before they unbuckle several belts across their chests and waists to free themselves. Without the weight of their loads, they each stand two heads taller than before.

"You keep the cloak," says the shorter. "I'll take that pretty sash round his waist. I haven't seen such fabric in ages. Beautifully woven purple linens and raw silk, hints of embroidered floral and filigree designs. A little touch up and I could live like a king for a month if sold to the right person in Mirus or Adamas."

He has indulged their foolishness for a time, but the thought of these two filthy degenerates touching his mother's shawl, the last and only possession he has to remember her, causes the hairs on Cheshire's arms to rise, as a chill charged with instantaneous hatred for these men courses through his body. And to make matters worse for the two peddlers, a familiar beige apron with traces of blood hangs rolled from the taller man's pack.

"I'll keep what is mine," Cheshire says, turning on the branch to face the two peddlers. "As opposed to the dead you are accustomed to stealing from."

"It's none of your business how we conduct ours. But I tell

you what. You know how they end up dead?" The shorter man pulls a rusted dagger from the leather frog on his belt and tosses it from hand to hand. "Do you think I wander from town to town waiting for people to die? Well, I do, but if there's no one there fresh at the ferryman's dock, I encourage them off the dock myself. Now, give us what we want or I'll split you open, take them, and string you up by your innards instead of your feet. Your choice, boy."

Cheshire turns quickly on the branch and hangs upside down by his knees, arm spread, taunting them.

"You'll regret those words. It's like threading a needle. Skilled hand, perfect shot, right through the eye," the short peddler says, overconfident. He cocks his arm back, the tip of his dagger gripped between his thumb and forefinger, and hurls it through the air. Cheshire can hear the flits as it spins. The throw is better than he expected, but Cheshire twists at the last moment, snatches the dagger out of the air, and flings it back at the short man, burying it deep into his right eye socket.

"Through the eye, correct?" Cheshire smirks.

The short man staggers a few steps and reaches for his companion before he collapses, blood oozing from his eye.

In one fluid motion, Cheshire drops from the tree, pulls the dagger from the dead peddler's eye, and plunges it into the tall peddler's inner thigh.

He falls back screaming as loud as his lungs can endure. A steady stream of blood pumps from the wound with every movement. He tries to pull the dagger from his leg, but the tip is deep in his bone.

"I wouldn't do that," says Cheshire. "You'll just die quicker.

Now, I can bandage it and stop the bleeding. And you may be able to make it to Rookridge to see a physician." Cheshire lies, knowing the wound is fatal. "Before I do, I need to ask you a question."

The peddler nods violently, in shock, color draining from his face.

Cheshire retrieves the bloody apron, and rips a thick length of canvas from a roll on the peddler's pack. In his hands, he knows it belonged to the woman on the road yesterday. He kneels beside the peddler, apron in hand. "Where did you get this?" Cheshire knows, but he wants to hear the words.

"From a corpse down the road, freshly buried," he says through short, choppy inhales. "There was a place on the road, recently cleared from debris. We took it to sell for a few coppers."

"That's all I needed." Cheshire grins and bandages the peddler's thigh tight with the canvas above the wound before pulling the dagger free. He wraps the rest of the canvas strip over the gash to pinch it shut, and secures it with a bowline knot.

"I'm sorry," he says. "I'm sorry."

Cheshire pulls the peddler to his feet with both hands and points in the direction of Rookridge. "You need to hurry."

The peddler, face as pale as the whites of his eyes, limps away towards the village. His bandages and trouser leg turn a deep crimson from his thigh to his boot. He leaves a thick trail of blood, a red snaking ribbon in the dirt, behind him.

Cheshire watches the life drain from the peddler as he staggers from side to side until his body goes slack and falls to the brush on the roadside. He rolls the shorter peddler and their packs off the opposite side of the road. He should string them up from the branches above, like so many others strewn throughout the Rookwood. They do not deserve the mercy. Cheshire will let the foxes, ravens, and insects have their say and rid the world of them.

He climbs a nearby oak and ties the apron around a high branch, out of reach of any who may pass. It flaps in the gentle breeze under the canopy. When the wind dies and it hangs still, he shakes the lingering thought from his head and leaps through the trees back towards Rookridge.

He has wasted enough time. It will be difficult to track Jonathan down in a village during the day, and convince him to abandon Mary Anne and return to the Hollow with him and March, and return to the way things ought to be.

CHAPTER 9

MARY ANNE

No matter how she sits, Mary Anne cannot find a comfortable position to escape the splinters of the turnip wagon she and Jonathan ride the rest of the way to Rookridge. Mary Anne brushes the damp soil off a turnip's welcoming white and purple skin. She has never eaten a raw turnip before, but her mouth waters from the thought of a single bite. If she had her wits about her last night, she would have jumped at the opportunity to partake in the cream puffs, tarts, or biscuits spread out along Jonathan's table. Perhaps then her stomach would not make the noises she hopes Jonathan cannot hear above the clunks of the cart's wheels.

She is grateful to the old farmer for the ride and for the chance to rest her tired, throbbing feet. He turns back often with a carefree, toothless smile surrounded by a salt and pepper beard, but with deep blues instead of blacks. During their ride, he is most hospitable and makes attempts at conversation. He asks how their morning was, why they were out so far in the middle of the Rookwood, and if Mary Anne and Jonathan were married and had children.

"My sister and I have had a rather eventful morning," Jonathan answers eloquently and without hesitation. "We were on route to Rookridge from Long Meadow, it's the small village to the north of the Rookwood, you must have heard of it. We are famous for our click beetle stew. You must try some if you are ever on your way northward."

"I think I've heard of it, but I've never been up that way," the farmer says. "Too far out the way, with the length of my trip already. But if you're coming in from the north, how'd I happen upon you on the eastern road?"

"The front axle of our wagon snapped. I mean, it was our father's and grandfather's before him, and more than eighty years old. I'm surprised it lasted as long as it did, but it snapped and spooked our lone horse and we had to watch it run off without us," says Jonathan. "We waited for a bit to see if he would return, but alas, we were stranded. Rather than give chase, we cut through the Rookwood by way of one of the trails we found, since the northern road winds so, to hopefully reach Rookridge by midday, and make our purchases along with a new horse to take us home. Unfortunately, my navigation skills are not what they once were, and we ended up walking in the wrong direction."

"Well, you two are lucky," says the farmer, fanning his weathered face with his straw hat. "Bandits and other unsavory types call this wood home."

"How intriguing," says Jonathan. He and the farmer

continue to trade stories and laugh the entire way to the village. Mary Anne marvels at Jonathan's ability to weave intricate stories vivid enough even she would believe them. But she can see his plan to keep the farmer talking about far away things so not to ask about the quiet woman riding in the back.

Jonathan's earlier words replay in her mind like a record caught on a single line of music, drowning out most of their conversation out, and Mary Anne is not able to rescue the needle. He instructed her to make sure her hood remains on. She wonders if it is to do with the two men who accosted them on their walk. She touches the spot on her ribs where the pistol pressed against her skin, imagining it tender with a bruise or mark. She has spent most of her days in her factory, business meetings, home working on finances, or her company's ship preparing the manifest for deliveries, at least until recently, and never dreamt she would live through such an ordeal. The other man cut a lock of her hair before they both ran into the woods. If a memento is all they required, she would have gladly parted with more hair to keep herself safe.

Do I need to keep the hood on in case those two return? she thinks. *Or are there others who would do me harm because I'm not of this world?*

"Welcome to Rookridge," Jonathan whispers as they cross through a large stone archway.

Mary Anne stands and balances herself against one of the wagon's posts as the village comes into view. It resembles the sketches and paintings in her childhood storybooks and comes to life before her eyes. Log cabins and half-timber buildings line the streets, each topped with weathered shingles or thatched roofs. The scent of manure and livestock wafts over from nearby fields and pens. Chickens and goats run freely through the streets.

The citizens of Rookridge are far more beautiful than any dream Mary Anne could create. Each of their heads of hair shines a different color, some vibrant, others dull but still colorful. The elderly cling to the small amounts of hue streaking through their gray or white hair. Mary Anne notices distinct absences of brunette, blonde, or even red headed women or men in sight, and suddenly fully understands how different she is in this world.

Women wear cotton bodices, capelets, and their dresses covered in dust from the unpaved roads, and the men wear loose fitting cotton shirts with no buttons, and swords hang from some of their hips.

Where are the motor cars and carriages? Where are the women in corsets and fancy feathered hats, or the men in Oxfords or suits?

A grim thought casts over Mary Anne. She may not only be in a different world, but a different time entirely, perhaps hundreds of years in the past. She humored Jonathan's theory of different worlds yesterday and this morning, hoping deep down she was just lost in the English countryside, but the evidence before her is irrefutable. March's words jump to the forefront of Mary Anne's thoughts, and they shake Mary Anne to the bone. She could walk forever and not find her home, because it does not exist here.

The cart reaches a bustling area of commerce Mary Anne believes to be the town's square or market. An anvil's ring keeps time somewhere in the distance over customers' negotiations with shopkeepers, and the brays, clucks, whinnies, and squawks of the animals within the square. Barkers from different vendors shout at potential customers, and musicians strum strange looking guitars atop stacks of boxes, adding to the overwhelming cacophony. Children laugh and chase each other while they play a game with a stitched leather ball through the dusty streets. A man without a table sells what Mary Anne believes are animal bones and the skeletons of birds on a worn mat. Another gentleman sells glass figurines of animals and people dancing at his stall. But it is the sizzle of roasted birds on spits at another booth which captures Mary Anne's attention. Their warm aroma twists her empty stomach.

Once the farmer stops his wagon, Jonathan helps Mary Anne down and then tosses a silver coin to the old man, who tips his hat as he drives away.

Mary Anne holds Jonathan's sleeve with one hand as though to keep him from evaporating into thin air and keeps the other hand firmly secured to the side of her hood. With the number of people in the town square, the crowd could easily separate them as they pushed by. Jonathan leads her through the crowd and into a clothier at the edge of the square in a line of wooden storefronts. Tall rolls of beautiful woven fabrics line both walls of the narrow shop like a grove of trees or columns in a church. They pass by in a blur as Jonathan escorts her to a small changing area at the back and asks her to wait behind the heavy curtains, which she agrees to without question.

She is not claustrophobic, but the compact space within the heavy damask curtains intensifies the sound of her breathing, her heartbeat, and the urge to panic crawls up her neck like rising water. The silence on the other side of the curtain makes her legs shake. Jonathan could abandon her here and now, walk out the front door, and disappear into the crowd. She would never be able to find him or his home, no matter how long she searched. But her panic recedes when she hears who she assumes is the store's proprietor greet Jonathan with kindness and familiarity.

Moments later, an old woman shuffles through the curtain into the changing area. Her plump features are full of warmth, her hands scarred with jabs and pokes from years of needlework, and numerous thick white braids wrap around each other in piles around her head, with those same needles jutting out of her hair like a pincushion. The woman has a simple but elegant pale blue dress and a beige linen underdress draped over her arm and secured with her wrinkled hands. But before she hands the dress over, she studies Mary Anne. Her rose-colored eyes peer through half circle spectacles.

Her long fingers with pronounced knuckles reach for Mary Anne. "May I?" she asks in a gentle voice, heavy with years.

Mary Anne looks down to see what the woman refers to and notices a small section of her hair hanging out of the corner of her hood. At first Mary Anne recoils, and tries to tuck it away, but realizes Jonathan brought her here for a reason, and if he trusts this woman, she must as well. Mary Anne takes down her hood and the woman's mouth drops, amazed, as she gently twirls her fingers through the loose ends of Mary Anne's hair.

"Beautiful," she says. "Not just your hair. You're quite a lovely young woman, despite your differences." The old woman winks.

Mary Anne smiles at the odd but genuine words. "Thank you," she says.

The old woman hands Mary Anne the dress, backs out of the changing area, pulls the curtain closed, and carries on with Jonathan once more. The laughter on the other side of the curtain helps to calm Mary Anne's nerves further. However, she is still reluctant to undress in this strange place, around these strange people. Nowhere seems private. But the alternative is to remain in her soiled and ripped nightgown.

She unties her cloak and hangs it on a metal hook behind her, slides the new underdress over her head, and unbuttons and wriggles out of her nightgown, dropping it to the floor. Complicated, but effective. The laces and open areas of the blue dress confuse Mary Anne at first, not understanding the orientation in which it is to be worn. But eventually she discovers the dress sits more akin to a coat, slipped on from the back and laced from the front, with the underdress exposed and serving as the front half of the ensemble. Mary Anne can imagine March wearing the outer dress with nothing underneath and calling it fashion.

The new garments hang heavier on Mary Anne's body than any other she owns. The material is thick and scratches against her skin, but as different as the garment is, it adds a bit of normalcy to the situation. She clips the cloak around her neck, makes sure her hood is in place, and emerges with her head higher than when she entered.

"Brilliant," says Jonathan, "but we are not finished yet." He locks the front door while the old woman sits Mary Anne on a small wooden stool facing a tall looking glass in the back corner of the shop.

Her experienced hands quickly braid Mary Anne's hair into the tightest bun she has ever worn. Then she holds up a piece of twine with long chunks of white hair, the woman's hair, stitched along its length.

"I cannot," says Mary Anne. "I shouldn't." Mary Anne does not feel able to accept the generosity of this woman. "This is too much. I do not know what to say."

"What's done is done," she says, tying the twine around Mary Anne's head and securing it to the bun. "I can't reattach it to myself now, can I? Either you wear it, or it goes out the door with the rest of the rubbish. If you can't tell, I have enough to spare. You wouldn't want to make an old woman's sacrifice go to waste now, would you?" She winks again.

"No ma'am, thank you again," says Mary Anne. "May I know your name, please?"

"Deidra," the old woman replies. She wraps the twine several more times around the bun and then conceals her handy work underneath a pale green kerchief.

Simple as the transformation is, the white curls hide every strand of her own hair, and besides the color of her eyes and eyebrows, she could pass for a woman of Wonderland. She will still keep her hood to cover her face, but at least this disguise lessens her worry.

Jonathan waits for her by the front door and nods with approval. Deidra walks Mary Anne to the door, then kisses and slaps Jonathan on the cheek.

"Don't you make me wait so long before your next visit,"

says Deidra. "I know you don't come into town often, but the least you can do is wave through the damned window at an old woman once in a while."

"You have my word," says Jonathan, returning the kiss on her cheek.

Outside, Jonathan walks with Mary Anne on his arm around the perimeter of the town square. She can tell he has a destination in mind, but wants to avoid the massive crowd at the square's center. But almost everyone they pass stops him and greets him as an old friend with a firm handshake, a tip of their hats or a curtsey. Everyone asks where March is and who the woman at Jonathan's arm is.

"She is my long-lost cousin from Ilex come to visit," he says to a burly gentleman who hugs Jonathan and spins him in the air. "A distant relation to March touring the village," he tells a woman closer to Mary Anne's age. "A blind woman looking for her father," he says to two young boys who kicked a ball over to play with Jonathan.

"I thought I was your sister," Mary Anne whispers between greetings. "Why change the story?"

"Because the more people who hear the same story can confirm its truth and continue telling it," Jonathan whispers back. "If everyone thinks you are someone different, even if disputed at first, people are less likely to remember the details. Then you become a ghost, a rumor, as opposed to a memory everyone remembers, and I have to answer for later."

"Clever," says Mary Anne. Then as they walk, regardless of her story, she greets all those who stop them with a cordial smile and nod, making sure to keep the white curls visible and her eyes concealed.

The muffled chime of Jonathan's watch chimes from his pocket, and as they make their way across the village, Mary Anne cannot help but notice a burned down storefront off the main square. Vines and other plants have overtaken the shop, twisting up along the charred remaining posts and rafters. A partial kitchen still stands, discernible by the iron stove which the fire could not claim, a staircase leading to open air, and metal people, Mannequins of a sort. All beautifully reclaimed by foliage.

The greetings continue, and Mary Anne's smile remains for the first time since she arrived. She has known Jonathan for less than a full day, and wrestled with trusting anything he and the others say, but finally allows herself to relax, slight as it may be, because the genuine admiration and respect the townspeople have for Jonathan sets her soul at ease, and proves perhaps he will keep his promise and see her home.

CHAPTER 10

JONATHAN

J onathan's timepiece rings from within its own tiny pocket sewn into his trousers, and the vibrations tingle against his hip.

Tea time, he repeats in his head as he greets old friends on the way across town. After twelve reunions, they reach the Dry Dock—the tavern on the far western side of Rookridge. Except for the clock tower, which Jonathan knows to be habitually five minutes slow, the tavern's pointed roof stands taller than the other buildings in Rookridge, like a temple calling to its worshippers. No matter the time of day or night, the Dry Dock overflows with travelers and residents of Rookridge partaking in its selection of stout drafts. The mandolin music and cavorting from within grow louder as Jonathan and Mary Anne pass through the short, rickety fence and sit at the furthest corner table in the yard. He seats Mary Anne facing away from the tavern, and himself opposite her, back to the wood, to keep a watchful eye on any who should approach.

"Look who's decided to show his face," the jolly, drunken tanner calls from the balcony. He sloshes his copper cup back and forth in celebration, his beard drenched in beer. "Good to see you, Jonathan!"

"Jonathan," the bricklayer shouts from the front door of the tavern. "Is that your woman with you? She drank me under the table and out of a week's wage last time she was in, and I demand a rematch."

"You have lost to her fourteen times." Jonathan laughs. "Are you trying to make it an even fifteen? Next time she'll take you for a month's wage. But no, March does not travel with me this day."

"Is it wise to stop?" asks Mary Anne, shrinking back inward.

"This is the closest village to the Hollow," says Jonathan. "We frequent here quite often for food, soap, and other essentials, and the villages have come to know us affectionately."

"I mean, is it wise to stop at such an establishment?" she asks.

"Everyone here is harmless." says Jonathan. "And since more well-wishers will be inevitable, we may as well take advantage of their short, inebriated memories while we wait for March and Dormy to join us. And besides, it is time for tea and a bit of lunch." He wants to take his time and lay out their food and tea service properly before eating, but Mary Anne's pained expression betrays her hunger.

She struggles against her decorum while she eats, taking

small bites of bread and cheese, and placing them back on their wrapping while she chews. But Jonathan can see how ravenous her hunger is by the way she stares at her food while it's on the table.

Even though he could not present the food properly, Jonathan painstakingly places the small silver tea service on the weathered table, fills the pot from the bottle thankfully not shattered in their skirmish, and watches the tea leaves transform the water into a rich violet.

Jonathan sips the sweet tea, and it coats his empty stomach and is enough to calm his own nerves after the day's events. He holds his cup below the table and adds a small drop from his flask before continuing to drink. To lessen the number of prying eyes, Jonathan takes his hat off and hides it in the chair to his right, but the villagers who know him, who watched him grow up in this village, would recognize him anywhere.

"Thank you, for everything," says Mary Anne. "I've not told you before."

"No thanks are necessary, but you are welcome," says Jonathan after he swallows a mouthful of cheese.

A long silence fills the space between them, and Jonathan picks at the splintered wood of the tabletop. A serving boy, in a buttoned coat too large for him and a leather traveling hat with a wide brim and tall crown comes from the tavern and places a loaf of bread on their table between them.

While she eats, Mary Anne's eyes follow townsfolk in and out of the tavern and explore the roofs of the surrounding buildings, collecting small bits of a puzzle to construct a question she hesitates to ask.

"You've a question on your mind," says Jonathan.

"Yes," says Mary Anne, eyes still wandering, "what year is it here?"

"It depends on who you ask," says Jonathan. "What year do you believe it is?"

"In my world, 1904," she says, fearful to be proven wrong. She looks to Jonathan for hope, but his eyes have none to give.

Jonathan takes out his timepiece and checks its fifth and sixth hands. "Time works a bit differently here," he says gently. "But it changes nothing. If there is a way to return you home, we will find it." He expects more questions from Mary Anne, but she sits in silence, mulling over this new information.

"I suspected, no, feared as much when we arrived in the village," says Mary Anne. "And you are correct, it changes nothing." She swallows audibly, trying to digest her own words in order to believe them. "Do you care for riddles?"

Jonathan perks up at the prospect of proper conversation. "I am not good at them, but I enjoy them."

Mary Anne smooths the dress in her lap. "A man lives in a house. All the walls of the house face south. Where is the house?"

"Well, for such a feat to happen, the house would need to be mobile, I suppose, like Dormy's wagon. She calls it home, therefore every wall can face south depending on which direction she parks, so the answer is wherever he wants it to be. I guess I'm not as bad at riddles as I thought." Jonathan is proud of his answer, but from Mary Anne's raised eyebrows, he knows he should not celebrate.

"That is not the answer I was told, but I think yours

works better," Mary Anne says with a humoring smile as if Jonathan were a child trying to solve arithmetic. But despite her furrowed brow, her smile remains. He wonders what her usual personality is, outside of the threat of death and loss of home.

"Do you have one?" she asks.

"I do not have a riddle, but I have a question," Jonathan says with caution, afraid to throw Mary Anne back into her doldrums of the day before. "And I do not mean to sour the mood, but I must ask, what is the last memory you can recall from your world? Knowing may help us discover how you arrived, and how to return you home."

Her smile shrinks by half, but remains in her eyes. "I cannot fully explain how it happened. But as I tried to return home, the fog set in as I ran through the grove of birchwood, which I've been familiar with all my life. I have always known my way home. But before I could leave the grove, I almost collided with another woman. I covered my face and braced myself to run straight into her, but she vanished. I searched the area, but there was no sign of the woman anywhere. Then when I tried to find my way home, the ground, the trees, the smell, even the wind felt different."

What little she reveals is intriguing, the presence of another woman who vanished, the fog, perhaps connected to the fog which crawled into the Rookwood. But silence discloses more information than her words. Jonathan can see the hesitation in her lips as they choose words carefully. Mary Anne is not ready to disclose all, but there is time.

"I wandered in the direction I thought my home would be

for almost an hour, I would assume," Mary Anne continues, "before I came upon the other young man."

Jonathan feels a fool to assume he was the first to meet Mary Anne, with the unfortunate exception of the Ace. But it stands to reason Cheshire would have crossed her path first, since he was the reason Jonathan ran into the Rookwood in the first place. He wants to know if it was a brief encounter or if they spoke before the Ace's attack, but before he can ask, Jonathan notices the mound of loaves piled on the table some time during the course of their conversation. He was focused on Mary Anne's story and never saw the other nine appear.

"I did not get his name," Mary Anne continues, "but he was yet another person half dressed, and rather rude."

"With lavender hair," says Jonathan.

"Yes." Mary Anne squints. "How did you know?"

The serving boy puts down the eleventh loaf of bread on the table and Jonathan grabs a firm hold on his wrist. Jonathan should have noticed before, but he was preoccupied with Mary Anne and did not think to give a second look to the server's appearance. But now, the short tuft of purple hair is clear through a hole in the leather hat which concealed his face until now.

"Hello, Cheshire," says Jonathan.

"You're getting slow." Cheshire removes the coat and hat in one swoop and places it on the back of the chair to Jonathan's left, but sits on the table's edge cross legged, face to face with Jonathan, blocking Mary Anne from his view.

He stares into Cheshire's vibrant lavender eyes, and his heart aches with joy and longing. It has been years since

Cheshire last appeared in the Rookwood, but he still does not look a day over his nineteenth year. Jonathan has missed everything about him. His eyes bright and beautiful as the day he last saw him. The mischievous slight grin ever-present on his face. His laughter and silence both in equal measure. The way Cheshire always looks with his eyes first before moving his head. And his touch, which Jonathan will have to wait for. Jonathan's own body stirs as he watches the muscles of Cheshire's torso tighten and relax with every breath.

Jonathan's eyes travel down his body to make sure his friend sits before him and not some specter or wish. It is a miracle his clothing has held up over the years—a threadbare vest, the long hood of his tattered cloak hanging out the back of his collar, the remnants of trousers climbing higher on Cheshire's thighs every visit, and his faded purple sash wrapped around his waist. Jonathan's eyes rise back to meet the two amethyst jewels which have never broken their gaze. He wants nothing more in this moment than to reach out and embrace him, feel his warmth, to inhale his ever-present scent of earth and leather.

"You are the one who left me to the brute!" exclaims Mary Anne. "It's because of you I almost died."

"Yes," Cheshire agrees with a dark glee, but does not take his eyes away from Jonathan.

"Cheshire," Jonathan begins, "may I introduce—"

"Mary Anne Elizabeth. I'm aware." Cheshire plops down in the chair with a dramatic huff and puts his bare feet on Jonathan's leg.

"How do you know who I am?" she asks, with a permanent look toward Cheshire as if she smells something foul.

"There are few things in Wonderland I do not know. Pour me a bit of tea, darling," Cheshire says to Jonathan while shoveling bread into his mouth. "This bread is rather dry."

Cheshire has an uncanny knack for knowing details before anyone else. A talent which has been, and will continue to be, dangerous. He refills his own cup and shares it with Cheshire before he pulls Cheshire's hood over his head, knowing a parchment with Cheshire's face hangs outside the Dry Dock's front door. Other notices cover half the drawing, but Jonathan will not risk any more unwarranted altercations this day.

"You do not know everything, old friend," Jonathan remarks.

"Yet." Cheshire winks at Jonathan. "But it's only a matter of time."

"To return to the matter of you two, did you at least warn her Death was at your heels?" Jonathan's attempt to chastise Cheshire falls as harsh as a drifting leaf on the autumn grass.

"Whatever do you mean?" Cheshire swallows his mouthful of sopping wet bread. "I saved her life. Therefore, you are welcome." He slides a loaf of bread in front of Mary Anne and pats the top of it.

"You threw me down a hill." Mary Anne's brows inch closer to each other, pinching the skin between.

Jonathan chokes on his tea. "What happened?"

"Lies and deceit." Cheshire leans forward in his chair. "First, she appeared out of the fog like a banshee, and then I led her to the small ravine on the north side of your property and strongly encouraged her to hide by way of letting her run off the edge and down its side. I told her to remain still if she wanted to live. I did tell you to stay there, did I not?" he says to Mary Anne. "But you did not listen, you climbed back out, and almost died, and now we are here. So again, you are welcome." He pushes the bread closer to Mary Anne and taps it once more. "You look hungry. Eat."

Jonathan has missed Cheshire's banter and knows there is no winning against him. These are not the circumstances in which he wanted their reunion, but he is thankful to have him close again. But Mary Anne has quite the opposite reaction to his presence. Her posture becomes more rigid every time Cheshire speaks, as if to grow taller, especially when he dismisses her.

Suddenly, Cheshire grabs a stone as big as his fist from the ground next to him and lobs it at something or someone behind Jonathan.

"What's the matter with you?" Jonathan grabs Cheshire's arm before he can loose another stone.

"There was a rather repulsive fellow at the gate staring in our direction," Cheshire says, watching his target disappear into the market. "And now he's gone. You're welcome."

"Can we try harder to bring less attention to ourselves?" Jonathan asks.

"The prize son of Rookridge, a strange woman in an obvious disguise, and the most hunted criminal in Wonderland sitting at the same table out in the open," says Cheshire, "and your plan was to be inconspicuous? Sure."

"Well, I did not expect you to join us," says Jonathan. "But I'm glad you're here."

"Criminal?" asks Mary Anne.

"Are you still here?" Cheshire asks her, before another word can leave her mouth.

"He exaggerates his reputation," says Jonathan to dispel Mary Anne's worries before they have time to grow.

"Do I? She can read it for herself on the parchment by the door," says Cheshire.

But before Mary Anne can look or comment further, a tall man, with white hair down to the middle of his back, saunters from the tavern and snatches what is clearly his coat and hat off the back of Cheshire's chair and walks back inside, cursing them all.

"I was going to return them," Cheshire calls after him. "The gall of some people."

"Indeed," says Jonathan, watching the tall gentleman disappear back inside.

Mary Anne studies Cheshire through squinted eyes.

"Is there something on your mind?" Cheshire asks, taking her expression as a challenge.

Jonathan massages the bridge of his nose, aware there is no way to stop the impending confrontation.

"As I try to understand this world, I have many questions of what I see and what I hear. I look out upon the village, its buildings and people, and with the exception of everyone's hair, I've seen it all before. Albeit in books, paintings, or other works of art. How can this not be a dream, when it is the inspiration of famous artists I admire? How am I in another world when everything here comes from my own?"

Cheshire loses his grin. "The amount of ignorance in your

statement astounds me. To assume everything originates in your world is pure arrogance."

"My world would not derive from a place of nonsense," says Mary Anne, her temper rising to combat Cheshire.

"That word, *nonsense*," says Cheshire. "People use it when challenged by an idea too complex for their simple minds to fathom. Your world and your thoughts are so small, limited to what you see with your eyes, and anything outside of what *you* consider normal, you reject. I have heard whispered tales of women from the other world who venture into ours. At first I thought you curious, but now to see you, I am completely unimpressed."

"How dare you?" Mary Anne stands and speaks to Cheshire through gritted teeth. "I will not have an impudent boy with poor upbringing speak down to me, as if I'm your inferior. You know nothing of me and *you* cannot possibly fathom my life and my world. Mary Anne's response is stern, confident, she scolds Cheshire as if he were a child, but she is unprepared for his wrath.

"You speak of things outside your comprehension, silly woman," he says with a calm, grim severity. "Sit down and allow me to make myself plain. You will never speak to me in such a manner. Ever. Do you understand? I do not care where you come from or who you are. This is my world. Not yours. You would do well to remember that the next time you decide to speak to me."

"Cheshire, stop," Jonathan says forcefully.

Mary Anne senses the seriousness in Cheshire and matches his gaze, but sits back in her chair to avoid further conflict.

"Fine. Enough of this dribble," says Cheshire, smiling again as if he did not drag Mary Anne's mind through the muck. "Where did you two leave off before I arrived?"

"Riddles," Jonathan answers, exhausted.

"Wonderful," says Cheshire, eating more bread. "I have a riddle for you, Jonathan." He hobbles his chair to Jonathan's side. "Why is a raven like a writing desk?" Cheshire asks, triumphant.

"Ravens are small, desks are not. A desk can be the same color as a raven, but not every desk. You can sit at a desk and you... cannot sit at a raven. You can sit on a raven perhaps, but it would be as silly as sitting on a desk, especially if you have a chair."

"I believe I know the answer," Mary Anne says.

"Not you," Cheshire replies.

"But I do," says Mary Anne, feeling the need to remain in the conversation. "Why is a raven like a writing desk? It is because Edgar Allan Poe wrote on both. That is the correct answer, is it not?"

"That was as wrong as wrong can be." Cheshire laughs.

"Wait," Jonathan says after a moment of clarity. "A writing desk and a raven, a carved one at least, are both in my study." Jonathan knows he is right, but Cheshire gives no acknowledgement except to chew the wad of bread in his mouth, moving it from one cheek to the other. "Have you been to the mill, already? Was March still there, or had they departed yet? How upset was she?" This game of questions has taken a turn, because Jonathan now has too many he wants answered and one he does not.

"You do not know the maelstrom headed your way," says Cheshire.

"My way?" Jonathan asks. "But you're here with us now."

"For now," Cheshire says, without looking away from his bread.

It pains Jonathan to know Cheshire is right, but he comes and goes as he pleases and stays hours, months, or anywhere in between. Jonathan wishes Cheshire would give up whatever crusade keeps him moving, and stay with him and March in the Hollow.

"Our journey, gods willing, will not be too long," says Jonathan. He tears a piece of bread for himself from the loaf in Cheshire's hand. "Dare I ask you to wait for us at the Hollow or will you ride the wind out of here as soon as we depart?"

"Where are you off to?" Cheshire asks.

"I thought you knew everything?" says Mary Anne with a smug look in her eyes.

Jonathan glances to Cheshire for his reaction, waiting for the tea kettle inside to boil over and burn Mary Anne, but he sits stoic, motionless in thought, ever a mystery.

"We're going to Mirus," says Jonathan. "We—"

"What the fuck ever for?" Cheshire does not let him finish.

"Jonathan escorts me to the capital to introduce me to the Duchess, who we hope will be able to return me to my home," says Mary Anne, with a hint of smugness in her tone.

"Would you care to join us?" Jonathan asks. "We can stow you away in Dormy's wagon."

"Right. You're having a laugh," says Cheshire. "You know I'll never get into Mirus that way."

Jonathan asked out of courtesy, not wanting to exclude Cheshire. The royal soldiers have hunted him since long before he came into Jonathan's life, and have taken every precautions to secure the city and keep Cheshire out indefinitely for his crimes against the crown. Whether the charges are true or fabricated, despite their severity, he will not place judgement on Cheshire. Besides, in Wonderland, there is little difference between stories, history, and lies. They have all done unspeakable things in their past. As much as Cheshire collects the secrets of others, what Jonathan knows of him is from observation, never shared, never spoken, and he does not press the matter, and thankfully neither does Cheshire with him.

"But I'll travel with you as far as I'm able." Cheshire winks at Jonathan. "Besides, you and March will no doubt need my skills on the way."

"Thank you," Mary Anne says prematurely.

"I'm not going for you," Cheshire says with a wide grin. "It happens I have important business of my own to tend to. And make no mistake. Should you get in my way, on the way? I'll kill you. I promise you that."

Mary Anne senses the truth in Cheshire's tone, her face frozen, and does not utter a response or change her face. Jonathan waits for the joke to end in an uneasy silence which drowns out every sound from the market and tavern, if it is a joke at all. He knows first-hand what Cheshire is capable of and hopes it will never come to fruition.

Cheshire finally laughs and Jonathan joins him to relieve tension at the table. Mary Anne does not join them, but her eyes swell to the size of saucers.

At first, Jonathan assumes she looks to him for a response to Cheshire's behavior, but there is something unseen behind him, something both he and Cheshire were too distracted to notice. She opens her mouth to scream, but cannot make a sound. Her body and her face frozen in a familiar horror.

As her eyes glance to the right, Jonathan puts both feet up on the edge of the table and pushes with all his might, hurling it into Mary Anne, sending her backward, and taking Cheshire to the ground with him, just in time to escape the swing of the ax which nearly claims all of their heads.

CHAPTER 11

TRAVELER

The traveler, having humored the little thief's antics long enough, yanks his coat and hat from the chair and throws them on as he returns to his stool at the bar.

"I was going to return them," the thief calls from behind.

He saw the thief swipe his coat and hat from the stool beside him, and would have stopped him immediately if not entertained by the sight of the short boy wearing his clothing as he left the tavern and returned several times. But after the tenth time when he did not return, the traveler knew to collect his property. He pulls one of the many leather tubes from his rucksack and puffs at its ornate silver mouthpiece. The water, heated by the hot stones in the base of his rucksack, gurgles as he draws the sweet smoke into his chest. He blows thick streams of smoke down the bar's surface for the other drunkards seated further down to scoop and swirl with their hands as a child would play with water.

A great crash from outside followed by a tumultuous collection of screams draws everyone's attention but his. The tavern erupts with panic as the villagers scatter like insects beneath freshly moved timber and bottleneck their way through the rear windows and door. The traveler finishes his pint, unbothered, and pulls on his matted beard to wipe off any spilled ale. With the owner gone, the first one through the back door, he reaches over the bar and grabs two full bottles for the road.

"The Reaper," a woman screams outside. "The Reaper has come to Rookridge!"

The traveler stops at this tavern because the people of Rookridge are simple and far removed from the capital and those aligned to its politics. He can sit and drink to his heart's content without anyone bothering him, except the barkeep to claim his silver. But now that the Butcher has found his way to Rookridge, regardless of why, the traveler will never be able to return. He takes a long draw again and blows a wall of smoke between him and the door, blocking out the soon-to-be massacre outside.

The empty backdoor should be his path, but his morbid curiosity will not allow him to leave. The traveler figures if he is not yet dead, then he is not the mark, but wants to know the unfortunate soul locked in the eyes of the Butcher. Last he heard, the Butcher was after one person, a phantom, in particular. The traveler swings his rucksack over his shoulder and walks through the smoke into the screaming streets.

Townspeople in the market try to hide or outrun the Butcher's ax as it cuts through fences, walls, and bodies as if they were wet parchment, slinging ribbons of crimson through the streets, staining paths, buildings, and townspeople. Bodies fall like wheat before the reaper. A man loses half of his skull and grabs at it momentarily, wondering what happened, before falling to the ground. A young woman crawls away from the destruction without her legs. Thick trails of blood gush from her thighs, until she can no longer move. An entire family falls to the ground, cut to pieces with a single swing. The father's hand still grips his son's, far from their bodies.

The small purple-haired thief from earlier is at the center of the fray. His eyes give him away. His two companions will soon regret their decision to be near him. They try to flee in every direction, but the Butcher blocks their escape with unnatural speed and the long reach of his ax. He swings with such force, the blade buries deep into the ground with each strike, flinging dirt and rocks with its release.

Debris flies by the traveler as he snakes through the remaining stalls. They offer little cover, but they are enough to keep him out of sight. He walks gingerly around the perimeter of the fight, curious as to the outcome. His eyes follow every movement, every step, every near-death strike from beneath the long brim of his hat. The iron taste and smell of blood grows thicker the closer he follows.

The thief breaks away in a different direction, attempting to pull the Butcher's attention. His plan has the desired effect. He runs erratically, avoiding every slash of the ax, until he dives through the open window of the bakery.

The Butcher hacks apart the facade, bringing the entire building down with three wild strikes. He drives his blade deep into the fallen rubble and beams, hatred behind every strike, until it reaches flesh. Blood spurts out as he pulls the blade free. His massive arm reaches deep into the splintered wood and pulls out the baker, bloody and mutilated. She hangs from his hand like a rag doll, her lower body held in place by a few sinews. Her body snaps apart as he flings her aside.

The traveler can see the wheels turn with dark intention under the black hood. The Butcher's attention turns to the other two in the thief's party running to the north end of town, and catapults towards them in order to draw out his quarry.

As predicted, the small one appears from an alleyway and brings up the rear of the chase, running at full gait to keep up. The Butcher, only a few steps behind the others, grounds his feet and twists his body, ax at the ready, muscles taut, poised to cleave them in two. But as the blade reaches the end of its arch, the thief hits the ground and slides under the Butcher, taking his legs with him, slamming their would-be assassin to the ground. The thief springs to his feet and uses his momentum to grab the other two and drag them to the train platform at the northern end of town.

"Impressive."

It takes the traveler back to his younger days in the service of the capital when he would fool-heartedly run headfirst into a fight such as this, whether it be his or not. But those years and obligations are in the distant past and dead as far as he is concerned. He puffs at his pipe again and keeps the smoke billowed in his face while he strolls around the Butcher at a distance, making sure to never put himself in his sight.

Within seconds, the Butcher is on his feet again. The thief's gambit gave them a few additional seconds, but the traveler doubts it will be enough. He sees their plan to reach and board the Wonderland engine as it departs, but whether they make it into a train car is irrelevant, because the Butcher's ax can slice through almost any material, and a wooden train car will offer no safety.

To save his own skin, the traveler knows he should be on his way, but he is compelled to watch, to see this fight to its end. It does not matter to him if the thief gets away or not. It is not his job to get involved. Not anymore.

The storefronts along the northern street create a narrow cattle shoot the townspeople try, and fail, to escape through. With a quickened pace, the traveler circles around the backside of the buildings to keep clear of the slaughter, but still be able to peek through the thin alleyways between stores. But what he cannot see with his eyes, he can picture vividly in his mind from each unique sound he knows well. The Butcher's swings are so quick they sound like an unnatural exhalation, as if the blade steals the last breath from whomever or whatever it destroys. Exhale. Scream. Exhale. Explosion. Exhale. Death.

A small crowd forms on the raised platform, half trying to push their way through the doors of the engine and the other half trying to watch the battle, believing themselves safe. Once the trio and the Butcher approach the platform, the townsfolk abandon all thoughts of the engine and flee like birds from a hunter, unsure of which direction will keep them alive.

The young woman runs up the stairs to the top of the raised platform and hides behind a stack of crates meant to be loaded. She grips her mouth to keep her breath and perhaps her screams under control. The traveler senses something off about her energy, her fear.

Without the hindrance of the woman by their side, the thief and his blue-haired companion hold their own against the Butcher, working in tandem as if they have fought together for years, with skill and passion in their steps. More than their age should allow.

The traveler walks up to the top of the platform to gain a better view, and happens to push the young woman into one of the open cabins just as the doors close and the engine pulls from the platform.

From the edge of the platform, he can see the weight of fatigue grow heavier on the thief and his friend. Their leaps and dodges slow significantly from before at the tavern, and with no weapons, these two bide their time before the Butcher claims their heads.

Perhaps this is where they are meant to meet their end. Or perhaps not, he thinks, fiddling with the hilt of the sword protruding from his coat.

CHAPTER 12

JONATHAN

He feels as though a crushing weight bears down on his chest. Not just from the exhaustion of his lungs and muscles, but of every death he is responsible for. This fight is not about winning, because there is no way to triumph against the pure unstoppable evil of the Ace. Jonathan and Cheshire struggle to stay inches away from every strike meant to be a killing blow.

But a stranger, a godsend, drops from the train platform above to shield him and Cheshire. Jonathan recognizes the long olive coat and tall leather hat worn by their savior, the older gentleman from the tavern. Though thankful, Jonathan cannot help but wonder why he would step in to help them. This sort of selflessness died out long ago in Wonderland.

Despite the Ace's power, this stranger can not only dodge but also deflect and bat away the Ace's attacks with a sword from long before the Age of Queens. The sound of their weapons colliding rings dull and sour, as if these two blades were never supposed to meet. The stranger dances around the Ace and swirls the length of his dust covered jacket as a distraction, and backs him away.

Jonathan climbs the steps to the platform and searches around the stacked crates and barrels for Mary Anne, but she is nowhere to be found, and the tracks are empty.

"Damn it," Jonathan shouts.

Cheshire follows close behind and opens a small hatch in the platform's floor and motions to Jonathan to follow him. Jonathan's broad shoulders are a tight squeeze through the opening. They drop underneath the platform, into a maze of wide wooden beams and cross braces. A tight fit, but enough to stand and maneuver, barely. The lattice walls around them offer little concealment or protection.

"Let her be someone else's burden," says Cheshire as he counts the beams, concocting some plan.

His suggestion is cold and cruel, but Jonathan knows if there ever were a chance, this would be it. He could escape both the Ace and Mary Anne, and return to the Hollow, with March, with Cheshire, his teas, and his table. It would be simple, but he cannot bring himself to do it.

"We can't. I can't," Jonathan huffs.

The stranger and the Ace now battle overhead, and a single blow from the Ace destroys a chunk of the platform between him and Cheshire, like a deadly clock pendulum.

"Does trouble follow you wherever you go?" asks Jonathan. He scrambles with Cheshire to the far side of the platform.

"What a stupid question," Cheshire says, watching the

battle through the slats of the floor above. "It's fucking difficult when trouble literally hunts me."

Jonathan continues to follow Cheshire through the web of posts and beams, but the ax destroys sections of the platform, blocking their path. Dust falls from between the cracks into Cheshire's eyes, and Jonathan grabs hold of his collar and yanks him back, in time to miss a strike which would have split Cheshire in half.

"Thanks," Cheshire says casually.

"What the fuck are we doing in here?" Jonathan asks.

Cheshire points to a short door in the lattice directly behind Jonathan. "Don't move," he commands Jonathan.

He continues to lead the Ace around the platform, controlling where the ax will strike. Seven of the eight support timbers creak and scream from the deep gashes cut through them. The eighth and last remaining post is right next to Jonathan.

Shit.

Cheshire dives for Jonathan and spears him in the stomach with his shoulder, knocking them both through the small door and skidding across the dirt as the ax cleaves the final support. The Ace and the stranger fall with the entire platform and massive wooden awning as it all collapses in on itself with a rolling thunder crack, and disappear in a cloud of dust.

Jonathan reaches for Cheshire, but he is nowhere to be found, disappeared from the street. He did not waste the opportunity and neither will Jonathan. He races back towards the center of town while listening for the slightest movement beneath the rubble. Jonathan wants to pull the stranger free, be it alive or dead. It is the least he could do to honor his sacrifice, but Jonathan knows the Ace is not dead, and will not remain buried for long.

In the distance, Dormy's wagon, a welcome sight to his drained muscles, speeds into view, its wheels caked with red mud. Without stopping, she hooks her ponies into a sharp turn, whipping the back of the wagon towards Jonathan. March hangs from the back, face pleading, arm outstretched. Jonathan pushes his legs harder as he hears the wood shift behind him, and leaps with his last reserve of strength. March snatches him out of the air and pulls him into the wagon.

He rests his head against hers for a moment to catch his breath, and then pushes his way through the wagon, swatting away hanging nets full of bottles, and dodging swaying stacks of boxes and crates.

Dormy opens the front hatch to the driver's seat for him. "The village. I'm sorry, Jonathan."

"It's little matter now. There's nothing we can do," he says, catching his breath. "Let's put some distance between us and Rookridge, shall we?"

"Where to?" Dormy asks.

"What's the next stop of the train?" he calls to March, who keeps watch out the back door.

"Briarwell," shouts March.

With a nod and a crack of the reins, the tiny ponies haul the massive wagon around the outskirts of Rookridge, over the tracks and on the northern road.

On their way out of the village, Jonathan faces the horrific aftermath dealt by the Ace's attack. Villagers are in shock, the market in shambles, horses cleaved in two and their entrails strewn across the ground, and townspeople Jonathan has known his entire life, friends, lay dead in the streets with their loved one's wailing, clutching their dismembered bodies.

Jonathan blames himself for the wanton destruction. They should have set out later in the day in Dormy's wagon, instead of stopping in Rookridge. Cheshire may have met them on the road, the Ace might have followed, and they would have outrun him as they have countless times. He climbs the ladder to the second level within the wagon, where March waits for him, and lays his head upon her lap. She runs her fingers through his hair and glides them along the curve of his ear. At least his body will be comfortable on the eight hour journey north to Briarwell, while his mind reels at the destruction he brought to Rookridge. He wanted them all to be together, March, Cheshire, and Dormy. But not like this.

PART II

CHAPTER 13

MARY ANNE

Mary Anne sits huddled against the wall of the train cabin, rocked by the tracks. She naively allowed herself to believe she was safe and assumed she would never again see the monster with the ax, who tried to kill her the night prior. The bloody images from the village, their faces, their bodies, their screams, will haunt her nightmares for the rest of her days.

There are drops of dried blood on her hands. *Whose?* she thinks. *The slaughtered children, some mother who will never again see her family, or one of the kind, old women from the market?*

Either way, she wonders if it was by luck or design that the man on the platform shoved her into the train car and shut the door. He saved her life in the moment, but may have doomed her as well. She must believe Jonathan will survive the confrontation with the murderer, because he has once before.

To believe otherwise is to give in to the despair that she will be lost forever in this world. But she remains hopeful in Jonathan's cleverness to escape and meet her at the next town where the train will station.

Rather than dwell in her thoughts, she elects to explore the cabin, and the rest of the train if need be, as a distraction. Until this moment, Mary Anne thought everything in Wonderland reminiscent of a fairytale or painting with knights and castles. Even after Jonathan's confirmation she is not in her own year, she finds herself on a train, out of place, out of time, eerily similar to those in England. If not for the intricate carvings in the lacquered woodwork of the benches and wall panels, the hooks for luggage instead of shelves, and the sculpted gold lantern hangers, she would think she was on her way to London. She moves from bench to bench, sits on their plush cushions, and stares out the window to watch the world pass by in a green blur. She contemplates jumping from the caboose, if she was brave enough, and following the tracks back to the village and Jonathan. But if he already left, she would be in an even worse predicament.

A train must have a conductor or engineer of some sort in order to operate, she thinks, determined to know her destination before they arrive. *I'm bound to meet one or the other if I continue to move forward.*

Mary Anne opens the front-facing door leading to the next cabin, but the roaring grind of the wheels on the tracks below and the wind in her face startle her. She clings to the side of the door as if the floor beneath her would soon dissolve. The cold air whips the white hairs across her face, further adding to her disorientation. She takes a breath and leaps across the small gap. The new cabin is identical to the previous, except for where the cushions on the benches were red, these ones are black. The colors alternate as she progresses through the train —red, black, and red again—and yet she can find no one else aboard the train, be they passenger or crew.

The next three cabins are as beautiful as those before, but these have private seating compartments with a single walkway along the right wall. As she walks, her heart pounds in her ears. Before, she could see clearly through the entirety of the other cabins, but now these provide hiding spaces for unknown dangers. As she continues forward, she realizes the pounding in her ears is not her heart, but the loud ticking of a great clock, and it grows louder the farther forward she travels. She opens the front door, and across the last gap is a frosted glass door, with a placard which reads *Engine* attached to its frame. Shadows of people move back and forth inside the cabin. Mary Anne adjusts her white curls, pulls her hood forward, and opens the door.

To her confusion, what she believed were the engineer or conductor within the engine room are, in actuality, large clockwork gears, whirring, ticking, powering the train. Mary Anne wants to explore the curious room with all its knobs and levers, but dares not risk her hand stopping the train in the middle of the forest. She crosses back to the previous cabin, closes the door, and realizes she is alone on this train without a driver, conductor, or passenger.

Before Mary Anne's mind can run away from her, a small boy, no more than five or six, peers around the corner of one of the compartments. Mary Anne is unsure how she missed him, but perhaps she was too focused on following the ticking of the engine.

"Mother, there's a lady out there," he says before disappearing behind the partition.

"Leave her be, darling," a woman whispers.

The soothing, tender voice pulls Mary Anne closer, and she peeks around the corner much the same way the young boy did. The woman's face radiates warmth and beauty.

"Oh, hello." The woman smiles at Mary Anne while picking her son up onto the seat next to her. "Would you care to join us? Walking around while the train is moving is the right way for an accident to happen. Please come in and sit."

Mary Anne does not hesitate to sit on the long bench across from the woman and her son. The little boy puts his hand on his mother's lap while he swings his legs, all the while smiling at Mary Anne.

"What's wrong with your eyes?" the boy remarks.

Mary Anne turns her head to look out the window and pulls her hood to cover the side of her face. She has been cavalier and careless while on the train, forgetting her eyes will give her away. Sitting in another compartment or returning to the first cabin would have been a wiser decision, but the woman's gentle tone, so similar to her own mother's, pulls at Mary Anne's heart.

"Alden, where are your manners?" says his mother. "That's no way to talk to a stranger or a lady. She's like your grandmother. Her hair once matched her eyes, but when she grew older, the color faded to white but her eyes stayed the same." But she has a mother's sharp eye. Mary Anne can see her staring at her dark brows, but chooses to say nothing.

"You don't look as old as my grandmother," says Alden.

"I'm not," says Mary Anne. "I lost my color prematurely, at an early age."

"There you have it," the woman tells her son.

"I must say, my hair is dull compared to yours," she tells the boy, returning his smile and admiring the shades of dark blue in both of their hair.

"Different is never dull," the mother replies. "Oh, look at me, prattling on in a conversation and I haven't even said—I'm Emilia, and this is Alden. Say hello, Alden."

"Hello!" he blurts out and bounces on the bench.

"Hello," Mary Anne says. "Mary Anne Elizabeth. It's refreshing to meet you both."

"Us? Oh, we are no one special." Emilia laughs.

Untrue, Mary Anne thinks. *These two couldn't be more special.* Their kindness and loving connection means the world to her and reminds her, as did Deidra, there is good in this strange world.

Even though Mary Anne met them moments ago, she sees her mother's gentleness and guiding hand in the way Emilia watches Alden. Mary Anne's mother raised her to be genteel to appease her father, who wanted nothing more for her than to find employment as a laundress, despite their flourishing shipping trade. But when her father was away, her mother taught her the importance of industry, pride, and confidence, not with words, but with her every gesture, glance, and step. The way Alden finds moments to mimic Emilia, her posture, her hand gestures, and her smile brings a warmth to Mary Anne's chest, not of fear or anger, but peace in the hope she will again sit at her mother's side. Though she wonders who will care for her this evening and the coming days.

"Do you know what the commotion was back in Rookridge?" asks Emilia. "It was muffled, but it sounded awful, whatever it was."

"I wanted to see what it was," says Alden. "It sounded like a battle."

"And that's why I asked you to stay by my side instead." Emilia taps a finger on the tip of Alden's nose. "Who would protect your mother if you went off like some adventurer and left me here?"

"It was nothing." Mary Anne does not have the constitution to explain, nor would she want to expose Alden's young mind to the truth of what took place in Rookridge. "A drunken brawl on the train platform between a few villagers."

"Well, it's fortunate my young hero didn't waste his bravery on fools," Emilia tells Alden, who scrunches his chin and pokes out his bottom lip with pride. "Well, Mary Anne, where are you traveling to this evening, dear? You've no bags or bundles to speak of, so the trip cannot be too long."

"To be honest," says Mary Anne, "I boarded the train by mistake without my traveling companion and without knowing our destination. Perhaps he will catch the next train and be able to meet me there."

"Sorry, dear, there's just the one. The Wonderland Engine."

Emilia points to a scroll hanging on the wall near the door with a map of the train track and follows the meandering circle in the air with her finger. "It makes a giant loop round most of Wonderland, one way, but always arrives at the same time."

"Like clockwork," says Mary Anne. "I suppose I've no choice but to ride until the next stop and wait."

"That's our stop!" yells Alden.

"Isn't that fortunate," Mary Anne says to Alden. "Do you live near the next stop?"

"The train gets us close, but we still have quite a ways to walk after we stop. We're from the village of Halma. Have you heard of it?"

"I am afraid not. I know little of"—Mary Anne catches her choice of words—"little about this area of Wonderland."

"No surprise there. Most people can't find our secluded village unless they've already been there. We're so far off the map, most of the time we're not on it. Our village is old, peaceful, but we're all close, family really."

"It sounds lovely," Mary Anne replies.

"It's home. Never known another." Emilia pulls Alden to her side and wraps her arm around him, causing him to yawn immediately. "You may want to get comfortable. We've several more hours before we reach Briarwell."

Mary Anne has grown accustomed to news contrary to what she wants to hear, and does not comment or complain. Instead, she watches Alden fight against sleep until his eyes flutter shut, and Emilia soon after. Mary Anne allows the rhythmic ticking of the train engine to lull her to sleep.

But the final lurch of the train as it comes to rest jolts

Mary Anne awake, and from the look of them, Emilia and Alden as well. Mary Anne barely recalls closing her eyes before they snapped open again, without dreams or feeling rested. It has happened before on occasion after working late without sleep.

She follows Emilia and Alden off the train and into pitch darkness, where a solitary lantern hangs on a crooked post to mark the train platform, which is not much more than planks of wood laid on dirt. Tall blades of grass up to Mary Anne's waist poke through the wide spaces between the wood. She can see little else beyond the lantern's glow.

The sound of a crank grows from the front of the train, clicking louder and faster until it stops with a sudden metal clang, and the train slowly snakes away into the night.

"Would you like to join us?" asks Emilia. She picks up Alden and rests his sleepy head on her shoulder. "I only offer if your friend isn't here. I hate to say, but it seems unlikely if he traveled the road while we were on the train. It is still a few hours' walk to Halma, and I'd certainly hate to leave you here alone."

"You're going to walk home?" asks Mary Anne with genuine concern. "But it's late, and dark, and could be unsafe. There could be bandits."

"Nonsense. There's no one this far out who'd do us any harm. Besides, we've made this walk hundreds of times over and the worst we ever came away with was a tripped ankle once. It's a small price to pay for the comforts of home. We only need walk a few more miles. There's a fellow from our village who sleeps in a wagon at the start of the path to Halma. He will take us the rest of the way while we rest. You really are welcome to join us."

"The thought is truly tempting," says Mary Anne, "but I must wait for them here. If I journey off the map, as you say, my companion will never find me. And if the roads here are as safe as you say they are, I have little to worry about."

"It was a pleasure meeting you, Mary Anne. I'm sure Alden would say the same." With her free arm, she hugs Mary Anne. "I hope you reach your destination."

Mary Anne cannot help but let it linger, and Emilia allows it as if she knows how much it is needed. She watches them fade into the dark, out of the lantern light, alongside the train tracks until she can no longer make out their figures. The thought crossed her mind while they embraced to ask if they would wait with her, but such a request would be selfish on Mary Anne's part. They have a long journey ahead to their home, but she will not keep them.

"Making friends everywhere you go?" March crosses the threshold of the light and beckons Mary Anne with her head before turning away. "Come on."

"Where are we going?" Mary Anne asks out of instinct, knowing any place would be better than the platform.

"Would you like to stay here instead?" March says. "I procured rooms at the small inn here in Briarwell. We've had enough excitement for one day, and all of us, including you I wager, need a good night's rest."

"Are there other rooms available?" Mary Anne asks.

"No. There are only three rooms." March turns to Mary Anne. "Myself and Jonathan's, Dormy's, and yours."

"But if I shared mine with Dormy," says Mary Anne, inching toward the lantern, "then one will be free for someone else."

Mary Anne does not wait, or know if March will approve, but she does not care. She unhooks the lantern from the post and holds it out, arm stretched, guiding her along the tracks until the light reaches Emilia, who turns around and smiles.

CHAPTER 14

CHESHIRE

In the village of Briarwell, Cheshire stands atop a fence post in the middle of the tallgrass fields, undulating like the sea, powered by the night breeze and bathed in serene shades of blue. The village's town hall, temple, forge, cowshed, cooper, and inn rest in the earth like a sparse constellation, each marked with a single lantern and connected by long stretches of rough dirt paths, and nary a tree between them. Only he and the others at the inn are awake at this late hour.

He should check on Jonathan, and should have checked earlier during their escape to Briarwell. Once certain the Ace remained buried under the rubble of the train platform, Cheshire dropped from the tanner's sign onto the top of Dormy's wagon as it careened out of the village. Jonathan needed comfort during the trip, and March is far better suited for the task than Cheshire. But he cannot deny the ache in his heart watching Jonathan's somber walk from the wagon to the inn. Their minds need time to settle, which means a cold bed for Dormy, a warm bath for March, and hot tea for Jonathan. He will call upon Jonathan later, but first he must take advantage of the empty village.

From Cheshire's recollection, besides the innkeeper, the whole of Briarwell's populace live in farmsteads outside of the village limits, and therefore, he has the freedom to explore each structure's interior. He is still unsure of what evidence he searches for, but when he finds it, he will know.

Cheshire begins at the forge, it being the closest building to the inn, and easily scales the tall stone walls and drops through the open roof into a rather predictable work area. The bellows still, the furnace cold, and piles of half-made armor and swords litter the shop's floor. Cheshire inspects every tool, under table, and flue before getting bored. As the night passes, he finds the other buildings in Briarwell far less interesting.

At the far end of town, the temple on the hill stands empty, except for the stone altars twice Cheshire's height and the town hall full of dusty books of histories and songs. At the cowshed he befriends the cows and horses and fills their troughs with sacks of grain left near the entrance. In the cooper, he checks between every rack, and shakes every barrel to discover its contents, but almost all are empty except for a few smaller casks filled with a rich mead hidden upon the stock.

He drinks from one of the casks on the cooper's roof, feet dangling and cheeks sticky with the delicious liquid. With wide eyes, he stares, mesmerized, by the swinging lantern below his feet. There is a point where the candle's warm orange glow meets the cold, blue night and their conflict creates a beautiful ring of purple. It is easy to overlook. Most would focus more on the light or the dark, but it is the in-between where Cheshire finds his solace.

A new light, a lantern swinging as if carried by hand, appears in the corner of Cheshire's eye as he holds out his tongue to catch the last drop of mead from the cask. It moves toward the temple back at the other end of the village. Without the convenience of being able to bound from rooftop to rooftop as in other villages, Cheshire traverses the long fence rails of the fields toward the light, but it disappears behind the temple before Cheshire can reach it.

He circles the temple four times but finds no sign of the lantern or its bearer in or around the towering stone structure. There are, however, three sets of fresh boot prints. One pair uncommonly large, the second's weight was heavy on one foot, as if he had a limp, accompanied by small holes made by a cane, and the third annoyingly generic. All faint at first, then they stop, facing the cooper, and explode outward with deep heel marks.

Cheshire stands in the impressions and looks to the cooper's roof, flat and tall with a distinct moonlit outline against the clear sky beyond. Anyone who knows the town could spot an unfamiliar object, and in his case, a figure atop the roof. But the deep heel marks mean they ran. Running implies guilt, and guilt is the result of concealing secrets.

Secrets Cheshire will discover. There are three different paths to follow, and Cheshire could easily track them during the night. But across the village, yet another light calls to him. The candle in Jonathan's room.

Back at the inn, the loose wood shingles of the awning clack softly with each step as Cheshire walks circles to spy in the guest room's windows on the second floor. A woman and her child slumber in one room, and Dormy hangs halfway off the small bed she shares with Mary Anne in the next. Dormy looks to have been reaching for a brass candleholder on the side table nearest her when she fell asleep. Mary Anne's kerchief and white hair pieces lay carelessly piled on the side table next to her. Cheshire meant what he said to Jonathan in Rookridge about letting the engine go and being free of her and all the trouble to follow. They have the same choice now. She is in a deep, motionless sleep and would not hear if they sneaked away during the night.

He follows the sound of splashing water around the corner of the inn, and slides through the narrow window of the washroom where March reclines in the bath, her skin wet and glistening from the candles placed at the corners of the room behind her. Cheshire steps down into the room on planks discolored and rotted from years of overflow, kneels, and rests his forearms on the edge of the trough.

"You're finally here," she says, not opening her eyes, "and at the same time. I should assume you rode with us the entire way without saying a damned word."

"Words are not my forte," he says, watching beads of water drip from the gentle curve of her under breast. "How is he?"

"Shaken." March raises her head and leans forward in the bath. "As you would expect. But nothing we've not been through before."

"And you?" he asks.

"Numb. As you would expect. It wasn't my birthplace, nor were they my friends. I hurt for Jonathan, not the village." She moves to the end of the bath to be closer to him. "I hurt for you as well. I know and understand what runs through your mind."

"A place you should not venture, no matter how brave." He grins.

"And in your heart," she continues, "no matter how deep you hide it behind your smile." She stands and the water cascades down her body and reflects the candle light. Cheshire raises his eyes to view this goddess of liquid fire before him. "I can see the hunger in your eyes. Good, you'll need it. But first, go see him. I'll be in shortly."

Cheshire jumps to the eaves of the second floor and pulls himself up to walk across the thick beams of the roof. He cuts across the inn, drops to Jonathan's windowsill, and sits, resting his back on one side of the frame and props his feet against the other.

Jonathan undresses and hangs his trousers and coat next to March's on the pegs beneath a shelf of old books and dried plants. His boots sit next to hers under the side table, and his hat teeters from the back of the old chair in the corner of the room. He fidgets with his timepiece, circling the crystalline face thrice, and lays it down next to his flask on the side table, making sure the chain lays in a perfect circle around it. He is aware of Cheshire's presence but stays silent. Jonathan lies on the bed, the cold sheets a welcome comfort to his tired body, and tucks his hands behind his head while he stares at the ceiling and lets out a drawn-out sigh.

"Marvelous, wasn't it?" Cheshire asks, taking in Jonathan's body in the flickering candlelight. When he sat face to face with Jonathan in Rookridge, he imagined arriving in the Hollow to find Jonathan seated at the head of his table, March on his lap. Cheshire would sit at the edge as he did in Rookridge and bask in the sights and sounds of their beauty and passion.

The evening and night to follow would have turned out differently if the Ace had not chased him. And even if their clash was unavoidable, the full day would have been spent in each other's arms and desires had Jonathan been at the Hollow when he arrived in the morning, instead of gallivanting with the strange woman. Regardless—at least here, far from where they should be—he has both Jonathan and March.

"Marvelous," Jonathan repeats. "M. Marvelous in meeting Mary Anne? Marvelous in the sense of almost being mauled? Or perhaps you mean the murdered men, women, and children."

"Yes."

"Fuck," says Jonathan. "An entire town destroyed."

"Not the entire town," Cheshire corrects him. "Just the northern portion."

"And Rookridge, of all places," Jonathan huffs. "It will never recover, it will never be the same, all those lives lost, the damage, the death..."

"All things recover in time." Cheshire does not believe the

words he says, but knows he must interject to keep Jonathan's mind from spiraling into a needless pit of his own creation.

"Take this seriously, will you?" Jonathan turns to Cheshire for the first time. "Do you not comprehend what we have done?"

"We?" Cheshire's voice drops. "You're right. *We* have a maniacal killer following our every step whose sole impulse is to take *our* heads, and because of it, *we* put everyone we care for or even come into contact with at risk of death. That is *our* problem, yes?"

Jonathan turns his head away toward the candle.

"Oh wait. It's my problem, not yours. I am the one who spends every day and night looking over my shoulder, hoping the Ace will not find me, or you, or March. And pray no one else will die on my account. So please tell me, Jonathan, how this is your burden to bear."

"I know all this," says Jonathan.

"I know you know. But the guilt is not yours to bear. Feel sorrow for those who lost their lives today and who will never again see their loved ones, feel loss for those you once knew whom you will see now in memory, but do not succumb to remorse. Guilt is mine and mine alone."

In silence, they both watch three beads of wax crawl down the thin candle, one after another, until they form one glob at the base of the brass candleholder. Though harsh, Cheshire hopes his words are enough to retrieve Jonathan's mind out of the mire. March's words and ways would have been gentler. At times such as these, Cheshire believes the years he spends away from Jonathan and March in solitude cost him part of his humanity and civility.

"It's been an age since we've had an adventure together." Cheshire's grin returns to mask his thoughts. He coaxes Jonathan to speak through his game. "W."

After a long pause, Jonathan finally speaks. "Well, they are difficult to come by when you wander for years on end, without word or warning of where you're going or when you will return, if ever. Worrying about you daily leaves an intangible itch in the back of my mind, wondering if I will ever see you again."

"You waste your time with worry. If I do not return, I do not return. I will have my reasons." Cheshire looks out the window to the crescent moon in her throne high above them. "Perhaps one day I will vanish from this world altogether."

"And the world, and I, will be all the poorer because of it," says Jonathan.

The sentimentality makes Cheshire uncomfortable. Jonathan is charming beyond compare, but his silver tongue will not work on Cheshire, at least in this fashion.

"Forgive me for not being as rigid and compulsive as you, planning every moment of the day from sunrise to sunset." Cheshire locks eyes with Jonathan's, staring at the candlelight dancing at their edge.

"Better than capricious and feral," says Jonathan, his gaze stronger than his words. "I'm surprised you still wear clothes at all or communicate with words, you savage thing." They share a much needed laugh, and when it trails away, Jonathan says, "Come inside."

Cheshire breaks Jonathan's gaze and looks to the tall elms at the edge of the village.

"What use will sleeping on a roof or tree be tonight?"

"Do you know the last time I slept in an actual bed? It's something I would rather not grow accustomed to again."

"I can tell you exactly when the last time was, now come inside."

Cheshire yields, shrugs off his vest and cloak, drops his trousers, and piles them next to Jonathan's boots. But he takes care to wrap his purple sash around his hand into a loose roll and lays it next to Jonathan's watch, mindful not to disturb its chain. The bed creaks as Cheshire climbs on and straddles Jonathan's thighs. The sensation of Jonathan's skin against his own, between his legs, sends a wave of gooseflesh up Cheshire's body.

"When?" asks Cheshire.

"The last you were in a bed was the last time you were with us, which would have been"—Jonathan's eyes jump back and forth, counting invisible numbers up Cheshire's body—"you've been gone almost seven years this winter."

With all the secrets Cheshire keeps, he is glad to share one —the secret of Wonderland's Time and its irrelevance with Jonathan. Wonderland's sun and moon dance across the sky like second hands of a giant clock catching every few thousand revolutions, if at all. Cheshire has been in his nineteenth year for over a millennium and Jonathan and March in their twenty sixth and twenty fifth just as long.

Jonathan purposefully tightens and shifts his thighs

underneath Cheshire. His thick arms appear double their size, having flexed them while his hands rest behind his head, fighting the urge to reach out. Cheshire fights the same animalistic urge he felt with March in the Hollow, and keeps his hands relaxed on his own thighs, but other muscles cannot hide either of their desires.

Soon after, March slinks into the room from her bath. Cheshire turns his head to her and watches the wet tendrils of hair roll against her breasts as they did this morning in the mill. She kneels behind Cheshire and caresses the nape of his neck with her open lips. Jonathan finally reaches out and strokes the length of Cheshire's thighs, kneading them with firm hands. Cheshire loses his breath, and his legs and abdomen spasm involuntarily at both of their touches.

March slides her hands under Cheshire's arms and runs her fingertips between the muscles of his stomach, following them as guides down between his legs. She moves closer, pressing her damp breasts against his back and hips against his ass. Jonathan sits up and softly kisses and bites at Cheshire's chest as his hands take hold with March's, and Cheshire's body throbs against their grip.

Cheshire grabs the back of Jonathan's head by its hair with one hand and reaches behind to grab March's backside in the other. He pulls them both into a tight embrace, writhing against each other, to feel the heat of Jonathan's body and breath from the front and the chill from March's body and the cold water dripping from her hair down his back.

He will not let either see his lip quiver or the tears forming in his eyes. For the first time in what seems an eternity, he lets go of every bit of tension, regret, sorrow, and hatred he holds within him, and releases each with a long shaking breath. Here, between Jonathan and March, is the only place he feels safe, feels that he matters, and the only place he has ever felt at home.

CHAPTER 15

MARY ANNE

The next morning, the sound of faint laughter wakes Mary Anne from a restful sleep. Her neck, shoulders, and legs stiff from not stirring once during the night. She believes the laughter might be her cousins come to visit. It always brightens her mother's disposition when they do, since her brothers do not think to return home often. But when she turns in what she thought was her bed, she discovers Dormy asleep next to her, clutching a candleholder to her chest as if it were flowers upon the dead at a funeral.

This is the second morning Mary Anne has allowed herself to wake, believing this all a dream. After two nights, there can be no questions. This is all very much real. She lies in bed and tries to imagine what new wonders and horrors this day will bring.

How will I almost die today? she thinks.

She turns away from Dormy to the small table next to the bed and drapes the old woman's white hair between her fingers, remembering Deidra's kindness, as well as Emilia and Alden. Disregarding Dormy, she jumps from the bed, opens the door to their room, and knocks on the thin door across the hall. But after knocking three times, she cracks the door open and finds the room unoccupied. Mary Anne cannot fault them for wanting an early start back to Halma, but she feels yet another layer of sadness compound on the rest already weighing on her shoulders.

The door at the end of the hall less than five feet from Mary Anne opens inward, and Jonathan stands before her dripping wet from a bath, with only a thin towel wrapped precariously low around his waist. A rush of heat consumes her face, her ears, and cascades down the rest of her body. Her tongue flops around her mouth, unable to formulate speech. She averts her eyes and squeezes past Jonathan even though she does not need to go into the washroom, except it is the closest open door and she feels the need to escape. But the doorway is thin, and she finds herself wedged between the door frame and his chest. Her underdress absorbs the water from his body, and she fears it will reveal the details of hers. She pushes into the room and slams the door.

"Is something the matter?" Jonathan asks from the other side of the door. "Are you ill? I could try to find a physic in the village if it would help."

"No, not at all," she says as confident as possible, but her face still flushed. She can hear his smile.

"I've drawn a fresh bath. Take your time washing up," says

Jonathan. "I'll gather the others and we will break fast downstairs."

His footsteps grow faint and disappear down the hallway, and temptation and curiosity creep into Mary Anne's thoughts. It would be simple to crack the door and watch Jonathan walk to his room. She imagines his back as sculpted as his front, and her heartbeat warms her face further.

Her thoughts flash to the brownstone across the alleyway from her home and to Thomas, her gentleman neighbor, who she would spy the same way through their second-floor windows. His physique pales compared to Jonathan's, but his soft hazel eyes and the slight upturn of his mustache as he smiled captured Mary Anne's attention. Their flirtation started playful and harmless at first. In the mornings, he took a considerable amount of time standing in plain view of her window, with a sly but kind smile, shirt open, trousers barely laced, while he fastens the cufflinks of his shirt before he left for his job at the finance district. She would wait to undress until he returned home, at first only stripping down to her long chemise, petticoat, and corset, never looking his way, but knowing he never broke sight with her.

But after several weeks, their visual, playful dalliance escalated, while the clothing they teased each other with became less and less. She could not resist the way he looked at her. Longing and loving. And after months of teasing one another, she found it difficult to resist the physical urges she denied herself for so long.

After so many rejections, she saw no harm or fault taking this one opportunity for herself, even if Thomas is a married man. His wife did not appreciate him and spent most of her time at social gatherings and garden parties to climb the social ladder through conversation and gossip. Or so Mary Anne tells herself. But she could see in his eyes the same void and yearning she felt deep, and as adults they chose to let each other fill it. So Thomas's home became the den of their passion while his wife was away, with Mary Anne's mother none the wiser. Until the end.

She needs to return home for her mother and her family's business, but also wants to return to his gentle, fumbling touch and crooked smile. But she shakes the memory of Thomas, and the thought of Jonathan, from her head.

Behind her, a freshly drawn bath waits in a small wooden trough as old and discolored as the floor planks. The odor of her body is not yet ripe, and even though she has not washed herself in two days, she dares not undress completely in this strange place. Besides the questionable cleanliness of the water, the lack of any latches or locks on the door would allow anyone to walk in upon her.

However, there is a mirror, and she has not seen herself in two days either. Hesitantly, she walks to it, and the woman staring back—covered with a thin layer of dirt from collar to hairline, and a rat's nest of hair oily and matted—is almost unrecognizable. The polished and strong woman she fought her entire life to become has been reduced to a filthy street urchin or beggars she would walk by on her way to shipping yards.

Mary Anne kneels beside the bath and scoops water into her trembling hands, splashing her face and neck wildly, then plunges her head below the surface of the water and releases the scream she has held at bay since her arrival. Her high-pitched voice transforms into a deep roar of warm bubbles exploding out of her mouth and crawling up her cheeks and ears to the air above. Mary Anne does not pull her head out in time to inhale and water rushes down her throat and lungs. She collapses to the floor, choking, gasping, water burning as it pours out of her throat and nose, and sobs for the first time since she arrived in this wretched land.

She wipes the snot and sopping wet hair from her face, and regains her breath and composure before she stands to look in the mirror again. This time, the woman looking back resembles Mary Anne more than before, and she stares and waits for the redness of her eyes to fade before she dries her face, hair, and underdress.

When she returns to her room, she notices the door down the hall ajar and the floor silent. She walks to Jonathan's door and reaches for the handle with the same caution she would a hot pan, and pushes it open. The room is empty, even of their belongings. She turns back to her door and swings it open to find Dormy gone as well. She listens for any sign of her companions, some shuffle of feet from below or chatter audible through the floorboards, but she hears nothing. Perhaps they left her behind once and for all.

She laces her dress as quickly as possible, but her hands shake and make the process difficult, adding to her frustration, and shoves her feet into her boots and throws her cloak around her neck. She carelessly places the white hair pieces on her head with no time to secure them correctly and ties the kerchief tight to keep them in place. Mary Anne's worry boils into anger, her heart thundering in her head as she clomps down the stairs two or three at a time. She runs through the small empty foyer and bursts from the front door to an empty street, and is about to scream again. But she swallows it when she realizes her entire party sits to her left at a table on the porch with breakfast. Jonathan sits with his teacup to his lips, March polishes a dagger against the leg of her trousers, Dormy focuses on the mound of eggs on her plate, and Cheshire stares unblinking at something in the distance.

"It's a bit of a dramatic entrance, don't you agree?" Cheshire asks the others at the table, shoving eggs into his mouth. He squints at the resentment clear on Mary Anne's face. "Are you always this foul in the morning?"

"Did you think we had left?" Jonathan stands and pulls out a chair for her. "I told you we would meet downstairs."

Foolish. Rash. These words resound in Mary Anne's mind following every heartbeat. She joins them at the table, ashamed of her quick assumption. But the short time she has known them still warrants some level of mistrust.

The innkeeper places a plate of hot eggs over easy, sizzling pork, and a hearty cut of bread on the table in front of her. Her mouth waters at the most aromatic meal ever to grace her presence.

Mary Anne picks up the crude utensils and begins hacking away at the pork. Once the fatty, salty meat touches her tongue, her entire body pauses, her heartbeat slows, and her eyes shut at its taste. Each mouthful of food sends a warm rush through her body.

"Thank you," she says as she chews, not following decorum,

but she will waste no time eating in case some other tragedy befalls them. But with fork and knife in hand, it is too late to stop or hide the chunk of dark hair from slipping from beneath her kerchief.

"You're welcome, m'lady." The innkeeper squints at Mary Anne. Beads of sweat grow upon his upturned lip and forehead.

"May we have more bread, please, good sir. Now?" Jonathan asks to draw his gaze.

Confused, the innkeeper nods and disappears inside.

"My apologies," says Mary Anne. "I should not have rushed this morning and taken more time with my hair."

"What's done is done," says Jonathan. A flick of his eyes signals Dormy, and she stands and adjusts Mary Anne's hair and kerchief, securing the white curls properly.

"Now that all are present," says Jonathan, "we must discuss an alternative course of action."

"Alternative?" Mary Anne asks.

Jonathan sets down his teacup, but keeps his finger in its handle. "I believe we're all glad to be finished with the happenings in Rookridge. And we have a significant lead on the Ace. Should he choose to follow, we would not see him for several days, and by that time we will be far from here. But we must come to terms with where we are now. Mary Anne, on this side of the country, the Engine travels away from Mirus, and our two-day journey has become four."

"Unbelievable." Mary Anne slams her fork on the table, startling Dormy, who tries to keep her smile.

March looks up, turns the dagger blade down in her fist and lays it on the table, with its tip pointing to Mary Anne. "We're all here because of you, whether we want to be or not. Act ungrateful again and rest assured we *will* leave you, no matter where we are." Jonathan tries to interject to save Mary Anne, but March stops him. "We left our home to make sure you reach yours. Stop thinking you're more important than us. Show some gratitude or fuck off." She stabs the dagger deep into the table and walks inside.

Jonathan and Dormy's faces cannot hide on some level, they feel the same, just not as blunt. Dormy reaches over and plucks the knife from the table and puts it in her jacket while Jonathan sips his tea. Without word or warning, Cheshire jumps from his chair, grabs hold of the awning, and pulls himself out of sight.

"I apologize for my tone," says Mary Anne. "I understand I'm an inconvenience, and I know I have taken you all away from your lives, but there is still much I don't know and it seems at every turn I'm farther away from home than I began."

"You're not wrong," says Jonathan, "but whether it takes us four days or four weeks, we shall see you to Mirus, and then we will all be home soon enough." Jonathan finishes his tea and stands. "We need to purchase more provisions for our journey, which will take most of the afternoon. We will not return through Rookridge, and there are few villages on the roads we will need to travel, so we must prepare."

Mary Anne can sense there is more to be said, more bad news to add to this already wonderful morning.

"We will gather what's needed and help Dormy prep the wagon, which will take most of the day. And with the off chance we may encounter the Ace on the road, it would be best it happen during the day. We will set out at first light tomorrow to be able to keep a weather eye open."

Of course she must wait another day. Mary Anne bites her tongue and continues to eat her food. She fears March will hold them to her word should Mary Anne speak out of turn again. But Mary Anne sees the truth in March's rebuke. She was ungrateful, but was not thinking of herself. She thinks of her mother and Thomas who wait for her.

Not wanting to feel left behind once more, she accompanies Jonathan and Dormy to the farmers and their carts lining the long dirt roads, and prepares herself for another day of silence and fabricated stories to the bumpkins of this village, until she hears a familiar voice and name from farther down the path.

"Alden, stop!" Emilia shouts and laughs as she chases him.

"I found you!" Alden stops and points at Mary Anne proudly in a dramatic wide stance.

"Forgive us." Emilia catches her breath and repositions the basket on her arm.

"No need," says Jonathan, tipping his hat.

"Hello Alden," Mary Anne beams. "Hello Emilia."

"These are the two you met on the train yesterday?" asks Jonathan.

"Yes, they were quite hospitable," she says. "I thought you'd left this morning."

"We're never ones to not repay a kindness," says Emilia. "We gathered food for the rest of our journey and hoped to return to the inn before you left. And the gods have seen fit for us to meet once more. We'd like to treat you to lunch before we set out on our way. I know I thanked you and the lovely woman who paid for our room last night, but it didn't seem enough."

Alden bounces with anticipation, pulling on Mary Anne's sleeve.

"May I?" Mary Anne asks Jonathan, not that she needs his permission, but rather because she questions if she would be safe away from his company.

"Of course. It will take Dormy and I several hours to gather everything we need. Enjoy your time," says Jonathan. And with a tip of his hat to both women and Alden, he and Dormy continue on the road.

Emilia suggests they eat at the table on the porch of the inn. Mary Anne initially wants to offer an alternative, since the emotions and March's dagger mark are still fresh, but realizes without Jonathan, there is a shiver down her back, some fear of the unknown, and her without her protector. At least at the inn there is familiarity, a place to hide, and March with her weapons should the need arise.

Already full from breakfast, Mary Anne does not partake in their lunch, but will join in their company and smiles, which fill her more than any feast could. Whether founded or not, she feels she can be herself around Emilia and Alden without judgement or comparison. She can see it in Alden's shimmering eyes and Emilia's gentle smile. She owes them nothing, nor do they feel responsible and burdened by her, as she fears Jonathan does despite his sincerity. Yet this woman and her son, whom she only met yesterday, want to spend time with her for no other reason than to be cordial. Mary Anne has almost forgotten what this feels like.

They talk for hours at the table outside the inn. Mary Anne wishes she could answer any of Emilia's questions, but after the third hesitant vague answer, she stops asking and allows Mary Anne to helm the conversation. She asks about their small village in Halma, what Emilia does for a living, what her family is like, and every other question she can think of to get to know this remarkable woman. The life she leads is demanding, but she is content, and unencumbered with worry. Mary Anne wishes she could say the same. But she lives vicariously through the simple tales Emilia describes of their routine to and from Rookridge for the food and supplies she cannot grow or raise herself, with adventurous embellishments thrown in by Alden. It is almost sunset by the time they finish their conversation.

"I apologize," says Mary Anne. "I've kept you late into the day and now you must walk back at night once more."

"Nonsense," laughs Emilia. "We stayed because we wanted to. Besides, I've told you once before, we're used to making this walk. And if we leave now, we'll be home long before we normally are." She stands and helps Alden from his seat. His little legs dance about, bursting with energy after being seated for so long.

"Thank you. Your kindness has been most refreshing."

Worry flashes across Emilia's face. "Tell me, my dear. I sense there is much you cannot say, but tell me plainly. Are your traveling companions not kind to you?"

Mary Anne grows immediately embarrassed. "No, no. I did not mean to imply any such behavior. Yes, they've been more than gracious." Emilia's motherly eyes squint dubiously. "I speak true. It's just... it's different with them." She cannot bring herself to say she feels beholden to them, and their time together more obligation and charity than compassion. "Thank you for asking."

"If you're certain, then I won't press." Emilia takes Alden by the hand and walks to the path leading to the train platform. "I hope you get to where you're going. Farewell Mary Anne."

"Thank you," she shouts as they grow smaller in the distance. She cannot bring herself to say goodbye, even though she knows this will be the last time she sees either of them.

But she is not allowed the time to feel any emotion, sadness or otherwise. A great rumbling thunder crack under a clear sky travels across the village, and Mary Anne knows whatever caused it, her companions are at the center, and it does not bode well for any of them.

CHAPTER 16

CHESHIRE

Cheshire wakes to the sensation of two mouths and four hands sharing and enjoying the lower parts of his body. He presses against the rough sheets and smooth bodies of Jonathan and March, hands gripping handfuls of their hair while gruff sighs escape his lips at their touch. With sleep still heavy in his eyes, they finally come to focus on a beautiful, undulating blur of skin and hair below his waist. Their eyes are not fully open either, somewhere between sleep and awake, not fully aware, just reacting to instinct.

The village comes to life outside the inn, a cock crows at the cowshed, the hushed conversations of townsfolk rise and fall as they pass, but it matters little to Cheshire. Nothing exists outside their little world this morning.

Jonathan staggers to the door, his backside tightening with every step, to listen for any movement or sign the others are awake, while March slides up Cheshire's body and curls around him, the tip of her breast at his lips, which he accepts eagerly. Out of the corner of his eyes, he sees Jonathan stand at the door and smile, watching for a moment before he returns. He pulls them both from the bed and leads them to the washroom at the end of the hall to prepare for the day ahead. However, Cheshire and March have different plans.

Inside, rows of large water buckets, prepared by the innkeeper early this morning, line the shelves along the wall and a long trough serves as the bath near the small window. They each carry buckets to the bath until it is halfway full, all the while continuing to kiss and touch one another. With a finger to his lips, Jonathan reminds Cheshire and March to remain as quiet as possible, to not disturb their unintended guests. Cheshire tries his best to make Jonathan break his own request, and with March's help, they succeed.

The trough is long enough to accommodate all three, and they take advantage of the space. They each take a turn standing between the others, Cheshire, March, then Jonathan, bathing each other. But their washing soon turns to worship, using their mouths as much as their hands, losing all sense of time. They each know what the others thirst for without ever saying a word. And despite the depth of their passion, they laugh every time they switch positions, their bodies slipping over each other like freshly caught fish in a net.

But when their mouths are not enough and the full compass of their desire needs to be released, they sink into the water. Jonathan reclines back on one end of the bath, pulls Cheshire down with him, hands strong on his waist. Then, with a gentle but firm hand, reaches down and guides Cheshire inside his body, connecting their spirits and souls once more. Cheshire's stomach quivers at the exhilarating sensation. No matter how many times over the centuries he, March, and Jonathan have been together, each time feels like the first and revitalizes his heart. He writhes against Jonathan at one end of the bath, breathes heavy, and leans his forearms on Jonathan's flexed chest, hands wrapped around the back of his neck. His forehead presses against Jonathan's, lost in his turquoise gaze, which sparkles in the rays of dawn slipping through the thin shuttered window. Each thrust sends small waves of bathwater splashing over the edge, and Jonathan's eyes fluttering.

Cheshire looks over his shoulder to see March reclining at the other end of the bath, arms resting on its edge, enjoying the sight of her two men entangled with one another. When she has waited long enough, she softly rakes her fingertips down the muscles of Cheshire's back, around his ass, and between his legs to caress their union. His legs quake at her touch. She kneels behind Cheshire, pulls him away from Jonathan, turns him around, and eagerly welcomes him into her. The slow and then quick circular movements of March's hips send goose flesh over his entire body. He leans her backward, body arched, and takes the tip of her breast into his mouth, massaging it over with his tongue. She releases a low moan with a chuckle hidden within, which drives Cheshire's fingers to flex and bend erratically as his hands travel up and down her back.

He hears the splash of Jonathan leaving the water and kneeling behind them, then can feel every muscle press against every part of his skin. Cheshire breathes quicker, ready for the moment he has waited for all morning, and craves every day he is apart from them. Jonathan kisses the back of his neck and slowly and passionately joins with Cheshire. An energy runs through them all, but Cheshire feels it most, channeling it, savoring it, and they tremble at the pure exhilaration of their sublime trinity. And here Cheshire stays for the remainder of the morning, between them, pleasing one other, soft and rough, until they all exceed the threshold of pleasure their bodies can endure three times over.

When morning passes and their bodies revel in the sweet aches inside and out, they soak in the water and their bliss. The water has lost its warmth, but its chill soothes their bodies, tender from the morning and night before. March leans against one end of the trough, and Jonathan the other. Cheshire lays between them, on top of them, his head resting on March's breasts and his feet propped wide on Jonathan's shoulders. Jonathan glides his fingertips over Cheshire's hard muscles as if tracing the surface of a still pond, wanting to feel the water but not disturb its peace, and mutters silently to himself.

"After the evening and morning we've had," says Cheshire, "you're thinking of your teas."

"Of course," says Jonathan. "If we were at the Hollow, I'd be inside setting the pot to boil while you and March continue to play at the table."

"Do you recall the Silent Fiddle tavern in Grey Harbor?" asks Cheshire.

"The shithole in the Wetlands?" Jonathan chuckles. "That was almost 700 years ago. What in Wonder would make you bring up such a memory?"

"I recall that was the one time in all our history when you

swore off tea for a month."

Jonathan's eyes and mouth grow wide and he cups his hand over his mouth. "Canary Tourmaline. I'd almost completely forgotten."

"Serves you right, with your bloody obsession." Cheshire laughs.

"The tavern owner duped you into believing he had the rarest tea in all Wonderland," says March. She dips her fingertips into the water and hovers her hand over Cheshire's chest, letting the drops run down his skin.

"He was rather convincing in his description," says Jonathan.

Cheshire shakes his head. "And all you had to do was get rid of his daughter's suitor to claim it."

"What was his name? Harold? No." Jonathan snaps his fingers, beckoning the memory like a dog. "Hayden."

"Eustace," says Cheshire.

"Fuck, Eustace." Jonathan rubs Cheshire's legs and laughs. "Pompous ass. It would've been a simple enough task if he would've stayed gone. But he wouldn't listen to reason or threats."

"Three weeks," says Cheshire, rising three fingers above the surface of the water, joining in Jonathan's merriment. "Three weeks we stayed in that shit stain of a town."

"Without Dormy's wagon, mind you," adds March, "so you felt obligated to stay in the cellar."

"Which is why you suggested we dress March in the daughter's clothing," says Jonathan, barely able to speak through his laughter, "and made sure Eustace walked under her window to catch the three of us fucking like spring rabbits. We never saw him again. I doubt they did either." Their laughter dwindles.

"It was an entertaining evening," says March.

"Threats only cut skin deep. To leave a lasting mark, your aim must be for the heart." Cheshire swirls the water with his finger. "He beat her."

"What do you mean?" Jonathan asks, confused.

"You never see the details. There were marks on the girl's legs and arms."

"How could you even tell?" Jonathan sits up in the bath. "We never saw her without her clothing."

"You didn't." Cheshire huffs. "I can tell a false smile better than anyone. And she used hers to hide her fear of Eustace's temper. Her father was a frail old man, who couldn't stop it. Of course he sought the help of someone kind and strong—you— to save them."

"I would have helped them in a heartbeat, if he would have asked plainly. And had I known what that bastard did, I would have run him through in the night and been done with him. Why didn't you tell me then? You've kept that for 700 years?"

"We all have our roles to play. You, the adventurer and hero, March the warrior, and I...I carry the secrets so you two don't have to. It's not much, but I can at least give you peace of mind. Besides, if I said anything, someone"—he points to March— "would have killed him outright."

"Damn right I would have," she says. "Gladly. We would have departed within the hour."

"Even so." Jonathan laughs again. "Canary Tourmaline."

"Your smug ass cradled the damn bottle all the way back to the Hollow. But the look on your face as soon as the first drop hit your lips and you realized—"

"It was piss." Jonathan and March can barely say through their laughter.

They cannot contain themselves any longer, and flop around, kicking water from the bath, laughing loud enough for the villagers down the paths to hear. They have had this same conversation twenty times over, but it never gets old. Even though years and, at times, decades may separate their time together, they pick up where they left off as if no time passed at all.

"Once our business with Mary Anne is finished," says Jonathan, "we will return to the Hollow. Together. And you'll stay no less than a month."

The mere mention of her name steals Cheshire's joy. His laughter trails off into a cough and he kisses Jonathan once more before jumping from the bath and shakes the water from his body like an animal. March steps out of the bath as well.

"Are you leaving?" asks Jonathan, his eyes fearful this will be the last time they will see Cheshire.

"You have your business to handle," says Cheshire, "and I have mine."

"Are you leaving?" Jonathan grabs Cheshire by his hips and pulls him back toward the bath.

"Why should I stay?" Cheshire says playfully.

March stands behind him and presses her hips against him, pushing him closer to Jonathan's waiting lips to give him his answer. "Your body betrays your attempt at indifference," she whispers in his ear before biting his earlobe, and then turning his head back to kiss him over his shoulder. "You've much time to make up for. Break fast with us, then off to your business with you."

Whatever reason they could give, it would not make a difference. Their touch will always be reason enough. And once they take Cheshire past the point his body can bear again, toes curling, knees buckling, and body quivering, for the fourth time this morning and sixth since last night, he catches his breath and finally answers. "Fine."

He kneels to kiss Jonathan on the top of his head, turns to kiss March on her cheek, and then walks back to Jonathan's room to collect his clothing at the same time the innkeeper climbs the stairs and turns into the hallway. The slim nervous man stammers, mutters some unintelligible noises, and blinks his eyes erratically as if dislodging something from them before running downstairs. He assumes the innkeeper did not expect to meet a naked man in the hall, or at least one still aroused from the morning's festivities.

Cheshire gathers his pile of clothes in his arms just as March enters to braid her hair. He grins and climbs out the window to let the sun dry his body on the roof. What he really wants is to continue making up for lost time with them both. But there will be more opportunities, he will make sure of it, and with Jonathan and March separately as well.

During the last part of the morning, Cheshire, Jonathan, March, and Dormy enjoy a delicious breakfast of eggs and pork belly prepared by the innkeeper who does not make eye contact with Cheshire. While the others partake in menial conversation, Cheshire focuses on the village folk who walk the roads this morning in search of the three conspirators from the night before.

Cheshire knows the identity of two. The wide pair of boots match those of the blacksmith he found marking the dirt and ash in the forge. In the town hall, there were years' worth of scruffs upon the floorboards made by the magistrate's cane. But he does not know their faces, and thus far, he has seen no one with a limp or a cane on the roads. And this morning no smoke billows from the forge. A thick chain and lock bar seal its front gate and townsfolk walk to the shop and turn away bothered, as if this is a rarity in their tiny village.

Mary Anne bursts from the front door, panting like a dog after a long run.

"It's a bit of a dramatic entrance, don't you agree?" he asks the others at the table as he eats his eggs. "Are you always this foul in the morning?" he scoffs at Mary Anne. Her incessant caterwauling makes focusing on the villagers difficult. He jumps to the awning and climbs to the roof once more to get a better view.

All afternoon, townsfolk come and go from the temple, but no one who would fit the characteristics he searches for. It does not matter what secrets they have, Cheshire will know them. And the longer he cannot find them, the stronger his impatience and irritation grows.

Even with his keen sight, he realizes finding the boots of the third conspirator will be a feat in and of itself, especially with the disgusting state of the villagers' feet. He jumps down to the awning and then grass to begin the long search by foot. Dried mud, halfway to their knees from centuries of daily travel of the dirt roads and fields they work, covers the boots of everyone he passes. But they neglect the stream not far past the village limits to the west, and the well near the inn the town is named after, where they could wash. At least he's able to keep his head down and covered, not that anyone would recognize him this far from the capital.

He spends the better half of the day searching each location over once more. He stops at the cowshed, and through a missing plank on the roof watches the milk maids go about their business in silence, hunched over with shoulders swaying back and forth as the milk rings out against the metal pails. The cooper offers no other evidence either, but it is amusing to hear the owner balk about ghosts raiding his stock in the night.

And the forge is cold, with no sign of the blacksmith. Nothing seems out of the ordinary, except for a slight scrape on the floor next to a solid stone block blowing carefully hung aprons, which more than likely serves as a bench. Mark on the floor would be commonplace here, but this one is recent and cuts deep through the years of soot and dirt in an arc. With a bit of brute force, Cheshire pulls the block away from the wall to reveal nothing at first, but upon closer inspection, he finds the back of the stone hollow. It housed something secret for some time and was brought out after his search last night. The tingle of triumph and anticipation dances down Cheshire's neck to the end of his fingers and toes.

In the temple, villagers drift among the towering stone altars to the gods and spirits this region deifies, and place offerings of food and trinkets at their bases. Large artistic carvings of fish, a tower, trees, a wheel, the moon, and the sun serve as central images on each slab, with tiny runes fanning out like starbursts. Candles placed on small stone shelves behind the slabs radiate a glowing aura on the temple wall behind them. There is a familiar scrape mark in front of the altar to the sun. The offerings on the ground almost hid it from view, but broken cobwebs which once spanned between old candles and flowers on the floor prove the slab moved in the same manner as the block in the forge, and probably by the same hulking man. Cheshire tries to peek behind the stone, but the shelves of the candles are obtrusive, and the space is not wide enough for his head. He is able to slide his arm into the tight space and feel engravings in the smooth stone with his fingertips.

Cheshire laughs silently for the people still in the temple. He scales to the top of the slab with the hidden markings, positions his feet against its edge, secures his back and shoulders to the wall, and pushes against the great stone. The villagers flee as soon as they comprehend what's about to happen, and it is fortunate they do. Cheshire clenches his teeth, grunts, and tightens every muscle in his body to fight against the weight of the slab, but there is not enough room for proper leverage.

He drops to the ground and runs to the opposite side of the temple. He cracks his neck and hops from one foot to another. After a few quick breaths, he sprints back toward the altar, leaps into the air, and lands on the slab's face with both feet and hands. Cheshire kicks off with all his strength, bounding back to the opposite wall, where he pushes off and launches himself at the altar again and again. After fourteen times, back and forth across the temple, the stone teeters. The great stone metronome gains momentum and calls out to Cheshire, saying it wants to fall. Cheshire scrambles to the top again, braces his back against the wall and digs his heels into the slab. He grits his teeth, and with a deep, guttural growl, pushes against the stone one last time. His thighs, calves, and ass shake and feel as though they are about to burst.

With the sound of a slow inhalation quickly growing louder, like the ominous breath of a cannonball flying in the air before reaching its target, the altar is betrayed by its own weight, and topples and falls through the air in a brief moment of weightlessness.

The altar lands with a deafening thunder crack, loud enough for the farmsteads beyond the village to hear, and breaks into several pieces. The impact rattles the whole of the temple and dust rains down from the ceiling.

Cheshire climbs atop the stone and mindfully avoids stepping on the cracks, as if walking on a frozen lake near the end of winter. He brushes away chipped bits with his feet to reveal more circles and runes like the other altars, but this central figure is of a person, a woman, he thinks. It offers little information about his search for the three men, but can serve as bait. He climbs to the wide beams running overhead and waits.

Within minutes, a squirming mass of curious villagers block the temple entrance. Some peer through the door in anger, others wail ridiculous cries at the loss of the altar, while others are bustling with excitement because something new happened in their mundane lives. But it's not long before three men push their way through the crowd to address them. The blacksmith, towering over the crowd and twice as wide as any one person, the magistrate, a grey-and-red-haired older gentleman with a cane, and the innkeeper. Cheshire snickers, realizing the innkeeper's reaction this morning was not because he encountered Cheshire without clothing, but because he somehow recognized him from the cooper's roof.

The blacksmith waves the people away while the innkeeper paces back and forth just inside the door, and the magistrate quells the whispers of the crowd and bids them return to their chores and tasks while they begin an investigation. The crowd is slow to disperse, but once the three men are alone, their attention turns to the altar's remains.

"It's a sign," the innkeeper stammers.

"Shut up," the blacksmith barks out, mourning the loss of his craftsmanship. "Who did this? Who could do this?" He is the mountain Cheshire thought him to be—neck, thighs, and arms thick as logs.

It's as if his mother fucked an ox and produced this gargantuan man, thinks Cheshire.

"Shut your mouth." The magistrate, knee wincing, is slow to sit on the cracked stone. From his build and gruff, his injury came from the battlefield—a retired soldier who put himself out to pasture. He pulls a dagger, too old to be a weapon, from inside his long coat. It is rare for Cheshire to cross something unfamiliar in Wonderland, but this knife is unusual, unlike any he has come across before. Three empty sockets, where jewels once sat, line the handle, and the blade, dull and rusted, curves to a tiny point.

"What did I tell you?" The innkeeper trembles. "I saw the one who followed us last night. He's at the inn with the rest of them. Have you seen them up close? Killers all, must be. We should've killed the lot last night when they slept and took the woman. But I overheard them talking. They said they're leaving in the morning. There's no way we could challenge them."

"We wait for night and strike quick and true," says the blacksmith.

This is all Cheshire needs to hear. He assumes they speak of Mary Anne. He would gladly give her over to them, if not for upsetting Jonathan. But since they intend harm to those closest to him, Cheshire will show them no mercy.

"Shut your mouth," the magistrate repeats in a hushed tone, but the aggression in his voice rises. "You saw the crowd. They bottlenecked the entrance as quick as blink. And we all turned to the temple as soon as we heard the crash. Whoever did this didn't have time to escape. They are still..."

The magistrate tilts his head to the rafters but never finishes the sentence. Cheshire drops, feet together and heels first, on to the magistrate's head, snapping his neck with a loud and final crack, and then jumps to the far side of the broken altar. The magistrate's limp body crumples to the ground beside the slab like a discarded marionette. The innkeeper screams with every frantic breath and runs from the temple back toward the inn.

But the blacksmith stretches his shoulders, cracks his neck, and blocks the exit. He pulls an identical knife, the one he kept hidden away in the shop, from his belt and tosses it side to side. "I'm going to break you like these stones. You're less than half the man I am." Cheshire's blank stare and lack of response fuels the blacksmith's rage. "I'll kill you, boy." He grabs the old man's knife and lunges, attacking with both blades, dwarfed in his grip.

Cheshire dodges, jumps, and spins away from every slow and thoughtless attack. The blacksmith believes himself formidable, but he is nowhere near the skill level or threat of the Ace.

The blacksmith finally grabs the end of Cheshire's cloak as he jumps overhead and slams it into the ground with a victorious, guttural yell. But the cloak has always been too large and long for Cheshire, and slipping out of it, even in the middle of a jump, is child's play.

Like a spider would descend upon its prey caught in its web, Cheshire takes hold of his cloak, still in the blacksmith's tight grip, and wraps it around the man's head, pinning his arm against his face. Cheshire digs his heels into the back of the blacksmith's shoulders and pulls tight.

The blacksmith swings blindly with his free arm, but the size of his muscles limit his reach. He roars and staggers back and forth, thrashing side to side to throw Cheshire from his back.

Cheshire pulls harder and steers the blacksmith toward another altar, tucks his knees to his chest and kicks with all his might, ripping his cloak from the man's head, sending him careening headfirst into the stone slab.

Blood gushes from the blacksmith's forehead as he turns and lumbers toward Cheshire. Whether it be because he cannot see from the blood flooding down his face, or because he is half concussed from his blow, he does not notice the altar rocking behind him until it is too late. It falls as the last altar did, but the blacksmith turns in time, drops both knives and catches it overhead. The weight strains every muscle in his body. His arms, shoulders, and legs shake violently and swell with blood and the determination to stay alive as the altar presses down upon him. He puts his forehead back into the same bloody mark and pushes, raising the stone slowly, his monstrous screams adding to his strength.

This feat does not surprise Cheshire. The blacksmith is probably the one who had a hand in lifting them depending on how old these stones are. But Cheshire will take no chances. He lashes his cloak around the shin of the blacksmith, right above the ankle, twists both wrists in the fabric, and heaves so hard his own fists collide with his chest, knocking him back. Another thunder crack fills the temple as Cheshire rolls and rights himself.

The blacksmith's body above his belt is gone. Smashed. The slab lies flat on the ground with an explosion of blood, bone, and organ bits from all sides. Cheshire envisions popping a grape between his tongue and the roof of his mouth, feeling its juices hit the inside of his cheeks, and pressing the thin layer of remaining skin flat.

"Half a man indeed," he says to the twitching legs. He should have had the foresight to collect one of the knives for closer inspection, but they are now dust beneath the weight of the stones Cheshire cannot move. But as fortune would have it, he knows where he may find a third.

CHAPTER 17

JONATHAN

There is no market to speak of in Briarwell, but farmers wheel in small carts piled with vegetables, fruits, meats, and cheeses to sell. They park them in the grass along the long, uneven stretches of dirt roads, which hold the memory of years of footprints and deep tracks cut from carts and wagons. Jonathan and Dormy take care where they step as they embark on their afternoon of shopping, but after tripping twice, Mary Anne walks on the short grass beside the road, with a hand on the wooden fence to steady herself.

Yesterday proved to be more challenging than Jonathan first thought. Keeping Mary Anne's secret is hard enough, but defending her, himself, Cheshire, March, and Dormy at the same time is beyond exhausting. Her presence is a liability if called to fight again, and he prefers she stays hidden in her room. It would be one less worry on his mind while he and Dormy prepare for their journey. But she refuses to stay, and walks a step behind them with an anxious eye as if they may still run. Jonathan knows he cannot expect her full trust, since they have known each other for two days, but he wonders what he can do to put her thoughts at rest. Perhaps it is as simple as keeping his word and delivering her to the Duchess.

As they walk, Jonathan smiles and nods to the villagers they pass. However, here, Jonathan and his companions are outsiders, and the villagers nod in return but their faces frown with apprehension. The people of Briarwell wear simple garments with a limited palette of grays, whites, and some greens, but mostly they are all varying shades of brown, bedraggled from the fields they tend. Jonathan's blue and silver coat, even though worn and distressed itself, marks him as a stranger.

Before they reach the first vendor, a small child runs down the Northern path. His arms swing wildly and a wide open smile covers his face.

"Alden, stop!" his mother yells from behind him.

"I found you!" The young boy plants his feet and points to Mary Anne proudly.

"Forgive us," his mother says, lifting her basket of vegetables higher on her hip and tussling the boy's hair.

"No need," says Jonathan, tipping his hat to her and her son.

"Hello, Alden," says Mary Anne. "Hello, Emilia."

Before her bath last night, March mentioned Mary Anne had given up her room to a woman and her son to save them from walking to Halma overnight. March grumbled, but the news of such a selfless act intrigued him, since he has seen little of Mary Anne's true character.

"These are the two you met on the engine yesterday?" Jonathan asks.

"Yes, they were quite hospitable," Mary Anne replies. "I thought you'd left this morning," she says to Emilia.

"We're never ones to not repay a kindness," says Emilia. "We gathered food for the rest of our journey and hoped to return to the inn before you left. And the gods have seen fit for us to meet once more. We'd like to treat you to lunch before we set out on our way. I know I thanked you and the lovely woman who paid for our room last night, but it didn't seem enough."

"May I?" Mary Anne asks.

Her worry of being left behind suddenly vanishes at the chance to keep company with this woman and her son. But it makes sense to Jonathan, since from the onset of their journey, Mary Anne has associated Jonathan and the others with her initial fear, doubt, and the horror of the Ace, whether or not it be conscious. But these two are pure and separate from her troubles.

"Of course. It will take Dormy and me a few hours to gather everything we need. Enjoy your time." He tips his hat to the woman and her son, and continues on the road with Dormy, looking back over his shoulder often as Mary Anne and her company make their way back to the inn. If Mary Anne stays in one place, it will also ease at least a portion of Jonathan's nerves, and he and Dormy can accomplish their errands much quicker.

Dormy tugs on his sleeve as Alden did to Mary Anne. "The quicker we work, the less the worry."

"Too right." He smiles. And by late afternoon, Jonathan and

Dormy purchase large bags of potatoes, an assortment of greens, a basket of apples and pears, and three large wheels of cheese. Whatever their price, Jonathan pays double while he compliments the quality of the selection, and each farmer thanks him with a hearty shake of his hand.

After the long haul back to Dormy's wagon, they secure the basket of apples and pears on top of one of the many boxes already precariously rigged to the exterior. The wheels of cheese wedge on top of a stack of books. One section of the wagon's roof houses a small garden Dormy cultivates, where Jonathan piles the greens in with the rest of the plants. The sack of potatoes hangs out the back window, and as they drive, will thump repeatedly against the wood, adding to the cacophony of wares. It takes skill to maneuver through the different compact levels of the wagon. The walls and floor are barely visible anymore, and the paths through must be walked sideways in order to fit. But anything they have ever needed, Dormy has provided, from a smith's anvil to thread and needle.

Dusk draws near by the time Jonathan squeezes his way back out of the wagon. And Mary Anne bids farewell to Emilia and Alden as they walk the road to the engine platform, with Alden turning back to wave every few seconds until they disappear behind the trees toward the engine platform.

A deep thunderous rumble travels through the ground into Jonathan's bones. It is enough to rattle the wares on and within Dormy's wagon and make the birds take flight in the distant trees. Jonathan wants to believe it is nothing, but this is not the rain season nor is there a cloud anywhere in sight. He looks to Dormy, who already stands atop her wagon, spyglass pressed to her eye, searching the horizon. March appears on the porch with one hand gripping the sword hanging from her hip and the other fiddling with the daggers belted around her thigh.

"Something happening at the temple," Dormy reports. "Villagers swarm the temple like ants to a carcass."

"Anything else?" he asks.

"A lot of screaming," she says, "crying, hands over mouths. The magistrate is trying to calm the crowd down."

"Cheshire," says Jonathan, knowing in his heart this mischief is his doing, "what have you done now?" Jonathan ushers everyone inside to the inn's common room and secures the front door.

"Mary Anne," he says, "if you would be so kind as to retire to your room until we have a better understanding of the situation."

She nods and climbs the stairs without protest.

"We should leave," says Dormy, watching through the shutters with her spyglass.

"No," says March, leaning against the wall beside the window. "If we leave now, we appear culpable. I wouldn't be surprised if the villagers blame us already."

Another thunderous rumble shakes the inn, and its old wood creaks as it sways and settles again. Glasses and steins rattle together behind the counter, and the small paintings hung on the wall sway back and forth.

March's eyes meet Jonathan's, confused. "Cannons?"

"No," says Jonathan, "something else."

"Help me!" The innkeeper bursts through the door. He kicks it shut and lowers the lock bar hinged beside the door.

His jaw shakes uncontrollably and his erratic breath fans strings of snot running from his nose to his beard. He trips over chairs and stools to lock the back door and bar each window.

Jonathan grabs a rag from the counter and hands it to the innkeeper to clean his face. "Sir, if you can tell us what happened, we may be able to help."

"He killed the others," the innkeeper sobs. "He killed the others and he'll kill me too. Please, don't let him kill me."

"Who's he talking about?" Dormy asks.

"Cheshire," says March.

"Calm down, sir." Jonathan tries to settle the innkeeper's nerves, but keeps him at a distance. Cheshire is not a murderer, but will kill with a reason. "Was it what happened at the temple? Can you give us more information?" asks Jonathan. "You're safe. The doors and windows are locked, and we will hear you out. What happened?"

"What about the windows upstairs?" March asks.

Horrified, the innkeeper runs for the stairs, but it's too late. Cheshire swings from the second floor and kicks the innkeeper in the chest, sending him rolling across the planks. He groans like a dying beast gasping to regain his breath, but manages to scramble to his feet and flings chairs, stools, and bottles at Cheshire while he chases him around the room.

Jonathan grabs Cheshire and wraps his arms around him before he can reach the innkeeper, but cannot hold on to him, even with March's help. Cheshire fights and wriggles through their arms and pursues his prey, who crawls away until his back is against the wall with nowhere to go.

"Help me!" the innkeeper cries. "Do something! You brought this devil upon us!"

Cheshire flips a dagger in his hand and presses it to the innkeeper's neck. Jonathan and March look to the empty slot on her thigh, unsure when Cheshire grabbed the dagger.

"You have something I want," Cheshire says. "You can give it to me before or after I kill you. It's your choice."

"That's not a choice," the innkeeper stutters.

"Cheshire, stop," Jonathan commands.

Cheshire looks over his shoulder at Jonathan, grinning from ear to ear, calm and calculating. Once his mind locks on what it wants, there is little Jonathan or March can do to deter him. He turns back to the innkeeper, who winces at the sight of Cheshire's full smile.

Jonathan waits for a twitch or reaction from Cheshire, but he remains fixed in time. Jonathan cannot even tell if he is breathing. The innkeeper's eyes dart to Jonathan, March, and Dormy for some hope of salvation. But Jonathan knows better than to attempt restraining Cheshire twice.

"Stop this, give the dagger to March," Jonathan implores. "Now."

Cheshire rises casually and walks past March to Jonathan and locks eyes with him, matching his resolve. The bottom of his eye twitches. Reluctantly, he presents the blade, but before Jonathan can grab hold, the dagger drops through Cheshire's fingers and spins blade over end toward the floor.

At first, Jonathan thinks it an ill-timed joke, but Cheshire's grin widens. He cocks his leg back, and with a jerk, catches the pommel of the dagger with the top of his foot and shoots it across the room. Jonathan understands too late why Cheshire handed him the dagger and not March. She would have been able to snatch it from the air, but Jonathan does not have her or Cheshire's reflexes. The dagger cuts the air with skillful precision and imbeds in the wooden post behind the innkeeper, through his mouth, severing his scream and any trace of life. The man who took them in and fed them this morning sits pinned to the wall, dead, with a look of terror frozen on his face.

Cheshire wastes no time rummaging through the innkeeper's pockets and yanking off his boots to check inside them. Not finding what he's looking for, he dislodges the dagger from the wooden post to flip the body over.

"Enough!" Jonathan grabs Cheshire by the back of his vest, but he swats Jonathan's arm away and produces an old, rusted knife from the back of the innkeeper's belt.

"Here." Cheshire tosses the knife to March. "Add this to your collection."

"What is it?" Jonathan asks.

March runs her fingers across the empty slots where jewels once sat. She passes the blade beneath her nose. "Blood. Old blood." She taps the blade on her forehead, trying to summon a memory.

"Explain this," Jonathan says to Cheshire.

"How the fuck should I know?" asks Cheshire. "What I know is, our gracious host and his two friends spied on us last night, each of them had a knife identical to this one, and they meant to kill us while we slept."

Above all, in spite of Cheshire's compulsion for

recklessness, he is honest, and Jonathan will not question further.

"Well, if they meant to kill us with these knives," says March, "they'd have a hard time of it. Only the tip remains sharp. And there's a hollow channel down the length of the blade to collect blood. In fact..." She raises the knife to her eye. The channel leads into the empty voids of the handle. She rubs the cold iron of her knife across pouted lips and holds it to her ear as if it would speak to her. "I have no knowledge of this knife."

"I thought you knew every weapon," says Cheshire.

"Do not question my knowledge," snaps March. "This is no weapon, despite the blood."

"Ceremonial?" asks Jonathan.

"Perhaps," says March.

During the entire scuffle, Dormy hid in the corner, her face covered by her jacket. Now her eyes follow the blade as if it is a rare treasure. With no other use for it, March trades her the knife for the dagger she pocketed earlier. With knife in hand, Dormy rushes to her wagon with the excitement of a child.

"Did you at least discover what our would-be assassins wanted?" Jonathan asks Cheshire, straightening his collar and hood.

"They wanted *the woman*," says Cheshire. "Mary Anne."

"Wonderful," says March, "and he wanted to kill us and take her."

"There must be others," says Jonathan. "He wouldn't have acted alone."

"Were. There were others. Two of them." Cheshire wipes

the blood from March's dagger on the innkeeper's shirt and slips it back into its leather sheath around her thigh. "And I destroyed part of their temple as well. It couldn't be helped."

Jonathan massages his forehead. With Rookridge fresh on his mind, at least he has the consolation of knowing the temple still stands, and those who are dead meant to do them harm. "We leave at first light, and if there are more of them, it's best to meet them here than on the open road at night. Everyone knows what to do. Shall we?"

Dormy secures the rest of the provisions in her wagon in order for a last-minute escape, should they need, and repairs the damage in the common room of the inn. March deals with the innkeeper's body, and Cheshire disappears. But Jonathan, however, walks into the mob at the temple, already whispering accusations about the outsiders. He listens to their assumptions and constructs scenarios to respond to each, but finds the truth a simpler course of action.

"We had no idea what happened at the temple. My companions and I have been at the inn all morning and afternoon, except for replenishing our food stores," Jonathan says to the farmer he purchased potatoes from earlier in the day, who confirms Jonathan's story. He walks through the crowd by the entrance to see the two broken altars, and stands near the farmer who sold him the wheels of cheese, but never looks his direction. "Such a shame something so awful would take place on such a beautiful day. Had I not been loaded down with groceries, perhaps I would have been able to witness what happened and bring the guilty party to justice."

"He's right," the farmer whispers to another behind Jonathan. "It couldn't have been them."

More whispers spread through the crowd, clearing Jonathan and the others of any involvement. But once they start describing another outsider by Cheshire's features, Jonathan offers another alternative to keep them distracted.

"When we arrived late last night," he says to an older gentleman, "I overheard two men arguing near the blacksmith's shop. I went to purchase new shoes for our ponies, but the conversation seemed intense." One by one, the villagers stop whispering to each other and crowd around Jonathan. "They spoke sacrilege, cursing one another's gods. Perhaps their dispute carried over to their worship and their anger overtook their sound judgement causing them to deface this beautiful temple."

By the time the sun sets, the entire crowd hangs on Jonathan's every word. They question minor details such as why, if they were in dispute, would they arrive at the temple together? But Jonathan, mindful not to seem too knowledgeable, lets their imaginations fuel their speculations. He does not know the two dead men in the temple, now their tomb, and part of him feels guilty for falsifying their deeds and lives to the people who lived with and respected them, but there is no quicker way to make people accept someone's death or murder, no matter how gruesome, than to make them believe the dead were against their gods.

The crowd drifts away through the fields and trees talking about the sad fate of the two misguided men, thankful they are no longer part of their community. Before he departs, he looks up to the overhang of the temple's roof and winks at Cheshire who has kept a watchful eye the entire time.

Back at the Inn, the common room shows no sign of the earlier scuffle, each chair and almost every decoration and detail in order and in its original place. Even the. blood-stained floorboards appear to have been replaced, and the dagger's mark in the post filled. But some steins and plates are missing and have no doubt found their way into Dormy's possession as a fee for her handiwork. March meets Jonathan downstairs, and together they bar every door and window on both the first and second floor of the inn except for their own room.

Upstairs, Jonathan knocks on Mary Anne's door, now opposite his, and grows nervous in the silence before she finally responds.

"Is it always like this here?" she asks through the door, her voice soft, her mind distant. Even though she was not witness to the innkeeper's death, the floorboards could not quiet his screams or their raised voices. He hopes Mary Anne remains oblivious she is the catalyst.

He does not have the heart to tell her their lives, at least Jonathan, March, and Dormy's for the time being, were peaceful before she appeared in the Rookwood.

"Yes," Jonathan answers and waits for Mary Anne to continue, but only crickets singing their melody in the night respond.

Jonathan returns to his room to find March undressed and in bed. Four swords stand against the wall in their sheaths, less than an arm's reach from her, and two belts of daggers drape across the small table next to the candle. He performs his nightly routine—folds and hangs his clothing, sips from his flask, and circles his watch with his thumb before laying it on the table across the room. March watches and smiles.

He lays with her, and she hooks her leg over his to hold him close. They share the same pillow and gaze into each other's eyes, mere inches away. Jonathan notices the devilish twinkle, like glowing embers in her eyes, eager for the chance of a possible attack. It's been nearly ten years since she fought a real opponent other than Jonathan, and a part of her is disappointed she missed the fight in Rookridge.

The bed shifts and creaks as Cheshire sits behind Jonathan. He reaches back and wraps his arm around Cheshire's waist to find his trousers still on. He should be undressed and sliding between them by now.

Jonathan turns his head to find Cheshire's gaze far beyond the window.

"We have a problem," says Cheshire.

CHAPTER 18

CHESHIRE

The temple would tower above the other buildings in Briarwell on even ground, but with its placement on the hill, Cheshire can see the breath of every field the village rests in, as well as the tops of the dense elms which surround it. He perches on the temple's point, cloak flapping in the wind as a weathervane, to be a sentry for Jonathan if he has need. If there are others who conspire against them in the village, they will either be among the crowd, or keep their distance. And there are no villagers anywhere except milling by the entrance of the temple. Not even in the windows of the other buildings, except for Mary Anne, who peeks out of her room occasionally. He slides down the side of the temple's roof, stopping at the stone point overhanging the corner to get a better view.

Below, Jonathan puts his silver tongue to work as he roams through the crowd, listening to everyone and speaking only when he must. No glance or head tilt goes unnoticed by Cheshire. They are all legitimately distraught over the men's deaths and the destruction of the temple, but soon villagers circle Jonathan as if he were a prophet, believing every word he says. It's Jonathan's eyes which are the key. The honesty and warmth behind his gaze can capture anyone's attention. By sundown, all the villagers come to their own conclusions and disperse to their homes beyond the meadow. Jonathan looks up and winks at Cheshire before returning to the Inn.

Cheshire stretches his shoulders and back, arching in both directions, and watches the last few villagers approach the tree line before his return to the inn. Some walk the roads, while others cut through the tall grass, leaving dark green trails behind them like slugs upon the earth. A particular woman and man catch Cheshire's attention. They pause shy of the trees, spooked, and both their heads, no larger than mustard seeds in Cheshire's sight, shift from side to side, looking at something unexpected in the underbrush.

Curious.

Whatever spooks them runs off as their heads and Cheshire's eyes follow a tiny shadow scatter through the elms. The couple change course and walk to the road, looking back to the trees as they go. Far to Cheshire's left, another farmer has the same reaction, and to his right, a family stops. The father picks his daughter up in his arms, and they retrace their trail until they return to the road as well. One occurrence could be dismissed as an encounter with a fox or wildcat. Many wild animals roam Wonderland's countryside, especially this far from the larger cities, but this is no animal.

Cheshire stretches his neck and widens his eyes. Suddenly multiple shadows come into focus and move under the darkening canopies. He scales the temple's peak and slides down the other side to see more shadowed figures concealed within the tree line. He tries to keep count, but they move slowly and in great numbers towards the northeast end of the village. The moon rises before the sun sets and offers little help, hidden behind slow rolling clouds from the east. The hanging lanterns of the buildings are the sole source of light in the village, and tonight their meager flames battle against pitch, not blue. But even in the darkest night, Cheshire can discern any shadow.

He walks back to the inn by way of the fences, and by the time he reaches the awning, the shadows have collected at the far end of the village behind the town hall. He climbs through Jonathan and March's window. They are in bed, bodies glowing in the candlelight, and curled with one another. Every fiber of his body wants to join them, but this night will bring blood, not pleasure. Cheshire sits on the edge of the bed, staring out the window, and Jonathan slides his arm around Cheshire's waist.

"We have a problem." Cheshire locks his fingers in Jonathan's.

"She's across the hall." March's muffled voice barely escapes Jonathan's chest.

Cheshire continues with a low, graveled voice. "There is movement in the tree line. A lot of movement."

"Probably friends of the men you killed come to seek retribution," says March.

"I don't believe they are." Cheshire sighs. "The men I killed were caught unaware by our arrival and proved to be unorganized. They wouldn't have had the time..." Cheshire trails off.

Jonathan turns his head, and Cheshire meets him, nose to nose. "How many?" he asks.

"I lost count at thirty," says Cheshire.

March gets out of bed and gathers her swords. "How long do we have?"

"Two hours. Three at best. Even with their numbers, if they haven't attacked already, they'll wait to enter the village until they assume we're asleep."

"Let's not disappoint them." March licks her fingertips and extinguishes the candle at their bedside.

Even though they prepare within the hour, their stalkers keep them waiting well into the night and close to dawn. Cheshire and March stand sentry on the roof of the inn, cloaked in darkness. With the moon hidden and the light of the lantern pulsing beneath them, they are as good as shadows. He perches at the north corner, and March stands at the roof's south end, dressed for battle. Two swords on her back, two on each hip, two flintlock pistols at her side, and an assortment of daggers on her thighs and boots. Besides her steel, there is little else. Trousers with the sides completely removed and thin leather cords keep small triangles of blue fustian centered on each breast. She has never looked more fearsome or alluring. March has fought and won more battles than Cheshire and Jonathan combined, and as her skill is unmatched, Cheshire's respect for her is unrivaled.

Long ago there were tales of a race of warrior women who

would charge into battle with exposed breasts covered in their own blood to distract and terrify their opponents. Cheshire is certain March does not descend from their line, but she is versed in all manners and history of war, and showcases her flawless, scarless skin to both confound and intimidate her enemies. And it is much easier to maneuver unencumbered. Cheshire would choose to fight without clothing at all, but only his cloak and vest stay tucked away in Dormy's wagon, and his sash is wrapped tightly around his waist and tucked into his trousers.

Even Jonathan waits shirtless beneath the awning of the inn, his large muscular arms crossed, chest tight, and broadsword leaning against the wall next to him. To look upon his height, muscle, thin waist, broad shoulders, and massive arms, anyone would believe he is a born fighter, but he is the gentlest of their threesome, with the most scars.

With pistols in hand, Dormy peeks out of the many hatches and portholes in her wagon, hidden by the hanging boxes and barrels. Mary Anne hides within the wagon as well with the ponies, no weapon, no backbone, cowering no doubt from the fight she brought upon them.

Cheshire turns his attention back to the village as the light at the town hall disappears. "It's about fucking time," he says. The town hall falls to darkness next. Then the forge.

March whistles two short notes down to Jonathan. The first short and the second one high.

March and Cheshire climb back inside, and Jonathan meets them to watch from the window of their room.

"The cowshed has fallen dark now," March says, with a hungry smirk.

The cooper's warehouse is the last to disappear.

"I would say there are over twenty cutting through the fields." March turns a sword in her palm to keep time.

"Another twenty will attempt to flank us," says Cheshire. "I saw them split once they reached the forge."

"Forty?" Jonathan asks. "Easy marks."

Finally, the men who have kept them waiting all night lumber from the tall grass and cross into the light, slowly, clumsily, as if they are part man and part bear. Their bodies clad with ragged leather armor, crudely made chain mail, animal pelts and furs, and sewn on plate metal. Throughout their numbers, they wield battle axes, swords, bludgeons, and flails.

"These men have no connection to the three from earlier," says March. "They're Death Mongers; mercenaries for hire from the Stone Hills by the Wastes." Her fingertips stroke the edge of her blade as if it were an obedient pet. "They wouldn't deal with farmers. Not enough coin in the business. But they certainly have turned out in droves. What the fuck have you done this time, Cheshire?"

"Wait," Jonathan points to two men below, "this one's on me. I recognize them." The two men he points to are out of place in the hairy bunch. One has an abnormally pronounced nose, and the other doesn't have a hair on his head, not even eyebrows, and a dead eye. They motion with their hands, and the mercenaries spread and circle the inn. "These bandits, Phillip and Rufus or something, attempted to rob me and Mary

Anne on the way to Rookridge. They cut off a lock of Mary Anne's hair and ran."

Cheshire recognizes the man with the nose and scar as the one who stared at them while at the tavern in Rookridge. "A lesson to be learned, darling. The three men who posed a threat to us yesterday are dead. You let yours live, and now they are outside ready to kill us."

"How do we proceed?" asks Jonathan.

"We handle this like the manor house in Breighton." Cheshire jumps over the bed, grabs the melted candle along with the spares beside it from the side table, and tosses one to Jonathan and one to March. After lighting his candle with the striking stone from the table, he holds the tip to Jonathan and March's.

Their memories catch as easily as the wicks. March hurries downstairs, and Jonathan walks to the rooms at the end of the hall. The small flame at the end of Cheshire's candle dances about erratic and beautiful, but as he drags it over the bedsheets, the fire crawls away with a life of its own. He tosses the candle through both open doors across the hall onto Mary Anne's bed and watches the flames devour the mattress, the wooden frame, and the rest of the room. Within seconds, the darkness succumbs and the night burns.

Cheshire steps out to the awning. The entire mob shields their faces from the unexpected inferno. The roar overtakes them, and the timbers of the inn begin to snap.

March rushes through the flames and slits two throats before the others realize they must now be on the defense. Jonathan kicks through a wall already ablaze, leaps at the mercenaries, and swings his broadsword wide, cleaving through one chest and then another. March dances with the fire. It moves with every swing and strike, almost as if her rage wills it to do her bidding.

She stabs a tall man with a long, braided beard through the gut, pinning him to a post holding up the awning, and sinks two of her daggers deep into the heads of other mercenaries. A stocky, pockmarked fellow manages to knock the blade from March's grip, but she pulls a pistol from her belt and fires directly into his eye through his head. She pulls another sword from her back and continues the onslaught without missing a step.

Jonathan keeps pace with her, using his fists, elbows, and legs to pummel anyone who comes within his reach, knocking out their teeth before nearly slicing them in twain with his sword. The sinewed muscles of his chest, back, arms, and torso tense and grow in the firelight. Mercenary after mercenary falls before them, throats slashed, entrails spilt, chests and heads pierced by March's blades and necks broken by the sheer power of Jonathan's fists.

They keep their backs to the fire, leaving their attackers to face the flames and smoke, stinging their eyes and impairing their vision. The men they face foolishly lift their arms to shield their eyes, giving March and Jonathan easy targets, and those who try to circle behind them, Jonathan kicks into the waiting inferno.

A volley of gunfire from Dormy's wagon spooks the mercenaries. Her tiny hands poke out from the various flaps and portholes, firing pistols into the crowd. Some mercenaries attempt to attack the wagon where her hand appears, but she scurries to another porthole to fire another shot at their heads. Not every bullet finds a target, but the noise and smoke are enough to add to their mounting confusion.

Though entertained by watching, Cheshire notices the crowd of mercenaries change their tactics and move in four or five at time instead of one or two. Jonathan and March hold their own, but there is only so much even they can handle. Cheshire drops on the shoulders of a large mercenary who tried to circle around Jonathan, locks his feet, tightens his thighs around his neck, and flips backwards with his entire weight, launching the man into the air and snapping his neck at the same time.

These men are ill prepared and ill informed. They were more than likely told to kill anyone in the party without knowing its members, and since Jonathan has history with their wranglers, they anticipated him and his strength. But the mercenaries, misled by March's appearance, approach her with little expectation of her skill until it's too late and they lay bleeding or dead at her feet. They also had no chance to expect Cheshire. He shoots in between their bearlike attackers unnoticed. He kicks a mercenary into one of March's waiting swords, then climbs onto Jonathan's shoulders and jumps off to knee the jaw loose on another mercenary. Those who cross him soon have their knees kicked in backwards with a loud crack and wait screaming for Jonathan or March to finish them.

Jonathan and March deal swift deaths. Cheshire smiles, like March, from ear to ear, making their deaths slow and painful. Cheshire dislodges two of March's daggers from the dead and slices at the living, aiming for the tendons on the back of the heel, the inside of their thighs, and any neck he can reach.

The sun creeps over the wall of elms as the inn collapses behind them and the battle nears its end. It is not the skill of the mercenaries which tire Cheshire and the others, as much as their numbers. Wave after wave pound against them like a tormented sea wearing down the rocks of its coast. Some mercenaries turn tail and run to escape the fate of their companions and their purses feeling not as heavy as before. But a few stout men remain, delusional, but determined to win the day.

March impales one of the last mercenaries with two swords, hilt deep into his back. Her bloody blades pierce through his body just below his collar bones. As he chokes on his blood, she places her foot firmly in the small of his back and kicks him to the ground, freeing her swords. Jonathan slices another mercenary across the chest with an upward stroke, nearly separating his left shoulder and arm from the rest of his body. Blood flings from his sword onto the gray cinders of the inn, where it sizzles and smokes.

The largest of the mercenaries swings his morning star and comes close to taking off Jonathan's head, but he is able to bat him away with his sword, landing a strike across his leg. The coward turns to March, assuming she will be easy prey. She blocks his swing with her blades, but the weight behind a single blow knocks her back ten feet, though she remains upright.

Cheshire charges the mountain, daggers in hand, and plunges them deep into his forearms. The man drops his weapon, the muscles controlling his hands severed. He roars with anger and pain and attempts to backhand Cheshire, but he dodges and collects two more daggers from nearby corpses.

While the mercenary tries to push the blades from his arms with limp hands, Cheshire dives through his legs and shoves both daggers through his ankles, slicing completely through his heels. Spit flies into the air as the last remaining mercenary screams in agony. He staggers, but on his first step, his feet snap sideways under his weight, only his skin keeping his feet to his body, and topples backward across a scorched beam.

March throws two more daggers to Cheshire. He jumps, snatches them from the air, lands on top of the mercenary, and with his full weight behind them, plunges them through each of his wrists, pinning him to the beam. Cheshire steps on the daggers to embed them further into the wood. He sits on the man's chest and bucks up and down as his victim screams and gasps for breath, unable to comprehend the pain in his feet, arms, and of his flesh burning away.

"You should never have tried to touch them," Cheshire whispers with a sinister grin.

In one final act of defiance, the mercenary tries to spit blood into Cheshire's face, but he quickly closes the man's jaw with his feet. The blood intended for Cheshire oozes from between the man's lips and pools in his ears. Cheshire straightens his legs, his heels digging into the soft triangle of flesh on the underside of his lower jaw. The mercenary's screams gargle and his neck muscles strain, fighting against Cheshire, but all it takes is one more quick snap to end the man's futile struggle. He convulses twice more before his body goes slack.

With every mercenary gone or dead, they regroup at the wagon. March breathes heavy, chest held high, and collects her swords and daggers from the dead, satisfied with her kills. Jonathan surveys the bodies to make sure all are truly dead. Dormy and Mary Anne reemerge from the wagon, Dormy from her driver's hatch and Mary Anne on the deck of the second level. Cheshire cannot help but notice the stark difference between Mary Anne and the rest. Streams of sweat cut through layers of ash and blood on his, Jonathan, and March's bodies. Dormy's layers of vests and jackets disheveled, her braids loose, and her hands black with gun power. And Mary Anne stands above them with only a slightly wrinkled dress.

Jonathan, March, and Dormy fought, and risked their lives, killed for her, while Cheshire fought to keep his friends safe. But Mary Anne has the effrontery to stand above them, looking down on them, unblemished. The more he looks upon her, the more the blood in his veins burns. Her presence threatens everything he cares for, everything he has worked for over the centuries. She is not one of them, does not belong here, and he wonders how long, if circumstances continue as they are, he will let her live.

CHAPTER 19

JONATHAN

The smoke-filled air chokes the first rays of dawn, its vibrant colors unnaturally muted as if all colors bled from the world. Jonathan grabs March and Cheshire in each arm and kisses both of their heads, their beautiful pink and purple hair matted gray with sweat and ash.

Although the heat pulses from the charred remains of the inn like a dying heartbeat, there is a chill upon the morning air. The ash and soot drift down around them, and from the rest of the village, the inn could be mistaken for being in the thralls of a dark winter. Jonathan wishes it could be so, but the illusion fades as he takes in yet another scene of destruction, bodies filling the road, and blood mixing with dirt and ash to create dark black puddles. The air reeks of blood, burned flesh, and excrement.

What the fuck are we doing here?

Mary Anne creeps out of the upper compartment, her face

motionless and numb, and covers her mouth and nose from the stench. Dormy emerges from the driver's hatch and stands on her bench. From inside the wagon, she was unaware of the full scope of their battle, and her jaw drops at the sight of the dead. She throws March her long gray coat and Jonathan his blue jacket. He searches the breast pockets until his fingers grab hold of his flask, and he takes a larger than normal drink, letting the cold, liquid fire run through him, calming his nerves and settling his mind.

Jonathan looks out upon the rest of the village, which should bustle with life by now.

Are the townspeople asleep? Are they hiding from the massacre? Another M word. Or worse, did the mercenaries murder them first in the middle of the night? He wants to run to every farmstead and make sure their careless actions did not wipe out an entire village.

"I wish you would've told me you were going to burn down the inn." Dormy unties a pouch from the belt of a dead mercenary. "Had I known I would have spent less time repairing and more time..." She does not finish for fear Jonathan would judge her, but nothing could be further from the truth. Most of Dormy's antiques and wares are stolen or found. It's second nature to her and more often than not, she is unaware of her actions until she empties her pockets. But she continues wandering through the bodies, collecting boots, belts, and as many rings and necklaces as she can stuff in her pockets.

"Dormy," says Jonathan. "If you would be so kind as to hitch your ponies to the wagon again. We will need to depart as soon as possible."

She quickly grabs two more items from the bodies next to her, and then does as Jonathan suggests. She leads them from the rear door and connects their harness to the center shaft.

"The two you spoke of earlier are not here," says March as she walks among the dead, collecting swords, knives, and the morning star as a prize.

"Damn it." Jonathan does not recall seeing them in the battle. He thinks perhaps he should have heeded Cheshire's advice, sought them out first, and killed them before they had a chance to run again. They brought a horde of mercenaries with them this time, and Jonathan does not want to think about what will fall upon them the next time they meet. However, to buy the service of such a band of mercenaries is beyond the means of two cowardly bandits in the woods. Jonathan must wonder who their benefactors are.

But before Jonathan can dwell on the thought, the villagers appear from the trees and approach the inn with caution and curiousity. *Thank the gods.* During the battle, he saw a few of their orange figures approach to investigate the fire, but once they saw the bloodshed, they ran back into the darkness. More and more gather at the edge of the circle of ash, taking in the dead bodies and the remains of the inn, and their mood turns to anger.

"Murderers!" they cry. "Heathens!" they shout. "Falsifiers!" they chant. The villagers scream, hurling insults and calling down curses upon them and their ancestors.

Jonathan looks for Cheshire, but he has disappeared with

the wind once again. March wipes blood from her daggers and stares at the villagers, daring them to challenge her.

"Let them come," she says under her breath.

"We will not harm this village more than we already have," Jonathan says through still lips.

March's grip tightens on the hilt of her sword, but Jonathan grabs her hands, and at his touch, she relaxes. He glances at Dormy, and she disappears into the wagon taking Mary Anne with her.

"It is fortunate you were all in bed when this attack happened." Jonathan raises his hands to hush the crowd. "We must be plain with you now. Our presence here is not happenstance. We uncovered a plot by the men who killed each other yesterday. They schemed not just to destroy your temple, but to destroy your entire village, your way of life. They hired these vicious men to come in the dead of night and wipe Briarwell from the map to steal all you own. Some of you saw them skulking in the shadows yesterday evening."

The villagers' shouts turn to murmurs, but their mistrust and confusion will not allow them to stop entirely. The day before, the villagers took Jonathan's story and dispersed it among themselves, expounding on it of their own accord. But this day they resist. Their disbelief stands firm. Jonathan watches the expression he knows so well on a few villagers scattered throughout the mob. Their gaze and their eyes tick from side to side, up and down as they try to understand the plausibility of what Jonathan presents. But a hint of doubt is all he needs.

"You do not know us," Jonathan continues, "but we would

not, nay, we could not let such a sinister act befall your peaceful village. The innkeeper, one of your stock, brave and true, helped fend off these assassins, but sadly lost his life in the fire. His sacrifice emboldened us to fight with lions' hearts to keep the evil of these men from spreading to the rest of your village. We regret the destruction and death brought upon you and understand if you require retribution for your loss, but know, in your hearts, we fought, through flame and blood, to ensure all of you could wake this morning."

"Thank you," a voice calls from the back of the crowd. "Thank you for saving our lives. My children's lives."

Those words pierce deep. Mothers grab hold of their sons, fathers shake the doubt from their heads, and a chain reaction begins. Another villager thanks Jonathan and March, and another, and soon they shout praises and curse the supposed despicable deeds of the magistrate and blacksmith.

"I, for one, never trusted the magistrate," a thin, shirtless man says.

"My grandfather warned me about him," a woman holding her son to her leg says. "I heard the magistrate tried to steal another man's wife."

A rotund man saunters to the front and addresses the crowd. "I heard he taxed us more to stuff his own pockets."

"And in league with the smith," another woman shouts. "He quarreled often with his customers, always with an upturned lip at us. I knew we couldn't trust him."

"I hope their souls rot," a young woman says from farther back. "Good riddance."

They were too blinded by their own emotions to realize it

was Dormy who spoke first from the back. She makes her way through the crowd and jumps back to the driver's bench, and March boards the wagon from the rear door. Jonathan joins Dormy on her bench, his thighs shaking as he sits for the first time in eight hours. He wishes the people would go about their day and clear the road. Then they could set out themselves, but the crowd mingles and spreads, forming a crescent shaped barrier around the wagon and inn.

"Jonathan," March says from within the driver's hatch, "to the south."

He holds on to the side of the wagon as he would the ratlines of a ship to get a better view of what approaches from behind them.

A procession of Mirusian soldiers on horseback gallop into view on the southern path. Every horse and rider clatters with armor polished to a mirror like sheen. Red and white banners whip behind them as they speed towards the wagon. At the head of the metal serpent rides the Red Knight of Mirus, in full crimson armor, a fire unto himself in the sea of grass and ash. Large spiked pauldrons increase his size and severity, as does the carefully crafted helmet made to resemble a horse's head, complete with black plumes of horsehair flowing down its neck.

Dormy looks to Jonathan for the signal to bolt. Her hands wrap themselves over and over in the leather reins, but without looking in her direction, a small shake of his head tells her they have no choice but to wait.

The soldiers stop and dismount from their horses behind the wagon and walk past to push the villagers back to secure the area. Five soldiers surround Jonathan and Dormy, swords drawn and ready to strike them down.

Jonathan slides his fingers into the small pocket of his trousers to feel the gentle ticking of his timepiece against his swollen skin. His pulse struggles to slow and match its mechanical heartbeat. And as he stares down the length of the iron swords, he thinks of his table, his cabinet, his tea, and spending the day with March and Cheshire, giving in to every carnal impulse.

What the fuck are we doing here?

The Red Knight turns his horse and stops in front of the wagon. He removes his helmet as if more burden than honor to reveal fair skin, a strong jaw, and dandelion hair pulled into a neat tail. "You there," he sneers at Jonathan. "Carter, are you to answer for this destruction and loss of life?"

"We're thankful for your arrival, good sir," says Jonathan. "We were actually on our way to Mirus, and stopped here for respite, when the village came under attack by brigands. I assure you, our presence here is purely happenstance, and we had no choice but to protect the village from these invaders."

Unconvinced, the Red Knight scoffs and unsheathes a broadsword with serrated teeth halfway up both sides of its blade and leans it on his shoulder.

"The villagers can attest to our involvement," says Jonathan, louder to catch the ears of the villagers.

"It's true," the rotund farmer says, "they saved us all."

"Leave them be," another woman shouts, causing a ripple throughout the crowd.

"Perhaps you could give us escort the rest of the way to

Mirus?" Jonathan asks innocently. "Or if not, then allow us to continue our journey. It's quite a way, as you already know."

The Red Knight strides closer to Jonathan. "Disembark and prepare to surrender all weapons and contraband on board this grotesque cart." He points his sword at Jonathan's head. "I will not repeat myself."

Jonathan's eye twitches at two distinct clicks from within the wagon. March has two flintlock pistols pointed at the Red Knight's head. "Wait," he says under his breath. If they are to take such a brazen risk and call down the fury of all the soldiers, they must all be closer. "On my mark."

"Soldiers," the Red Knight shouts and flicks his hand toward Jonathan and Dormy. The soldiers follow their command and inch closer, their eyes moving from Jonathan to Dormy, deciding who will suffer their first blow.

"Jonathan?" Dormy grips her reins tighter.

He counts down the soldiers' distance with the seconds of his timepiece. The closer they are, the more will fall under the weight of the wagon once it lurches forward, and the less power those who remain will have behind their swings. Finally, the vambraces to two soldiers click together and Jonathan breathes deep, ready to give the command.

Dormy will crack the reins with all the strength in her arms, and March will burst through the hatch and deliver shot after shot with an archer's accuracy. The pistol fire will spook the horses on the road in front of them and the wagon will mow down any soldier in their path. But a herald's trumpet from behind them kills their plan quicker than any blade and shakes Jonathan to his core.

The Red Knight pulls on the reins of his horse to turn and orders the soldiers to clear the bodies lying in the path, then dismounts and stabs several of the dead mercenaries to cover his own sword in blood. Two men remain with Jonathan and Dormy while the rest fling the dead into piles on the grass like sacks of grain.

A knot rises in Jonathan's throat. He tries to swallow it down, but it refuses to budge. He does not turn back this time, yet the sound of approaching hooves pounding and kicking up dirt, and the rattle of wheels of a great carriage from behind increases his panic. With the path clear, a grand carriage, the Duchess's carriage, drawn by four powerful white steeds, passes by as if time crawled in this moment. Silver figures, filigree, and ornaments cover every red wooden panel, door, wheel, and roof. The coachman tugs the reins and stops the horses near the villagers, who gawk and point at the lavish carriage.

How is she here? He slides his blood-covered sword through the driver's hatch to hide it from view. *How could she have known? When did she hear? The attack in Rookridge was two days ago. Has she been to Rookridge? What will she say? How do I tell her about Mary Anne?*

The coachman climbs down and pulls a small step ladder from beneath the carriage and secures it in place below the door before holding it open for the Duchess. She pokes her head out of the door with a handkerchief over her mouth and nose. Her voluminous gold and scarlet dress bells from side to side as she descends the small ladder. The Red Knight approaches her and presents his bloody sword. She nods and waves him away to join his men.

Jonathan jumps to the ground and uses his sleeve to wipe the stains from his face. He should hear the clinking of armor, a lingering crack from the cinders, or the Red Knight barking orders, but the only sound in his ears is the soft squish of ash and mud as the Duchess walks closer.

This is all wrong. It's been wrong since the beginning.

They should have arrived in Mirus four days from now. Dormy's wagon would climb the winding streets of the city, enter the castle gates, and roll to a stop in front of the great stairs of the castle. The Duchess and her courtiers would descend to greet them. Jonathan would present Mary Anne and they would exchange curtsies and pleasantries, but instead Jonathan comes face to face with the Duchess in a field of men, dead by his hands, and covered in blood.

CHAPTER 20

MARY ANNE

She fights her way through Dormy's junk to get to the back door on the lower level of the wagon. She is not sure how she came to be here, nor does she care, but she knows in her heart the woman who stepped out of her carriage is the Duchess. She is the end of Mary Anne's journey and this nightmare.

March leans against boxes near the back door and uses water from a small barrel hanging on the wall to wash blood from her hair. Mary Anne pauses, assuming she will try to stop her from leaving the wagon, but March does not raise even her eyes. With no resistance, Mary Anne explodes from the door, tears welling in her eyes, and her boots beating the ash beneath them, past Jonathan toward the Duchess. But two soldiers cross their swords to block Mary Anne's path.

"Let me through," she commands. Deliverance, salvation, less than twenty feet away, yet still out of reach. Mary Anne never wished harm on any soul, but in this instance, she wishes the two soldiers would disappear or fall dead before her. She pushes against the soldiers' armor and swords and reaches her arm between the blades toward the Duchess, straining, and fears the webs between her fingers will tear. One blade cuts through her underdress and into the tender area under her arm. The burn snaps Mary Anne back to her senses and she recoils from the sting.

"Oh, separate, will you?" The Duchess waves the soldiers away. "Look what you've done to the poor dear." She snaps her fingers and the Red Knight brings a linen rag from his saddle and wraps Mary Anne's arm roughly. She studies Mary Anne's face, her eyes bouncing back and forth from eyes to eyebrows, and she smiles.

"Thank you," she says to him and the Duchess. Mary Anne takes in a long breath through her nostrils to suppress the need to bawl. She will not let the Duchess see her cry, and uses the cuff of her sleeve to wipe away the tears in her eyes before they can stream down her cheeks.

The Duchess is a beautiful, Rubenesque woman in a thick maroon and gold dress with bulbous sleeves, and an oversized hat adding to her size and grandeur. The lip color she wears does not extend to the ends of her mouth, making her smile appear petite between her full cheeks.

"How do you do, your majesty?" Mary Anne curtsies, without a clue how to address her.

"Majesty?" The Duchess smiles and walks closer to Mary Anne. "I like you. I am no majesty, my dear, far from it. You may address me as Madam or Duchess. Whichever you prefer."

"Yes, madam, Duchess," says Mary Anne. "I am pleased to make your acquaintance, madam. We were on our way to Mirus to meet you, actually. Forgive me, madam. My name is Mary Anne Elizabeth, from—"

The Duchess holds up a finger to her own pouted lips to keep Mary Anne from saying where she is from. "So, you're the one all this fuss is about." She leans closer to Mary Anne and whispers, "It's not often a woman from your world enters Wonderland, but I assure you, the fewer who know, the safer you will be."

It's true, Mary Anne thinks. Her jaw trembles. *The Duchess knows of previous women who have found themselves stuck in Wonderland. And therefore, it stands to reason, she will know the means to leave.* Mary Anne has waited for this moment since the first mention of the Duchess. "I would like to go back home. Please, madam," she whispers.

"Are you sure, dear?" the Duchess asks. "I can't blame you. Wonderland is not everyone's cup of tea."

A nervous laugh escapes Jonathan.

The Duchess looks past Mary Anne to the wagon. "Jonathan Carter." The Duchess's voice drops in tone. "How did you happen upon this woman?"

Jonathan steps down and approaches. "Hello, madam. By chance, I stumbled upon Mary Anne Elizabeth in the Rookwood. We had no means to help her, so we thought, with your position in Wonderland, you might."

"Can you help me, please?" Mary Anne asks, but wonders how the Duchess knows Jonathan. It seems silly to think of considering the short time she has been in this world.

The Duchess reads Mary Anne's face immediately. "How do I know young Carter? Apparently he has been shy about the acclaim and reputation of his family. Why, there's hardly a city or village in all of Wonderland who hasn't heard of the work of Theophilius Carter and his son, the Queendom's premier and most sought after hatters." The Duchess looks around at the villagers of Briarwell, who stand at a distance. "Well, maybe not this village."

Their time in Rookridge makes sense to Mary Anne now. The townspeople in Rookridge held Jonathan in such high regard, and even in Briarwell there were a few who pointed his direction as they walked earlier. This is a vital and reassuring detail of her hero, and she wishes she knew this from the beginning. But once she looks upon his blank expression, she can tell this is a part of his life he did not want revealed.

Perhaps this is why he chooses to live in the middle of nowhere. But why? If he is famous or successful throughout the country, why hide from it?

"But," the Duchess interrupts her thought, "to your question, yes, my dear, I know of the way to return you home. It is a simple matter," the Duchess says warmly.

Every risk and pitfall suddenly seem worth the torment she has suffered these past three days. She does not have to wait four more days, dodging more unforeseen perils or madmen bent on her death. Her way home stands before her.

"I am ready." Mary Anne pulls away, plants her feet, adjusts her dress, and closes her eyes. She pictures the stairs leading up to the landing of her home, the dark lacquer finish of her front door in the noonday sun, and the bronze door handle so close she can reach out and touch it.

"My dear, what are you doing?" the Duchess asks with a gentle voice.

"Going home." Mary Anne opens her eyes to see the Duchess staring back, confused. "I'm ready."

"Mary Anne, I am good, but I am not that good. Alas, I do not have magical powers and cannot wave my hands to send you home." The Duchess speaks to Mary Anne as if she still believes Saint Nicholas is real.

Now Mary Anne can barely sense her heartbeat, fearing it will fade away into nothing. To her understanding, the Duchess was supposed to be the end, not a stop point on a needlessly prolonged journey. A sour taste creeps from the back of her throat.

The Duchess takes Mary Anne by the hand and cups it in both of hers, firmly, motherly. "I can return you home, but such a feat must begin at the castle. I wish it were possible to do so right here and now, but it is not. If you can wait a while longer, I assure you, you will see your home again."

Mary Anne pulls her hands from the Duchess. She reacted quickly to her first words, letting her emotions get the better of her, and now she pays for her assumption, elated one second and devastated the next.

"Come along now, back to the castle with us." The Duchess's hands wait, still outstretched, and her cheeks plump with her reassuring smile. "If you are still willing?"

She cannot control the trembling of her hand as she reaches out, and snaps it back to her chest to keep her fear hidden from the Duchess. "Yes. Please." She knows she has no other choice. She will continue on this misadventure and see where it leads. But she will not go alone. She looks over her shoulder at Jonathan. "May I make a small request?"

The Duchess's eyes follow Mary Anne's. "Of course, dear."

She walks back to the wagon, fear and guilt burning in her stomach and chest. Jonathan and the others have been through much for her already, and in his current condition, their surroundings, and especially the past three days, he has every right to refuse to agree to the request she is about to ask.

"Thank you for everything you've done for me, Jonathan," she says in a hushed tone. "I have no right to ask this, but would you accompany me to the capital? You've saved my life more than once, and I am truly thankful. And I would be amiss to say I'm not frightened. I know I must go with the Duchess, but I don't know her well enough to trust her yet. But I do trust you. Please."

Dormy shakes, unable to make a sound, but from her smile Mary Anne assumes she is excited at the prospect of continuing their journey to Mirus. March, however, who watches from the upper level of the wagon, disappears inside without a word. Mary Anne looks to Jonathan for his response, with fear and guilt churning in her stomach and chest, creating a volatile heat that makes her want to vomit.

But Jonathan takes a rag from Dormy and wipes the blood and dirt from his face, neck, and chest. "I did promise to see you safely to Mirus. What kind of gentleman would I be if I did not keep my word?" The twinkle in his eye shines bright against his gray skin. "Besides, we're already packed and supplied for the journey. We will follow."

"Thank you," Mary Anne says quieter than a whisper. She walks to the carriage as the Duchess speaks to a small gathering of villagers and hands them two full pouches of coins, offers her condolences, and pledges a handful of the soldiers to remain and help them rebuild.

The coachman helps Mary Anne into a small compartment in the carriage, luxurious and borderline garish. Wine-colored quilted fabric covers each wall and ceiling with hand knotted pink tassels along each seam, plush velvet cushioned benches, and a double layer of sheer organza curtains and thick brocade. She questions if she rides in a carriage or the stomach of some beast.

When the Duchess finishes her business with the villagers, she climbs into her own separate compartment in the carriage, much roomier than Mary Anne's, and gives the order to turn and depart Briarwell. Mary Anne's heart sinks into her feet, and she opens the curtain to see Jonathan smile and hold up a hand. When the carriage passes the train platform, Mary Anne looks off into the direction she believes Emilia and Alden walked to Halma. There is little chance she will ever see them again, but she is grateful to have witnessed such true, genuine kindness and love between mother and child.

The carriage soon leaves the uneven paths of Briarwell and turns on the wider dirt road to Mirus. The ride in the Duchess's carriage will be peaceful, but lonely. Mary Anne assumes the alternative would be to sit across from the Duchess, wavering back and forth between forced conversation and awkward silence during their four day journey.

"I hope it is not an inconvenience," Mary Anne asks the Duchess through a small wooden sliding partition, "I asked the others to accompany me to Mirus. I should have asked your permission before asking them."

"Nonsense, dear. I understand completely," says the Duchess, "and would have thought it odd if you hadn't asked them. You've grown close and want to keep them nearby. I don't blame you in the slightest. After all, Jonathan Carter is quite the upstanding young man."

While Mary Anne stood outside Dormy's cart, before she boarded the carriage, all she wanted to do was wrap her arms around Jonathan, her savior, to say thank you. But she restrained herself. She does not know Jonathan well enough yet to warrant such a show of affection. Now she travels away from him and his kindness, and hopes he will keep his word again and follow. She survived four days in Wonderland thus far with Jonathan's help. She will last four more on the road to Mirus, this time under the protection of the Duchess, and hopefully be all the closer to home.

CHAPTER 21

CHESHIRE

Cheshire claws at the trunk of the elm where he perches. He has not looked upon the Duchess's smug, repugnant face for a millennium, since he was in his tenth year, and never thought he would see her this far from the safety of Mirus. In all his memory, he cannot recall a time when she dared cross beyond the city walls, and for good reason.

The Duchess glances from Mary Anne to Dormy's wagon and the crowd of villagers. She suspects he is near. She hides her paranoia well, or she truly believes the forty Mirusian soldiers traveling with her keep her safe. But Cheshire, Jonathan, and March could dispatch them with slightly more difficulty than the mercenaries the previous night. In less than a minute, his hands could be around her neck, denying her breath as she has denied him entry to the capital. Her eyes would bulge and her mouth would purple and swell until her last remnant of life rattles and dwindles to nothing.

But he slows his breath and calms the rage clouding his thoughts and judgment to watch their lips and follow their distant conversation. Jonathan assumed correctly, and the Duchess will take Mary Anne immediately back to Mirus with her, presumably to aid in her return home.

It turns out Mary Anne is not worthless after all.

Cheshire does not know why the Duchess wants to help her, or why she traveled this far to find her, nor does he care, but Mary Anne's arrival presents a unique opportunity never before possible. She has brought the Duchess to Cheshire.

The soldiers at the Great Gates search every merchant's wagon, cart, and noble's carriage before being granted entrance, but Cheshire wagers the Duchess's vanity will never allow herself to be seen lowered to the same level as the people she pretends to preside over. If they search the Duchess's carriage outside the Great Gates, he will fail, but be able to fight his way out and escape as he has before, though it has been many centuries since his last attempt. But if the soldiers let the Duchess through, as he believes they will, then unbeknownst to her, she will be his way back into Mirus.

PART III

CHAPTER 22

CHESHIRE

Cheshire sits high in the rafters of the Last Hand tavern, a stone's throw from Mirus, leg dangling while he drinks from a stolen tankard of the unconscious drunk below. The warm ale courses through his stomach, a welcome change from pond and river water.

The catacombs and their arcana—old magic—allowed him to travel the near one thousand miles between Briarwell and Mirus in two days. Half the time it will take Dormy's wagon or the Duchess's carriage. And while he waits for the others to catch up, he watches and listens to the motley clientele of the Last Hand from his perch.

The midday sun bounces soft light through the squat frosted windows into the dark tavern, keeping the drunks and disreputables partially in shadow. At one end of the packed tavern, a portly man glides his bow elegantly against the gut strings of a weathered vielle tucked under his chin. A brawl breaks out between two large men with hair poking out the back of their collars over a plate of half-eaten turkey legs.

Not yet with the nerve for a brothel, four young women, from neighboring farms, hunt men of Mirus to entertain outside the walls and away from their wives. A farmer with a beard down to his waist slips on a puddle of beer and slams the back of his head on the unswept floorboards, still holding his drink high and never spilling a drop. In the far corner, a group of three well-dressed men of Mirus play games of chance forbidden within the city, stain their pristine linen robes with brown splotches of ale, and sing along to the lewd chanty filling the tavern.

Pinned to the far wall next to the door is a parchment with the drawing of Cheshire's assumed likeness and the words *QUEEN SLAYER. ENEMY OF THE QUEENDOM. Reward 100,000 gold pieces for the capture of the fugitive.* There must be over twenty layered on top of each other, each growing older the further back they go. Unlike Briarwell, these parchments are as common as leaves on trees this close to the capital.

A shirtless drunk with a full rug of hair down his chest and back stands on the bar, thrusting at an imagined woman, cheering his own conquest.

"Get your hairy ass down, you beast of a man, before some hunter takes aim at your tit and I have to clean up your fat disgusting carcass off my bar." Cara Ogden, proprietor of the Last Hand, slaps the man on his calf with her wrinkled hand.

"Fuck off, old wench," the drunken man slurs.

The vielle and all conversation, arguments, and laughter disappear as if Cheshire suddenly lost his hearing. One of the men who stopped his brawl coughs, the men of Mirus snicker in the corner, and the vielle player removes the small hat from his bald head.

Cara Ogden, small of frame but large of spirit, looks at the rest of her customers, swipes the inside of her bottom lip with her tongue, and turns back to address the hairy man. "You're new. I'll give you the benefit of that. But I'll still ask you one last time to get the fuck down off my bar or get the fuck out."

The man squats down on the bar, both his hands on his knees, and belches through gritted teeth in Ogden's face. "What will you do about it, ya wee pup?"

Cheshire grins, knowing the drunk has sealed his fate. Ogden turns her head to the right as if to look over her shoulder, and every degenerate in the Last Hand, regardless of status, descends upon the man. They strip him of the rest of his clothing, boots, and weapons. A few of the patrons slap him across the face and bare ass every time he curses at them. His words go unheard, overpowered by laughter and taunts. The crowd carries him to the door, throws him out, slams it shut, and looks to Ogden for her approval.

"May the gods help you all, ya pack of hedge-born sots," she says, wiping her hands on her leather apron.

The tavern erupts with cheers and a new robust song from the vielle. One of the largest men kisses Ogden on the top of her head, as he would his own mother. She makes her rounds through the tavern, dodging swords poking through worn scabbards, checking on the unconscious farmer to make sure he still breathes, then ever so slightly looks up at Cheshire, careful to not draw attention. They used to talk years ago, but anything they would say to each other now would take them both to a time they do not want to relive.

She sighs, not surprised, and leaves Cheshire with a nod to let him know she will still honor the arrangement to pour the soldiers or the Castle Guard of Mirus a heavy hand, making them forget their wits and duties, for him to question them once they stagger out the door. If he is finally to gain entry to Mirus, he will need as much information about what has changed within the towering city walls. But for the past two days, no soldier or guard has entered the Last Hand.

However, two figures Cheshire never thought he would cross, and has chosen to avoid, slither through the front door. On a normal day, criminals of varying severity walk into the Last Hand. Cheats, swindlers, thieves, poachers, bounty hunters. And any of them would appear a saint next to the Twins, Lysander and Uriah, the last blood of the line of the Old Kings of Wonderland.

"Shit," Cheshire says under his breath.

They stand at the door and wait for the crowd to bask in their presence. Their polished gauntlets, linen tunics, and freshly washed hair sparkle as the sun outlines them in the doorway. A low murmur of 'shits' and 'fucks' travel through the tavern, the crowd all too familiar with the Twins' reputation. The robed men from Mirus nervously clear their table and move across the tavern, the vielle pulls sour notes, and the four women with hungry eyes do a poor job hiding their discussion of their intentions behind their hands.

Lysander drops onto the vacant bench and lays his long sword across the empty table, knocking the previous men's drinks to the floor. He eyes the four women and runs his fingers through his full braided beard down to his chest, a predator luring in his prey.

Uriah, on the other hand, brushes his hand against his alabaster cheek and swings his long hair over his shoulder as he sits. He leans his silver glaive against the wall and lays his whip beside Lysander's sword. For twins, both men couldn't be any more different in build, hair, and movement. Their eyes, however, share the same dark and salacious design.

Cheshire climbs to the highest beams and slinks across the timbers, careful not to disturb the centuries of dust, and cautiously moves one part of his body at a time as he travels to the opposite side of the tavern, until he lowers himself slowly to the large cross beam directly above their heads.

The four women slink over to Lysander and Uriah, unaware of who they are or under the misguided notion they are the hunters. The Twins grope and inspect the women's waists, thighs, and asses, testing them like ripe fruit. They pull two of the women onto their laps and dismiss the others. With a gentle hand, the women try to lift Lysander and Uriah's eyes to theirs, but Uriah jerks his head away while Lysander swats the woman's hand from his face. Lysander unlaces his woman's bodice and pulls it open, ripping a seam, and massages her bare breasts with rough hands. Uriah runs his arm far under his woman's dress and between her legs. Both women inhale and clench their teeth, hiding their newfound fear behind their smiles.

"I think you're both mistaken," says Ogden. "There's a brothel in Mirus for you to take your business."

"Beer." Uriah looks past her to the man behind the bar.

"You can speak to me." Ms. Ogden flaps her rag onto the table.

"You can get our drinks." Lysander does not look at Ogden either, his attention is firmly on the breasts of the woman straddling his legs.

"Why do you still stand here?" says Uriah, offended she does not immediately follow his orders. "Beer."

The whispers in the tavern fall silent again. This time, hesitancy fills the eyes of every man and woman in the tavern. Ogden holds her hand up, and the crowd goes back to their business.

"Well," says Uriah, "will wonders never cease?"

"You own this establishment?" asks Lysander, not for an answer, but to belittle Ogden.

"Drinks," Uriah says through his teeth.

"And meat," says Lysander.

Unbothered by their taunts, at least in their sight, Ogden brings tankards back to the table in one hand, and a plate of large turkey legs in the other, leaving a trail of spilled beer and juices behind. She sets them on the table and walks back to the bar, both annoyed to serve them and relieved to be at a distance.

"Look what the cat dragged in," Uriah says while licking his woman's neck.

"What do you mean?" she says.

"Shut up," says Uriah. "I wasn't talking to or about you."

"He was talking about our spy." Lysander bites the breast of his woman. "The mythical little bastard himself."

"Don't think we didn't notice you across the bar," Uriah says in a hushed tone he knows Cheshire will hear and also go unnoticed by the crowd.

The hair on the back of Cheshire's neck stands on end.

"I think you should heed the advice given to you earlier, and leave," Cheshire says from the shadows above.

The women both look up, but Lysander and Uriah grab their chins and lower their heads.

"That would ruin our fun," Uriah says, looking into the eyes of his woman. "If you want to keep your eyes, keep them on me."

She nods, bites her lip, and runs her hands over the muscles of his hairless chest.

"Leave," Cheshire repeats. "Now."

Lysander's voice drops. "Does this make you uncomfortable, boy? Have you even tasted a female? Had her in your mouth or felt yourself within her? Or perhaps you're more inclined to other predilections?"

"No matter who I bed"—Cheshire chuckles softly—"it's of their own discretion. Unlike yours who demean themselves because of the sludge running through your veins."

Uriah rolls his eyes and huffs. "We should move to a more private location to enjoy these strumpets fully. Do you agree, brother?"

"Agreed. Our men wait outside with our horses." Lysander lifts the woman off his lap and pushes her in the direction of the door. "They'll take you to our temporary residence, where they will prepare you for our arrival."

"Now, get off." Uriah heaves his woman off his lap.

Lysander points to the other two women whom they discarded earlier, and motions for them to join. Confused, they do as commanded and head towards the door.

It should be none of his business, but Cheshire wants to catch them before they reach their horses to warn them of what lies in store. Uriah hears the slight shift of Cheshire's feet above him.

"Take a step towards them, and I will spear all four with one throw." Uriah glances up, directly into Cheshire's eyes, and then returns to his drink.

"Join us." Lysander bites into a turkey leg, juices oozing down his beard, and rips off the meat clean off the bone.

"We've never officially had the honor," says Uriah.

"And you never will," Cheshire replies.

Once the women leave, Uriah returns to Cheshire's words. "Now, where were we?" His over-articulate diction crawls beneath Cheshire's skin. "Ah, yes. Sludge and women demeaning themselves."

"Wives, mothers, and daughters have fought to share our bed and cocks," Lysander says as he pulls gristle from his teeth. "Or carriage, or horse stall, or broom cupboard."

"Interesting," says Cheshire. "I've heard you take them, whether they, their husbands, fathers, or sons protest."

"And why shouldn't we?" Lysander chugs from his tankard. "That *sludge* gives us the right to take anything or anyone we want. Wonderland is ours."

Uriah changes the subject before Cheshire can respond. "Our two men sent us a raven and told us they spotted you in Briarwell."

Cheshire recalls the man with the large nose and the one with the milky eye who led the band of mercenaries to kill them, and who Jonathan allowed to escape twice. The next time he sees them, Cheshire will be certain to correct Jonathan's mistakes.

"I happened to be there," says Cheshire. "With as much money as you two possess, I would think you could hire better quality assassins. A waste of money if you ask me."

"Our men informed us only of one man, a brute, accompanying the woman we seek." Uriah nurses his drink. "Had we known you and your ilk traveled with her, we would have spent more coin. Then we could have swept more pieces off the board in one go."

Again with Mary Anne, he thinks. *Always Mary Anne.*

"There is still time." Lysander rocks his sword back and forth on the table. "Our paths will cross again."

"And to keep the game interesting"—Uriah smiles—"since we were informed of your involvement, we sent word ahead of us to Mirus. Every soldier and guard already know you're skulking nearby, and they are assembling the proper countermeasures to keep you from the city. And should we see hint or hair of you within the city walls, we will proclaim it from the rooftops."

Cheshire's fingers press deeper into the wood, seething and searching his options. Lysander and Uriah sit far apart, out of reach of each other, making it difficult for Cheshire to take them both down together. He could drop onto Uriah, the smaller of the two, killing him instantly, but Lysander had the forethought to lay the tip of his blade towards Uriah. As soon as

Cheshire lands, Lysander would run him through. A knee to the top of Lysander's head would at least stun him, but Uriah is the quicker of the two, and would have glaive and whip in hand before Cheshire could make his next move.

"Boy," Lysander sneers, "we can feel the murderous intent radiate off you. If you were anywhere near capable, you would have sought us out long ago."

"Besides"—Uriah strokes the length of his glaive—"will you risk the lives of everyone in here? One or two, I'm certain you would. But everyone? I would hate for you to be responsible for destroying the Last Hand a second time."

Cheshire looks to the large chunks and gashes in the walls, crudely repaired with mismatched bricks and mortar.

"Now be off with you." Lysander pounds his chest to release a guttural belch.

"No, no," says Uriah. "Let him remain and stew. We have whores to attend."

They drop a few coins on the table, gather their weapons, and head for the door. "Charming establishment," Uriah says to the crowd. "We hope to visit again soon." They leave without flourish or ceremony.

Cheshire climbs to the roof and crawls through a loose section of thatch as Lysander and Uriah mount their horses and gallop towards Mirus.

Sons of whores, he screams in his head.

Entering Mirus would not have been easy to begin with. The Duchess has made sure of it over the years with explicit orders to every soldier and member of the Castle Guard to kill him on sight, as well as the Ace to hunt him down. Mary Anne presented a unique opportunity. The Castle Guard will double, soldiers will patrol the streets night and day, and the Ace will be close outside the city walls. Since he left as a child, he has reentered Mirus twice, and the soldiers found him in less than a day. Cheshire can outrun most, but not a swarm of biting ants numbering in the hundreds, if not thousands. The gambit he is about to play is perilous enough without Lysander and Uriah's added interference.

Cheshire climbs to the thin branches overhanging the roof of the tavern and travels away from Mirus, leaping the sizable gaps between trees to a portion of road with solidified ditches in the dirt made from passing wagon wheels during the last rain. Within the hour, the Duchess's carriage appears on the horizon, a red speck in a sea of gray and green trees.

His mind whips through scenarios as the carriage draws closer. He could lie in one of the ditches and cling to the bottom of the carriage as it drives over, but from afar he may still be visible to the watchful soldiers at the wall. If he trusted the carvings on the side of the carriage, he could cling to the side, though he would still have no cover. He thinks of thirteen more plans, all possible but not practical, until he sees Mary Anne seated next to the coachman, and the additional coachman and soldier seated backward at the rear of the carriage. In Briarwell, he saw Mary Anne board the carriage into an empty compartment. If she rides atop with the driver, the compartment should be empty.

As the carriage draws closer, Cheshire grabs the branch above him with one hand and crouches against the trunk. His toes fidget with anticipation. When the carriage is feet away from the largest dip in the road, Cheshire pushes off the tree and flies through the air, weightless, the wind whipping against his ears.

The carriage slams into the ditch with a loud bang and clatter as Cheshire lands on the roof, inches behind Mary Anne and the coachman, rolls off the opposite side and catches the thin metal piping of the roof with his fingertips to stop his momentum. The soldier at the rear turns. Cheshire looks into the two windows to see the Duchess in the front compartment and the empty smaller one behind her. He tucks his knees to his chest and shoots through the small window feet first into the empty compartment, landing silently on the gaudy soft cushions.

He sits in disbelief and forces his thundering heart and frantic breath to surrender to his will. Never did he think it would be the Duchess herself who would bring him into the city, but he must hope the soldiers will only check the exterior of the carriage. He wants to smile, but will not do so prematurely for fear he will jinx how far he has come.

"Watch how you're driving!" the soldier shouts from the rear.

"It was unavoidable," the coachman shouts back.

"Not to worry. I'll have a crew come and smooth the road again," says the Duchess.

Her voice grates against Cheshire's soul and ignites his blood. His eyes bore through the small wooden partition and into the back of the Duchess's bulbous head through the veil trailing from the points of her hat.

How easy it would be to reach through and throttle her, to hear her last breath rattle from her vile, gaping mouth.

He could easily pull a piece of wood or metal ornamentation from within the cabin and shove it through the back of her skull to repay her for everything she has done. But he needs her alive for now. Getting into Mirus takes priority, and arriving in the city with her corpse would surely implicate him and complicate his plans infinitely. He sits on the cushioned seat and watches her through the partition, listening to her sickly-sweet humming.

It is not long before the soft trot of hooves on dirt transform to clacks against the stones of the long, narrow bridge leading to the city gate, and a shudder runs through Cheshire's body from his toes, up his spine, to the base of his skull. He can hear the Great Gates to the city rumble open and the call to get the carriage into the city quickly but check the undercarriage as it passes. His assumption and risk pay off. The Duchess will not have her carriage searched like the peasants, gentry, and merchants entering the city.

But the Duchess stops humming and flinches in her paranoia, ready to look behind into the compartment. Cheshire falls to the floor and tucks himself beneath the seat directly below the partition just as he hears the Duchess grunt when she turns. His body tenses, and his toes and fingers spread and dig into the floor and cushions, poised to either strike or flee. He stays still and quiet as a gravestone, knowing she watches the empty compartment as they cross the long bridge above the Boroughs and wind up the snaking streets of Stonehaven. She does not look away until they reach the Crest, where she can wave and bestow benediction to the Mirusian elite who come out to welcome her until they reach the castle's gatehouse.

He slinks back into his seat to watch the Duchess, and get his bearings and see who he may be up against through the thin gossamer curtains.

Chains thicker than Cheshire's arms clank and scrape through old wooden gears, raising the black portcullis. The tall gates crack open inch by inch for an eternity. His entire body trembles from his knees to his stomach to his eyes. Over a thousand years he has fought to get within the castle walls, now they open of their own accord, and for a moment he does not know what to do. The carriage rounds the expansive stone bailey and slows to a stop yards from the great, stone stairs. For the first time since he slid into the compartment, Cheshire takes his eyes off the Duchess to look through the curtains at the front doors to the castle, and everything around him falls silent. The carriage rocks wildly as the Duchess steps to the ground.

He realizes how careless he was in the moment. She could have turned and seen him, and all would be for naught. He crouches and raises his eyes enough to peer out of the window to see the Duchess and Mary Anne, and the pointed arched doors beyond them. The Duchess pauses and turns back, sensing something amiss.

With nowhere else to go, Cheshire slides the partition to the Duchess's compartment open with one hand and never looks away from her repugnant face.

As she returns, he slips through the small opening and shuts the partition closed again as she opens the door to search the compartment he was just in.

When he lands, he knocks her poorly-emptied chamber pot with his foot and its contents slosh side to side. The stench reaches into his throat, gagging him. He crouches and holds his breath while she inspects the cabin longer than she needs. It is small with no places to hide, but her paranoia will not allow her to walk away, and Cheshire knows she will check her compartment next.

Cheshire glances out of the opposite window. *Ten castle guards on the battlement, facing outwards. Six patrolling the bailey. And those are only the guards I can see.*

The chink of their chainmail and clatter of their pauldrons bounce against the stone walls and say there could be double if not more. He wraps his cloak around his waist and quickly and quietly opens the opposite door and shuts it again while he hangs from the thin silver handle outside. The Duchess flings open her cabin door, expecting to catch him. He waits to hear the click again. She waits as well.

He knows he is out in the open for any castle guard to turn and see. The guards patrolling the perimeter of the bailey are reaching the end of their path and will turn around at any moment, and the carriage door still does not shut. They are not as heavily armored as the soldiers, and he could kill many of them with ease if he needed to escape, but hopes it will not come to pass.

"Driver," the Duchess calls out.

"Yes, madam?" he answers.

"Is there anything on the other side of the carriage? Is there anything caught on the wheel, perhaps?"

Fuck. Cheshire scrambles against the side of the carriage, fingertips and toes clinging to the silver horse and bird carvings until he curls himself under the seat of the rear coachman, inches from his feet. *I'm a right slack wit,* he tells himself. Two guards at the far end of the bailey turn back toward the carriage, talking to each other, distracted for the moment. If they look forward, they will notice him.

"No, madam," says the coachman. "Nothing in the wheels."

"Is everything alright, madam?" Mary Anne asks.

Her voice scratches against Cheshire's ears. His lips snarl.

"Oh yes, my dear. One can never be too careful," the Duchess says as the carriage door finally latches. "Very well," she says to the coachman. "Thank you for your time and service." Her footsteps, along with Mary Anne's, grow faint against the cobblestones until they reach the steps. "Oh, but please do a thorough inspection of the carriage before it reaches the stables."

Cheshire keeps his eyes on the two guards facing him, and another on a parapet who heard the movement of the horses. He lowers himself below the carriage and wedges himself between the rear axle and the floorboards.

Four guards draw closer and walk with the carriage—two beside, two behind.

The reins crack and the carriage lurches forward and circles the bailey to make its way to the stables. The turn is wide and will cross mere feet from the gates, where the pair of towering bald simpletons, slow at their job, have not closed the gates to the outer wall yet.

Not fucking fair, he screams in his head. He is here, at long last, on the castle grounds. In his mind, every soldier, the Duchess, and even Mary Anne die by his hands to get inside the castle walls. But that is a fantasy. There are too many guards, too many eyes, and too many unknowns. A single misstep now would cost him everything. Cheshire swallows hard to keep his anger at bay and to digest the hard truth—he must leave the castle now to find a way in later.

Cheshire lowers his feet to the ground, stepping along the cobblestones, and pulls himself to the middle of the undercarriage. His fingernails claw against a bolt holding part of the axle together, twisting it until it comes loose, and catching it before it falls to the ground. Time is running out and they are almost upon the gate. He scrapes against another bolt until it comes loose and the metal frame pulls away from the carriage as it jostles. Just in time. The space between the wheels aligns with the gap left in the gate for only a second, and Cheshire holds his breath and darts through the wheels, past the massive legs of the behemoths, and tumbles through the gates as they shut.

He slams his back to the wall, chest heaving, to keep out of sight from the guards above and waits. The road between him and the Crest spans nearly thirty feet with no covering except sparse poles with pennant flags. On the other side of the wall, a loud crash of wood and metal dragging against stone startles the horses. Their rhythmic clopping is now a chaotic dance on their hind legs as the coachman shouts to control them.

"What happened?" a castle guard from above calls to the coachman, his voice distant, facing downward into the bailey. And soon the others join him, their attention cast to the panic inside the wall.

Even though difficult to accept, and not what he wants, Cheshire knows the smartest strategy is to bide his time and find another way to enter the castle. After all, the long game matters most. He unwraps his cloak, pulls his hood up, and disappears onto the rooftops of the Crest. But he can smile and laugh. Despite the Duchess's exhaustive efforts, her own folly has allowed the *Queen Slayer* to return to Mirus.

CHAPTER 23

MARY ANNE

On the morning of the fourth day, the coachman asks Mary Anne if she would care to join him on the driver's bench. Had she known this was an option, or had he offered earlier, she would not have spent the prior three days asleep in the carriage to escape her boredom. During the brief interludes she was awake, she watched forests become plains with large granite outcrops, then endless mind-numbing stretches of tall grass, then forests again.

However, a discrepancy itches in her brain. From her studies and experience with her family's shipping business, she knows the number of miles a horse, even shire horses which pull the Duchess's carriage, can travel in a day. But these stopped a grand total of three times during their trek and even drove continuously through the night from what she can recall. Looking at the trees and hills pass on the road, it appeared the carriage moved at the same speed as the train. She chalks this curiosity up to being in a different world and does not question the matter further.

Now, since she is in the open air, she allows herself the luxury to marvel at the surrounding landscape. The trees dwarf those of the Rookwood. Tall, thin, and almost uniform, like giant blades of grass. Different from the tangle of roots and canopy of the Rookwood. Walking trails brush aside the dried blanket of leaves and wander off the main road to distant, unknown corners of their world.

"What is this forest called?" she asks the coachman.

"Queenwood," he replies.

When Mary Anne was a child, her mother would tell her the story of a young girl in a red cloak wandering into the forest. These trees are identical to those she imagined the girl skipping through on the way to visit her grandmother.

Her thoughts of home fade like the fog as the belief in the impossible suddenly becomes all too possible for Mary Anne as a towering, solitary stone column rises above the treetops, scraping the heavens and defying all logic and sense. Unable to take her eyes from it, she turns as far as she can on the bench as they drive past. She closes one eye and holds up her hand in front of the column to attempt an arbitrary measurement of size and distance, and subtracts fingers until it is less than the width of her pinky. It grows thinner, but never shorter. The coachman nudges her and gestures forward to where the road and the trees disappear to a point on the horizon.

She turns around and squints. *What does he point at?* she wonders. *The trees are lovely, the road long, the mountain rising beyond the trees are no different from any other mountains.*

She could not be more wrong. As they draw closer, details on the mountain—rooftops, chimneys, towers, an entire city the likes of which she has never heard of, seen, or dreamt—take shape and grow larger. And at its summit, a genuine castle. Her heartbeat quickens to match the pace of the horses' gallop.

Suddenly, the carriage dips into a deep hole in the dirt road. It sways violently and almost tosses Mary Anne from the bench.

"Watch how you're driving!" the soldier riding with them yells.

"It was unavoidable." The coachman rights himself on the bench and catches his breath.

"Not to worry," the Duchess's muffled voice says. "I'll have a crew come and smooth the road again."

Soon after, Mary Anne gasps when they exit the forest and she can see the city's true majesty. A work of art the likes of the great Italian painters.

The ride becomes smooth once the horses cross onto the long cobblestone bridge to the main gates of the city. Long red and white banners hang from metal lampposts along the bridge and flap in the wind blustering from the sharp ravine below. Mary Anne holds fast to the curved rail of the bench when she realizes the sheerness and depth of the drop to a sparkling river, the width of a thread from her perspective. The same tall trees of the Queenwood pepper the rocky cliff face and shrink to the size of grains of rice at its bottom. And halfway down, a small wooden cabin rests precariously on an outcrop of rocks.

"Welcome to Mirus, Mary Anne," the Duchess says from within the carriage.

The portcullis rises and iron gates taller than the houses of

Mary Anne's street open to reveal a bustling metropolis concealed within the sweeping white stone walls. They continue through the gates and over a mirror image of the bridge leading to the city, except not as deep and filled with an overcrowded shanty town below.

Mary Anne loses count of the twists and turns as they wind further up the narrow streets. Citizens wave and shout as the carriage passes, but her attention never breaks from the grandeur of the castle gazing back at her. Tower after tower pierce the sky, buttresses adorn its lofty walls, and countless balconies and exterior staircases with ornate balustrades wrap the castle like ivy.

When the carriage stops and waits for the gates to the castle itself to open, Mary Anne turns and looks down the slope of the city for the first time, and imagines God reaching down, pinching the castle between his fingers, and pulling the city into creation. Her entire village of Lyndhurst would fit within the castle walls, and London itself could hide within the city four times over. The white stone houses and shops of Mirus with their multicolored wood and stone-tiled roofs transform her own world to lackluster shapeless forms of greys and browns. The gates slowly swing open with a thunderous rumble to reveal an expansive stone courtyard stretching toward the castle.

"The castle," Mary Anne says to herself. "Its arches, doors, and windows would shame Christ Church and Notre Dame."

The carriage circles the courtyard, and the coachman stops in front of a grand staircase leading to the pointed doors. Mary Anne remembers another fairytale her mother read to her of a young girl who attended a ball and arrived in a beautiful carriage. Although Mary Anne did not arrive inside, she allows herself to feel as special as the young girl from the story. Out of place, but full of wonder.

After the coachman helps Mary Anne down, her eyes travel up the exterior of the castle. Her breaths become heavy, and she digs the fingernails of her middle fingers into the meaty part of her thumbs to reassure herself this is not a dream, and for the first time she hopes it is not.

She turns to the Duchess for guidance and finds her opening and closing the doors to the carriage, searching for something.

"Driver," the Duchess calls up to him as she searches the floor of her compartment.

"Yes, madam?" he answers.

"Is there anything on the other side of the carriage? Is there anything caught on the wheel, perhaps?"

The coachman leans over and checks the opposite side of the carriage. "No, madam, nothing," he replies.

"Is everything alright?" Mary Anne asks hesitantly. "Madam."

"Oh yes, my dear. One can never be too careful." She shuts the door and addresses the coachman. "Very well. Thank you for your time and service. Oh, but please do a thorough inspection of the carriage before it reaches the stables."

He nods and drives away, with the clacks of the horses' hooves becoming fainter as they circle the courtyard once more.

Mary Anne follows a step behind the Duchess as they ascend the stairs. *Where are Jonathan and the others?* she wonders. She turns back to the gate, hoping to see Dormy's cart sway into view. Instead, two giant men, identical and bald as newborns, push the heavy gates closed and lower a lock bar the size of a tree trunk into its resting position.

When they reach the top of the stairs, a doorman dressed in green finery bows his head and opens the door for them. "Welcome back, madam."

"Thank you," says the Duchess.

"Thank you, sir," Mary Anne mimics. She pauses at the threshold to take in the long hallway, tall grey pillars, and lofty arches down its length.

Never in her life could Mary Anne imagine a sight more grand. She should feel amazed at the vision before her, but the whole of this new experience makes her feel small, hollow. Unsure of how long she has gazed at the ceiling, she looks back to the Duchess and discovers she is gone from the hallway.

In her place, well into the distance, a tall spindle of a man in long black and white robes and white hair down to his knees clears his throat. "Mary Anne, you're already late!" he barks before disappearing into a door or another hallway hidden behind a pillar.

Mary Anne walks down the hall and searches every offshoot and hallway, but cannot find any trace of the tall man.

"Hello?" she calls, with no response. She turns back to the front door, closes one eye, and places the doorman between her thumb and forefinger.

He was smaller, though there is no accounting for his height, she thinks. *It would stand to reason the correct hallway would be further along.* She continues her pursuit and needs to measure the doorman once more before deciding on which hallway to follow.

With no sign of the man, she turns down one empty hallway after another.

"Hello?" she calls again.

"Mary Anne, stop dawdling." His voice echoes from a hallway to her right.

"Wait, please!" Mary Anne shouts after yet another turn. The volume of her voice reverberating through the halls startles her. She could return to the doorman and ask him for help, but in her haste did not think to memorize her path. She attempts to retrace her steps anyway, afraid she will lose herself even further.

After several turns, she pants with frustration, unsure why the gentleman did not simply wait for her. She hopes the Duchess will not be cross with her for being unable to follow the gentleman sent for her, retract her offer to help, or find Mary Anne lacking.

But when her thoughts are about to plunge headlong into more despondent possibilities, she stumbles upon two figures, laborers of some sort, with green hair at the far end of another hall. They make hand gestures to each other, speaking without speaking, and point to a particular spot in the ceiling.

"Excuse me," Mary Anne says loud enough for them to hear. "I'm in need of assistance."

The girl rests an enormous wooden mallet over her shoulder, and the boy slides a long handled hammer into a loop on his belt alongside four others and two tools Mary Anne is unfamiliar with. She does not know who they are but feels some comfort in their appearance. They both wear stained trousers, heavy boots, and long open leather vests without shirts held in place by belts with a dozen leather pouches and tools. Even the girl. Their oily, shoulder-length green hair swings back and forth as they walk. Smeared dirt and grease cover their clothing, arms, and the portion of their chests exposed between their vests. It is as if they belong in Jonathan and Cheshire's savage lifestyle, as opposed to the pristine elegance of the castle.

"Could you help me?" Mary Anne asks again. She waits in silence as they walk casually toward her without a response.

"Yes," says the boy.

"I'm looking for—"

"Chamberlain Weiss," says the girl.

"The tall man with the long hair," says Mary Anne.

"Chamberlain Weiss," she repeats. "Follow us." She and the boy walk past Mary Anne and turn down another hallway, never looking back to see if she follows.

Mary Anne keeps up with these two better than Chamberlain Weiss, through another series of corridors. The metal tools hanging around the boy's belt clank and jiggle against each other and his slender frame in the silence, only awkward to Mary Anne. The weight of the girl's hammer increases the sound of her footsteps. Her arms are sizably larger than his, and would need to be in order to carry, let alone use, such a large hammer. It is almost as long as she is tall, and its head does not match the handle.

They climb a wide stone stairway to a higher section of the castle, and in the distance, Mary Anne can hear the faint conversation of the Duchess and Chamberlain Weiss.

"Where is she?" the Duchess asks in the distance. "Did you

lose her? How could you have lost her? She just arrived! Of all the incompetent—"

"No, madam, she never followed. I waited for her. I did." Chamberlain Weiss lies. "The girl must have ventured down another hall distracted by something."

"Go and find her," the Duchess pleads.

Mary Anne and her guides round the corner and nearly collide with Chamberlain Weiss, who towers over all three of them. He lowers his spectacles to glare at Mary Anne.

"Why have you stopped?" the Duchess asks.

Chamberlain Weiss steps aside to reveal Mary Anne. "I found her," he says.

"There you are, my dear." The Duchess clasps her hands and holds them to her lips, sighing with relief. "I sincerely apologize for your treatment. Weiss forgets in his impatience others do not have the unordinary leg span he possesses."

"I got lost trying to follow him. All the hallways blend together," Mary Anne confesses. "Luckily, these two brought me to you." Mary Anne meets the Duchess in front of an enormous set of metal doors with decorative vines and curls.

"At least I can count on someone." The Duchess speaks in a hushed tone and winks to Mary Anne. "William. Patricia. Thank you, as always."

"Our pleasure," they say together and leave back down the stairs.

"Now, back to the matter at hand," says the Duchess.

"Thank you," says Mary Anne. "After four days of running for my life, I'm ready to return home. Shall I be home in time for dinner?"

Chamberlain Weiss chuckles, but coughs it away. "Perhaps not by dinner."

"Then when?" asks Mary Anne, the uneasy feeling in the pit of her stomach returning.

"That remains to be seen," the Duchess says gently.

"In Briarwell, you said you could help me." Mary Anne does not hide her frustration. "I traveled all this way with you, farther from where I knew my home was because you said it was simple."

"My dear, returning you home is a simple matter." A tone of authority mingles in the Duchess's soft voice. "I never said it was easy. Or quick. Those are different entirely."

Mary Anne cannot believe the inconsistencies in the Duchess's story. Those are not the words the Duchess spoke in Briarwell, or perhaps they were, and Mary Anne chose to see her regal air and gentle ways instead of listening. She did say the feat begins, not ends, at the castle. She finally accepts her predicament is far beyond her control and has been since the moment her foot first touched Wonderland soil. "Where do I begin?"

"Are you sure you don't want to freshen up first?" Chamberlain Weiss asks. "It's been a long journey."

"Thank you, but no. Where do I begin?" Mary Anne repeats.

"As you wish." Chamberlain Weiss gestures to the gigantic doors they stand in front of. "We begin here. The grand throne room." He and the Duchess step back and watch. "After you."

She places her hands on two small areas of smooth, cold

metal between the intricate designs and pushes. The doors do not budge. She tries again, harder this time. Nothing.

Chamberlain Weiss turns and stares uncertainly at Mary Anne, then at the door, and back to her. The Duchess spins a ruby ring on her forefinger slowly, her gaze soft and focused somewhere far away, head tilted up, listening.

"Did I do something wrong?" Mary Anne asks, worried.

"Not at all, my dear." The Duchess walks to a stone bench across from the doors and groans as she sits. "Join me." She pats the empty portion of the bench next to her.

Mary Anne's thoughts return to business dealings she took over once her father passed. The older financiers in the consortium would give her crumbs. Just enough information to keep her begging for more, not enough to satisfy and make her feel equal. This woman, the Duchess, says she wants to help, but there is information she withholds.

"Speak plainly, please." Mary Anne sits and starts the conversation. "Do not speak gently. Be honest. What must I do to return home?"

"I admire your courage." The Duchess straightens her posture and her dress before continuing. "You are not the first woman to find herself lost in Wonderland. Little is known about how, but it happens. And from what I've learned in all my years, crossing worlds, from Wonderland to yours isn't easily done. From our side, at least. In fact, only one has the power to break through whatever thin vale divides our worlds. And she is the Queen."

"Is she here?" Mary Anne asks with a new sense of urgency.

"Or rather, is she within the throne room? Can she help me? May I speak with her?"

"No." The Duchess places a hand on Mary Anne's knee. "She's not. We've not had a queen for some time." Her thin eyebrows raise, coaxing the answer from Mary Anne. "And therein lies both the problem and the solution."

The Duchess speaks in riddles, Mary Anne thinks at first. *No, not riddles or crumbs. A test.* She wants Mary Anne to discover the answers herself rather than spoon feed her. *Only the Queen has the power to leave Wonderland, but the throne is vacant. Which is a problem for the country perhaps, but also the solution.* The spaces between the puzzle pieces of her thoughts shrink until they click together. "I... *I* must become Queen if I want to return home?"

"Correct," says Chamberlain Weiss.

"I told you, the answer is simple. But it is not easy." The Duchess squeezes Mary Anne's hand in her own. "Are you ready for such a task?"

"Yes," she answers simply. "I cannot decline, even if I don't know what the task entails."

"Wonderful," says the Duchess. "In order to become Queen, you must first prove yourself worthy."

Worthy. The word sends a chill like an icy dagger sliding up Mary Anne's spine. She is not sure of the qualifications of a queen, but perhaps the life she has led until now—her own personal wants denied to support her family, the dedication to her work, and the obstacles she overcame—will help her case. Except for a few decisions, her life has been one selfless sacrifice after another, all to benefit others. "Prove myself to whom?" she asks.

"To Wonderland," the Duchess replies.

"Its people?" asks Mary Anne.

"Partly," the Duchess continues. "Not anyone is deserving of the crown and title and everything accompanying them. Wonderland itself must accept you as a candidate. The doors were merely a test. They're sealed shut and will only open for a woman worthy of becoming Queen."

"They didn't move. Not even an inch." Mary Anne questions her assumption of her own worth. If a life dedicated to others is not enough, then what is? She wants the Duchess to tell her what happens if the doors never open, but she knows the answer without needing to hear the words.

"Yet. They did not move, *yet*. We hope." The Duchess grabs both of Mary Anne's hands and holds them tight. "My dear, I know it's quite a lot to take in, but understand, this is the only way for you to return home. And I will be here every step of the way. I promise."

Those last words from the Duchess are enough for Mary Anne. She will hold on to the spark of hope, no matter how minuscule. "How does one become worthy?"

The Duchess snaps her fingers and calls Chamberlain Weiss forward. He produces the largest book she has ever seen from within his robes and lays it on Mary Anne's lap.

She treats the book with both fear and reverence, afraid to touch it, but eventually extending her hands to it as if it were a cornered animal. Her fingertips explore the worn, faded black leather binding, frayed corners, and rigid spine. Small tabs, some ribbon, some wood, others metal, peek out from the thick stack of pages like a hundred small tongues. The spine crackles as she opens it upon her lap. The jagged edges of pages lost long ago rise from the first crease. Teeth to match the tongues. She glides her fingertips across thin brittle pages covered with symbols written with a heavy quill.

"Rest this evening. It has been a long journey. Weiss will show you to your room." The Duchess pats the cover of the book. "Read as much as you can. We begin your official lessons tomorrow. From what I've seen of you thus far, I believe you have the determination, the character, and the will to become Queen and take yourself home."

"Yes, I shall." Mary Anne lies. She does not want to disappoint the Duchess or feel more inferior in her eyes than she already does. But she could not bring herself to admit out loud that she cannot understand a word or recognize a single letter upon the page.

CHAPTER 24

JONATHAN

In the upper compartment of Dormy's wagon, Jonathan and March kneel to restore each other's clothing. He closes and buckles her cropped leather jacket while she raises and laces the front of his trousers with a forceful tug and kisses him, simple and lingering. Jonathan can feel March tuck her lips and turn her gaze out the window, contempt weighing heavy in her eyes. Jonathan looks out the window as well, aware of what troubles her.

All four days he filled his time and thoughts, as he always does, with tea and March, to not think of their destination. It took Jonathan the first day, with March's help, to pack away the thoughts of Briarwell and Rookridge. On the second day, Jonathan made up for the promise he could not keep because of Mary Anne's untimely arrival, and spent from sunrise to far past sunset pleasing March, even while she steered the wagon to let Dormy rest. And taking breaks only for tea. The third day they sparred atop the wagon while they drove across the vast grasslands of The Winds. Without a tree for over hundreds of miles, the winds roam free, fierce, transforming Dormy's wagon to a ship set upon a grass sea, and whip through Jonathan and March's long coats like unfurled canvas. They spent this morning in silence holding each other until they crossed into the Queenwood, knowing the imagined adventure in their shared mind without Mary Anne would soon come to an end.

Through the small front window, the gates of Mirus increase in size until the red iron grows beyond the wooden frame. The sunlight dims as they cross into the late afternoon shadow of the wall.

The wagon lurches to a halt outside the mammoth gate. Jonathan can hear the scrape of plate armor grow louder as soldiers approach from all sides. He kisses March on her neck, slides down the ladder, and emerges from the driver's hatch to greet over twenty soldiers in full armament and red and white tunics flowing down to their shins.

"Gentlemen," he says, "wonderful to see you again."

"State your purpose in Mirus this day." A paunchy soldier with a long mustache curled at its tips approaches the wagon. He bangs his silver chest plate with his palm to punctuate his importance.

Dormy flicks a small latch on the side of her bench and a wooden flap swings down to reveal a worn parchment nailed to the wagon. "Statement of Commerce, sir," she says proudly.

The soldier leans over, breathing through his mouth as he reads the clearance. "Yes, well, this seems in order, but we must be thorough. Prepare for a full inspection of the wagon.

Everything must be removed and searched before you'll be allowed to enter."

"Jonathan..." Dormy whispers, her hands shaking on the reins.

"Courage." He winks and knocks loudly on the hatch behind him. "Why the precautions?" he asks the soldier.

"Not that it's any of your business, but we've heard reports of vicious criminals in the area." The soldier grunts as he leans on his knees to inspect the undercarriage.

"I wonder who that could be?" Jonathan smiles.

"Any of us, really," Dormy says under her breath. "Depending on who you ask."

She and Jonathan drop from the driver's bench and stand out of the soldiers' way. March meets them from the rear with a shabby cloak draped around her, and its hood pulled down to conceal her face and hair.

After half an hour of labor, four soldiers become nine, and after an hour, nine becomes sixteen to expedite the unloading process. Jonathan, March, and Dormy share tea while they are forced to wait and watch while the soldiers untie and pile boxes, sacks, and barrels from the exterior of the wagon, and search their contents, along with his and March's personal trunks.

"Oh, shit," a thin soldier mutters when he sees the interior of the wagon. He squeezes through the rear door and carelessly knocks over stacks of books, dishes, and boxes.

The clatter of the mess crawls under Jonathan's skin. He looks to Dormy, whose face is frozen between grief and horror.

Her breaths are short and quick—it looks as though she vibrates.

The lead soldier saunters over to the trio, and from his face and line of six wagons behind them, Jonathan knows he will deliver unwelcome news. "Well, you three are free to enter the city, but your, uh, wagon needs to stay here for the night."

"No, no, no, no, no," Dormy repeats under her breath, shaking her head in terror.

"Excuse me," says Jonathan, "we've accompanied her into Mirus several times before and she's never had to leave her wagon behind. What's the reason?"

"As you can see," says the solider smugly, "there's quite a queue forming behind you. Some of them from the Crest. So most of my soldiers will tend to those more... deserving, while one or two tend to your trash heap. Be glad I'm gracious enough to let you lot in. Come collect your things tomorrow."

"March," Dormy pleads in a whisper, on the verge of tears. "Please."

March huffs through her nose and pulls her hood back. "No," she commands the soldier. "She will not leave it."

For a moment, the solider is dumbstruck. He fumbles with his words and, not knowing what to do with his hands, past his bent thighs and chest plate in search of something invisible. "Forgive us, Lady Audrianna," he stammers. "We didn't know you were onboard. I mean, we weren't told to expect you."

"And you never will be," says March. "Now let us pass."

"I'm afraid I can't." The soldier wipes his brow. "We have protocols, orders, we must follow, we've always had to follow. Every coach, wagon, cart, carriage, and wheelbarrow must be searched from top to bottom. I can't let you pass. I wish I could, but I can't. Not even for your family. These orders come from the Duchess herself, with detailed strictures."

"Fine." March steps closer to the soldier. "Then I suggest you order the soldiers you would have allocated to search those who you deem more *deserving*—"

"A thousand pardons m'lady." The soldier bows his head repeatedly. "I meant no disrespect."

"And," March says over him without break, "as many other soldiers as you can gather to attend to our traveling companion." She looks over her shoulder to Jonathan. "Darling, how long will it take you to prepare tea for the three of us?"

It could take Jonathan upwards of an hour to prepare in the Hollow. He would take his time and appreciate every movement, and savor every drop of tea as if it were a holy ritual. He wishes he could do so now, but knows March wants to prove a point.

"A cold brew?" asks Jonathan. "From tea selection to final sip, a half hour's time."

"A half hour's time," March repeats, staring daggers at the soldier. "Perform your search. But we will be on our way in half an hour, and not a minute over. Am I clear?"

"Yes m'lady," says the soldier.

"And if anything is broken, the smallest bobble," March says coldly, "you will hear from me again."

"To me," the soldier shouts and whistles to the other soldiers, spit flying from his lips. He waves down eighteen more soldiers from the top of the wall to help in the search. Collectively, thirty-seven soldiers work to clear out and search the content of Dormy's wagon. "Now move you sluggish sacks of shit."

Jonathan notices they smartly leave anything too small to conceal a body, Cheshire's body, to make their work go quicker.

The driver of a gilded carriage waiting three back in the queue shouts, "Hurry up. We haven't got all day."

"Shut your face," the lead soldier barks back. "Lady Audrianna returns to Mirus. And you will wait there until she is satisfied."

March groans under her breath, not wanting the news of her presence to be widespread, but it is too late. Onlookers from wagons and carriages and distracted soldiers cannot help but steal a glance.

Dormy watches on, tears in her eyes, as if a loved one is about to go under the surgeon's knife. March massages the back of her neck and holds her hand to try and soothe her nerves.

Jonathan grabs a teapot and three cups from the wagon, along with three small crates to sit on, and prepares their tea. Cinnamon Rhubarb. They sit and enjoy the dumb show of soldiers racing back and forth. Even Dormy forces a smile every now and again.

With thirteen seconds to spare, the soldiers finish their search, restore the wagon and all of its contents, and usher Dormy back onto the driver's bench. Instead, she walks the perimeter, pointing and accounting for everything in its place, and then enters the rear of the wagon to inspect the soldiers' care.

The lead soldier huffs out of breath and dabs his drenched neck and forehead with a rag from another soldier's belt. He tries not to look in March's direction, who stares at him with a raised eyebrow.

Satisfied, Dormy reemerges, nods with approval, and takes her place at the reins. Jonathan and March store the crates they used as chairs and climb the side of the wagon to the upper deck.

"Forgiveness, Lady Audrianna," the soldier says.

"Yes, yes," she says, pulling the hood back over her head. "Now open the gates and move."

The soldiers surrounding the wagon resume their posts and the Great Gates of Mirus open for them. Dormy whips the reins, and her small ponies pull the wagon over the stone threshold into the city.

"Thank you, sir, for your dedication to the realm." Jonathan tips his hat to the soldier.

"At least my name is good for something." March grabs an apple from a sack hanging from the side of the wagon and breaks its skin with a loud crack.

Jonathan wipes juice from her cheek. "I saw your face. You relished the moment."

March bites into the apple again, juices spilling down her chin. "I will make the best of an unpleasant situation."

The wagon crosses the lengthy causeway built over the Boroughs. Both Jonathan and March look down into the peaceful derelict portion of the city. Smoke rises through crooked chimneys from meager fires within overcrowded homes. Planks are removed from walls to poorly patch holes in weathered roofs. Newly constructed rooms cling precariously to the side of existing houses. A small, shoeless boy without a shirt stands and waves to them from one of the many crowded wooden roofs.

March tosses her apple to the child. He catches and holds it close to his chest, staring at the partially eaten fruit as if it's the first meal he has seen in days. She forcefully cuts the twine securing the sack full of apples with one of her daggers, swings it back and forth a few times, and lobs the entire sack down to the child. Her aim is true, and upon impact, apples spill and bounce across his roof, collecting at the short, upturned lip along the perimeter. Jonathan hangs from the netting on the side of the wagon to watch the boy collect as many as he can in his tiny arms, all the while dancing excitedly.

"Do you want me to drop you at the castle?" Dormy asks.

"Thank you, no," says Jonathan, pulling himself back to the deck. "I doubt your wagon will be welcome in the upper ring. Go about your business and we will to ours."

The wagon clambers through the tight dirt streets of Stonehaven, the heart of Mirus, nudging shop signs, brushing against other wagons, and causing townsfolk to duck into doorways or alleys to avoid being run over. From the deck, Jonathan puts his foot against a cottage and pushes off to tilt the wagon ever so slightly in order to clear its second story, while March uses her swords to close shutters before the wagon rips them from their hinges.

After snaking back and forth through the city, they reach The Row, the largest market in the city nestled deep within Stonehaven. Dormy backs her wagon into a large empty stall kept reserved for her and turns for the side to face the street where customers who know her well wait for the spectacle of her shop. Neighboring fabric and jewelry vendors scoff and roll their eyes at her arrival.

By the time Jonathan and March emerge from the rear door, Dormy has secured her ponies and begun setting up shop. She unfurls an awning from the side of the wagon and raises it on two thin posts. Using all of her weight, which is minimal, she leans on a large lever near the driver's bench. It falls with a thunk, and the side of the wagon facing the street swings out like a jewelry box to showcase her collection in the wagon's main compartment. She extends hidden shelves and compartments from various places until her wagon is twice its original size. She opens her arms wide and garners applause from the waiting crowd.

Jonathan unloads three collapsible wooden tables and sets them up at the front of the stall. He wants to ask if Dormy needs anything else, but she has already completed seven purchases. Seeing she needs no help from them, Jonathan presents his arm to March, which she accepts and leans her head on his shoulder as they disappear into the crowded Row. He remembers most of the townspeople, but they are far too busy shopping or passing through to their daily work or chores to stop for a greeting.

To delay the climb to the castle, he and March walk the wide curve of the main thoroughfare of the market, alive with the sound of commerce. Shouts, barters, bargains, complaints, and thanks fill the air in a muddled cacophony. Jonathan both appreciates and pities how nothing has changed since their last visit years ago, except for the large stretches of triangle canvas between the storefronts to keep out the garish sun.

He and March escape the main crowd through cramped side streets, weaving away and back to the main market to return to some of their favorite shops. All the storefronts of the side streets lean precariously in toward the street creating a jagged fissure of sky above. At a dead end of one of the streets, Jonathan pays a hefty sum to the traveling merchant who brings teas from the western coasts for his entire stock to be delivered to Dormy's wagon before nightfall. March purchases several gowns and coats from a clothier who is grateful for her business but sighs with disappointment, knowing March will deconstruct his handiwork beyond recognition to fit her own style.

As dusk approaches, Jonathan and March ascend the steep stairs through Stonehaven until they reach the broad arched, cobblestone streets of the Crest, the highest tier of Mirus. The sandstone and marble buildings glow in the evening sun, and the overabundance of perfumes waft through the air as if the city were on fire.

Several citizens of the Crest pass by in their posh and extravagant attire. A woman looks over her thick fur collar to turn her nose up at Jonathan. A thin man with a corseted coat scoffs at March for the amount of skin she shows. This treatment continues their entire walk through the Crest. If the townspeople took the time to look past their wardrobe, they would realize Jonathan sold each of them the hats they wear. He will return with a fancier, more appropriate outfit later and be more than happy to overcharge them again for his repair services, with them none the wiser.

"Five hundred and thirty-one steps," Jonathan counts as he

climbs. If Dormy drove them here, it would take over a dozen turns snaking back and forth across the entire breadth of the city.

Finally, they ascend the last staircase, which ends with the looming castle in front of them and a picturesque view of the valley and mountains behind them.

They approach the giant wooden gates to the castle walls, and Jonathan knocks. The thick wood barely makes a muffled thud. He tries again feebly. March uses the knocker on a small door disguised within the gate, and the clank of iron on iron penetrates the wood and echoes in the courtyard on the other side.

"Never noticed that before," says Jonathan.

After several repeated wraps, the door swings inward and the Red Knight emerges, minus his armor, and shuts the door behind him. "You lot again," he says. "Bit far from home, aren't you?"

"Too far," says March.

"What do you want?" The Red Knight sighs, unable to be bothered.

Jonathan removes his hat and scratches through his matted hair. "We've followed the Duchess and we've come to see Mary Anne, the young woman accompanying her."

"No," the Red Knight says with a blank face.

"No?" Jonathan asks, bewildered.

"No. They're far too busy for the likes of you at the moment. Now be off before I signal for the hounds to be released." The Red Knight walks back through the door, winks at March, and then slams it shut.

"I'm going to cut his fucking eye out," March says as she walks away from the gate. "Can we leave now? It's been a long journey, and we need to rest. We'll try again tomorrow."

As the sun sets, they stop and share tea on a beautiful terrace on the edge of the Crest before the long descent back to the Row. While they drink, a few townspeople who pass on the street recognize March, even though she has her hood drawn, and grab someone near to them to whisper as they walk away.

Jonathan looks at March and furrows his brow to say, "You know they will tell your mother you're in the city."

March twitches her right eye. "If she doesn't know already."

Jonathan raises the corner of his mouth. "She will come looking for you."

March rolls her eyes behind fluttering lids and exhales. "She'll send one of her servants before she dares lower herself to Stonehaven."

The lamp lighters climb the curled posts to finish their work for the evening and disappear down into Stonehaven, leaving Jonathan and March alone on the street. Except for a well-laced gentleman who approaches and leans against their table between them, his eyes devouring March's breasts. Jonathan looks around the rude gentleman to see if March wants him to intervene, but a simple wink lets him know she will handle the situation.

"You're a delicious strumpet." He rubs his chest with his right hand to showcase the jeweled rings he wears on every finger. "If you're finished with this customer, I could fancy a quick fuck. I know of a partially secluded alley and I'll pay you handsomely, more than this gentleman ever could."

March tilts her head and smiles at Jonathan. Even though the streets are empty, he still shakes his head. Not because March would ever do something as disgusting as go with this degenerate. They themselves have succumbed to a moment of passion in the Mirusian alleyways, and will again before their task is finished. But the foolish man does not recognize who he speaks to. March's hair is matted with sweat. Loose strands dangle over one eye, and her braids flow between her breasts, which is all the man sees. He knows this man will die at March's hands if she leaves with him.

He repeats his offensive offer and flings his coat open to show a wide leather pouch with silver studs hanging full from his belt.

March grabs his wrist with one hand, and with the other shoves a dagger he never saw her pull from her sleeve straight up into the soft meat between his legs. A trickle of blood stains his white trousers and crawls down the blade. His legs dance as if he hung from the gallows, and his head trembles, mouth agape in disbelief and horror.

"I think it's time you leave," she tells him, "or I'll nick something that will save many more women your trouble." She pulls her dagger back and wipes the blood on his thigh.

He staggers off, wincing with every step. "Fucking disease riddled whore."

March flips her dagger in hand, ready to sink it into the back of the man's neck, but Jonathan holds up his hand, asking her to wait.

"Darling, this is our first day in the city. Let's not add to our death toll just yet." Jonathan flings his tea saucer down to the cobblestones and it skips under the man's heel as he walks away. He slips, arms flailing, and stumbles backward over the terrace down to the streets of Stonehaven. He lands with a crunch and wheezes all the air from his lungs.

"Dead?" March asks.

Jonathan looks over the balustrade. "No. Unconscious."

"Pity. I'll catch him soon enough." March slides the dagger back into her sleeve.

"Privately, please." Jonathan takes a long sip from his flask. "Back to the wagon then, before we cause more of a ruckus?"

"We've spent enough nights with forks and books and bobbles poking us in our bits. I've a better idea."

Well after sunset, Jonathan and March walk into the Verdant Inn, which sits on the lowest edge of Stonehaven. One thousand sixty stairs on the way down, by Jonathan's count. It is a decently clean establishment with potted ferns and saplings filling the room and ivy climbing up the walls and across the ceiling to create a false yet beautiful canopy. It's the closest they can get to the Hollow in the city.

The old innkeeper stands from her chair behind the counter and adjusts her spectacles. "How may I help you this evening?" She touches her feather quill to her tongue.

"Your rooms," March says. "We want the lot."

"I'm afraid such a thing isn't possible. I already have guests checked into two rooms for the night." The innkeeper lays her quill down on her log book, thinking March's request a joke. But after March tosses a leather pouch with silver studs onto the counter and handfuls of silver and gold coins across the wood, she corrects herself. "How long do you want them?"

She gives the current guests the excuse of a sudden infestation and returns their coins. It's no loss compared to what March pays her. With the Inn to themselves, Jonathan and March lock and bar each door and window and retire to a room on the top floor, where ivy from the common room crawls through the cracks between the floorboards and up the walls. They undress and stand together at the window for a moment to take in warm air and hard sounds of sleeping stone and metal.

Jonathan misses the hollow. The insects, trees, animals, and wind serve as a serene, ever-present lullaby, but the high walls of Mirus block out any such comfort. They slide into bed, and the stuffed straw mattress feels as soft as any down compared to the planks in the wagon. March wraps her arms around Jonathan's neck, hooks her leg around his waist, and pulls him into her. Their soft moans fill the room as they drift in and out of sleep.

The last thought before Jonathan succumbs to his heavy eyelids is of Cheshire.

"He's fine," March whispers, sensing his worry. "We will see him again when we leave."

Selfishly, Jonathan wants the bed behind him to move and feel Cheshire's warm body press against his back. But he knows the danger Cheshire faces if he were to enter the capital. Mirus is no place for a Queen Slayer.

CHAPTER 25

CHESHIRE

Cheshire dozes out of sight in a stone cupola atop a Crest clothier's shop for most of the afternoon, waiting for night. He drifts in and out of unconsciousness, listening to the dull, meaningless chatter from the streets below. Peacocks dressed in their finery discuss their indecencies, jewelry, not so secret whores, and brag of their wealth and number of servants. The clatter of soldiers' armor as they patrol the streets adds some variety to the incessant drone.

Once the sun hides her face and the moon rises to smile and greet him, Cheshire stretches as best he can in the small square and climbs atop the cupola's metal vane. Up the hill in the distance, at least two hundred castle guards stand sentry along the parapets of its outer wall and fifty soldiers patrol at its base. Their torches give away their positions. When he was last in Mirus, the Castle Guard and the ever-present watch of soldiers and archers on the city wall were positioned at least forty paces apart. They were enough to thwart all of his efforts to reenter the city—not to mention the mounted trebuchet, crossbows as wide as a griffin's wingspan, and cauldrons of oil. But now their numbers are so great, the soldiers on the city wall and the Castle Guard on the parapets stand shoulder to shoulder, and the walls burn in solid, continuous arches of fire.

Is this because of Lysander and Uriah's warning? Or has this been the normal state of things since my last visit?

With no clear path into the castle, he must wait for a better opportunity, whatever it may be. Cheshire shifts uncomfortably in the unfamiliar open air and looks down into the city, realizing his antiquated memory at the sight of the changes made during his near thousand-year exile. The garish buildings of the Crest stand double in height and their pointed red-tile roofs attempt to mimic a fake crown around the city. Long wooden bridges and walkways snake high over the streets of Stonehaven but below the roofs, creating an entirely new level above the first. And the Boroughs, hidden from view, forgotten, grow further into disrepair and neglect.

Cheshire yearns for the cold of the catacombs waiting for him outside the city walls. If they crossed beneath Mirus, he would have gained access long ago, but the closest entrance is twenty miles away. However, the castle and city have their own complex of catacombs, cut off from the rest of the land. Once Cheshire finds his way inside them, there will be nothing the Duchess can do or hide from him. The problem is the only entrance he remembers is beyond his reach at the moment, deep within the castle.

"What do we know?" Cheshire digs memories from the

back of his mind to gain his bearings. He closes one eye and points to the locations he remembers. "The Crest, the Row in Stonehaven, the stretch of smiths as long as the market at the Forge, the Crooked Market if it still exists in the Borough, the harbor on the far side of the castle, and the castle itself. That's it. Fuck."

There should be more townspeople, more activity, in the streets. The increased presence of soldiers has imposed an unintentional curfew, leaving Cheshire alone with the soldiers. From his perch he watches six soldiers stand two by two, stoic and silent, at the four corners of the intersection below him. Additional pairs of soldiers pass every ten minutes by Cheshire's count. A woman wrapped in a silk robe with plumes of feathers around her wrists and neck walks onto her bedroom balcony and asks them to walk quieter. The soldiers ignore her and keep to their patrol.

Thick ropes with dark hanging lanterns span the wide Crest streets, and Cheshire uses them to cross farther down the hill until he descends into Stonehaven, the partially clouded night his ally. He climbs atop the bell tower of a temple and looks over the sleeping city—the clutter of stacked houses and the markets, chimneys, pointed roofs, and random soft treetops among the harsh angles. Below, soldiers stand at every corner and meander through the streets by torchlight, transforming the city into a mountain of glowing embers.

Cheshire stalks several pairs and waits in the shadows near others hoping to uncover some crucial information, but every soldier he encounters remains silent. Even when they walk in pairs, neither utters a sound nor looks at each other. If they need to change direction or call the other's attention, they motion with their hand and point, with nods and shakes the sum total of their conversations. They have been warned to keep their mouths shut. Which would also account for their absence in the Last Hand. However, not all Mirusian soldiers can be completely obedient or intelligent. Cheshire needs to find the right one.

He keeps to the dark sky and tails more mute and unhelpful soldiers on his way to the Row, and at its center, Dormy's wagon, closed for the night. After the soldiers pass, he drops from the taller buildings framing the Row onto the wagon's roof and peeks through the upper window expecting Jonathan and March to be coiled around each other. Instead, he finds the compartment empty. They are likely in more hospitable accommodations after their long journey. He wishes he knew where, because since their time together in Briarwell, Cheshire's body aches and craves their touch. He adjusts himself in his trousers and climbs to the lower level where he crosses over Dormy, curled asleep on a pile of rough burlap flour sacks, to snack from a basket full of dates, walnuts, and plums.

Two more sets of soldiers pass by like clockwork while he eats, and light from their torches sweeps through small cracks and sparkles against glass bottles in hanging nets and crates. As a third pair passes, Cheshire's ear twitches at the grating sound of armor approaching and hushed voices hidden within the metal scrapes.

He pockets a handful of walnuts and plums to eat later, and when the wagon is dark again, Cheshire climbs back to the rooftops and follows the soldiers to the quadrangle at the far end of the Row. The quadruple-stacked living quarters rise to create tall, looming walls and keep the square below in darkness, except for the light from the tavern at its east end. Cheshire jumps to a wooden pole near where the guards have stopped to rest and dangles his cloak below him to match the large pennants on the adjacent poles. Their high gorgets obscure their mouths and speech. Cheshire can only hear the sporadic words they emphasize to each other.

"... important prisoner... next time... shackles... double..."

"My ass... duty, not my... dangerous... keep moving."

"... cells... hide from..."

Cheshire's skin burns with curiosity against the humid night air and the hair on his neck bristles. *After all this time, have two asinine soldiers unknowingly told me where my mother is kept? This seems far too convenient. But I cannot afford to not find out.*

Several faint glows of nearby torches move and flicker through the tunnels leading out of every side of the quadrangle beneath the living quarters. Cheshire wants to drop and beat the information he lacks from these two, and would if he were anywhere else, but to do so would give away the game. His mother may wait for him locked away in the prison, and he will find out where she is this night.

However, he has no knowledge or memory of the prison's location, and it will take longer than a single night to find where it is. He will enlist the aid of the soldiers to lead him to it.

The taller of the soldiers motions to the tavern and leaves his post. His partner, at first reluctant, soon follows, and raucous laughter and foul conversations greet both when they enter. The warm light from within pushes through the film-covered windows and casts a soft orange path on the cracked dirt, ending at the empty pillories at the square's center.

Without knowing how long the soldiers will disregard their post, Cheshire slides down the pole and sneaks to the dais the three pillories stand upon to inspect them.

No locks. The soldiers must keep them on their persons to keep townsfolk from stealing them, he reasons.

He raises and lowers the top board of the center pillory, and a pin rattles loosely in the wrought iron hinges. All of his fingers are too large to push the pin out of the narrow barrel, but the nail from the sign attached to the top board can fit. The words on the sign read "Public Drunkard" written in red. With little force it pulls free, and he positions the nail's tip at the bottom of the pin. One solid punch against the sign is enough to pop the pin free from the barrel. It clinks on the wooden platform and rolls softly to the dirt. He makes quick work of the other two pins and pockets all three. The noise of his punches stir some mongrel and its distant bark echoes through the night.

The taller soldier hears the dog and steps out of the tavern, drink in hand. Cheshire drops and lies flat behind the platform, which is a hair taller than it needs to be, to hide him. His breath pushes the dirt away as he peeks above the edge.

A large, drunken, belligerent man with shoulders almost as broad as Jonathan's pushes past the soldier, who gives him a warning. The drunk turns and shouts a slurred insult back at the soldier about his mother fucking a goat or being a goat. The soldier spits after the drunk man and returns to his comrade.

The drunk staggers out into the night, stomach sloshing, and looks around the quadrangle for his way home, which he left in one of the bottles in the tavern. Cheshire stands and leans his back against the center pillory in plain sight.

"What are you looking at?" the drunk asks.

"I'm minding my own, enjoying the night air." Cheshire grips the sign from the pillory tight in his hand behind him. "Do you need help to find your way home?"

"Does it look like I need help from a little runt like you?" Even in the dark, the man's eyes are glazed and red.

"My mistake, sir." Cheshire flips the sign in his hand and cracks it against the side of the man's skull, sending him face first into the ground, less a few teeth. As the dog barks again, Cheshire flings the sign, spinning it through the air. It shatters four panes of the tavern's long window with an explosion of glass and curses from within. He runs for the nearest house and climbs all four stories in a matter of seconds and watches both soldiers run from the tavern, kick up dirt, curse, and throw their helmets at the unconscious man.

"What's this now?" The shorter soldier kicks the man's leg.

"Piece of filth," says the taller soldier.

"Well, at least he saved us the trouble of carrying him out here. Let's lock him in and then get back to our drinks." The shorter soldier steps up onto the platform and lifts the top board of the right pillory, only for it to fall completely off its hinge and thud against the platform. He tries the other two with the same result.

"What'd you do?" The taller guard sits the man up.

"They broke. I think."

"All of them?"

"Yeah. What do we do with him? Leave him here?"

"No." The taller soldier studies the grimace on the tavern owner's face through the shattered window. "On second thought, I don't think he'd make it till morning if we left him here."

"So much for drinks."

Both soldiers lift the man, throw one of his arms over each of their shoulders, and exit the quadrangle to the north. The man's feet digs trails in the dirt behind them. They recruit four more soldiers on their way to help bear his weight.

Cheshire follows on the roofs above as the soldiers walk the entire curve of Stonehaven through the Forge until they reach an intimidating stone structure built against the city wall. He positions himself across the dirt road as the soldiers pass the drunk to guards, who drag him inside, and then continue back to their rounds, the two talkative men now silent around the others.

He counts seventeen prison guards in total, all in long black and red tunics with polished silver pauldrons, greaves, gauntlets, visors with thin slits for their eyes, and short wide swords sheathed at their hips. They pace slowly on the three levels of the prison, their hard shadows crawl against the stone fed by iron braziers extending from the walls. He could kill them all one by one, if there was a way to surprise them. Unlike the soldiers on patrol in the city, these guards stand alone at different points of the imposing structure and have a timed routine to look at another's location every minute. Four grey and black hounds with muscled shoulders sleep by the only entrance, their lips snarled to show sharp teeth. One misstep and the hounds and every guard within earshot would descend upon him.

He pulls a plum from his cloak and eats while he paces across several rooftops, searching for any unguarded window, door, or hatch, but can find none, and the few windows he can see are less than a foot wide. He throws the pit down the street and it softly bounces off a lower shingled roof. Every guard turns toward the sound, hands on their swords, and the dogs jump to their feet, shoulders arched. Cheshire sits on the edge of an awning and watches their movement, their routine, and plays out several scenarios, each ending with his capture. He pulls a shingle loose for each failure. Twenty-seven sit in a pile next to him.

After several hours of waiting and watching, two figures walking side by side pass on the street below. The woman catches Cheshire off guard when she glances up and stares back. She says nothing or raises no alarms to his presence. She lowers her eyes and continues walking with her companion, as if she never saw him. Something about her face plucks a cord within Cheshire's mind, and the vibrations fill gaps he forgot were there.

He follows them both through the streets of Stonehaven and down into the narrow streets of the Boroughs. Cheshire jumps across the crowded buildings like stones in a stream. They lead him through the bowels of the city and down narrow alleyways barely wide enough for both to walk side by side. Cheshire jumps ahead and slides down the wall in front of them, his arms and legs braced between two rickety houses.

Upon seeing both of their faces and green hair, the plucked memory becomes still and solid. "Patricia. William," he says.

"Welcome back," says Patricia, not the least bit surprised.

"It's been quite a while," says William.

Cheshire searches past their names and remembers they played together as children. Despite the multitude of questions plaguing his mind, he asks the one at the tip of his tongue. "How did you know I was on the roof?"

"We maintain the city." Patricia slides her hammer off her shoulder and leans on it like a cane. "We know every plank, every stone, every detail. Spotting something as out of place as you was easy."

Cheshire grins. "Impressive. Then, perhaps you could help me with an endeavor. For old Time's sake."

"Depends what it is." William wipes the sweat from his brow, leaving a grease streak in its place.

"What do you know of the prison cells?" Cheshire crawls back up to the awning.

"Everything," says Patricia. "We designed them."

"And built them," says William.

"I want to get in."

"Get caught," they both say.

"I'd rather not. Not this early in the game. There must be another way." Cheshire stares unblinking at them. "Will you help me?"

They look at each other and then back to Cheshire. "This way," they say together, and lead him to a small stone culvert in the lowest level of the Boroughs next to the city wall.

William removes an iron pin from a solid iron flap

embedded in the stone, releasing the aged pungent stench of shit and piss as it falls to the ground. "It's a long way, but this section of sewers passes below the cells."

"My thanks." Cheshire strips, ties his clothes into a bundle, and hides it in the closest thatched roof. He keeps his sash and wraps it around his face to cover his mouth and nose.

William tosses the metal pin from hand to hand, and Cheshire snatches it out of the air, in case they have the idea to lock the flap behind him.

Cheshire stoops into the dark tunnel and decades of shit squish up between his toes and cake his feet. The farther up the tunnel, the harder it is to see with the tears stinging his eyes. He holds the pin between his teeth and cheek to use his hands to steady himself against the curved walls as he plods through the sewer. After what must be five miles, an iron grate blocks his way at the end of the long tunnel. On the other side sits an expansive dark room with a dim orange glow creeping down the walls from far above. He scrapes the shit off his fingers and reaches through the spaces between the iron to explore the edge of the grate, searching for bolts or a latch.

There is a gap thinner than his smallest finger running along the top and sides of the grate, except for one spot where a piece of metal juts up and disappears into the wall above him. He wipes his eyes on a clean portion of his arm, his sweat causing them to burn more. He rubs his hands on the tunnel's curved ceiling, searching for any recess or evidence of a latch. One of his fingertips sinks into a small hole, too smooth to be an accident or imperfection in the stone. All his fingers are too large to explore it, but conveniently, as if planned, the pin William tossed in his hands fits perfectly.

Cheshire pushes it into the hole until it clicks against metal and an inch still protrudes. He braces his feet against the drier side of the tunnel and pushes up with his legs. The end of the pin digs into his thumb, and finally it clicks and disappears into the stone above. He barely has to push on the grate with one hand, and it falls forward into the muck. He enters not a large room, but a pit dug one hundred feet deep into the granite mountain Mirus sits on, and steps knee deep into the putrid cesspool of viscous shit and piss.

Overhead, fifty prison cells hang like bird cages. Three lit braziers circle the top rim of the cages with the shadows of bodies in them.

If my mother is here, I'll drown the Duchess in this shit myself.

A single platform built out from the wall on one side of the pit rests high above at the same level as the cells. Cheshire wades to the far side of the room through the muck and steps on what he believes to be full leg bones and a rib cage beneath the putrefied surface. His toes trace the curves of the bones and he realizes quite a number of prisoners have died, either trying to escape or taking their own lives to evade their sentence.

He scales the steep rock face and waits beneath the platform listening to the sound of swinging iron chains and the occasional small crack from the fires, waiting for soldiers footsteps upon the wooden planks.

After an hour, he pulls himself onto the platform to find a carved arched door far to his right and a row of wooden levers, kept in place by metal rings spanning the wall. Each lever connects two iron chains pulled tight up the wall and through a complex of wheels and gears across the ceiling and back down to the cells. Wooden placards hang from the levers with names and offenses of the imprisoned. None of them bear his mother's name, but he cannot rule out deception and misdirection. His fingers dance in the air, accepting the temptation, and he grabs the round knob of a lever and drops it. The chains clunk through the gears and a cell lurches down louder than Cheshire expects.

He returns the lever to its original position to stop the descent and waits to hear a reaction from the hounds or soldiers through slivers of windows overhead. They stay silent, accustomed to the sounds within the prison. Cheshire raises the lever next to the first he tried, and the chains above scrape against gears as the cage with the drunk from earlier travels to the edge of the platform. The man lies in an uncomfortable heap, shoulder pressed into his jaw and hips torqued at an odd angle.

Cheshire opens the gate to the man's cell and slaps him across the face to check if he is still alive. A weak groan escapes his smooshed mouth. As he steps from the cell and closes the gate, Cheshire notices the drunk's cell and the others, both occupied and not, have no locks or shackles.

No need for them with a hundred-foot drop into the pit below.

He looks to the other cells with lit braziers, each at a different height and distance. The prisoners' arms and legs hang freely through the holes of the metal lattice of the cells, and their hairy faces are plain in the torchlight.

This is not the place the soldiers spoke of. It can't be.

Cheshire reads the placards on each lever, even those still hanging for unoccupied cells. These men are nothing more than common thieves, poachers, and tax evaders.

There must be somewhere else in the city to hold who they consider important prisoners.

The soldiers from the quadrangle know the information he needs, but he never saw their faces, and though Cheshire is usually patient, he is too close. It will take too long to track them down. Any soldier could have the same information, and even though ordered to stay silent, Cheshire could make them speak. The possibility remains they know nothing and he would waste more time and effort. He could lure the guards in and force them to divulge what he needs, kill them, and hide their bodies in the pit below. But someone would eventually notice their disappearance.

Cheshire looks to the drunk who graciously helped him before and is in a position to help him again. He pulls the man from the cell and lays him on the planks, then grabs his name placard and throws it into the pit below. He lowers his voice in pitch, similar to the gruff, slurred ramblings of the drunk, and yells at the windows and climbs back into the pit, clinging to the support braces underneath the platform.

In less than a minutes, two soldiers crunch into the room. "What is this?" says a voice from overhead. "Who got him out?"

The scrapes of armor grow louder and stop directly over Cheshire's head as the guards search the cells and pit.

"Looks like the ass got himself out. Damn escape artist is what he is."

"That's not possible. Smells like a drunk. What'd they bring him in for?"

"I dunno. His log's gone."

"Probably threw it into the shit so we won't remember."

"Who the fuck cares." A guard's gauntlet clangs against the man's head. "Think you're clever? Throw him back in."

"He'll just escape again. We should toss him in the dungeons."

"I'm not lugging him all the way into the castle. We should toss him down and be done."

"Shut up and put him back in. Since his log has disappeared, we don't know when to let him out. So put him as far back as the cage will go and let's see if he can escape again. We'll let me stew there for a week, if we remember him at all."

One soldier extinguishes the braziers on the man's cell and the other pulls the level to send him across the pit. They watch his cell swing and clack against the far wall before they leave, chuckling to each other.

Though the man has served his purpose, Cheshire will not let him be forgotten in the dark. He waits an hour below the platform with no entrances or checks from other guards. He climbs back up, pulls the lever, brings the man's cell back to the platform, and takes a torch from the wall and relights the braziers of the cell.

"Thank you." Cheshire smiles and pats the man's face through the bars. And with a final push of the lever, sends the man back to the same position the guards left him.

Cheshire climbs down the wall, jumps into the cesspool with a horrible deep squish, and crosses to the grate and pulls it shut behind him, catching the pin as it falls from the hole. He entertains himself on the five mile walk down the greasy sewer. The slight angle of the tunnel allows him to use gravity to his advantage and slide most of the way, careful not to lose his balance.

Outside the tunnel, the dark night sky gives way to the soft blue before dawn. Two buckets of water, soap, and a scrub brush left by Patricia and William sit below the awning with Cheshire's clothes. He shakes the caked shit from his feet and feverishly scrubs his body until every part of his skin is red and tender. He takes care to dip his sash in the soapy water and massage the smell from its fibers before he dresses.

The first rays of dawn will rise over the city wall soon, and he must make it back to the Row and Dormy's wagon, where he intends to sleep until nightfall. A renewed vigor courses through him. The prison guards gifted Cheshire with an important detail, yet unknown to him. If they were to take any prisoner to the dungeons, the soldiers would never be allowed to walk them through the castle gates, let alone the front doors. There is another entrance somewhere in the city, and tomorrow night he will discover its location.

CHAPTER 26

MARY ANNE

The next morning Mary Anne wakes to bright sunbeams spreading through the room. She stays in bed for a while and admires the dust particles floating in and out of the streaks of light. She stretches her sore arms and legs and still cannot reach the edges of the bed.

Six nights, she thinks. *The first at Jonathan's, the second in Briarwell, three curled in the Duchess's carriage, and last night in the most comfortable bed.* She watches the yellow tassels hanging down from the velvet canopy overhead sway in the breeze, and almost gives into the temptation to doze again. But a knock at the door startles her awake.

"Mary Anne," Chamberlain Weiss calls from the other side, "are you awake?"

"Yes." She jumps from the bed, wipes the sleep from her eyes and mouth, and straightens her underdress.

"Are you rested?" Chamberlain Weiss sweeps through the

door, his long robes and hair flowing behind him, and inspects Mary Anne's face. "Yes, the dark circles under your eyes are much less prominent this morning. Good. We have much to accomplish and little time to do so." He circles and scrutinizes her from head to toe and sighs.

Mary Anne half expects him to poke or prod her with a stick. She knows she is not what they would readily consider queen material, but she cannot help to be offended. She straightens her posture and smooths her dress again to appease him.

Chamberlain Weiss adjusts his spectacles, even though he does not look through them, and claps his hands to summon a servant girl from the hall who carries a wrapped bundle. Mary Anne believes this girl to be a servant, even though her clothing indicates otherwise—a floor-length black and white dress covers her entire body, from wrist to ankle, and a coif and half mask conceal her hair and eyes making her appear to be dressed to attend some high-to-do masquerade rather than serve. The girl curtsies delicately, head bowed. Mary Anne returns her curtsy out of instinct.

"Don't curtsy to the servants." Chamberlain Weiss sighs. "It confuses them."

"Hello," Mary Anne says politely, uncomfortable to have anyone bow to her.

"She cannot respond to you, so there is no use or need to speak to her," says Chamberlain Weiss, exasperated. He flutters his hand, and the girl opens the door to the adjoining room. "She will be your attendant for the extent of your stay with us." He waves Mary Anne through the open door.

Already rested from her full, undisturbed night's sleep, her muscles relax further at the steam rising from the glorious clawfoot tub with golden trim and lion's paws for legs at the center of the room. Not some filthy barrel in a rundown hovel. In a genuine castle with no discernible risk of attack or danger.

Beautiful.

Thin glassless windows line the exterior wall and present the morning light in long strips on the dark stone floor, and the breeze billows tall gossamer curtains and beckons her closer to the bath like the curled finger of a lover. Mary Anne turns to the servant girl, but she is already gone and the door closed. At long last, she steps out of her dress, unafraid, drapes it across a gilded chair against the wall, and lets her body breathe in the cool morning air.

Mounds of bubbles and the welcoming scent of lavender draws her to the tub. She dips her hand in the water, expecting it to be warm, but finds the heat jarring at first. Mary Anne lowers herself into the tub, hissing inwardly and panting sharply as the hot water climbs her skin. Once acclimated to the water, she relaxes again and sinks up to her chin. She takes care to wash every part of her body and hair, rubbing away days of dirt, sweat, dried tears, and worry until her pink skin glistens.

Why could I not have entered Wonderland here? she says to herself. *Then I could have appreciated this world for what it offers and started my journey home sooner. Have the other women who crossed into Wonderland all used the same method to return home?* She recalls Chamberlain Weiss's words. *"Not everyone is deserving."* So were all of them, any of them, able to become Queen? If not, what happened to them?

To keep her thoughts from straying and ruining her relaxation, she closes her eyes and slides farther into the water. She takes one last breath before the water covers her nose and fills her ears. The circle of dry skin on her face shrinks until she submerges into yet another world. She finds solace in the rhythmic pounding of her heartbeat intensified by the water. Her body floats off the bottom of the tub and for a moment she exists weightless, without a thought running through her mind.

She emerges from the water, sits up, and smooths her hair back, pushing the water down the back of her neck. Once the water leaves her eyes and she breathes again, she discovers the servant girl standing just out of arm's reach of the tub with a beige, cotton robe held open for her.

"How long have you been there?" Mary Anne hides below the side of the tub and gathers the remaining bubbles on the surface of the water to preserve modesty. *This may be customary here, but I'll not stand wet and naked in the presence of anyone.* She covers her chest with one arm and raises out of the water to grab the robe from the servant girl with the other. And once she turns her back, Mary Anne wipes the water from her face and slowly steps from the bath, cautious of her feet upon the slick floor. She turns her back to the girl as well and secures the robe tight around her waist.

The servant girl reaches for Mary Anne's hair, towel in hand, startling Mary Anne.

"I can manage myself." She steps away. "Thank you." The girl tries again, reaching for Mary Anne, her lips pressed with worry. "Thank you, but no."

The servant girl backs away, head lowered. At first the

thought of a servant intrigued, playing to Mary Anne's vanity, but seeing the girl stand before her and realizing she must wait on her every need does not sit well. On closer inspection of what she can see of the girl's face below the mask, her skin is youthful and pale, and her pressed lips are painted a deep maroon. Mary Anne must be her senior by only a few years.

"I understand you have duties to perform," says Mary Anne, "but I would much rather have a friend than a servant for the remainder of time I am here." The servant girl shakes her head. "What is your name? May I please know your name?" The girl grips her hands tightly in front of her and keeps her eyes downcast. "I will need to call you by some name, and I will not call you *servant* or *attendant*. Grace, perhaps? It's a suitable name." Still no response. "Well, until you decide to tell me your name, I shall call you Grace."

The hint of a smile sneaks into the corner of Grace's lips.

"Hang on," says Mary Anne, noticing the empty chair. "Where's my dress?"

Grace leads Mary Anne back into the bedroom to show her a breathtaking mauve dress laid out for her on the bed.

"Is this for me?" Mary Anne runs her fingers along the gold threaded seams. "It's lovely."

"Of course, it is." Chamberlain Weiss huffs, leaning against the wall by the door adjusting his white gloves. "Now dress quickly, because we have a long day ahead of us."

Mary Anne waits for Chamberlain Weiss to leave. Instead, he sniffles and raises his eyebrows, waiting for Mary Anne to move.

"I'll not dress with you in the room, sir." Mary Anne holds the collar of her robe tight.

Chamberlain Weiss guffaws. "Simple woman, there's a changing screen behind you. I did not, nor do I want, for you to disrobe in front of me."

He tells the truth. A tall wooden folding screen she did not notice the night before stands in the corner with red and purple scarves draped from its rounded peaks.

"I'll still not change with you in the room."

"As you wish. I will wait in the northwest courtyard. Your attendant will bring you to me when you're finished primping."

"Grace," Mary Anne says matter-of-factly.

Chamberlain Weiss turns his head as if slapped, eyebrows arched upward. His hair swings with a flourish around his knees. "I beg your pardon?"

"She's unable to tell me her name, therefore, I'm going to call her Grace."

He rolls his eyes and whips out of the door, pulling it closed behind him. Once he is out of the room, Grace reaches to open Mary Anne's robe.

"We've been through this once before." Mary Anne laughs. Grace bites her bottom lip and fidgets with her fingers.

"I've had no one dress me, except for my mother when I was young. Please do not take my shyness as a sign you are doing anything wrong." Mary Anne worries her refusal could cause an unintentional reprimand or punishment from Chamberlain Weiss for not carrying out her duties. She must suspend her own discomfort for now, for Grace's sake.

She walks behind the screen, turns her back, and unties

her robe. Grace slides it off her shoulders, down her arms, and hangs over the changing screen. Mary Anne instinctively covers herself, one hand across her breasts and the other hanging down with her hand positioned between her legs. She thinks of March, naked as the day she was birthed, walking through Jonathan's home, and knows her body will never look the way March's does, nor does she want it to. But Mary Anne is helpless to the jealousy picking at her soul, wishing she could stand with an ounce of the confidence March possesses, instead of hunched and cowering from a girl younger than she.

Grace retrieves the new dress from the bed and motions for Mary Anne to raise her arms out to slip the dress over. Begrudgingly, Mary Anne turns, unwraps her arms from her body, and thrusts her arms into the air. An icy shiver covers every inch of her exposed skin. Grace pushes the sleeves up Mary Anne's arms and raises them above her head for the dress to slide into place. It gets stuck momentarily at her shoulders, leaving her blind, her body exposed, but at least covering the flush of embarrassment across Mary Anne's face.

She leads Mary Anne to a tall, oval looking glass in the opposite corner of the room where she meticulously laces the back of the corseted bodice sewn into the dress.

Mary Anne's eyes follow the golden threads around her pointed cuffs, the arms through the sheer fabric of her sleeves, and her fingers trace the golden brocade designs swirling on the bodice. The weighty fabric of this dress is not as comfortable as she imagined or compared to the dress Jonathan bought her in Rookridge. To complete the ensemble, Grace collects Mary

Anne's hair in a golden snood and slips on brown heeled boots, lacing them up to her shin.

As she studies herself in the looking glass, a woman as unrecognizable as the soiled face in Briarwell stares back, and she wonders where the woman is who would smile at her from the small, square looking glass above her bathroom sink in Lyndhurst. This woman may look regal, but she is just another veneer.

Mary Anne carries her book and follows Grace through another complicated series of lofty hallways full of large clay vases and paintings, all twice Mary Anne's height, and down spiral staircases which lead to a new area of the castle with Baroque cloisters circling a lush verdant lawn. Grace gestures to the cluster of young willow trees at the center of the courtyard where Chamberlain Weiss sits on a stone bench too short for his long legs.

I shouldn't have lied, she thinks. *I should have been honest and told them both I couldn't understand the language.* She reverts to a schoolgirl, clutching her book to her chest, afraid to tell her headmaster her work is unfinished. In this case, the consequences could be far more dire.

"Are you not coming?" Mary Anne whispers to Grace, knowing better than to expect a response. But Grace surprises her and shakes her head, hands clasped in front of her.

"Will you at least stay? I don't think I could find my way back to my room if I searched for a week." Grace nods once and steps back into the shadows of the cloisters. "Thank you."

Mary Anne inhales, filling her chest, and breathes out all worry. She is not a schoolgirl or at university and will not allow herself to feel so, and Chamberlain Weiss is not her head master. Head held high, she walks to meet him with the veneer of confidence she has used all her life.

Chamberlain Weiss picks his head up from his time piece as she approaches. "It's a start," he says, referring to her dress. "Please, sit."

"Will the Duchess join us this morning?" Mary Anne joins him, but inches to the far edge of the bench.

"She must deal with matters of city and country this morning. Every morning, she gives audience to the people of Mirus to hear their grievances and see how she can render aid. Since she spent several days abroad, you can imagine there are many who've waited to speak to her."

"Fascinating," says Mary Anne. "Should I not be there with her?"

"No. Not yet at least." Chamberlain Weiss pulls his spectacles below the bridge of his nose. "Until she joins us, I'm to prepare you and see how far we get. What have you read thus far?"

She breathes in deep again, ready to confess and prepared for an admonishment or lecture. "I should have been plain with you and the Duchess yesterday. I thumbed through every section last night hoping the strange symbols would make sense, but I cannot understand the language the book is written in."

"Not to worry." Chamberlain Weiss waves his hand in the air. "It's Old Prodigium, the first language of Wonderland. There are few who can still read it. Mainly the highly educated, like myself."

"Why then was I asked to read it if you knew I could not in the first place? A trick?"

"A test, Mary Anne. To gauge your response." He scrunches his nose to raise his spectacles and study her. "To see if you would be truthful, when you would be truthful, or see how long you would carry on with the charade."

"A test. Did I fail?" she asks.

"I'm not the judge." He shrugs. "Merely a guide. An advisor, you could say." He gestures with his hand for Mary Anne to move closer. "Now that you're rested and presentable, shall we begin?"

"I do have a question before we begin. You mentioned yesterday, Wonderland will decide if I am a worthy candidate. But how does Wonderland decide? Is there a poll? A census?"

"I'm not sure where the confusion lies." He embellishes every word as if orating to some unseen audience. "The land itself must accept you. Ask the dirt beneath your feet, the beasts in the forests and fields, and the stones of the mountains if you wish. Wonderland will answer you when it is ready, and not before. Now, can we begin?"

She moves closer and opens the book across both their laps. He flips two pages and points at a bold heading with the same angular characters as the rest of the page. He clears his throat before reading. The words he speaks are beyond foreign, but they sound like a mix of Gaelic, Corsican, and perhaps even Latin.

"If the Queendom throne sits vacant," he reads, "a pawn may ascend, if proven worthy to fill the seat and give the land power once more." He translates and glides his finger across the words to help Mary Anne understand.

Surely the selection of a queen cannot be based on a game of chess, she thinks. In school she studied lineages and divine right determining the monarchy of countries and empires, but not a simple game.

"Six Tenets must be fulfilled to ascend as sovereign Queen," Chamberlain Weiss continues.

"Tenets?" Mary Anne tilts her head. "Am I expected to search for lost artifacts or complete puzzles?"

"My dear, nothing so droll or boorish." He chortles. "The six fall into three categories." He turns the page. "Education. Manifestation. Coronation. The very first is exceedingly simple." He points back to the text and reads. "The first Tenet is to Declare Wise Counsel." He looks up from the page and smiles. "You must choose an advisor to assist you. And be aware your declaration is binding."

"Must I choose now?" she asks.

"If you did, we'd be on our way to the third Tenet." He hands the book to Mary Anne and rises. "On the other hand, if you're in no rush, I can check back with you tomorrow. And also, to make you aware, I have served devoutly as advisory under the previous queens of Wonderland."

The passage said choose. But this is no choice. Chamberlain Weiss presents himself as the only option. How much of this is actually theatre? she asks herself. Mary Anne understands Chamberlain Weiss wants her to choose him here and now. But if she must name someone to help her, only one person in all of Wonderland has earned her trust.

"Jonathan," Mary Anne says without hesitation.

"I beg your pardon?" The blood runs from Chamberlain Weiss's face. His hand lays across his chest to cover his wounded pride.

"Jonathan," she repeats. "I choose Jonathan Carter. If I am to have someone to help me get home, I choose him." Mary Anne rises. "Please understand. He's the one person I fully trust at the moment. And I hope after declaring someone else, you will still be able to help me. I'm not sure if this is unorthodox or no—"

"You can't do this. This isn't done. I am the most qualified to be advisor to the Queen. You've no idea what you've just done." He pulls a white fan from his cloak pocket and taps it against his gloved palm. His head darts to the balconies surrounding the courtyard.

"I'm sorry," she says. "I feel he is the correct choice."

After Chamberlain Weiss fans and calms himself, he sits on the bench again and picks up the book, turns the page, and reads. "The second Tenet is Acknowledgement of Worth. For a Queen to rise, the pawn must first accept and confess their own worth as a pawn."

Mary Anne blinks and looks to the grass beneath her feet, as if they would have the answer to the cumbersome translation. "I'm not sure what that passage means."

"Do you want to be Queen?" he asks.

"Of course. I must."

He scratches beneath his nose with a bent finger. "Do you realize the difference between a pawn and a queen? A pawn is the furthest thing from a queen. In order to become one, you must accept you are the other. To be considered worthy of even being a candidate to become Queen, can you honestly say, are you ready to say you are a pawn? Nothing. Insignificant. Worthless."

A deathly cold washes over Mary Anne and fills her from her foot to follicle. If there is a heartbeat in her chest, she cannot feel it. She is a paradox. Deep within her soul she knows she is not worthy, and has been made to feel as though she was never good enough by almost everyone in her adolescence and adult life. And to say it out loud would be admitting to herself and to them, they were right all along.

"No," she says. "I won't."

"Can't?" asks Chamberlain Weiss, confused.

"Won't. As many wondrous things as I've seen during my time in Wonderland, asking me to admit such a thing is truly impossible."

"I'm somewhat taken aback," he stutters. "You realize you can't move forward. You can't become Queen. You can't return home."

"I'm aware," she whispers.

"Then what are we doing here, Mary Anne?" He slams the book closed and steps away. "You said you wanted to return home. The look in your eyes said you wanted nothing more. The Duchess traveled across the country to find you. Your companions risked death. And from what I've heard, countless people died in Rookridge and Briarwell as soon as you arrived, and I do not believe in coincidences. But now, you can easily dismiss all they've done and all that's happened, because you cannot simply say you—"

"I. Will. Not." She waits for him to call her a fraud, a failure, but his dismissal cuts more than the words could.

"Clearly you are not ready." He removes the glove from his left hand to snap for Grace. "Take her to the bailey," he orders. "I'll have the palanquin made ready."

"Are you kicking me out?" she asks, horrified.

Chamberlain Weiss's movements become erratic, twitching as he chides Mary Anne. "No. But since you've lost all motivation to return home, there's little *I* can do for you. Your *advisor* has arrived in the city by now, so go and spend the day with him. Perhaps he can coax sense back into your brain."

"You do not understand," she whispers through clenched teeth, unable to keep her tears at bay. If it were possible for her to shrink and hide inside herself, she would curl into a ball and hope to disappear from any world completely.

"I don't. And it's not my place to. I'm not your advisor, and I'm not the one who wants to leave Wonderland." He turns and exits on the far opposite side of the courtyard, leaving Mary Anne alone.

She rises and follows Grace through the cloisters and back inside the castle. Every step is labored by the embarrassment and rejection weighing on her body like anchors, whispering to herself over and over again, "impossible."

CHAPTER 27

JONATHAN

The Crest slumbers, unlike the people of Stonehaven and the Boroughs, as Jonathan climbs the white-marble stairs and empty streets to the castle. He finishes the cup of Pearl Chamomile tea and places it in the leather cup holster on his belt.

The sun crests over the horizon by the time Jonathan reaches the castle gates, the world drenched in the blues and greys of predawn. He takes hold of the heavy knocker and raps against the door three times. The deep clanks echo in the bailey. After no response and three minutes' time, by Jonathan's watch, he steps back and looks to the top of the wall. The parapets hide the guards from his view, but he can see tips of their spears and longbows sway gently.

"I've no other plans today," he calls to the guards above and those ignoring him on the other side of the gates. "Right then."

He knocks nine more times and waits, then three, five, and finally twenty-one. He almost reaches another sixteen before the door swings inward and the knocker is pulled from his grasp.

"Are you daft or simple?" the Red Knight says, the sleep not yet out of his throat and his yellow hair a mess.

"Good morning to you as well." He smiles and tips his hat. The Red Knight slams the door in his face.

"Did you really walk all the way here to ask me one question?" Jonathan grabs the knocker and at the first squeak of the hinge, the Red Knight whips the door open again. "I'm here to see Mary Anne. May I enter?"

"I am not a doorman," the Red Knight says, glaring.

"But you are a man at a door. So may I enter?" His attempt at humor falls flat.

"I will kill you where you stand."

"At least let her know we've arrived in the city?"

"I am not a messenger. I am charged with the safety of all Mirus and most of all, the castle. I will let no one simply walk in without express invitation or summons."

"I do have invitation," Jonathan says, removing his hat. "Mary Anne asked us to follow her in Briarwell."

"Show me proof and then you may enter, not a moment before. Besides, the invitation came from the strange woman. Not the Duchess. If you are in fact needed by the Duchess, or her guest, then you will be summoned. And then I shall allow you to enter. Not before." The Red Knight slams the door and lowers the iron lock bar.

Jonathan will have to wait until called upon. He takes his

flask from his jacket pocket, sips and turns to look at the forest-covered mountains outside the city wall.

He hopes Mary Anne, preoccupied and now in the Duchess's company, has forgotten about him. If so, he and March could purchase a single horse, depart the city by midday, and return to the Hollow, his table, and his teas. Their return trip would take considerably longer without Dormy's ponies, but they could take their time, stay off the main roads and live out another wild adventure, this time of their choosing.

After a few months, and several large bags of gold and silver coins, Dormy would find her way back to the Hollow. Cheshire is another matter altogether. If he has made it into capital, convincing him to leave would be impossible in every sense of the word. At least not until he finishes exorcising whatever demons have pushed him here.

Jonathan imagines being at the Hollow this morning with Cheshire and March, in the thralls of one another, basking in their glow as the sun kisses their bodies as well. Years ago, when Cheshire stayed almost a year, they did not wear a stitch of clothing during his stay, which made tea time all the more entertaining. A cock crows from below in Stonehaven and pulls Jonathan from his daydream.

Back in the Row, he pushes through a packed crowd of townspeople from all three tiers of the city. News of Dormy's return to Mirus spread quickly and her customers have grown twenty-fold since yesterday. To get near the wagon, Jonathan cuts behind the other vendors lining the street. They perk up as he approaches, since they have not had a customer of their own all morning, but he asks their forgiveness as he crosses beneath their awnings. When he reaches the wagon, he notices it is not just Dormy's reputation which has drawn the crowd.

March stands on the deck of the wagon, tossing down the wares out of Dormy's immediate reach to expedite her transactions. She wears worn leather trousers and one of Jonathan's linen shirts, too large for her small figure, sleeves rolled to her elbows and tied loosely at her waist. Both men and women customers alike stare with blatant lustful thoughts, while others glance up to appease their secret desire, and yet more stare contemptuously and confused why a daughter of Mirus, a member of the wealthiest family in the capital, would act in such a fashion. She unapologetically is who she wants to be regardless of lineage or expectations, and the townspeople, especially those from the Crest, cannot stomach her conviction.

Your tea is ready, her wink tells Jonathan, never breaking her rhythm with Dormy.

A warm cup of Seaside Jasmine waits on a barrel at the back of the wagon. The aroma and a gentle warmth cascade down his body. He finishes his cup quicker than he normally would, while still giving proper respect to the tea leaves, then hangs his hat and jacket on a peg inside the wagon, and assists Dormy on the ground with her sales.

She barks for items and he and March fulfill her orders. "Crate of scrap metal. The copper, not the iron, lashed to the rear. *The Oyster Maiden,* fifteenth book from the floor, third stack from the cauldron. Eight yards of silk. Sack of flour. Necklace with a nightingale, pearl missing from the eye. Jar of pork fat. Empty pickle barrel."

Customers continue to pour into the Row from both ends

to shop at Dormy's wagon. Vendors and shop owners mingle in the crowd to spy and draw patrons back to their stalls, but none will budge.

They work through midday, when the sun clears the tallest buildings of Stonehaven. March finds opportunities to drop a walnut, berry, or bolt onto Jonathan below, for him to look up and catch the smile in her eye. They sweat and laugh while they work, and could not be happier.

"Gold ring with stags embossed," Dormy shouts.

Inside the main compartment of the wagon, Jonathan finds the small wooden jewelry box beneath a stack of porcelain plates and fumbles too long in the small drawer packed with an assortment of jewelry. Dormy pushes past him and plucks it out immediately, drops in three newly acquired rings from her unsuspecting customers, and returns to her sales. Her ability to keep up with the demand amazes Jonathan and always has. Even if he and March were not helping, she would still manage.

March whistles a nightjar's chirp from the deck. Jonathan jumps from the wagon and searches the crowd for what March sees.

A red, iron horse head, the Red Knight's helmet, crests above the townspeople and pushes his way through the crowd. Jonathan's stomach immediately feels empty at the sight of the Duchess's ivory-colored palanquin following the Red Knight, carried by eight additional soldiers.

The crowd whispers in awe, and townspeople reach out to brush their hands against the elaborate oak and alder reliefs carved into the wood. Some try to peek through the small mesh screens behind the carvings, hoping to catch a glimpse of the

Duchess. Jonathan glances at March and she knows to meet him at the rear of the wagon.

The soldiers set the palanquin down in the shade of one of the wagon's awnings between the wagon and the stone wall behind them, and then position themselves on the other side to block any prying eyes. The Red Knight opens the door facing away from the crowd.

Mary Anne steps out, and Jonathan breathes again. She looks a completely different woman than he met in the Rookwood. She stands straighter, more poised, yet worry still pinches her brow.

"May I present, Mary Anne Elizabeth," the Red Knight says. His helmet adds a metallic tinge to his voice.

"We've met." Jonathan would pay ten gold coins to see the expression behind the Red Knight's visor.

"Hello, Jonathan," says Mary Anne. "It is wonderful to see you again. March, you as well."

March leans against the wagon and returns a quick raise of her eyebrows. *Fuck you,* they say.

"Hello, Mary Anne." Jonathan wipes the sweat from his brow. "Your disposition has much improved since last we spoke."

"Not needing to run for my life and a warm bath does wonders for the complexion." She and Jonathan are the only two who chuckle.

"But you're still here. Could the Duchess not help you after all?"

"It's complicated." She recounts her adventure within the castle, describes its beauty, getting lost, the throne room door, the Tenets, and the conversations with the Duchess.

"Wait. Queen?" Jonathan catches up to the conversation. "You must become Queen?"

"I had the same reaction. It sounds impossible, but the word has little meaning here I find." She smiles at Jonathan, referring to his advice in the Rookwood.

"Well then, I wish you well. Your Highness?"

"Oh, don't, please. Call me Mary Anne. I need someone to keep me grounded in this fantasy."

"As you wish, Mary Anne. Well, from your attire and your company, it seems you're in excellent hands. I cannot say it's been a pleasure"—he laughs—"but it has been an adventure. We wish you fair travels on your return home."

Jonathan can see March's smirk out of the corner of his eye.

But Mary Anne looks at the ground and fidgets with her dress. The empty sensation returns to Jonathan's stomach.

"I've done something without your consent, and I fear you will protest." Mary Anne wrings her hands. "You see, I had to declare an advisor. Someone to help guide me through the process of the tenets. And..."

Jonathan knows the words she is about to say, three simple words, but it does not lessen his fear or dread.

"I chose you," she continues.

Jonathan's ears and eyes go numb. The bustling sounds in the Row turn to hollow wind, and he looks through Mary Anne, past the city and mountains to the Hollow, moving farther out of his reach with every passing day. Cobwebs collect on his cabinet, weevils take up residence in his grain store, and his table sits empty while rain and leaves fill his neglected teacups.

"Jonathan?" Mary Anne's voice pulls him back to the market. "You're cross with me."

"No, not in the slightest." Jonathan shakes the dream from his mind and fumbles with his words. "Unexpected. But what do I know of royal matters? I'm not sure how I can help."

"I don't know either, but I had to choose, and yours was the first name to come to mind. I don't know or trust anyone else," she says in a half whisper. "You, at least, kept your word, and that is enough."

"Perhaps we can discuss more details before—"

"Her decision," the Red Knight cuts Jonathan off, "is official and cannot be undone. You are to be her advisor while she fulfills the Tenets."

"How long?" Jonathan asks, not ready for the answer.

"Days. Months. Years." The Red Knight bites his words. "Hard to tell."

He does not have to look, but he hears March climb back into the wagon, and feels the pain in her heart.

Every step away is a step back, he repeats, thinking of her. The numbness spreads and consumes Jonathan's face and chest. If there are words in his mind or breath in his lungs, they are outside his reach.

"I'm sorry," Mary Anne says.

He can hear the emptiness in her apology, but he understands. There was no choice.

"Forgive me." He collects himself. "I made a promise to see

you home and I have not yet fulfilled that promise. I accept whatever duties there may be. What duties are there?"

"Advise." A half smile grows on her face. "I'd like to become familiar with Mirus's people and the city. All of Wonderland, really. And I wanted to ask if you and the others would accompany me."

"All of us?" He chuckles. "You're brave. Well then, perhaps a tour is in order?" Jonathan slips on his jacket and hat. "Will your escort be joining us?" he asks the Red Knight. "Shall I walk beside the palanquin or perhaps ride on top?"

Before the Red Knight can reply with a snide remark, March whistles from the deck again. Different. Urgent.

Jonathan rushes to the front of the wagon where the crowd of customers stands back twenty paces, and in their void, the Twins, Lysander and Uriah, smirk from atop silver-clad white stallions.

How could so much go wrong on such a beautiful day. Jonathan sighs.

"I must say," Lysander says to Uriah, "fortune smiles upon us."

"Agreed, brother." Uriah flips the long hairs from his face. "Hello, Audrianna. Jonathan."

March crouches on the deck, her hands reaching for the pistols hidden behind the small planters at her feet.

"There's no need for such actions." Uriah snickers. "You're not the reason we've come." He takes a small lock of brown hair tied with twine, Mary Anne's hair, and passes it under his nose.

"We want the girl," Lysander says with a deep growl in his voice.

Jonathan grabs Dormy by the shoulder and moves her behind him, feigning ignorance.

"Don't play stupid." Lysander's thick fingers circle the pommel of his sword. "The Otherworlder."

Jonathan watches the eyes of the crowd swell. Their whispers spread faster than even he could ever catch or dispel. The Red Knight and soldiers emerge from behind the wagon, hands on their hilts. Jonathan swallows the nervous lump in his throat, knowing this is what Lysander and Uriah want.

"You two have no business here," the Red Knight commands. "Be on your way."

"Wrong." Uriah addresses the crowd. "The people of Wonderland, the citizens of Mirus, have a right to know about your plans. Your machinations."

"This is not the time nor place." The Red Knight tries to maintain the control he never had to begin with.

"You plan to seat another woman on the throne," Uriah continues, shouting for all the Row to hear. "What good has ever come from a queen? Division. War. Hardship across the land. And not just a woman, but an Otherworlder."

The crowd's whispers become murmurs. And when Mary Anne appears from around the palanquin, the murmurs become gasps. Every townsperson in the Row stares, mouth agape and eyes wide. Some townspeople strain their neck to get a better view of Mary Anne. Others scowl and turn their faces. A few others run out of the Row to spread the news.

"There she is." Uriah licks his teeth.

The soldiers draw their swords and kick Dormy's tables over for barricades, her wares spilling onto the dirt.

"You have no right to sit on the throne, which is ours by blood and right," Lysander roars.

"Your reign and line ended long ago, if history serves correct," says Jonathan.

"Now you're little more than spoiled, pampered children without their toy," says March.

"How dare you?" Lysander rears his horse. "Our forefathers sat upon the throne and their blood will sit there again."

Uriah trots his horse around the edge of the crowd. "Do you, citizens of Mirus, want another queen on the throne? An outsider? An Otherworlder who has no claim of love for your land?"

The market falls to silence and then a woman bends down slowly, picks up a stone from the ground and whispers, "Death to the outsider."

An elderly man at the front of the crowd says, "Hail to the God Queen Mother," under his breath.

"A whore will never rule Wonderland," a woman says louder. The people next to her glance at her with disgust.

"Our world, not hers," a young man shouts from the back.

"A queen must be on the throne," a young girl says fearfully.

Jonathan ushers Mary Anne to the rear of the wagon and backs himself into the driver's hatch to grip his long sword lying inside, hoping he does not need to use it again. He watches the eyes of the townspeople dart from one person to the next. Beads of sweat form on their brows wondering who will ignite the powder keg set by Lysander and Uriah. Jonathan can almost hear the air crackle as the fuse shrinks. The crowd is divided in belief, but not physically. They turn to one another wondering where their neighbors' allegiance lies and who will spark the violent brawl at the tip of everyone's trembling fingers. And at the center, Lysander and Uriah sit proudly upon their horses, smiling at Mary Anne.

The Red Knight takes off his helmet and drops it to the ground. "Enough of this foolishness." He takes the ram's horn from his belt and blows a long, sour note in the air, and in less than a minute, Mirusian soldiers swarm the Row. Twenty, thirty, then upwards of forty. Half position within the crowd to quell the tension, while the rest circle Lysander and Uriah, swords and spears drawn.

"I'm not sure why this show of force is necessary against us. We haven't come to fight." Uriah smiles like a serpent. "We've not moved, let alone reached for our weapons."

"Don't play stupid," the Red Knight shouts. "We see your machinations."

"Whether or not you're here to fight, we will defend Mary Anne," says Jonathan. "She will become Queen, regardless of your interference."

"Mary Anne," hisses Uriah. "How proper. We shall see."

"Leave," Jonathan says through his teeth. The muscles across his chest and arm tighten as he grips his sword harder.

"This woman is under the protection of the Duchess and Mirus," the Red Knight says loud enough for the Row to hear, after the other soldiers have quieted the mob. "Any violence against her will be an act of sedition and will result in the immediate execution of all involved. Do I make myself clear?"

Half the crowd disperses, divided, their faces telling their allegiance.

"What a shame." Lysander grips his reins. "They would hold an Otherworlder woman in higher regard than the hardworking men of Mirus. Do what you like, but there are only so many soldiers, and the people of Mirus and Wonderland are legion."

"But as you wish." Uriah runs his fingers through his hair needlessly. "No harm will come to the girl by our hands. We shall reacclimate ourselves to the city which once belonged to our family. Perfectly within our rights."

"We will see each other again." Lysander turns his horse and says, "Farewell," as he trots away through the crowd.

"Should you need us, we're staying in the Crest. If I'm not mistaken, two doors from your mother, Audrianna." Uriah glances up to her. "Have a most pleasant day." He swings his hair, tugs on the reins, and trots after Lysander out of the Row.

Jonathan knows March's pistols are in her hands. She could end them both here and now with a single shot to the back of both their heads, but there are citizens in the crowd and even more throughout the city loyal to them and who will not accept the end of the Old Kings' line.

Tension and whispers swirl in the air, but the Red Knight commands the remaining townspeople to return to their business. Most listen, several kind hearts help Dormy reset her tables, and stragglers stay to peek around the wagon to see Mary Anne.

Jonathan finds Mary Anne behind the wagon. She sits on the ground, back against the stone wall, and knees to her chest. She has never looked smaller.

"I can't do this," she says. "I can't. I don't see how it's possible." She stumbles over her words. "Wonderland and its people must accept me to become Queen. But how can I ever win over a person when half of them call me whore and want me dead? Not to mention conspirators who rally forces against me."

Her worries have merit. As long as Lysander and Uriah are in Mirus, they will poison the people's minds against Mary Anne at every turn. In order for her to overcome, Jonathan and the others will need to reassess how to find their way out of this unforeseen tangle. He can trust March to stay by his side. Although dubious toward Mary Anne until now, March's hatred for the Twins surpasses what she feels against her.

He reaches out a hand to help Mary Anne up. "Stand, please. The ground is no place for a queen. And you must not let them see you affected."

The Red Knight saunters to the back of the wagon, flicking dirt from his helmet.

"What is our next course of action?" Jonathan asks him.

"Lysander and Uriah don't want to keep their schemes secret. We will keep a close watch of who they speak to, where they go." The Red Knight slides his helmet back over his head and clips the latches to secure it in place. "There are already four thousand soldiers on patrol in the capital and another five hundred on the outer ramparts. And twenty thousand more who can be ready within a fortnight. Most are loyal to the crown."

"Most?" Mary Anne asks. She hides her hands behind her back to keep their trembling secret.

The Red Knight holds open the door of the palanquin for Mary Anne. "We will return to the castle immediately and consult with the Duchess. As advisor, you will need to be alive. They said no harm would come to Mary Anne. They said nothing of you lot. I suggest you move inside immediately."

Taken off guard, Jonathan points to his watch in his trousers, his flask in his jacket, at March, and his trunk of teas lashed to the side of Dormy's wagon.

"No," says Mary Anne. "I can see you need time to prepare. And from what I've witnessed, you and the others can take care of yourselves, should the need arise. Besides, with over four thousand soldiers in the capital, I would hope to be safe within the castle walls. Tomorrow afternoon?"

Her answer surprises Jonathan. Mary Anne has pressed the importance and urgency of returning home at every turn. But now, a troubled calm covers her face, as if she has realized she will be in Wonderland much longer than expected. "Are you sure?" he asks.

"Yes. I've work to do on the second Tenet and it would be best to do so alone, I feel. It turns out I'm not in as big of a rush to return home as originally thought." She nods with a sad smile as the Red Knight closes and latches the door of the palanquin. He snaps and orders the remaining twenty soldiers in the Row to join the escort to the castle.

Jonathan reaches for the flask in his breast pocket, takes three swigs, and slumps against a barrel, shaking. The feeling comes back to his face with the unwelcome sensation of one thousand insects scurrying across his skin. He runs his hands down his face, clammy palm relieving the heat and tinkling, and wants to think of the comforting images of home, but his thoughts are frozen, and his body as well. He is not ready for this. Before he daydreamed of the Hollow, but now he wants nothing more than to bolt from the city and disappear with March and Dormy. But he could not return to the Hollow, the soldiers would hunt them down and he will never allow them to find his home.

Jonathan focuses on individual grains of dirt at his feet until the edges of his sight blur and shimmer. He gives into the cold isolation his mind sinks to, unable to control or fight against it, but at times like these, with the world encroaching upon him, he embraces the chance for his mind to retreat into nothing.

CHAPTER 28

MARY ANNE

The Red Knight and soldiers carry Mary Anne's palanquin to the castle at double the pace they walked to the Row. She bobs and jostles back and forth and has to brace her hands against both sides to keep upright. This is not how Mary Anne imagined her first day in the capital would begin. She wants to think of the two men in the market and why they set against her, but returning to the safety of the castle walls is her only concern.

She anxiously looks out of every screen for the two men from the market in case they appear in the soldiers' blind spots. Townspeople stare and gesture at her from the other side of the screen. They cannot be privy to what took place in the market, but she wants to know what they say none the less. But the rhythmic crunch of the soldiers' armor and boots against the cobblestones overpower her senses.

When they cross into the upper tier, they stop just before a small bridge and the Red Knight sends two soldiers ahead to scout the area. In the uncomfortable quiet, Mary Anne can feel every eye upon her, from the well-dressed men and women on the street, and from their windows and balconies above. Even the soldiers' eyes glance to Mary Anne through the side of their visors. The sound of her breath suffocates her in the small wooden cage.

The scouts signal to the Red Knight from across the bridge, and the metallic procession quickens through the twisting streets until they reach the gates of the castle. Soldiers with spears and shields at least seven feet tall pour out and position themselves in rows in front of the castle gates, under the orders of the Red Knight, as the others carry Mary Anne through. The two giant men who operate the gates stare down at her with blank expressions as she passes, and then turn three iron locking mechanisms into place once the gates shut.

The Duchess waits at the top of the stairs and beckons Mary Anne with quick, shaking hands. Once out of the palanquin, Mary Anne picks up her dress and runs to meet her.

"My dear, are you well?" the Duchess asks, taking both of Mary Anne's hands into hers.

"I don't know," Mary Anne answers truthfully, shaken.

"Come with me." The Duchess wraps one arm around her. "Tell me what happened, dear." She leads her up the stairs, through more winding hallways to a new wing of the castle.

"In the marketplace," says Mary Anne, slowing her breath. "I went to speak with Jonathan, and two men approached on horseback. One brawny with a beard and the other thin with long hair."

A disgusted sound falls from the Duchess's mouth. "Never you mind those two."

"They said they wanted me." From the lust in their eyes, Mary Anne fears they want more from her than to step away from the crown.

"They are Lysander and Uriah." The Duchess heaves a heavy sigh. "They are the last remaining blood of the First Kings of Wonderland. Every so often they emerge from between the legs of whatever poor woman they've seduced and incite trouble. To them, women are inferior. Property. And should sit at the foot of a throne. Never on it."

"There were people in the marketplace who believed as they did, called out curses and wished me dead. The Red Knight and the soldiers had to intervene to calm the street."

"Some still cling to the old ways," says the Duchess. "Everyone is entitled to their opinion."

"How am I ever to become Queen with opposition? How do I make them accept me?"

"Make them?" the Duchess asks with a raised eyebrow. "You cannot force them to accept. You must win their favor."

"How?"

"How, indeed? Remember, simple, not easy." At the end of a winding hallway, the Duchess opens a small wooden door to the base of a tower. Two staircases with wide stone rails wind up the walls, spiraling into a single point above. "I've something to show you."

"Up there?" Mary Anne squints to estimate the tower's height. "A trip to the top would take an entire day."

The Duchess shakes her head with a sly smile and pulls a

golden lever at the base of one of the staircases. Iron chains rattle and snake up through channels recessed in the tower walls Mary Anne did not notice before. The rattle grows louder as what appears to be the bottom of a wooden bucket comes into view. But her jaw drops as an elegant, gilded elevator settles at their feet.

The Duchess opens the thin, retractable gate and ushers Mary Anne inside.

"Will wonders never cease?" Mary Anne cannot take her eyes from the polished wood, swirls adorning the metalwork, the dial on the back wall with tick marks for floor numbers, and a curled golden lever.

"May I?" Mary Anne asks.

The Duchess steps in and closes the gate. "Whenever you're ready."

Mary Anne grips the handle and pauses. *This shouldn't be possible,* she thinks. Though not a history scholar, she realizes the amount of anachronisms in this world grows by the day. Jonathan's timepiece was the first to feel out of place once she realized there was a time discrepancy. Elements of March's clothing seem oddly modern by Mary Anne's standards, compared to the rest of the people she has seen while in Wonderland. Though fundamentally different, the train is, for all intents and purposes, a steam engine with the innards of a clock. And now the elevator she stands in resembles those in London. She must give credence to Cheshire's words and assume not everything does originates in her world.

She pulls back on the handle, and the elevator ascends. It twists slightly as it rises higher into the tower, past beautiful landscape paintings and statues on every floor which sink below Mary Anne's feet. The Duchess names the different regions depicted in each painting, but Mary Anne still ponders the elevator.

It slows and stops at the highest possible floor with nowhere to go but a single arched door in front of the gate. The Duchess opens both and sunlight floods the small space. Mary Anne shields her eyes and follows the Duchess out onto the balcony of the highest tower of the castle. The dizzying height overwhelms Mary Anne, and she slumps to the ground to keep from seeing over the edge.

"Do mind the wind." The Duchess offers her a hand. "Stand up dear, you'll dirty your dress."

Her hand shakes in the Duchess's palm, but she rises and presses her back to the wall, eyes clenched, as if the next gust would carry her from the tower.

"It's safe up here," the Duchess answers before she is asked. "Open your eyes. You're missing everything." She places Mary Anne's hand on the parapets.

Mary Anne slowly allows her eyelids to flutter open and her fear falls away with the wind as she takes in the full glory of Wonderland. In the distance, mountains as beautiful as stained glass rise above a gentle mist at their feet, and their tops cut through a sky more blue than any ocean she could envision. And in the valley between them, distant hills and forests disappear into the horizon.

Below, the afternoon sun shines on the entire expanse of Mirus, with different colored roofs marking the separate tiers of the city. Red, brown, and grey. She rounds the balcony to the opposite side of the tower and grows weak in her knees at the sight of the expansive hedge maze garden consuming the castle grounds. And beyond, the sea sparkles below as if made of every color of precious gemstone in her world and theirs.

"All of this is Wonderland?" she asks.

"Magnificent, isn't it?" The Duchess stands beside Mary Anne and looks down into the garden. "This and more. Mirus has been my home for many years, and its splendor never ceases to steal my breath."

Mary Anne shakes her head and smiles, unable to find any word suitable to describe the grandeur before her. She completes the circle of the balcony, back to the city side and notices the pillar she rode past yesterday rising above the trees, cutting the horizon in half.

"What is that, madam?" Mary Anne asks. "The giant stone pillar."

"You've a keen eye. That is a Pinnacle of Wonderland. Far off to the east, you can almost see another." She points close to Mary Anne's face for her to follow. "And then farther still to the north, one juts out between the mountain tops. Six in all, each marking a different region in Wonderland."

"Their mere existence seems..." She stops herself.

The Duchess chuckles. "There's much to digest. But the wonders of this country stretch far beyond the land. It's the people as well. Below you there are thousands, and beyond the walls countless more, all wishing Wonderland once more had a queen upon the throne."

The weight of such a thought is more dizzying than the height of the tower. "Are you sure?"

"The people and the land need a queen on the throne," says the Duchess.

Mary Anne waits for her to continue, but the Duchess leaves her comment hanging in the wind like bait. "Why?" Mary Anne finally asks.

"During the reign of kings, which was most of Wonderland's history, the country was under the heel of war. The kings were obsessed with the conquest of other lands and the subjugation of those who lived in their own. It took one woman, the first Queen, to defy them. She rose to power and ended their tyranny and brought peace and prosperity to Wonderland."

"But Lysander and Uriah spoke of division and hardship."

"Their tongues spew only half truths or lies. When a queen sits on the throne, Mirus resonates with vitality and the country thrives." Whether it be the warmth of the Duchess's smile or the beauty of the land, Mary Anne's curiosity swells and overshadows her worries.

"The first Queen. Was she from Wonderland or my world?" Mary Anne asks.

"No." A soft smile grows across the Duchess's face. "Queen Dinah was of Wonderland and of royal blood. She deposed her own grandfather, King Muiread."

"How... how did she accomplish such a task?" The tale captures Mary Anne's attention. She expects the Duchess to describe a warrior queen, proud, strong, fearless, leading battalions of knights as they descend upon the castle. She wears shimmering silver armor from head to toe with angel wings engraved on her back.

"Queen Dinah was a gentle soul and had a proclivity to

books and exploration," says the Duchess. "Whether it be by happenstance or destiny, she somehow unearthed the Book of Queens from a sealed reliquary, forgotten to time, deep within the castle. She completed the Tenets, became Queen, and saved her country and her people."

"She sounds lovely," says Mary Anne. "What happened to her?"

The Duchess loses her smile and locks eyes with Mary Anne. "She was murdered. Taken before her time, at the height of her accomplishments, by a foul, loathsome, selfish villain."

A chill down the back of Mary Anne's neck shakes her, realizing no one, not even a queen, in this world is safe.

"That's the abridged version, of course, and a tale for another day." The Duchess takes a deep breath and collects herself. "But because of her, Wonderland was able to emerge as a new country with a new purpose. A Queendom. The book she found, the book now in your possession, is the only reason we know women from your world are able to become Queen. Royal blood or Otherworld women. No one else can."

"But how could she overturn a kingdom?"

The Duchess's cheeks rise high and tight with her returned smile. "Mary Anne, think of what we spoke of yesterday outside the throne room. The answer will come. Let go of any thought of reason clouding your judgement and ask."

She considers her miraculous, albeit frightening, emergence into Wonderland, the throne room doors which will open of their own accord, pillars stretching into the heavens, and a land which can make decisions. She lets herself ask the question hanging on her lips since she first saw Jonathan's candles. "You speak of magic?"

"Mary Anne, magic is for street performers who entertain for coin." The Duchess speaks through her wide smile. "I refer to the Grand Arcana. It's the real power flowing through Wonderland. And the only person in the world who can wield it, is a queen."

"I... I... I..." Mary Anne stutters, unable to wrap her mind around the existence of real magic.

"Tenet Four covers the Arcana." She tilts her head to look into Mary Anne's eyes. "Weiss tells me you're having difficulty with the second Tenet.

"Yes," Mary Anne answers simply. The sick wave of humiliation crests out of her mind and down her body. She inhales, ready to defend her actions with Chamberlain Weiss.

"Don't speak." The Duchess holds up a finger. "Until you're ready. I say this with all sincerity, you need no excuses or justification, because they won't help you. The second Tenet, simple as it is, is the most revealing and difficult, in my opinion. Take your time."

Mary Anne knows the Duchess speaks the truth. Her kind yet honest words are enough to ebb the tide of Mary Anne's thoughts. She does not want to take time for self-discovery. She wants to return home. But there is no choice.

"Weiss says he can do nothing for me until I complete the second Tenet," she tells the Duchess.

"Balderdash." The Duchess laughs. "Weiss has a proclivity for the overdramatic. There is plenty he can still teach you about Wonderland and its people. But he is correct, you cannot progress forward until it's completed. So, think through whatever it is which blocks you, but don't let Weiss, Lysander, or Uriah diminish your resolve."

"Thank you." Mary Anne matches the Duchess's smile, and boards the elevator with her once more. "Thank you again for your encouraging words."

"I'm tasked with the safety of Wonderland and its people until a new queen takes the throne. As far as I am concerned, you fall under both categories. So it's both my duty and my pleasure."

In England, Mary Anne's world and thoughts were small, but here a vast unknown country lies before her, whose borders are so far they are unfathomable. Again, her heartbeat overpowers her thoughts, a mixture of fear and excitement. The journey she finds herself on is beyond her wildest imagination. She is unsure how long it will take her, but whenever she does return home, it will be as a changed woman.

Grace meets Mary Anne at the bottom of the tower, and the Duchess bids them farewell for the day. She asks Grace to take her to Chamberlain Weiss if she knows his location. She nods and leads Mary Anne to the same courtyard where he paces in a circle in front of the bench where the book sits.

She thanks Grace, sits on the bench, unlaces her boots, and sets the book on her lap. Chamberlain Weiss's ears perk as she approaches but he tries to maintain an aura of professionalism. He sits next to her, eyes waiting.

"I'm not prepared for the second Tenet. But I am ready to learn," she says. "Please. Teach me."

CHAPTER 29

JONATHAN

He can see March kneel in front of him but cannot move or respond to her calls. She takes him by the hand and leads him into the wagon, a passenger in his own body. She stands face to face with him, and he watches her mouth move but cannot hear her words.

"Jonathan." Her distant voice finally breaks through. "Come back to us."

He blinks and finds himself standing in the upper compartment of the wagon at dusk, with March's doe eyes pulling him back from his oblivion.

"Us?" he asks.

She steps aside to reveal Cheshire reclining on sacks of flour.

"We've only had to wait two hours," Cheshire says, a playful grin upon his lips.

Jonathan feared Briarwell was the last time he would see

Cheshire for another decade. He wants to tell him to leave immediately for his own safety, but he cannot bring himself to say a word. In this moment, to be whole with March and Cheshire gives him the strength to calm the storm within his mind and push down the thoughts of the castle, the Duchess, Mary Anne, Lysander, Uriah, Weiss. He will resume the struggle against them tomorrow.

Jonathan kneels, lays his head against Cheshire's stomach, and wraps his arms around his waist. His head raises and lowers with each breath. March sits beside Cheshire and runs her fingers smoothly through Jonathan's hair, while Cheshire circles his fingertips on the back of Jonathan's neck. His body relaxes and releases a soft whimper against Cheshire's muscles.

He kisses the firm skin below Cheshire's navel and releases the pent-up yearning within them all. They topple stacks of books and baskets, which Jonathan will correct later, as they all push their trousers to their ankles with their feet, kissing each other and laughing softly. Dormy climbs over them a handful of times for the items she needs and, as always, never interrupts.

When Jonathan feels the tendrils creeping up from the cockles of his mind, he slides between Cheshire and March and reaches behind him, pulling Cheshire in with March's hands guiding, welcoming the sharp, exquisite sensation. He wraps his free arm around March's waist. She welcomes him as well, pressing hard against his hips and hooking her leg over his and Cheshire's body. Jonathan trembles with the union of their three bodies, the tangle of their spirits. The rhythmic pulses against his body free his mind of worry, fleeting as it may be.

"You can't," he whispers to Cheshire through his short, panting breaths.

"Can't what?" Cheshire asks, pausing, his face pressed against Jonathan's back.

"You can't leave us again—" Before Jonathan can finish his thought, Cheshire resumes, stronger than before. He turns Jonathan's head back to stop his words with a passionate kiss. March gently grabs his chin and turns him back to her to share the kiss. She matches Cheshire's tempo, causing Jonathan's body to shake involuntarily, succumbing to the pure ecstasy of the moment.

Well into the night, the dim moonlight spills into the wagon and onto the trio, parched, drenched in sweat and bliss, and Jonathan at peace for the moment. Cheshire rests on Jonathan's right, head on his chest, and March on his left.

"How long had you been in here before we came in?" Jonathan asks Cheshire.

"Most of the day, sleeping on and off in a crawl space. The bit with Lysander and Uriah finally woke me."

"You've been here the entire day and didn't say a word?"

"It was the safest place I would manage before the dawn." Cheshire turns to face Jonathan. "Besides, I wanted to watch you two follow Dormy's commands. Move as if you didn't have a care in the world. Drink tea. Watch both of your muscles as you stretch and work."

"Why?"

"Because since I've returned you've done nothing but run and plan and run more, all because of Mary Anne. Even when we all laid together, I could still tell your mind spun with worries of her, coming here, and when you'd be able to return home. I wanted to have a moment of peace for myself where I could watch you both the way I remember you, the way I want to see you."

The moment of sincerity catches Jonathan off guard. Cheshire divulges little emotion no matter the time he spends with Jonathan and March. His true thoughts remain hidden for everyone behind his beautiful, enigmatic smile. Perhaps Cheshire's own veil of worry has lifted since he has entered the castle, cracking his exterior ever so slightly.

But he knows the capital is the most dangerous place for them all to be, most of all Cheshire. To him, the castle is a prize at the end of a long hunt, but to Jonathan it is a cage. So many things could go wrong within the city walls, and he worries he will lose Cheshire.

"Cheshire," says Jonathan, worried if he lingers any longer, he will be discovered.

"You say my name differently." Cheshire taps his fingers on Jonathan's chest. "Do you know that? Than anyone. There are times it actually makes me consider staying with you and March for good."

"He has that effect," says March. She reaches across Jonathan and runs her fingers through Cheshire's hair. "Will you stay the night with us?"

"For a bit. I've much to attend to," Cheshire says with his grin growing ever wider. "But since we can't be in the freedom the Hollow affords us, I'll find better arrangements for the three of us. Somewhere we no longer have to restrain ourselves from prying ears."

"Indeed," says March. "I've grown tired of catering to the needs of others over our own."

"I'm glad you're here with us," says Jonathan. "For the trouble I fear quickly approaching over the horizon." He wants to stay in the moment, but cannot keep the thoughts of the next day from creeping in.

"*Us* as in you and March and Dormy. Or does *us* now include Mary Anne?" Cheshire asks in a sharp tone. "I'm unsure when she became one of our party."

"Since we stumbled upon her," says Jonathan. "And I do mean we, since you were the first to come upon her."

March's eyes slowly raise to Cheshire, with partially playful accusation. His eyes widen and his mouth hangs open, like a child trying to deny breaking a dish, when it lays in pieces at his feet.

"You've fought with us before," Jonathan continues. "Will you not again?"

"I fought in Briarwell because they threatened your life, March's life, and Dormy's." Cheshire lays back against Jonathan's shoulder, looking out the window to the night sky. "It was only afterward I discovered Mary Anne could be of use to me. But now I'm here, and that's over."

"You'll help because I'm asking." The conversation took a turn Jonathan did not expect.

"You assume much," says Cheshire. "I suffered her only because of you. But she's served her purpose as far as I'm concerned. Make no mistake. There is not trouble on the horizon. It knocks upon your door. It sits with you now. I give you both fair warning. Things are about to get much worse in the city and the castle, by my hand. Remember my words in Rookridge. If there comes a time when I must choose between my path and hers, I will not hesitate to sacrifice or kill her myself." Cheshire's words hang in the air, charging it with a pure undeniable tension they can all feel crawl up their skin.

"Mary Anne has chosen me to be her royal advisor," says Jonathan, not sure what else to say. But perhaps knowing Jonathan will be with Mary Anne will frustrate Cheshire's thoughts of murder. At least for now.

"What the fuck does that mean?" asks Cheshire after a pause.

"I haven't a clue." Jonathan runs his hands through Cheshire's tangle of hair. "I'm to find out tomorrow at the castle."

"You'll be spending a lot of time in the castle then?" Cheshire asks with a distinctly brighter tone than before. "Good. I'm going to get inside the castle one way or another. And once I do, I doubt I'll leave anytime soon. If you wish to see me more"—Cheshire presses against Jonathan—"you should be inside the castle as well. I'll be glad to have you two near."

"But how will you—"

"I have my ways."

"Yes, you do."

He holds Cheshire against him, to keep him close. As long as Cheshire is with him, Jonathan can keep him safe. But his eyes close for what he thinks is a second, and when he opens them, March sleeps with her head on his chest, and the right side of his body is cold, and Cheshire gone.

Too late to walk back to the inn, Jonathan slips his arm

from under March and looks out the window. Outside, Dormy still welcomes customers by lantern, and pairs of soldiers keep watch every twenty paces. He pulls a shabby wool blanket from a shelf and lies with March again, covering them both, wishing Cheshire would have stayed. But Jonathan knows night is the opportune time for him to go about his business, whatever it may be. He nuzzles his lips against March's forehead. The worries of tomorrow try to crawl back into his mind, but he breathes March in and pushes them back into the darkness. Her light will keep him safe through the night.

"Every step away is a step back," he whispers in her ear, "to you."

CHAPTER 30

CHESHIRE

Cheshire sits near the window and stares at the moon beyond the fading light of the sunset. Her smile will not make his work easy this night, but he is grateful to see her none the less. He reaches down and runs his fingers through March and Jonathan's hair, careful not to disturb their dreams.

He imagines what would have happened if he allowed Mary Anne to die in the Rookwood the night they crossed paths. He would have left her to die at the hands of the Ace, waited for the Ace to search elsewhere, and then joined Jonathan and March lying in the soft grass of the Hollow beneath a sky dominated by thousands of stars, their bodies cocooned around each other to fight off the chill in the night air. If not the Hollow, then the catacombs, sheathed in their icy embrace, hundreds of miles away. But he is thankful fate played a different hand, allowing him entrance to Mirus.

He pulls his trousers on and wraps his sash tightly around his waist, kisses Jonathan and March on the forehead, and climbs down the ladder. Before he can depart or pocket more nuts, Dormy stops him.

"What grand adventure are you off to?" She holds out a small basket of biscuits and fruit for him.

"I'm searching for something." He grabs several biscuits and shoves them into his pockets with the nuts and plums from earlier. "That's for me to know." Cheshire leaves by the rear door and jumps to an iron flagpole attached high on the wall.

"Come along now." Dormy follows him. "It's only fair. Consider it payment for everything you've nicked from me. What are you looking for?"

"A way into the castle," Cheshire concedes. "Nothing too important."

"I could help. I could stow you away and drive you right through the front gates."

"If they search your wagon every time you enter the city, imagine what would happen if you tried to drive through the castle gates. They'd dismantle every piece to make certain I wasn't on board."

"Oh." Dormy grabs hold of her upper arm. "Best not then."

"But perhaps you can help me." He hangs upside down by his knees, eye to eye with Dormy. "You come to Mirus often. By chance, do you know William and Patricia?"

"Bill and Pat?" She smiles as she grabs a lantern off a hook above the door and tries to light it. "Of course."

"Bill and Pat," he repeats. "Where can I find them?"

"That's easy. They live in a small cabin on the cliff side below the wall, just outside the main gate."

"Outside? That does me no good. I just got into the city. I'm not about to leave again. Not yet."

"You need them or a way into the castle?"

"One in the same." Cheshire thinks of the street near the prison and whether Bill and Pat walk the same route every night out of the city. If he returned to the jail, he could wait the entire night and not see them again. If they leave by the main gates, Cheshire could catch up to them, but the long causeway over the Boroughs offers no places to hide, and soldiers line the entire bridge. "Damn the soldiers," he says under his breath.

"The soldiers?"

"Yes. They're everywhere in the city." Cheshire drops and takes the striking stones from his pocket. "Like ants. Definitely makes searching more difficult."

"A shame you can't find what you want where there aren't any soldiers." Dormy holds out the lantern. The sparks catch on the wick and a soft orange glow envelops them.

"Interesting point." His eyes follow the edge of the soft orange orb they stand in. Weak, but it pushes against the dull blue night. "Thank you." He climbs to the roofs of the nearby buildings. "By the by, you have customers."

Dormy gasps and runs with her glow to the tables at the front of her wagon.

Cheshire looks to both ends of the Row where soldiers stand guard as before with their torches. He runs to the west end overlooking the quadrangle to find more soldiers and torches. On the adjacent streets, more soldiers, all with torches.

The houses and shops on every street are awash with orange all the way to their rooftops, but only where a soldier stands or walks. He questions why they would make themselves stand out if they were hunting him. Unless their purpose has not been to hunt him, but to draw his attention.

Cheshire races across the rooftops back to the temple from the night before, and from its bell tower he can see clearly now he knows what to look for. The orange glow from the jail rises against the city wall far in the distance to his left, the Crest glows like a dishonest halo above Stonehaven, orange smoke rises from the Forge, and even the Row glows dim below him. And the torches of the soldiers patrolling the streets illuminate the innards of the city, reflecting off walls and windows. He cannot see the soldiers, but he can see the glow from their torches meander through the streets.

Last night, the flames lured him like a moth, as if the soldiers were guarding something important. The Duchess knew he would watch them She counted on it. A clever ruse to draw his attention to the wrong places. But tonight, he softens the gaze and looks for the darkness, the gaps between the lights, and more importantly, where there are no lights at all.

He leaves the bell tower to investigate two small patches of darkness at opposite ends of Stonehaven. After two hours crossing the city twice, he discovers both are small graveyards with low headstones, few trees, and no structures large enough to hold a secret. Soldiers walk the perimeter but never enter out of reverence or fear. Frustrated, he returns to the bell tower to discover what he missed.

Cheshire watches the orange march of the ants well into the

night and is about to give up on his theory until one small glow appears out of nowhere in the middle of a street far to the east. He keeps his eyes trained on the street and the moon as she travels overhead.

In an hour's time, another glow approaches the same area and then disappears. Cheshire's thighs and toes twitch with anticipation, but he waits and watches the moon. After another hour, he looks back just in time to see another glow appear.

"I win."

He leaps from the temple and traverses the roofs of living quarters and shops as he makes his way to the east, keeping to the dark paths between patrols. When he reaches the street and spot in question, he perches in the shadow of a brick chimney on a high rooftop and searches for a gate, tunnel, or doorway. But the only difference between this street and any other is the unremarkable stone courtyard opposite him. The paving stones of the courtyard match those on the wall, except for inlaid arched stonework across all three walls. And six wide, shallow basins of water form a circle at its center.

By the moon, he does not have long to wait, and within minutes four soldiers approach from the west. One pair continues their march and turns down a side street far to Cheshire's right, while the second pair breaks off and pauses in the courtyard, their eyes searching the rooftops. Once the soldiers assume no one watches them, they douse their torches in one of the basins and walk towards the back wall of the courtyard and disappear in the blink of an eye.

He leans over the edge of the roof, stretching his neck to search for the men. He slides down a drainpipe between houses and is certain the soldiers are not lying in wait, before crossing into the courtyard, every step cautious, as if each brick could spring a trap. There are no visible doorways or tunnels. He walks closer to the back wall where the pair of soldiers disappeared, and a sliver of shadow appears where it should not exist. With an outstretched hand, he walks toward the center-most archway expecting to feel the smooth stone on his palm, but the wall sits further back within the archway. The identical stones used on the ground and walls create a masterful illusion, making it appear every archway lies flat at first, and even second, glance.

Cheshire steps past the threshold of the wall and peers into the dark tunnel to his right, disappearing deep underneath Stonehaven. He looks back to the moon and figures another pair of soldiers will emerge from the tunnel within the half hour. But without knowing the length or outlet of the tunnel, he could end up in a lion's den, overcome by soldiers, or run into them on their way out. But he will take the chance.

The tunnel appears out of place, an afterthought rather than Mirusian design, resembling more of a mine shaft than a catacomb. Its rough grey walls and low ceiling are held in place by fat timbers spaced five paces apart. His eyes adjust quickly to the darkness as he travels deeper below the city. Ripples of excitement course over his skin at the familiar feeling the tunnel gives, mixed with the threat of the unknown.

The echoes of clinking armor soon overcome his footsteps. So far, there have been no offshoots to the main tunnel. The soldiers should appear in front of him. Not long after, two dark figures come into view farther down the winding tunnel. They walk abreast with their hands upon the walls to guide them, leaving Cheshire no room to pass.

He stands in the middle of the shaft waiting for the soldiers to be less than twenty paces away, and grabs a walnut from his cloak, throwing it over their heads. It clacks several times as it bounces down the hall behind them. The soldier on his right spins and pulls his sword. Its pummel hits against the other soldier's breastplate, who tries to swat away the sword but backhands the other soldier across the face. Cheshire presses his back to the humid wall and slides past in the middle of their blind scuffle. He pockets the walnut when he reaches it and continues farther into the depths. By now, Cheshire figures he has crossed the edge of Stonehaven and should be well below the Crest. But finally, after a half hour, a glint of light as small as a grain of sand appears at the end of the shaft.

Cheshire can feel every hair on the back of his neck stand, and a shiver travels down his back to his crotch. He quickens his pace until he reaches a full run. The orange speck grows wider, filling his vision, and the air grows stale and warm as he draws closer.

The shaft opens into a massive cavern with gnarled, pointed rocks hanging like fangs above and the path becomes a long, crumbling bridge, no wider than the shaft, dividing the cavern in two. It ends at a towering iron door, covered with green patina over the etched designs and carvings matching those of the castle. A knot forms in his throat and grows larger with every step closer to the doors. Cheshire rests his forehead against the oddly cold metal and rocks it back and forth. His fingertips run up the curved iron columns set in the doors and circle the etched vine and leaf detailing as they would caress Jonathan and March's bodies.

He wipes the small tears from his eyes and looks down into the sleeping dungeon far below the bridge. A single staircase to his left leads down to three levels of arched cells with iron lattice, ladders, and more hanging cages filling the misty depths. Directly underneath the bridge, six soldiers play at cards and drink around a crudely made table near a solitary brazier on the dungeon's lowest level.

By Cheshire's measure, new soldiers should arrive in just over half an hour. He pulls his hood over his head and wraps his cloak around his body. Its faded colors blend in with the dark brown and greenish stones. He climbs down the stairs on his hands and feet, as low as possible, and inspects the cells on the highest level. The iron lattice of each cell is three rows thick, each with its own gate, with holes smaller than the width of his hand. Most are completely empty except for three, which hold bodies at different levels of rot and decay. All men. The same holds true for all the cells on the second level.

As he is about to risk exploring the bottom floor, two soldiers emerge from the shaft, descend the stairs, and replace two others at the table. The rotating soldiers climb the stairs in single file and leave into the shaft to start their patrol in the city. Even with the addition of the two new men, or when small pebbles fall from the bridge above, the soldiers never look away from their game. With no living soul in the dungeon, there is no need to be vigilant. Cheshire keeps to the shadows and creeps along the walls of the dungeon floor on the opposite side of the bridge from where the soldiers sit, and finds every cell empty except for stretches of cobwebs.

If the dungeon is empty, why do the soldiers remain? And who were the soldiers in the quadrangle speaking of?

The last area of the dungeon to search is the section of cells closest to where the soldiers sit near the brazier. He lies flat to the ground and crawls, inch by inch, toward the bridge in the shadow of one of its supports. Every time the soldiers whisper or cough, he freezes, hoping they have not spotted him. As he crawls, his hand sinks into a large round metal grate ahead of him. His first thought is of another sewer, but there are several more grates in rows across the dungeon floor. He pulls himself to the grate and peers down into the dark cylinder, which sinks out of even Cheshire's sight.

Oubliettes.

He stays on his stomach and drags himself to grate after grate, but there is no way to know if they are empty or house a prisoner, as far as he can tell.

However, the first soldiers he followed said they moved a dangerous prisoner recently, and by the years of grime and dirt packed within the small crevice between the grate and stone, any prisoner in the oubliettes he has already seen have long been bereft of life for quite some time. Cheshire resumes his crawl, checking each one, until he reaches the bridge and sits with his back to one of its wide stone supports. While he rests, he notices none of the cells have locks on them, the same as the pillories in the quadrangle. It would stand to reason any cell without a lock would be empty. This discovery would have saved Cheshire an hour of searching, but at least now he can safely check the cells on the other side of the dungeon without circling into the brazier's light.

He peeks around both sides of the bridge support to see every cell on the far side of the dungeon without a lock. But the oubliettes have no need for latch or lock. Cheshire peeks out again to search the dungeon floor, but from his angle, the ridges of the grates blend with the stones, making it difficult to see their outlines. He crawls back to the dungeon's wall, climbs back up the bridge, and positions himself over the soldiers, sliding one eye over the edge, cheek and nose pressed to the stones.

The circle around each grate is indistinguishable, filled over from years of dirt like the others. All except one—the dark ring partially covered by the table the soldiers play at. He could easily dispatch all six, but there would be no way to escape or hide his deeds before the next set of soldiers arrives, which will be soon.

His solution lies among the rocks strewn across the dungeon floor, broken off from the bridge by time. Cracks almost the width of his hand zig zag across the ancient bridge, some with the glow from the brazier below cutting through. But he will need something stronger than light. He brushes a small pebble off the edge and watches it bounce off a soldier's pauldron, with no reaction from any of them, and then a stone the size of his thumb. It clicks against the dungeon floor, and the soldiers still pay no attention.

Though his mind races, the weariness in his body signals dawn's approach. He sneaks back down the stairs and hides in the nearest cell during the next shift. Two soldiers in, two out.

And once they have passed into the shaft, Cheshire stalks them, knowing every step farther into the darkness ticks down the clock. With a gentle hand Dormy would be proud of, he relieves one soldier of the dagger from his belt and makes his way back to the bridge.

He pushes the dagger into the largest crack along the middle of the bridge and drags it back and forth, digging into the rock. Tiny stones and dust click off the soldiers' armor below, but their whispers do not break. Cheshire's arms and chest strain as he forces the dagger deeper with every bit of his weight until it sinks down to its cross guard.

A deep crack thunders through the dungeon and a long chunk of the bridge, larger than Cheshire, breaks free and falls as all sounds in the dungeon vanish, as if Mirus itself took in a breath in anticipation. The stone slams to the dungeon floor as if launched by a catapult and crushes the heads of three soldiers, killing them instantly. Its impact throws two more backwards through the air and against the dungeon walls. The last jumps free at the last moment and scrambles to help the others.

Cheshire flips the dagger in hand and aims at the top of the standing soldier's unprotected head, but realizes such a wound would leave evidence. He races down the stairs to the dungeon floor and picks up a large piece of broken stone and slams it against the side of the soldier's head. He collapses like an empty suit of armor, blood trickling from his ears. Cheshire heaves the stone overhead with both hands, and hurls it at the soldier sitting dazed against a wall, splitting his skull. His legs and arms spasm and then fall limp. The remaining concussed soldier staggers to his feet and pulls his sword, but Cheshire slides through his legs, grabs his cape and slams him back to the ground. Before the soldier can react, Cheshire straddles the soldier's head, slides his forearm behind the soldier's neck, grips his face with his opposite hand, and leans back, snapping the soldier's spine.

He sits for a moment to collect his breath, checks every soldier to make sure they are all dead, and clears the splintered remains of the table and the larger broken stones from the grate. He reaches into the dark holes of the grate and tries to lift it. The veins in his neck and arms bulge, but the weight is greater than his strength. But not his mind.

Against one of the bridge's supports stands a long square rod, a specifically made pry bar, tapered to a blunt point at one end. Next to it, a large crank with rope thicker than Cheshire's arm spilling out and coiling on the ground, with a crude leather harness at its end. Cheshire drags the heavy rod, meant to be carried by multiple men, to the grate, lifts the thick end onto his shoulder, and guides the point through a hole in the lattice until it supports itself. He pushes down, stands, and even jumps on it to try and rock it free, but the grate resists him.

Less than three quarters of an hour remain before the next pair of soldiers arrive. Half an hour if they heard the crashing of the bridge. Cheshire's eyes search the dungeon for another rod or sack to pile stones in to add weight, but there is nothing in the dungeon except six soldiers, each double his own weight easily. He grabs their bodies and, one by one, lifts their dead weight and balances them on the highest end of the metal rod. After the third, the metal groans. After the fourth, the opposite side of the grate lifts out of the hole. And with the fifth, the grate rises into the air high enough for even a grown man to enter.

"Hello?" he calls down into the pit, but only his voice responds. Cheshire has perched at the edge of the tallest cliffs, scaled the highest mountains, braved the deepest rivers and ravines across Wonderland all while facing the Ace. Never once was he afraid. But only now does he feel the uneasy sensation in his stomach and tingle in his body, as if the floor were about to drop out from under him.

He tugs at the coil of rope and kicks it over the edge. It hisses as it unfurls into the darkness of the oubliette. It snaps tight, rattling the chains of the counterweight hanging precariously high on the adjacent bridge support. He grabs the rope and climbs down into the nauseatingly tight cylinder until it opens into a black void. Above, the circle illuminated by the glow from the brazier is little more than the size of a saucer above.

He stops his descent, doubts creeping to the front of his mind. *What if this is all for naught? What if it's empty? What if it isn't?* Now that he is here, he does not know which is worse. His heart aches as if his own hand squeezes it to muffle its screams.

He calls out again once his feet find dirt. "Hello?" His swallow fills the void.

His eyes soon find the huddled mass within the darkness. Tears pour down his cheeks and his jaw shakes violently. He will kill the Duchess for all she has done to his family.

"Will you walk a little faster?" he sings feebly through tears. "Said a whiting to a snail. There's a porpoise close behind us, and he's treading on my tail." He walks closer, his stomach spasms as he breathes erratically. "Will you, won't you, will you, won't you, will you join the dance? Will you, won't you, will you, won't you, won't you join the—"

A cold air surges through his body, as if his soul fled or was ripped away. Whoever sits against the wall in the dark is too large, their limbs long, and shoulders broad. And dozens of empty wine bottles lay in the dirt.

His legs tremble with each step closer to the black mass. He kneels and reaches out to the long, crusted, mud-covered tangle of hair and moves it aside. His heart fights against his grip and screams within his chest. His face burns and he hopes the heat evaporates the tears from his face. He grabs the soiled collar below the rat's nest of the man's beard and sits him upright against the wall.

"I know your face." Hatred hisses from Cheshire's gritted teeth. "It's not supposed to be you. Why is it you? Is this all it takes? The mighty Gryphon, General of Wonderland. Failure. I heard tale of your death centuries ago. But here you are imprisoned not within an oubliette, but within a bottle." Cheshire punches him across the face, saying, "Wake up," with each blow until his words become guttural screams and his fist cramps. He grabs the Gryphon's face, fingers digging into the mud and skin to force his eyes open. "You were there. You saw. You know the truth. Make no mistake. I will free you. And once you're sober, you will tell me what happened to my mother."

CHAPTER 31

JONATHAN

He counts his steps. Not toward the castle, but away from March curled beneath the sheets in the wagon, with only his fading warmth. He smells his wrist and then the inside of his shirt to breathe her in.

The men and women of Stonehaven rarely return his pleasantries when he nods or tips his hat to them, preoccupied with their own worries. To combat the growing sense of isolation in his mind, Jonathan searches out the differences in the city since he last walked its streets. Though the people of Mirus have not changed, Pat and Bill's minds and hands have not been idle. Since his last visit, they have finished their system of high ways above the streets of Stonehaven. Its bridges and pathways fill the gaps between houses and storefronts, supported by wooden posts thick as trunks and brackets attached to each building. Townspeople clop upon the wooden planks as they walk overhead in the sun. But Jonathan prefers to travel to the castle in their shade.

While distracted, Jonathan almost collides with an older woman walking contrary to him and apologizes for his carelessness. She accepts with a nod, nervously, and continues on her way without stopping. As she passes, Jonathan catches sight of the hilt of an old knife at her hip, concealed by her woven cloak. Prior to five days ago, he would have dismissed this as merely a weapon to defend herself from the questionable characters who have taken up residence in the shadows of the high ways. But even in a glimpse, he recognizes the same knife Cheshire pulled from the dead body of the innkeeper in Briarwell. The years he has walked through the streets of Mirus, Rookridge, and every other town he and March have visited, he cannot recall ever spotting these knives before. Three in one city is coincidence, but to see the same blades almost a thousand miles apart in a matter of days is conspiracy.

He turns into a small alley and circles back to the Row, wanting to search every man and woman he passes, but he keeps his eyes forward and a smile on his face. If correct in his discovery, Mary Anne, and perhaps those with ties to her, are in danger once again.

Back at the wagon, Jonathan sighs with relief. Dormy tends to the shabby, stitched-together of the Boroughs, the smudged merchants and workers of Stonehaven, and the perfumed servants from the Crest, who dress better than any of them. Dormy returns Jonathan's nod with a quizzical expression, her eyebrows furrowed and nose twitching, sensing something amiss.

He climbs into the rear of the wagon to find the knife Dormy took and realizes the infinite number of places it could be. It cannot hide too deep, since it is a recent acquisition, but he could search for a week's time and still not find it.

"Was your appointment so short lived?" March leans against the rear door.

"I never made it. The knife. The one from Briarwell. Do you know where Dormy keeps it?"

Her eyes narrow. "You saw another."

"I believe so. But I must be sure."

"Damn." March huffs and searches two crates with assorted utensils, rusted daggers, and old fishing knives.

"Is there anywhere else to search?"

"There's everywhere else to search. But the simple option would be to ask her. We just have to give her a reason to leave her customers and come in." March smiles and picks up both crates. "Close your eyes, darling."

Jonathan obliges and hears March dump the crates on the floor. The metallic clatter ripples up Jonathan's spine. He opens his eyes and stares at the misshapen iron porcupine of cutlery. His fingers itch, needing to pick them up.

The noise summons Dormy within seconds. "What's happened? What's what?" she asks, then glances back and forth from the pile of knives back to the customers at her tables. "Touch that and I'll bite your fingertips off."

Jonathan bends down and sorts them back in their crates, not as they were, but as they make sense to him. Over a hand's length in one crate and lesser in the other, in descending order of rust and cleanliness, and he cannot speak until he finished.

"Forgive us, Dormy," says March, "but we need to see the knife from Briarwell. Do you still have it?"

"Of course. I have everything." Dormy pulls the knife from within her coat and hands it to her.

Once Jonathan finishes his task and sets the crates back on a crowded shelf, March tries to hand it to Jonathan, but he cups her hand around the blade to show only what he could see out of the woman's belt, positions it on her hip, and steps back.

"It may be the same," he says, tilting his head from side to side, "but then again—"

"Twenty-seven," says Dormy.

"I beg your pardon," says Jonathan.

"Twenty-seven. It's hard not to notice them, when you notice them. That's how many I've seen, poking out of belts or the top of boots. Twenty-two yesterday, and five this morning."

"And those were just the customers who approached her tables," says March.

"Thank you," says Jonathan.

Dormy nods and hops from the wagon to return to her customers.

"It would seem my suspicions are no longer suspicions." Jonathan takes the knife from March and tucks it within his own jacket. "Twenty-seven. Twenty-eight, potentially. And you are correct," he tells March. "Those are only the ones we are aware of."

"Is it possible they are from Briarwell and followed us here?" she asks.

"They couldn't have. Even on horseback, it would take them at least two more weeks to catch up with us. But word has spread. The woman I came upon dressed in Stonehaven garb, simple skirt and tunic, kerchief, and her face seemed familiar. I've seen her in town before. So, whatever order they belonged to, there were already members here in Mirus."

March disappears to the upper level and returns with his belt, scabbard and sword already attached, and ties it around his waist. He kisses the top of her head and then walks from the wagon. But she follows, buckling her waist harness, carrying four swords from her collection.

"You should stay to look after Dormy. If these fanatics wanted to kill us in Briarwell, we must assume the same here."

"Look at her." March points to the ever-growing crowd. "There are more eyes on her than on Mary Anne. She'll be fine. Besides, she's not a fool. Look at her coat." The muzzles of four flintlock pistols lift the back hem of the corduroy jacket. "Whomever this clandestine group is, they will not risk revealing themselves in public. Not now. Not yet. You need the extra set of eyes."

"Always."

They take the busy main thoroughfare of Stonehaven rather than the side streets below the high ways, and walk between wagons, carts, and their mules and horse as they trot through the city. Jonathan nods cordially to all he passes, his eyes darting to their belts and boots. But soon the sheer number of townspeople overwhelm his senses. His eyes jump erratically and his breaths become short.

"Rest your eyes." March reaches down and squeezes his hand firmly. "Head down. Concentrate on the earth beneath your feet."

He tilts his head until the brim of his hat blocks everyone's faces, relaxes his eyes, and listens to the rhythmic slow crunch of his steps on the loose dirt. After he regains his breath and faculties, he asks, "What is your count?"

"I've added six thus far. Wait. Seven, off to our right. The boot of the woman near the fountain playing with her child." March releases his hand and places it back on the pommel of one of her swords. "Yours?"

"Four. All from Stonehaven. I've seen none carried by those from the Boroughs. Do you think they keep these symbols on their persons all the time?"

"Doubtful. Then again, we've never known to look for them," says March.

"Then why now?" He spots the handle of a knife peek out from within a gentleman's breast pocket as he reaches to unlock the front door to his home. "Five."

"The simplest answer is the pain in our asses. Mary Anne."

"But how do they know? What are their intentions? In all our years, we've never had dealings with any of them. Never seen them. Or rather, never thought to look for them. What's the connection? What does it all mean?"

"It means trouble. For Mary Anne. And for us." March slides her arm inside Jonathan's jacket and around his waist, and he wraps his arm around her shoulders. "And a prolonged stay in the capital."

"If we were home," he asks, "what would we be doing right now?"

She smiles. "I can do better than that. If we were home, you, and I, and Cheshire, would pack for an extended adventure."

She slides her arm beneath his shirt and traces the grooves of his back muscles. "With Dormy of course. Books. Swords. Teas. Each other. It's all we need. All we've ever needed."

"To what destination will the adventure take us?"

"The Pool." Her eyes shimmer in the sunlight, reflecting the water she speaks of. "Our own undiscovered, secluded cove."

"The glowing beetles guiding our way as less and less sunlight pierces the canopy," adds Jonathan. His thoughts join March, and they no longer walk through the crowded streets of Mirus. The people and buildings become the welcome shadowed forms of trunks, bushes, and rocks, down the long, secluded path to the Pool, the canopy above so dense it is as if they walk in a cave instead of a forest. He can feel the slight chill in the damp air upon his face.

"The sparkling spring fed by two small waterfalls in the cliff face," March continues. "It exists outside this world. And when the few small shafts of sunlight hit the surface of the water, and their dancing reflections combine with the gentle pulsing light of the beetles, it's truly ethereal. The only place in the world where night and day exist at the same time."

Jonathan wants to continue the dream, but a glint off to his left catches his eye. At first he thinks it one of the beetles, but the forest around them dissolves back to the market within a breath. Another knife sits in the belt of a farmer driving by. Then another pokes out from the satchel of a young man with spectacles. With this growing threat, Jonathan realizes they will not see the Pool or the Hollow any time soon, and the words March speaks become fantasy. If she would have stayed in the Hollow, at least Cheshire could be with her and keep her safe.

"Jonathan," March says softly. "You're a thousand miles away."

He did not realize his face grew downcast while she spoke. "I wish we were," he says. "I'm sorry I brought you into all of this. It was never, never my intention."

"Stop it." March yanks Jonathan by the collar into a narrow alley and pushes him against the gray stones of a cobbler's shop. "I never asked for an apology. Never once. Nor will I ever. I'm here of my own accord. For you. For us. I do not need an apology. Ever."

"And that is why I give it."

March rests her forehead against his chest, and he rests his chin upon her head.

"We will be home soon enough," she whispers.

Jonathan inhales. She smells of home. After countless years, the scents of the Hollow have become her own, and no matter how many baths, the sweet fragrances remain. The linseed oil on her swords. Oak and leather. The dirt and rock path from the mill to the table. The slight smell of extinguished candles. Thirty different teas in her hair alone. She smells of the wind in the Hollow, which is why he breathes her in as often as he can. She is life.

"You are my home," says Jonathan. "But for us to return to the Hollow, this all needs to end. So I had better start. You can head back to the Row. I'll continue on."

"Do you think I'll let you walk into those gates alone?" She laughs.

"It's not the castle which makes me worry. It's the Twins,

lurking somewhere in the Crest. And then there's your mother. There may be a chance she doesn't yet know."

"She owns two thirds of the Crest. If Lysander and Uriah stay two doors from her, it's because she allowed them, invited them. And what they know, she will know. Regardless, I will not cower from any of them. So on we press."

They pass out of Stonehaven and continue through the Crest with the same foul looks from the townspeople as before and arrive at the castle gates without incident from the Twins or March's mother and without spotting another knife. A member of the Castle Guard, and not the Red Knight, opens the door for them graciously. But Jonathan shudders when the iron catch of the door falls into place behind him. He keeps his eyes lowered to the cobblestones until they become stairs, and then the pale tile of the interior castle hallways. The scent of the castle is undeniable, old stone, like a long-forgotten mausoleum opened recently.

"Good evening, sir. Where am I to find Mary Anne?" Jonathan asks the doorman behind him, who keeps his nose and chin high in the air with no response.

"This way." Weiss's unmistakably sour, nasal voice shoots from down the hallway like an arrow. "Now." His robes share his disdain, whipping into an arched door. Its iron-ring handle jangles as it slams shut.

"I see he hates you no less," says March. She pulls Jonathan by the arm to keep pace with Weiss, whose stride is unforgiving. "Maybe more."

Their footsteps echo against the vaulted arches above, and all Jonathan can think of is walking under the heels of a giant's boots, trying to crush them, but the faster they walk, the faster the boots chase. Eventually, it's Jonathan who leads March to escape the incessant sound following them. When they arrive at the door, Jonathan stares at the handle, gently swaying, his hand inches away, sweating.

A single kiss from March on his cheek calms and focuses his thoughts. He can hear a conversation on the other side of the wood, not yet heated, but approaching a slow boil. The Duchess, the Red Knight, Mary Anne, and Weiss.

"What a wonderful pot to be dipped into," he says.

"Dipped?" March chuckles. "We've been dropped." She straightens his hat and the dusty color of his jacket. "I'll wait out here, should you need me." Jonathan still hesitates to move closer or put a hand on the door. "You can't walk back to me, until you walk away," March says with a beautiful sad smile. "Play your part well." She puts a hand on the door, pushes it open for him, and leans against the wall, out of sight from those within.

The door croaks a long death rattle as it opens. He enters the long, narrow sterile meeting room. Grey stone walls—unadorned with portrait, painting, or banner, lined with empty iron braziers in the shape of flames and thin windows no wider than the palm of a hand—reinforce the severity of this gathering. March pulls the door shut behind him.

Mary Anne, framed in a shaft of sunlight from one of the windows, sits at a table longer than his in the Hollow—a skeleton of a table covered in dust, devoid of life or care, except for the runner of woven scarlet fabric down its length, kinked every few feet.

Fifty-two, he thinks, counting the identical, tall wooden chairs which stand around the table's perimeter. Parishioners worshiping at their false altar of oak. Jonathan shuts his eyes to keep from counting the bronze, round head nails decorating each chair, but he knows he will before this meeting concludes.

The Duchess, at the head of the table, where he would sit, gestures to an open chair opposite Mary Anne. She sits where March would, and he at Dormy's place. The dance and screech of fat chair legs against the stone floor adds to the awkwardness and tension already thick in the large room as he sits. The Red Knight, with an upturned lip, sits resting on his elbow to Jonathan's left. Weiss, with lips pressed into a trembling line, sits diagonal, next to Mary Anne, where Cheshire ought to be, his posture rigid as the back of the cushionless chairs. Mary Anne smiles from across the table, like a jeweled necklace adorns her face. But it does not ease his sorrow.

Jonathan lowers his eyes and wrings his thumbs beneath the table. Despite the atrocities wrought by the Ace in Rookridge, or the scorched bodies of the men he killed in Briarwell, the sight before him is the most harrowing. A disgraceful perversion of his own table.

CHAPTER 32

MARY ANNE

Jonathan enters the stale room and his uncomfortable half smile and bright blue eyes sparkle from beneath his top hat. Mary Anne cannot hide her smile. Even though she saw him yesterday, time in the castle drags, and it seems the market was an eternity ago. She notices he wears a linen shirt underneath his blue frock for the first time since she met him. *Not that it makes a difference,* she tells herself. But he looks uncomfortable, as if he wears someone else's skin.

She can sympathize. Even though she sits at the table with the Duchess in her finery, the Red Knight in his polished armor, Chamberlain Weiss in his official robes, and herself in a dress more lavish than any she could ever afford, she cannot help but feel like an imposter among them.

Jonathan endearingly pulls the chair out, wincing at the loud scrape it makes against the floor, and sits. His eyes bounce to each person seated at the table and then each empty chair to the end. He envisions his table back at the mill just as Mary Anne did when she first came in the room. However, Jonathan's face turns downcast the farther he travels up the table.

"This is quite the gathering," says the Duchess.

"Unorthodox," says the Red Knight.

"Overcrowded," whispers Chamberlain Weiss.

"Nevertheless," says Mary Anne, "I thank you all for your attendance. I look forward to your council."

"Well spoken." The Duchess leans forward and fans her fingers onto the table, bunching the long table runner. "Now to business. As we know, helping Mary Anne complete the Tenets must be our highest priority. Our first task is to discuss Lysander and Uriah, and how to rid the city of them. While they are here, they will most definitely frustrate our every effort. Suggestions?"

"Perhaps we could pay them off," says Chamberlain Weiss. "Bribe them. Not that our coffers could withstand the sum they would demand. But there must be something their vile little hearts crave."

"Their vaults and wine cellars are full, and women flock to them in every city." The Red Knight scoffs. "What could we offer them? Besides what they want."

The brief glance at Mary Anne does not sit well with her.

"Then we force them out," says Chamberlain Weiss. "We have the numbers. Four thousand soldiers in the city alone. I'm sure they are formidable opponents, but they cannot resist an army."

"And incite a rebellion?" The Duchess leans back in her chair, tapping her chin with a curled, plump finger. "No. The loyalty to their family runs deep in the Crest. And if they and their purses rise against us, we'll have no chance. No, force and money will do us no good with these two."

This news and the Duchess's demeanor differ sharply from their time together on the tower yesterday. She was optimistic and made it seem as if Lysander and Uriah were annoyances rather than genuine threats, not just to her becoming Queen, but to her life. And it appears Jonathan's mind is hundreds of miles away at his own table, wishing the rest of him could join. Mary Anne can taste the dry, bitter guilt in her mouth. No matter the amount of chivalry he displays, she knows he does not want to be here. But she needs him.

"What do you think, Carter?" Chamberlain Weiss hisses.

"I'm sorry? Think about what?" he asks.

"Mary Anne named you her advisor," Chamberlain Weiss says in his over-articulate way. "You are here to advise. So advise."

"Yes, but advise on what exactly?" he asks again.

"Idiot." Chamberlain Weiss turns to Mary Anne. "You see, this is why I questioned your choice. You need an advisor who understands—"

"Do not speak to him that way," she says sharply. "I don't understand the animosity in this room, but Jonathan is brave and noble."

"Noble." Chamberlain Weiss chortles. "He's common. As common as they come."

"We cannot all renounce the families we were born into." Jonathan straightens in his chair and raises his eyes to meet

Chamberlain Weiss's for the first time. "I am up to the task. I need only know what the task entails."

"Are you?" the Duchess asks, eyes piercing.

"I believe in him," says Mary Anne. "After all he and his friends have done, I believe him."

"Oh, I am well aware he can certainly cleave a man in twain and fight off a horde. I saw the aftermath." The Duchess smirks. "But he is not your protector anymore. You have named him your advisor."

The Red Knight stiffens in his seat. "I'm sorry," he says, "you're mistaken. I slew the brigands in Briarwell."

"Of course you did." The Duchess dismisses him.

"Can Jonathan not be both protector and advisor?" Mary Anne asks.

"Perhaps." The Duchess squirms in her chair, annoyed at Mary Anne's questions. "But if he runs headlong into danger every time a threat arises, then he cannot give counsel to you, now can he?"

"I am confused at this turn," says Mary Anne. "As we left Briarwell, you said—"

"I said he was an upstanding young man, which is fine for grass fields and bumpkin peasant towns," the Duchess corrects her. "But Mirus is quite the opposite. He is as out of place as you are, Mary Anne."

Jonathan's face betrays him. Mary Anne can see it's true, but also knows Jonathan to be brave and self-sacrificing, which is what she needs at this moment. But here, in the presence of the Duchess, Red Knight, and Weiss, he shifts in his chair and keeps his eyes lowered to the table. Yesterday, she said his name because he is the only person she fully trusts in this world, but her decision makes him miserable. She can see it now.

"Then I will name another advisor."

"It's too late for that now." The Duchess waves Mary Anne's suggestion from the air like candle smoke.

Mary Anne looks to Chamberlain Weiss, and says, "I name... I name... I..." Her mouth puckers and her tongue presses against the roof of her lips, ready to name Chamberlain Weiss, but she has no control over her faculties. No breath or sound can escape her mouth. She gasps and tries again. Her neck tightens and stomach shakes, but nothing still.

Chamberlain Weiss picks at his fingernails, and the Red Knight scratches at the grain of the table. The familiar expression from the Duchess tells Mary Anne she should have known better.

"I do not understand." She panics. "I cannot speak another name. I want to name—" Her throat clenches again.

"Of course you can't, my dear. Wonderland won't allow you to." The Duchess shakes her head. "You've begun the Tenets, and they and the Arcana are binding."

"Why was I not told this at the beginning?" Mary Anne fights back a grimace aimed at Chamberlain Weiss. "You assumed I would choose you, so you did not read the entire passage."

"You did not let me finish," he snaps. "Yes, of course I expected you to name me, because I assumed you took this seriously and wanted an advisor with some semblance of experience in working with queens. Not some... physical distraction."

Mary Anne feels the heat surge over her face, and cannot tell if she blushes or if all the color has left her cheeks. Her eyes have strayed to Jonathan's figure on more than one occasion, but she has never given in to lustful thoughts. If Chamberlain Weiss could call out her behavior in the short time he has seen them together, then Jonathan can as well, and March. She hangs her head, utterly embarrassed and unable to look at Jonathan.

"Do you think we play at games here, Mary Anne?" The Duchess's face turns stone and her eyes daggers. "You merely want to return home. Those of us at this table, with the exception of Jonathan, are tasked with holding a queenless nation together, and its seams are already stretched tight."

"The burden of the Queendom weighs heavy on all of us," says the Red Knight.

A weight presses down on Mary Anne's shoulders, as if some great man forcefully holds her in place. She feels the sensation flow down her arms, back, and then her chest. She can feel the thump of her heart in her feet, fingertips, and face.

"What am I to do then?" she asks.

"Take this seriously," the Duchess implores. "If you're only concerned with yourself, if returning home is your sole objective then it will all be for naught. Wonderland knows your-"

"You speak of Wonderland as if it is alive," Mary Anne shouts.

The room falls silent. Not even the shift of wool or linen, creak of wood, or breath hangs in the air.

The Duchess's calm, hushed tone chills Mary Anne's blood. "When we sat across from the throne room doors, I told you

Wonderland must accept you. The Arcana courses through the land like life blood through a body. It keeps Wonderland alive. You took my words as hyperbole?"

She did. Or perhaps she only heard the words which would expedite her return. Again.

"You accepted the Tenets," says Chamberlain Weiss. "The first is complete and you cannot stop them until you ascend or fail. Your fate and Wonderland's are now intertwined."

The Duchess takes hold of Mary Anne's hand. "I apologize for the harsh words. I do. But I will speak plain with you during this journey."

"We, here, understand your burden," says Chamberlain Weiss. "Our lives depend on your success. So we will help you at all costs."

Their words lift the weight, part of it, from Mary Anne and allow her to breathe easier. And the smile from Jonathan across the table is enough to lift the rest. She did not mean, nor could she have known, the effect of her arrival on any of them, especially Jonathan.

"Well then," says the Duchess, "back to the business at hand. Let's deal with the Twins before something else falls into our laps."

Jonathan winces. Mary Anne thinks it could be from the horribly uncomfortable chairs, but he reaches into his coat and reveals a rusted knife. He holds it by the end of the handle with two fingers like a dead rat and lays it upon the table. Silence fills the room again, just as deafening as before, except this time, Jonathan joins Mary Anne, looking to the others for answers. Whatever the trinket Jonathan brought into the room causes all in attendance to look worried. More than speaking of Lysander and Uriah.

"You had no word of this?" the Duchess asks the Red Knight. The corners of her small, painted lips twitch.

"We've been somewhat preoccupied." He picks at something in his teeth with his tongue and points to Mary Anne.

"Jonathan has been here all of ten minutes and produces a more meaningful contribution than the lot of you." The Duchess covers her mouth to collect her thoughts before continuing. "That knife is a symbol of religious zealots. Damned fool. Yet another problem to contend with. Where did you come upon this?" she asks Jonathan.

"Briarwell," he replies. "There were three men, each with identical blades. They plotted to kill us."

"I see. And where are these men now?" she asks.

"Dead."

"By your hand?" she probes.

After a brief pause, he finally answers. "Yes."

"Good, then. Perhaps nothing to worry about after all." The Duchess leans back in her chair.

"Forty. We've seen forty since we arrived yesterday," Jonathan continues.

"This is a fucking nightmare," says the Red Knight.

"I don't understand," says Mary Anne.

"There are a great number of gods the people of Wonderland worship, depending on what corner of the country you find yourself. Fifty-two, or some obscene number. I lost count long ago. But, the more well-known deities include The

Suicide King, Bas, The Old Maid, and The Mother. This dagger belongs to a disillusioned faction of those who worship the latter. They... they believe women from your world, Mary Anne, are The Mother made flesh."

"They refer to them as God Queens," adds Chamberlain Weiss. "Actually, God Queen Mother, to be more precise. But that is a mouthful."

"This is positive, yes?" asks Mary Anne. "Would they help us with Lysander and Uriah? We could rally them and ask for aid."

"No," says the Duchess. "Not advisable. They believe these God Queens are The Mother trapped in human form. Like a rare wine in old leather wineskin. Those knives are used to free The Mother from her confines."

"Free? How?" Mary Anne asks, fearing the answer forming in her mind.

The Red Knight leans forward in his chair. "Puncture the wineskin. The wine flows. And what do you do with wine?"

"Drink it," Mary Anne says matter-of-factly. "Drink? You mean they drink the God Queen's blood?"

"They spill her blood with those knives," the Duchess continues. "They drink the blood to take The Mother's power into them. Then they take their own lives with the same blades to release her back into the ether."

The pounding in her chest returns, and now in her eyes as well. At every turn, obstacles arise. Lysander and Uriah, and now a fanatical cult. But despite the threats they pose, Mary Anne knows the most dangerous adversary she must face in order to return home is herself. And she has no idea how to triumph after losing the same battle all her life.

CHAPTER 33

CHESHIRE

From the dungeon floor, Cheshire can hear the soldiers approaching through the shaft, counting down the minutes before they swarm into the dungeon. He kicks the latch to the counterweight, and the rope whirs and smokes as it races through the crank and metal loops along the bridge. The large stone slams to the ground, shaking the dungeon. Every cell in the dungeon rattles, and dust hisses and drizzles down from the cavern ceiling above. The Gryphon's body flies from the hole and skids across the stones, like a freshly caught carp yanked from a lake.

One by one, Cheshire pulls the dead soldiers from the bar until the grate of the oubliette falls shut with a resounding clang. He replaces the pry bar against the pillar and then pulls the soldiers' bodies atop the grate once more, positioning them as naturally as he can. When finished, streams of warm sweat wash down Cheshire's body in the dank air. He unties the

Gryphon from the leather harness, squirms under his arm, and pushes against the ground with all his strength to raise him to his feet. Spit shoots from pressed lips, spots flash in his eyes, and his head and thighs want to burst under the Gryphon's dead weight.

"I've not come all this way just to have you ruin my efforts."

Once upright, the Gryphon towers over Cheshire and feebly tries to support his own weight like a newborn fawn. Cheshire takes the brunt, over twice his own weight, as they stumble up the stairs to the bridge. The Gryphon loses what little control of his legs he can gather and slams Cheshire against the dungeon wall again and again. The stench of sick and the foul odor of decades, if not centuries, without a bath cut deep between Cheshire's eyes. He gasps for air, but the air does not soothe his burning lungs, parched throat, or cracked lips. He digs his fingers under the Gryphon's ribs and curls them upward to coax him upright. The pain jolts him to his feet.

At the top of the bridge, Cheshire shows their escape from the encroaching soldiers lies on the other side of the iron doors, sealed for centuries. "They will be upon us soon," he tells the Gryphon, "and I can't get us out the way I entered. But I'm sure the knowledge to get into the castle is in your slush of a brain, so fucking help." A delayed gurgle from the Gryphon is the only response. "Do something or I swear to all the gods I'll toss you from this bridge and end both our suffering."

The Gryphon raises a limp arm and swipes at a small column embedded in the door, but his hands slide off, accomplishing nothing. Cheshire squints at what he first thought a solid decorative column, but it is actually divided into four smaller sections. Layers of grime and dirt fill and obscure the cracks between them and the runes upon them.

Combination tumblers, Cheshire thinks. *Of course.* He claws and scrapes the filth away with his nails to reveal the clear Prodigium runes.

"Again," he commands the Gryphon, guiding his wandering hand back to the door, while measuring the distance of the soldiers running down the shaft by their sound. They will reach the dungeon in five minutes, but he will be within their sight in four.

In his drunken state, the Gryphon barely has the strength or coordination to move the tumblers. He lays the tip of his forefinger on the metal and flicks against it for each turn. But it is enough for Cheshire to decipher his meaning and turn each tumbler to the other runes carved around them.

A heavy click vibrates the doors from the other side. Cheshire uses their combined weight to push against the door and then tries pulling, but they refuse to move.

"Match," the Gryphon says through a hoarse inhale and gestures to the adjoining door.

Cheshire drops the Gryphon to the ground and a tingling sensation climbs his body and leaves out the back of his neck like a cold steam. For a moment he feels weightless, dizzy, but he scrapes the second set of tumblers free and shifts them to correspond with the other door. But as he brings the last rune on the bottom tumbler into position, all eight spin and shuffle to their original positions. The tumblers not only need to match, but are spaced and made to be operated by a pair, and the partner Cheshire finds himself with can offer no help.

He wants to rest, catch his breath, allow his muscles to relax, and stop his legs from trembling, but he has less than a minute before the soldiers will be close enough to see him and know of his escape into the castle. He closes his eyes and runs and orchestrates a way to demolish the bridge in seconds. Raise the counterweight, wrap the rope around the broken section, kick the release mechanism as they cross over, and bring it down, killing them all. If more soldiers arrive, they could not reach him, since the only staircase to the floor below is on his side. He wagers from the amount of dirt in the tumblers, the soldiers do not use or have the knowledge of these doors, and so, once on the other side, they will be unable to follow. But he wastes precious time on a plan he has no time to execute.

Cheshire opens his eyes and turns, reenters the sequence as before, aligning the top three sets of tumblers. The final tumblers sit at Cheshire's eye level, staring back at him, but he cannot reach both at once. And though the Gryphon may be of no help, he can still be of use. The Gryphon stands at least two heads taller than Cheshire, and on his knees, they would be comparable in height. Cheshire positions the right tumbler to be one turn away from the ending sequence, pulls the Gryphon to his knees and leans his forehead against the door next to the tumbler. He places his hand on the left tumbler, reaches out with his leg, and kicks the Gryphon over. His head scrapes against the metal and slides the final tumbler into place as Cheshire turns at the same time.

Two heavy clicks this time, followed by the ticking of large gears. Three iron circular plates, spanning the seam of both doors, break free of years of crust and turn until thin slits running horizontal in each align vertically with the break in the door. They crack open with a slow rumble and exhale a cold, suppressed breath.

Cheshire laughs deliriously, tears in his eyes, wishing there were time to savor this first victory in his thousand years of searching. He strains to pull one of the doors open wide enough, drags the Gryphon through by the collar of his jacket, and pulls the doors shut. Once closed, he can hear the metal plates turn back into place, the tumblers scrape and shuffle, and iron rods and gears slide and turn in the darkness.

He presses his ear to the cold metal and in just over one minute's time, soldiers huff past the door and down the stairs to the dungeon floor, none the wiser. His shoulders burn as he removes his cloak and vest. He collapses into a thin layer of dust covering the floor like new fallen snow deep within a wood. He stretches his arms and legs, soaking in the cold of the stones through his skin to heal his muscles. Loose cobwebs sway in the gentle breath of the castle. His heartbeat gently rocks his tired body back and forth.

The groans behind him also sharpen the hard truth, as well as Cheshire's eyes. He is in the castle, yes, but in order to go any farther, Cheshire will need to attend to the Gryphon's current state and keep him alive long enough to question him. But even though the doors to the dungeon have not been opened in years, there is no way for Cheshire to see boot prints or any other sign if the corridors are still in use. They must keep moving.

Cheshire gets to his feet and leaves the Gryphon to search for any detail of the corridor in front of him, but this unfamiliar darkness chokes the halls like smoke in the castle's lungs. He realizes the reason he knows there are cobwebs is because he saw them in the dim light of the dungeon when the door was open. He stares at a single point until his eyes water and the hazy form of an arch appears above his head, and then the slight shift in value of the floor from the walls, but nothing more. His moment of triumph turns in his stomach like old milk. For the first time in almost a millennium, Cheshire must guide himself with his hands against the wall, blind.

After an hour of walking at a turtle's pace through the depths, and several stubbed toes and knees from unforeseen sudden turns in the dark maze, the sounds of his breathing, muffled by the stale air and dense walls of the corridors, lifts high above him. His foot finds the edge of a stone step, and another, and then the curve in their run. He follows the spiraling staircase upward until the black veil over his eyes turns into a fog of grays and blues. Boot marks become visible in the decades of layered dust upon the stairs, but even they have years of dust covering them.

Twelve spirals up the stairs end at a single door inside the castle, or so he hopes, where faint daylight reaches underneath and dances over his toes. There are no sounds of movement or voices on the other side, armor or otherwise. Perhaps the Duchess's overconfidence keeps all the guards in the castle grounds and soldiers patrolling the city. Even in her paranoia, she did not believe he would make it this far. But to be underestimated is a great gift. One she will soon regret. A flash of warmth from within his body fights the cool air pumped through the castle and brings his weary muscles back to life. He cracks the door open and grimaces at the loud squeak of its hinges.

He pokes his head into the hallway and rejoices at the sight of the pale gray walls, still as tall as he remembers. From the height of the walls, and the waypoint, he can tell he is on the ground level. He slides through the door and slinks down the hallway, past woven crimson and white tapestries at the height of the walls and suits of armor which date back to the War for the Realm. The long hallway he follows becomes a waypoint with five other adjoining hallways shooting off into different directions like a starburst.

Footsteps approach from one hallway, but with their echo Cheshire cannot discern which. He backtracks and hides behind the edge of a tapestry closest to an armor on display. The soft, quick steps of boots pass. He peeks out to see the back of a servant woman holding up her long twill dress and apron in one hand and carrying a stack of folded sheets in the other. Another crosses through the waypoint into another hallway with some haste, adjusting her kerchief and cursing under her breath. He waits for another two to pass before he pokes his head out again. And the longer he waits, the more he realizes there is no place he can realistically hide the Gryphon.

His salvation comes from a familiar hum, like an angel singing from the heavens, too soft for others to hear at this distance, but he can recognize March's soothing voice anywhere, even in a crowd of thousands. Certain no servants are near, he leaves the tapestry and peeks around the corner to discover March leaning against a wall halfway down the long hallway, which means Jonathan is close as well. In the door she watches opposite her, more than likely.

In the silence after she finishes her tune, another voice, the Duchess's, no matter how faint, grates against the inside of Cheshire's skull. Soon the voices of the Chamberlain, Red Knight, Mary Anne, and Jonathan carry through the closed door and down the hall. If there were a place to hide the Gryphon within the castle, he would eventually be spotted, heard, and then discovered by someone in the castle.

Perhaps I've thought about this endeavor backwards. The Gryphon has been assumed dead for centuries. So news of the miraculous resurrection of Wonderland's beloved General would spread far and quick, if he were seen. Since there is no way to conceal the Gryphon, it will be easier to keep him alive in plain sight.

He skulks through the hallways until he reaches the smoky kitchen toward the rear of the castle, which is only two turns away from the door leading back to the dungeon. The door to the kitchen remains open wide for Cheshire to peer through. Not much has changed. Stacks of casks line the far wall. One woman stokes the fires of the large stone ovens along the back wall, and her small son jumps up and down pulling on the bellows. At the row of tables dividing the room, three older women carve a massive slab of salted pork and gossip about the other servants who work on the ground floor. The old cook, thin as a nail, plods in and out from the rear door to the storehouse and topiary gardens behind the castle to bring in baskets of vegetables. After three trips, the cook bats away her overly frizzy hair from her face and asks the other women to help her bring in a side of beef. They all follow her out the door, even the child.

Cheshire's stomach groans for the stacks of freshly baked bread, meats seasoned with coriander, and the smell of overripe bananas piled on a nearby table. He grabs a large wooden bucket from the stack in the corner and pumps water in from the copper spigot on the back wall. As it fills, he shoves his face into the cold bursts of water, gulping mouthful after mouthful until his throat and stomach ache. Water splashes across the already wet floor and soaks him down to his trousers.

With the bucket full to its brim, he shakes the water from himself and wipes the excess water from the bucket with a discarded rag and wraps the bottom with it, to keep drops from leaving a trail. On his way out of the kitchen, he grabs a steaming loaf of bread with his teeth. The crunch of the hard crust makes his mouth water, and the aroma of warm yeast and hint of cinnamon fills his lungs and his stomach. He carries the bucket and bread back through the hallways, mindful of any other servants, and descends the stairs to the dungeon. After once through the darkness, Cheshire remembers the way and retraces his steps, without his hands on the walls, back to the unconscious Gryphon.

He places the bucket next to the Gryphon's head and takes a moment to savor half the barley loaf, soaking up the bucket full he drank in the kitchen. Cheshire holds the bucket steady with one hand and twists his fingers tightly into the matted rat's nest of the Gryphon's long hair, hoping this plan will work. And if not, he will be one less worry. Cheshire shoves the Gryphon's face under the surface of the water and holds it there. After a few seconds, the Gryphon's body finally jerks and convulses, arms and legs flailing, fighting to breathe. He struggles against Cheshire's grasp, spilling water from all sides of the bucket, but Cheshire pushes his face deeper into the water and swats away the Gryphon's arms with his legs.

"Quickly now," says Cheshire.

The Gryphon convulses twice more before the final bubbles climb to the surface of the water and his body falls limp. Cheshire holds his head under a few more seconds for good measure, then rolls the Gryphon's lifeless body over to his back, and crouches by his stomach. At the count of thirty, the Gryphon still has not stirred, so Cheshire drives his fist deep into his swollen gut. Bile, water, and what must be the content of an entire wine cask erupt from the Gryphon's mouth like a broken dam. He turns to his side and gasps for breath and then vomits out more thick streams of mixed liquids. The rancid pool crawls out in all directions, seeping into cracks between stones.

"The hell are you doing here, boy?" the Gryphon asks with a hoarse voice after several gasps. His words are still slurred beyond comprehension, but at least now they are somewhat coherent.

Cheshire grabs the Gryphon by the tattered lapels of his long coat and pulls his face closer. "I've given you a second chance at life. You're most welcome. It's more than you deserve, and more than you've ever done for me. Now, before my generosity runs out, you will answer me. Where is my mother?"

"Leave," the Gryphon rasps.

Cheshire slaps him across the face with such force his fingers vibrate and the meaty part of his palm burns.

"Leave," the Gryphon repeats.

"Answer me." Cheshire's breaths become quick and sharp, and his stern commands become frantic pleads. He unleashes a barrage of punches across the Gryphon's face, fueled by the repressed rage meant for the Duchess, and does not stop until the open cuts on his knuckles burn and the iron smell of his own blood fills his nostrils. "Answer me. Answer me," he cries, spit flying across the Gryphon's face. "Answer me!"

The Gryphon concedes and sighs, then gurgles and spits out another glob of bile, and talks with the strings still hanging from his lips. "She's dead," he wheezes. "She died many, many years ago."

"You lie." Cheshire backhands him across the cheek. "You lie. Why would you say such nonsense?"

"I buried her myself," the Gryphon says through severely cracked lips, each word requiring significant effort. "Far from here. Safe. Away from the capital. In a cliffside cemetery near the black sands of the Wrecks." Even in the darkness, Cheshire can see the small tear trickle from the corner of the Gryphon's eye. He has no reason at all to fabricate such a story.

Cheshire's thoughts flash back to the last time he saw his mother when he was all but ten, kneeling before him, her forehead pressed against his and tears streaming down her flushed cheeks. "Go," she said, "far from this place. Outlive Wonderland." She kissed his forehead. "Now run, my heart. Go."

Finding his mother has been the sole purpose of his

extended life, and now the Gryphon rips the fabric of Cheshire's world in half with only a few words. A numbing fire overtakes him all at once, and Cheshire cannot feel his trembling face, shaking arms, or his breaths. His veins run cold and hollow as the endless catacombs, and for the first time in all his life, he is lost. He wants to listen to his mother's words again and run. But there is nowhere he can hide from the thousand years of sorrow he repressed, about to be unleashed as a torrent and drown him from the inside.

He cannot think. He must move. He uses the numb void inside him while it lasts and fights against the crushing weight on his shoulders and chest to stand again, dons his cloak and vest, and pulls the Gryphon to his feet. This time only needing to support half his weight, Cheshire guides him through the hallways and up the spiral stairs. But when they reach the door, the Gryphon musters the strength to push against the stone frame to keep Cheshire from opening it.

"Stop this," he says. "What are you doing?"

"If what you say is true," Cheshire says through gritted teeth, "then my list has gotten much shorter. And now at the top is killing the Duchess. Painfully. Slowly. Not as difficult as killing a queen. And you will help me."

"No." The Gryphon tries to fight back.

"I don't have a choice. And now neither do you."

Cheshire slips under the Gryphon's long coat. The layers of sweat, dirt, and sick are suffocating and the pungent stench brings him to the edge of vomiting. He digs his fingernails into the soft skin of the Gryphon's underarms, and once his arms retract from the pain, Cheshire forces him through the door into the castle hallways. He wraps his arms around the Gryphon's torso to keep him upright and steer him first to the kitchen and then to the meeting room where Jonathan and March are.

On the way to the kitchen, Cheshire can hear a servant girl gasp and run. She, or another servant he will soon encounter, will run to the bailey and alert the Castle Guards. The clock begins anew.

Full suits of armor crash to the ground and tapestries rip as the Gryphon tries to find any means to stop Cheshire, but his strength and coordination are that of an infant in his current state. When they reach the kitchen, the four women inside scream and curse and throw pots before they flee. Cheshire can hear the reverberating gong from the ones which find their mark on the Gryphon's skull. He puppets the Gryphon through the castle, toppling vases and pulling paintings from their nails, until they turn the last corner in the waypoint and head towards March.

"Who the fuck?" she whispers as they approach, drawing her sword.

Cheshire squirms his head under the Gryphon's arm and out of his coat, coughing up the putrid air from his lungs.

"Fuck. What have you done?" she asks. "Wait, is this?"

Cheshire cannot bring himself to smile. He kicks the Gryphon through the door with both feet and sprints down the hallway without a word, leaving a bewildered March behind to help Jonathan put the pieces together. He turns a corner and ducks behind a heavy purple tapestry to hide from five soldiers who run past with a servant girl at their heels.

He reaches the waypoint and races down a familiar hallway with paintings of the different regions in Wonderland down its length. Mirus, The Wastes, the Warrens, the Wetlands, the Winds, and finally the Wrecks. He cannot help but stare at the painting of the Wrecks, its black shores, gray waters, dark mountains and sea stacks, low clouds, barren trees, and the skeletal remains of hundreds of ships.

His mother lies somewhere out in that forlorn, isolated place. Though just paint and canvas, the cold and desolation of the painting reaches out and grips Cheshire by the neck, choking him. He grunts short and choppy breaths through his teeth, clutches at his chest and throat, and stumbles away to free himself.

At the dead end of this hallway, a large and unremarkable bookcase sits forgotten. He remembers it taller. The books and edges of the shelves are clean for appearances, but cobwebs fill the spaces far to the back between pages and wood. He runs his fingers across the spines until he finds *Obelisks of the Ancient World* and pushes it back into the bookshelf until he hears a click. On a different shelf, he finds *Prayers of the Old Ways* and pushes it back as well. Click. *Everwood: A History* on the bottom shelf. Click. And finally, the sequence ends with *Nomadic Tribes of the Outlands*. Click. The final tumbler falls into place and the castle breathes a sigh of relief from behind the bookcase.

He presses his head flush against the wall and feels cold air blast against his face. The bookcase is heavy and has not moved since Cheshire last opened it, but he gathers the last of his strength to swing it open from the wall and step in without hesitation. He pulls the bookcase closed, and the locking mechanism catches, and the tumblers reset.

The castle and the city belong to him now, no matter what the Duchess does. The emptiness inside him fills with the all-consuming flood of grief and pain. He feels it in his chest and throat, ready to suffocate him. His stomach convulses and his face strains to hold it at bay, but the tears pour from his eyes as he weeps, loud and uncontrollable. Spit hangs from his mouth, unable to close it as he wails. Someone may hear him, but he does not care anymore.

The thought of never again seeing his mother's face, her gentle smile and radiant purple eyes, and the lullaby she sang to him every night, which brought him comfort for so long, now tears his immortal soul in two. He fears without the hope of one day finding her, the image of her face will fade from his memory. He collapses to the floor, his stomach still spasming and his cheek pressed to the cold stones.

Cheshire does not have the energy or will to move anymore, but the tears still flow from his eyes. "Would not. Could not. Would not. Could not. Could not join the dance," he whispers with his last few breaths of consciousness.

CHAPTER 34

JONATHAN

Jonathan continues to follow the conversation as if it were a shuttlecock, lobbed back and forth between the players seated at the table. Weiss suggests Mary Anne stay within the confines of the castle, and not even venture out to the castle grounds for her own safety. The Red Knight asks to call in soldiers from their patrols around the Queendom and enlist new recruits from nearby farmsteads to bolster their numbers. But the Duchess returns swift rebuttals to both ideas, not wanting to cower from the likes of Lysander and Uriah. It's clear from their intentional twitches, pointed inflections, and throwing their words at each other like daggers, trust is in short supply. And as long as there is no consensus, no one wins this game.

He cannot help but let their conversation fall to a drone as his hands explore the sides of his chair. Twenty-one nails line the perimeter of his seat, and from what he can see on the Red

Knight's chair next to him, twenty more up each side and pointed top, which means there are six thousand four hundred in the room, assuming none are missing.

Suddenly, the door to the chamber bursts open and a giant sloven of a man, smelling of human excrement, vomit, and wine, lurches in and doubles over on the table between Jonathan and the Duchess. Mary Anne and Weiss dart behind their chairs to shield themselves. The Duchess recoils, startled but curious. The Red Knight jumps to his feet and stumbles backwards to the wall. His chair falls to the floor with a loud bang.

Besides his initial shock, Jonathan stays in his seat and turns to lock eyes with March at the doorway.

She tilts her head and widens her eyes. "Cheshire," they say.

He's in the castle, Jonathan thinks. *Was he right outside the door? Rash. Stupid. What game is he playing?*

Sweat races down the Red Knight's face, jaw trembling, and he pulls at his breast plate and underlying chainmail to give his neck room to catch his breath.

Jonathan reads the blank expression on the Red Knight's face plainly. A secret he wanted to remain hidden has been laid bare before his eyes and he cannot conceal his guilt and shock. Jonathan looks back to the unconscious man lying on the table and reaches out for the tangled mass of hair to look upon his face.

"Move away from him!" screams the Red Knight, drawing his sword.

"What is the meaning of this?" The Duchess rises and pulls Mary Anne close, backing away from the table.

"This man is a prisoner." The Red Knight tries to collect himself. "A murderer. Rapist. He must have escaped from the dungeon. I'll put an end to him right now." He swings his sword high overhead, ready to bring it down on the man's neck.

Jonathan turns back to March and squints. *Cheshire? Are you sure?* his eyes ask before he makes a costly mistake. She nods, quick and small to go unseen by the others. Although reckless, Cheshire's actions are never arbitrary. There is design here. He pulled this man from the depths beneath the castle and brought him all the way here for a purpose, and Jonathan will see it through.

"Wait," he says, but the Red Knight's strike speeds towards its target. Jonathan unsheathes his sword and swings up in a mighty arch to bat away the Red Knight's killing blow with a bitter clang.

The whites of the Red Knight's eyes fill with red pulsing veins, and his face contorts with frenzy as he turns his murderous rage to strike at Jonathan. But before he can lift his sword again, March descends upon him, two swords drawn. The cramped space between the chairs and wall hinders his wide swings, but March dances around him and deflects every strike he attempts, slicing at every exposed space between his armor and backing him to the far side of the room.

"Answers, now," the Duchess shouts over the piercing metal strikes in the narrow room.

March disarms the Red Knight with a harsh flourish and holds him against the wall with the point of her sword pressed into his cheek, dangerously close to his eye socket.

Jonathan pulls the man back into a chair and pulls the

crusted hair from his face to discover who the Red Knight does not want them to see, and who Cheshire brought to the table. One of his cheeks and eyes is badly swollen with fresh blood upon it. But as Jonathan studies the crusted face further, distinct features take shape. "Nine Hells. This is the Gryphon. Greatest general in Wonderland's history."

"Impossible." The Red Knight tries his best to push past March, but her sword digs into his flesh. "He died years ago. I assure you, this is a dangerous criminal who escaped, made his way into the castle and must die before he can do any more harm."

"Nothing is impossible," whispers Mary Anne.

"Quite right, my dear." The Duchess steps away from Mary Anne and stands at the head of the table. "Enough of this," she commands. But March stands resolute, blood trickling down the Red Knight's face.

"March," Jonathan says in a gentle tone, and she immediately backs to Jonathan's side, returning her swords to their scabbards.

Weiss fumbles his way around the table to the Gryphon, grabbing the back of each chair to steady himself. He dares not dirty his white gloves and pulls his closed fan from a pocket in his robes and uses it to flick the hairs from in front of the Gryphon's face. "It's him," he says. "Irrefutably."

"The Gryphon is dead." The Red Knight seethes.

"Presumed dead," says Weiss, suspiciously. "After countless man hunts across the entire country, no one ever recovered his body. And then you campaigned to become his replacement."

Weiss taps his fan against his lips, but spits daintily, remembering he used it on the Gryphon's hair.

"You knew." The Duchess glares at the Red Knight. "Our greatest champion, missing for years. You knew where he was."

Jonathan can see the muscles in his neck and upper lip twitch. The more the Red Knight tries to hide his guilt, the worse his condition. "You were the one who locked him away."

"You have seconds to explain your actions before I have you thrown into a cell of your own." The Duchess brings her words down on the Red Knight like a hammer on a smith's anvil. "Why?"

"Have *I* not served you faithfully and without question? My every waking moment consumed with the safety of Mirus and its people." The corners of the Red Knight's mouth foams as he shouts, veins bulging in his neck and temples. "I have defended this castle, slaughtered all who would threaten this city. And this is how you repay my loyalty?"

"All?" the Duchess sneers. "Don't take me for a fool. In Briarwell, you presented a bloody sword to me with not a drop of sweat on your brow, to take credit for work your hands have never seen, while Carter and Lady Audrianna stood before me covered in ash and blood, and the perspiration of fighting to keep themselves alive. And this is not the first time I've overlooked your arrogance and presumption I'm less intelligent than you. And now in our home, two factions move against us as we speak to undermine everything I have worked to maintain without a queen on the throne." The Duchess hears the roar in her voice, takes a deep breath, and continues.

The clatter of armor grows louder from the hall, and soon

five soldiers file into the room, hands poised on the hilts of their swords, while four more wait in the hall.

"Soldiers," the Duchess commands, pointing to the Red Knight with a shaking fist, "remove this man from my sight. Know he is stripped of all rank, title, and land for being a traitor most foul to the Queendom. Escort this man off the castle grounds immediately and place him in the hanging cells until I command his release, which will be for his confession and execution. Should he try to escape, kill him on the spot."

Jonathan and March step aside for the soldiers to surround the Red Knight. His demeanor shifts, calms, as the soldiers approach. Jonathan looks to the slightest motion of March's eyes, for they see more than anyone here, and she watches every minuscule movement of the soldiers. She slowly tightens her grip on her swords.

"Confession *and* execution," the Red Knight says, as the soldiers lead him to the door. "True to form, you've given me no options."

March's right foot slides back to widen her stance. Her eyes tick from soldier to soldier.

"You've given *me* no option." The Duchess slams her hands on the table. "You endangered the entire realm and hid away the Queendom's most loyal protector. He is invaluable to Mirus. We walk precariously upon the edge of a blade. One misstep to the left and we fall prey to Lysander and Uriah, and their supporters. A misstep to the right and the zealots will overrun us like an avalanche against a pebble. Your incompetence let this happen. They are at our doorstep and *you* knew nothing about it."

The horrible realization comes to the forefront of Jonathan's mind. *Or perhaps he did.*

"Someone has to hold the blade you speak of," says the Red Knight in an ominous, low whisper. "All this time, you believed it was you. But it's the people who determine which way the blade turns. Stupid woman. Your governance and the reign of any woman who will seat herself higher than the blood of Wonderland will soon come to an end."

"How dare you spew that vile doctrine to me?" The Duchess stutters in disbelief. "Execute him at once," she orders the soldiers.

March's fingers break the seals between cross guard and scabbard. In her mind, she asked the question everyone else ignored. Why are there soldiers here and not the Castle Guard? Her eyes snap to Jonathan and shout, *Look at their faces!*

"Change of plans, men," the Red Knight says.

The soldier to the left of the Red Knight bears a scar on his right cheek visible through the slit in his helmet. The soldier to the left meets Jonathan's stare with one good pale green eye and one dead with a milky film.

March recognized them in an instant from Briarwell. Jonathan should have noticed them the moment they entered the room. These are the two men who met him and Mary Anne in the Rookwood, who took her hair and gave it to Lysander and Uriah. The hair they flaunted in the market. These two have always worked for them, and whether they be proper soldiers or not, Lysander and Uriah have a foothold not just in the capital, but in the castle.

"Kill them all." The Red Knight takes a dagger from his belt and stabs it into the face of the young soldier directly behind him, killing him instantly. Then he pushes past Jonathan and March and out of the room with both of Lysander and Uriah's men at his side to shield him. The remaining six soldiers block their escape and pull their swords, as if all went according to plan.

The two soldiers already in the room attack wildly, but they find the small space between the wall and table limits their movements. March pulls a chair out from the table with her foot and Jonathan thrust kicks it into the two remaining soldiers. They try to knock it out of the way with their swords, but the chair is too large and heavy, and the wood too old to be cut. March runs up the chair's back and topples both soldiers beneath its weight. And as they fall, she plunges a sword through each of their visors with such pinpoint accuracy, her blades never hit the metal of their helmets. And with a quick yank downward, she splits their heads. Blood pumps from their wounds in waves through their gorgets as they choke on their blood and gurgle their last breaths.

Jonathan turns his sword reverse grip in his left hand with the flat part of the blade down his forearm as an improvised shield for their strikes to slide off. He steps between the four soldiers to cancel the use of any broad attacks in close quarters, and blocks their attempt to run him through. They learn their swords are useless and resort to pummeling Jonathan with blows to the ribs, abdomen and back. He guards his face and drops to one knee, cocks his shoulder back, and swings for the inner thigh of one soldier. His leg pops out of socket from the power behind Jonathan's blow, and he crumples to the floor howling in agony. Jonathan stabs his sword into the soldier's helmet and pushes up to get back to his feet.

March jumps on top of the table to clash with the remaining soldier blocking the door.

Two of the soldiers move for Mary Anne hiding with the Duchess in the corner of the room. Jonathan charges one, palms his helmet, and shoves him against the wall with a loud dull gong. The soldier slides to the floor disoriented, with a large dent in his helmet. He pulls it from his head, blood trickling from his temple and ear.

March dances around her opponent's strikes intended to cleave her legs. She spears one of her swords into the table in time for the knight's swing to clang off of it. He spins in order to strike from the opposite side, but March sinks her second sword into the table, blocking the soldier's attack. With her hands free, and the soldier's back to her, she pulls a dagger from her belt and plunges the blade down through the break between corset and helmet, severing his spine.

The last soldier on his feet pushes past the Duchess and grabs Mary Anne with his free arm. While he is focused on Mary Anne, Jonathan slaps the end of the soldier's blade toward the ground and drives his knee into his wrist, knocking the sword from his hand, then pulls his helmet from his head. The other soldier behind Jonathan gets to his feet and grabs his shoulders.

Jonathan flips the iron helmet in hand and lets it fall onto his closed right fist. He spins and with his left arm, knocks the soldier's hands away, freeing himself. And with his right hand wearing the helmet like an iron glove, he swings and punches with the full weight of his body. Without his own helmet for protection, the soldier dies instantly of a shattered skull. The structure of his face crumples and distorts between the helmet and the unforgiving stone wall.

The final soldier recovers his sword and swings it overhead, ready to bring it down on Jonathan's neck. At the apex of his strike, March flings a dagger across the room and embeds it in his skull—the handle sticking out of his cheek and the sharp, bloody point jutting out behind his temple. Before he falls, she pulls her blades free of the table and runs from the chamber to give chase to the Red Knight and two others.

Mary Anne stands with the Duchess farther down the room at a safer distance. She nods to Jonathan to tell him she is unharmed.

After a drawn-out awkward lull, the intensity in the chamber fades and Weiss breaks the silence. "Well done," says Weiss, cowering in the far corner of the room. "But we cannot interrogate dead men."

"There's no need," says Jonathan. "The two who absconded with the Red Knight are Lysander and Uriah's men. They've followed us since Rookridge."

The Duchess exhales through her nose and composes herself. "Chamberlain, send word to the Castle Guard. No soldiers are to set foot within the castle walls until we can discover who is still loyal to us, if any."

"Of course." He stutters and cannot leave the chamber fast enough, walking the long way around the table to avoid the blood and Jonathan.

"Do we have yet another obstacle in our path?" asks Mary

Anne, defeat growing in her voice. "If all the soldiers are loyal to the Red Knight, then they could abandon the city and leave us defenseless, or turn on us and kill us all."

"Not all of them." Jonathan slides his sword back into his scabbard and removes the dagger embedded in the skull of the innocent, dead soldier. "This unfortunate man must have tagged along out of a sense of duty. If he were aligned with them, he wouldn't be dead. So he's proof that there are still some loyal to the Queendom. Hopefully, he's not the last."

"But there's no way of knowing who we can trust," says Mary Anne.

Jonathan looks back to the Gryphon slumped on the table and remembers the tales his father would tell him in his adolescence of the Gryphon's acts of heroism during the War of the Realm. Men and women from across the nation rallied to him, fifty-two thousand strong, to fight against the king's tyrannical rule. He trained the armies with honor and a kind hand to protect the Queendom and her queen. Surely, he can do it again.

"There is one option." Jonathan returns and sits in his chair next to the Gryphon. "Sir? I'm not sure what to say or ask. As a young boy, I heard stories of the bravery, the adventures, and the loyalty of the Gryphon."

"That is history." The Duchess walks to the opposite side of the table, with Mary Anne in tow.

"Our circle of allies shrinks," says Jonathan. "And it is history only because the Red Knight made it so. If there is any trace of the legend we all know left in him, then why not add him to our numbers? And perhaps the return of the Gryphon will reinforce the allegiance of the soldiers who remain loyal and could sway others back to our side." Jonathan sits next to the Gryphon cautiously, hoping his theory will bear fruit. "I know you have been mistreated, wrongly imprisoned, and forgotten by the country you dedicated your life to, but could you still find it in your noble heart to help us in our time of need?" He hopes the Gryphon can hear his words, not just for Mary Anne's sake, but for his own.

A crowd of servants stands at the door, listening and whispering questions to each other about the Gryphon.

"My loyalty and life remain with the crown," the Gryphon wheezes.

"Wise counsel." The Duchess sighs. "At least something has gone right this day." She snaps at the servants at the door. "Make the preparations. A long bath. Clean chamber in the castle. Fetch a healer we can trust and take his armor off display and shine it anew. Oh, and bring buckets of water to remove the blood of these traitors and dispose of their bodies." She dismisses them, and they curtsy and run off to their duties.

March returns to the room, chest heaving and a vexed expression darkening her face. A simple shake of her head, if not her just her presence, is enough to tell Jonathan they escaped. "They fled, through the main doors, into the bailey, and out into the city. No other castle guards thought anything amiss until I arrived. They're gone."

"They had no reason to expect foul play. We hope," says Jonathan. "Madam, how closely did the Red Knight work with the Castle Guard?" he asks the Duchess.

"He didn't," she says, with a hint of relief in her voice. "The

Guard and soldiers have always kept separate ranks. There may be some crossover, but I doubt it. The Red Knight saw the Guard beneath him. No glory staying within walls." She takes Mary Anne by the hand. "I'm sorry, my dear. I'm sorry you had to witness these unspeakable actions."

"I'm sorry as well," says Jonathan. From the blank look on Mary Anne's face, Jonathan can tell, though shocked, she has quickly grown accustomed to death happening in her presence.

"Will you and Lady Audrianna escort Mary Anne back to her room?" the Duchess asks Jonathan. "I'll also have a chamber made up for you two as well."

"We can't," says Jonathan.

"You most certainly will. That was not a request," says the Duchess. "Do you believe it safe outside these walls now?"

"Yes," says Jonathan. "But we have a friend in the city. It won't be safe for her either."

"The small one with the wheeled monstrosity? I'll send for her immediately." The Duchess pats Mary Anne's hand before releasing it. "Not to be insensitive, Mary Anne, but whatever holds you back, I suggest you find a way to overcome it. Perhaps your advisor can offer some aid in this regard."

As they walk up the winding stairs to their rooms, Jonathan follows a step behind Mary Anne, and March a few steps behind him, all in pensive silence. Even from behind, he can tell by Mary Anne's posture that the Duchess's words affected her. This explains her shift in demeanor in the Row yesterday. At first, he thought news from the Duchess or Weiss dimmed her resolve, but something internal, personal, holds her back.

"It now seems I must catch up," he says when they reach the

eleventh floor. "If I may ask. What the Duchess mentioned earlier. Does something trouble you?"

Mary Anne keeps her stride and waits until they climb two more floors before answering. "I am not ready to speak of it just yet. And that's the problem. It is something I must come to terms with and I know I can't." She stops on the thirteenth floor and waves to a fancily dressed servant girl, her handmaiden perhaps, waiting for her down the hall. The muscles of Mary Anne's face tighten, and she inhales in a long breath to hold back her tears. "I'm sorry. Good night," she says and walks to meet her handmaiden.

Jonathan watches until she disappears into the chamber door. Her handmaiden walks closer and opens the door of the room next to Mary Anne for Jonathan and March. He looks to March to follow, but she descends the stairs instead.

"Where are you off to at this hour?"

"To conduct my own search of the castle for any stray soldier lying in wait. If I have to sleep in this forsaken place, I will do so peacefully, damn it. As peacefully as possible. I'll start here and work my way down."

"I'll meet you at the bottom then."

She kisses him, and they part ways. March down the corridor with their rooms, and Jonathan down the stairs. An anxious quiet fills the castle as dusk approaches, leaving Jonathan with his thoughts, which he does not want to face alone. Instead, he focuses on the soft click his boots make on every stair and adjusts his steps to match the ticking of his timepiece, all the way to the ground floor and out the front doors.

Outside, he sits halfway down on the castle steps and feels the bruises forming on his ribs and back. He pulls his flask from his coat and swallows a mouthful. He hisses inward through his teeth for the air to ease the burning sensation.

The sunset casts an ombre of orange, pink, purple, and blue across thin clouds blanketing the evening sky, more beautiful than words. It is the first time since his arrival Jonathan looks above the buildings and walls of Mirus and sees a sky he would see above the Hollow. He takes comfort knowing this sky, these colors, stretch across the land and shine down on his table. Jonathan imagines the porcelain and metal tea services sparkle and reflect the multitude of colors, creating a kaleidoscope of beauty and wonder. He watches the sky until the clouds disappear and night overtakes the heavens. Muted stars pepper the sky, not as clear or bright as the view from the Hollow.

Once the torches of the guards are lit, he checks on Dormy in the bailey. It did not thrill her to leave the Row, nor were the guards thrilled when they had to search her wagon again before finagling it through the gates. But at least she is safe within the castle walls. Jonathan peeks through the rear door of the wagon and discovers Dormy seated on the floor and leaning against several stacks of books, chin against her chest, snoring in a deep sleep. He carefully lifts her over his shoulder and climbs the ladder to the upper compartment.

She has every odd and end in her wagon, but as long as Jonathan has known her, she has had nothing even resembling a bed. He pulls a few sacks of flour close together with his foot, covers it with a folded piece of canvas from a nearby shelf, and lays her down. She falls back harder than Jonathan expected, but she remains asleep, still snoring, dead to the world.

As he leaves the wagon, he cannot help himself and counts the torches along the top of the castle's outer wall. Sixty castle guards stand vigilant along the wall's curve, another fifty wait around the bailey, and no doubt there are at least another hundred or more around the perimeter of the castle's gardens. The men on the ground sit against the wall, heads in their hands, or held low. Others shift nervously, their armor scraping in the quiet night air. They all, along with Jonathan, wonder how many Mirusian soldiers have aligned with the Red Knight, and by association, Lysander and Uriah.

Jonathan approaches a pair far to his left, tossing pebbles across the cobblestones, playing a simple game of distance to distract themselves from their worry.

"Hello, gentlemen." He picks up four oblong pebbles from between the gaps of the cobblestones, not part of their game. "Beautiful night. The moon is full and the breeze robust and refreshing."

The guards remain stoic, if not a little annoyed at Jonathan's attempt at conversation.

"May I join?" he asks, to which the guards shrug indifferently. He turns one of his pebbles between his forefinger and thumb while keeping the rest cupped in his palm. After the two guards have their turn, he skips his pebbles, enjoying the rhythmic clacks against the large cobblestones. They continue to play in silence, and Jonathan ensures his rocks always land in the center of the cluster spread across the ground the guards had before he arrived. Never farther, never closer.

"I take it Weiss told you all the tragic events with the Red Knight earlier," says Jonathan, risking conversation again.

"What do you think we're all here for?" the mustached guard says, skipping the next stone in his hand. "We got the order and came to the castle, not knowing if we should expect a battle or not."

"Left my wife at dinner," the other says. "I love her rabbit and cabbage. Would have fucked into the night too. But instead, I'm here."

"I am sorry," says Jonathan. "We're all on edge this evening and must make the most of it, I suppose. Did Weiss also mention the Gryphon's return?"

The pair stop their game and remove their helmets. "That's a right disrespectful thing to speak of," the mustached guard says. "You mean someone finally found his body?"

"Yes, but very much alive. He's here in the castle."

The guards stare dubiously, dumbfounded, unable to decide whether to brand Jonathan a liar or believe him.

"What's he going on about," another guard whispers loudly from the wall.

"He has the nerve to come out here and say the Gryphon's returned, alive, and here inside the castle," the smooth-faced guard says. "We should knock some sense into him for—"

"Is that why one of the castle girls ran for the physician earlier?" the guard on the wall asks.

"Yes," Jonathan replies. "It will take him time to heal, but he will soon join your ranks and hopefully be able to increase it tenfold."

Without another word to him, the two guards leave their

game and walk to others sitting around the bailey, and the one atop the wall runs to the next in line. Their chain of whispers spreads faster than dry kindling and ignites a spark of hope for the first time in many years. Word will spread into the city by daybreak, to the citizens of Mirus, and hopefully reach the ears of the soldiers loyal to the crown. Rumors are not much, but they will erode at whatever plans Lysander and Uriah have until the Gryphon is well enough to become flesh from whisper once more.

Jonathan turns to find March, finished with her search, leaning against the wide pillars framing the main door to the castle. He climbs the steps to meet her, puts his arms over her shoulders while hers wrap around his waist, and they begin the walk back up to their room. Without a word, Jonathan knows she is not satisfied with the results of her search, but as he is about to ask, they both hear the distinct sound of sobbing.

CHAPTER 35

MARY ANNE

Inside her room, Mary Anne stares out the arched windows into the fading evening light, and rocks back and forth as Grace unties the corset strings of her dress from behind. She should have said something to Jonathan, but she continues to keep him at arm's length. She does not want to disappoint him, like so many others she has in her past. She does not resist as Grace unties her boots and lowers her dress and long chemise to the ground for her to step out of. Nor does she cover herself while Grace selects a white silk robe from the wardrobe on the other side of the room and slides it up her arms. Mary Anne wraps it closed and ties the belt around her waist.

Her thoughts drift out of the window to the city below. Somewhere in the shadows and torchlight, her adversaries sleep, or plot her demise. Lysander. Uriah. The Red Knight. A cult of fanatics she has not yet fully given credence to. She met these enemies in her first few days in Wonderland, without provocation or cause, and they will not relent in their quests to kidnap and kill. That is, while she remains.

"Grace," she says. "Do you know the way to the throne room doors?"

Grace turns, with Mary Anne's dress and chemise in her hand, surprised at the question, and lays the bundle down on the table against the wall, careful not to disturb the lace tablecloth or candelabras. Her fingers fidget in front of her, as if wanting to speak for lips she keeps pressed. But she clasps her hands together and nods slightly.

"Take me there," says Mary Anne. "Please."

Grace nods again, hesitantly, and then opens the door for Mary Anne.

Mary Anne follows and sears the path into her memory. So many hallways look similar, but she recites the path in her head again and again until they reach the hallway where she first sat with the Duchess. Grace waits at the end of the hall, where Mary Anne almost collided with Chamberlain Weiss.

Mary Anne approaches the doors, almost hidden in shadow. Upon her last visit, the day she arrived in Mirus, she did not take in their true scale and magnificence. Without the ambient light of the sun bouncing against the pale castle walls, the tops of the black iron doors disappear into darkness high above. They could be thirty feet tall, fifty, or even one hundred. Regardless, Mary Anne stands in front of them and has never felt more inferior in all her life.

Her hands tremble as she reaches out for the sleeping giants and places her palms on the wide iron bands running up both sides of the center seam of the door. She pushes gently at first, then harder, with more force again and again, but the doors will not move, or even make the slightest sound. Mary Anne leans against the door and pushes with all of her weight. Her heavy breaths become cries, then screams, and finally a roar and tears as she pulls away and beats against the door wildly with the underside of her fists. She does not feel the pain or the nicks in her flesh from the jagged pieces of iron. Small splotches of her blood grow upon the door and her fists with every hit, and slowly trickle towards down her arms.

Mary Anne turns and slumps to the floor, draws her knees to her chest, and holds her face in her hands, overwhelmed by the possibility she may not return home, ever. She does not want her life to be at risk or worry about what attack may come from around the next corner, even in the place she thought she would be safe. She wants to be home in Lyndhurst, not worried about her mother, and laying with Thomas, wrapped in his warm embrace, his fingers running down between her thighs as he holds her from behind. She is starved for any physical contact, making her feel even more alone in this strange world.

"Mary Anne?" Jonathan calls from the end of the hallway.

She presses her face harder into her bloody palms, wanting to disappear entirely. How could Jonathan have found her, and in this state? She wishes he would walk away, but his gallantry will not allow it.

"Seems an odd bookend to our journey to find you like this once more," he says with a light-hearted tone as he approaches. "Mary Anne, you're bleeding." He kneels next to her, rips two strips from the bottom hem of his shirt, and gently pulls her hands from her face to bandage them. The words to ask what happened are at the tip of his tongue, but the bloody stains on the door answer his question.

The sensation of his gentle touch on her skin sends a shiver up her arms. This is the first he has reached out and touched her, as if he knew the need growing inside her. She cannot bring herself to say anything to him. Not even thank you. If there were a way to reverse time to where she never came down to the door, she would. Or go back even farther and never leave her home to never wind up in Wonderland.

"Do you remember our first walk through the Rookwood?" he asks. "Not the one where you were unconscious, but the one we walked together to Rookridge. You had such a troublesome time believing in the impossible. Not that you weren't able to comprehend it, but because you weren't ready to accept it yet. It meant letting go of what you thought was real, what you believed true all of your life, what brought you comfort in the unfamiliar. But if my ears did not deceive me, you spoke those words to the Red Knight earlier."

Mary Anne can only bring herself to shrug and shake her head.

"You've seen more, experienced more," he continues, "whether it be bad or good, and allowed yourself to believe in the impossible, even if for the briefest of moments. Hold on to that fleeting thought. I can only imagine how insurmountable the journey ahead of you seems. I'm not sure I completely understand it, but regardless, listen to your own words. Nothing is impossible."

She lifts her eyes to meet his. "In order to move forward, to prove I am even worthy to be a candidate to become Queen, I must first admit I am worthless. Nothing. And it should be the simplest task. All my life I've felt I was a disappointment to my father from the beginning for wanting to be more than a laundress and someone's wife. And to my mother for not being the strong, quiet, confident woman she was." Mary Anne cannot stop the flow of tears or her words. "Inadequate as a lover to failed suitors, except one. A mediocre businesswoman at best in the eyes of the consortium, who tolerate instead of accept me despite my education. I spent every waking moment of my adolescent and adult life working to prove my worth in school, university, at work, and at home, knowing in my heart I could never meet the measure for any of them. They saw me as worthless, and deep down I know it to be true, but I cannot say I am worthless and mean it because if I do, it will prove everyone else right. Even here, I am a failure to the Duchess, and myself..." she trails off. "And a burden to you from the start. You, and March who are perfection in every sense and could not want for anything." Her last words vomit out before she can stop them.

"As your advisor," says Jonathan with a soft smile, cupping her bandaged hand in his, "I feel I'm inclined to tell you your reasoning is flawed on two points. You think your actions and others' opinions are what give you worth, which could not be further from the truth. The race you run after their approval is never ending. And for what? What have your accomplishments bred? Success, perhaps. Fortune. But from what I know of you, those are not what you seek. So why hold them in such high regard?"

Why indeed? she thinks to herself. *Father's respect. Mother's approval. The consortium's acceptance. Thomas's love.* All these have always been out of reach, no matter how fast she chases after them. And stumble after repeated stumble, she would rise again and continue without acknowledgement or reciprocation. Even Thomas's love is truly beyond her grasp. He confessed his love for Mary Anne many times, both in the throes of passion or while they sat together, before she had to return to her own home before his wife returned.

"Have you ever paused to wonder," Jonathan continues, "if the most deserving could not be those who believe they are the least deserving of all? Just a thought. If you believe you deserve the crown, how is your motivation different from Lysander and Uriah?"

"Chamberlain Weiss said I must accept that I am worthless."

"He tends to be overdramatic." Jonathan huffs. "And sharp with his words. Always has been."

"I don't know if I can," she answers honestly. "My entire life I've been racing towards a certain end, and to let go is not so easily accomplished."

"Not yet," says Jonathan. "But ask yourself, wouldn't it be nice to stop running for once?" He takes Mary Anne by both hands and helps her to her feet. "It's late. And we told the Duchess we would escort you to your room."

Mary Anne looks over Jonathan's shoulder to see March leaning against the wall an arm's length behind him, arms crossed, head down, and one foot up against the bricks. She was so enthralled with Jonathan, Mary Anne took no notice of her.

She leads their procession up the stairs, Jonathan a step behind, then March, and Grace at the rear. As they climb, Mary Anne remembers there was a second point Jonathan never mentioned. She stops and turns. "There was something else you wanted to say downstairs."

"Quite right," says Jonathan. "I wanted to say simply, perfection, as you put it, is an illusion, a mask. We, all of us, are all broken or damaged to some extent." He extends his arm back and March takes hold of it, locking their fingers. He pulls her to his side and puts his arm around her shoulder. "You just don't know our stories, yet. But each of us has suffered a significant loss or endured some tragedy in one form or another. Those things shape us, but they are not who we are."

Mary Anne looks into the genuine sparkle in his sad, twinkling eyes, and looks to March for some snide remark. But her eyes are soft and sincere as she leans her head against Jonathan's chest.

They walk up the last few floors in silence. Mary Anne feels a pressure on her shoulders. Not the weight of the herculean task ahead of her to become Queen of Wonderland, but the simple guilt of not being honest with Jonathan the first time he asked. Back then, they barely knew each other, and she would not divulge such information. However, after his sincerity, she feels the need to tell him the whole truth. If they are to share their stories, she will begin with hers.

"I ran," she says, taking the group off guard. "I'm not sure how I got into Wonderland, but I ran from my home in a frenzy. I was having an affair with my neighbor, unbeknownst to his wife. It carried on for a year and two months until we were careless and didn't draw the shades tight enough. My mother discovered us. One evening when I returned home from work, after I changed for bed, she confronted me and said if news of this infidelity spread, it would ruin his prospects and career, not to mention my family's reputation and standing. I told her I wouldn't allow it to. We had kept it a secret for more than a year and could continue to do so, being ever more cautious. She wouldn't allow it. She said if I did not end my affair that evening, she would tell his wife and put an end to it all. And I would be left to pick up the shattered pieces. My embarrassment and rage consumed me, my eyes burned, and my whole body shook. I wanted to... I don't know what I wanted. I was afraid, so I ran from my home and out of town into the forest to get away from everyone and everything. That is the last thing to happen before I arrived. As far as I can recall."

"Now she becomes interesting," March says. And Mary Anne cannot help but laugh softly.

They continue to their intended floor, and Grace ushers Jonathan and March to the door of the room next to Mary Anne's. The thought of his close proximity worries the Mary Anne who arrived from Lyndhurst. She would object and request Jonathan move to a different floor. The Mary Anne who survived the past week in Wonderland, however, is intrigued by the idea.

After the day and evening she endured, Mary Anne soaks in a hot bath, washing the blood from her hands and face, enjoying the water's sting on her body. Once relaxed and the water tepid, she dries herself, and Grace wraps her in a fresh, unbloodied robe before she leaves. Mary Anne does not know where she retires to, and would not expect an answer if she asked, but is grateful Grace will be at her side first thing in the morning.

Mary Anne sits on her bed, ready for a full night's sleep, but a sound from the small balcony of her room draws her attention. At first she thinks it is the wind, but the unmistakable sound of moaning reaches her ears. She feels the heat of her blush overtake her cheeks. It sounds like March. She creeps to the edge of the arched windows leading out to the balcony and stretches her neck past the stone columns to listen. Purely out of curiosity, or so she tells herself. A welcome shudder falls like rain down from her shoulder to her thighs when she realizes the moans belong not just to March but Jonathan as well.

The balcony to their room, illuminated by the pulsing candles within, sits across thirty feet of open air, separated by her washroom. She steps back from the windows, face flushed, and a warmth tingling through her body. She goes into the washroom to splash water on her face from the curved stone basin below the looking glass. Before her hands can break the surface, the sounds of their moans, whimpers, and panting intensify. The orange lit edge of their balcony is mere feet away through the last window of the washroom. She stands next to the window, back pressed to the wall. From their sounds, Mary Anne can imagine what takes place. The moments Jonathan's moans are muffled. The moments March falls silent and Jonathan moans louder. And when both moan in harmony with each other.

Flustered, Mary Anne catches her breath, collects herself,

and walks for the door to her bedroom. A small orange spot of light no bigger than a buttonhole on the cold blue stones next to the door catches her eye. She raises her hand to it, and the spot jumps to the back of her hand, and then her palm as she turns her wrist. She turns back to the shared wall and follows the faint beam of orange twinkling light to its source. A tiny hole in the mortar between the giant stones of the wall. Perhaps she never noticed the hole before, only bathing during the day and the room next to her unoccupied before tonight. She follows the thin beam of light across the room as a moth would be drawn to a flame, and recognizes the circular eyepiece of a spyglass inset within the stones.

She swallows and her hands tremble at the thought. She should turn around, walk back into her room, get in her bed, and sleep. But each step she takes toward the door in her mind, she takes toward the wall until the bright orange circle is inches from her face. From this distance, she can see their distorted and blurred figures writhing up and down in the curved lens. She does not know the reason why a spyglass would be concealed within the wall, and for tonight she will not question it. With her hands on the wall, she moves her right eye closer, closer until the image of Jonathan and March comes into focus, their bodies bathed in the candlelight. She cannot and will not look away. The temptation has her, and she will not fight against it.

CHAPTER 36

CHESHIRE

Not even the moon can brighten the dark hollowness Cheshire feels within. No matter what befell him during the day, the sight of her gracious crescent smile, as if she smiled solely for him, would be enough to wash him clean. This evening, she reaches her arms through the window of Jonathan and March's chamber to embrace Cheshire. But he sits, legs crossed, at the foot of their bed in the shadows out of her reach. He cannot bear to see the smile which so often reminded him of his mother's.

Well into the night, the bed jostles and Jonathan wakes behind him, inhaling the first deep breath after waking. Cheshire stays as still as a gravestone. March moans softly as she wakes and sits up with Jonathan. Their whispers seem miles away even though Cheshire can feel Jonathan's feet shift beneath the bedsheet. He and March get out of bed and kneel in front of him.

Their beautiful faces contort with grief and anguish when they look into Cheshire's vacant stare. Their expression would break his heart if it had not already shattered. Cheshire's dry eyes burn, bloodshot and swollen. The paths of his tears cut clear through the dirt on his face and down his neck. Jonathan reaches out and raises Cheshire's chin with a curved finger. The moon tries to reach Cheshire, her light glistening in the tears pooling in Jonathan's and March's eyes and running down their cheeks, as if his mother sent her tears through them.

Jonathan slowly wraps his arms around Cheshire and hugs him tightly. March sits beside Cheshire and rests her head against his, and softly strokes his arm and runs her fingers through his hair. Cheshire thought he had no tears left. But at their embrace, they begin anew, as powerful as before, down his face and onto Jonathan's neck and shoulder. Cheshire spasms as he weeps, slowly at first. Then they become quicker and consume his entire body. Jonathan and March tighten their hold on him.

It is not until the first signs of dawn creep over the horizon that Cheshire lifts his head from Jonathan's shoulder and inhales a deep breath for the first time this night. He cannot stay in this condition. Jonathan and March loosen their embrace. Cheshire exhales and shakes as he stretches the sore muscles around his eyes and jaw, and wipes the tears, snot, and drool from his face.

"You need to leave the city," he tells them in a dry, exhausted voice. "I will be responsible for what comes next, and I want you two nowhere near."

Jonathan and March do not say a word. They do not need

to. Their silence and touch are enough to tell Cheshire what he already knows. No matter what he says or how he pleads, they will never leave him. And though grateful, now he is terrified to lose them.

"Damn you. Damn you both. You are honorable and true." Cheshire looks into both their eyes. "To a fault. And that tears at my soul, because I know it will be your undoing. And I cannot bear to lose either of you. I can't. You both should have stayed hidden away in the Hollow, far from this fucking city, and these fucking people, and their fucking schemes."

"And you should be there with us. Lost to the world," says March "What has it done for any of us but drown us in pain and sorrow?"

She speaks truth. Even though none of them have shared their secrets with each other. Cheshire has always seen the pain and the lies locked away behind Jonathan and March's eyes as well as his own when he looks into a river or lake. Their hurt as much as their love unites them.

What comes next cannot be undone once Cheshire begins. The Duchess has spent a thousand years corrupting the citizens of Mirus with fear. Fear of him. Fear of the Queen Slayer. And he will exploit this fear to bring her plans to ruin. He knows Jonathan and March will stand beside him. In the end, they will watch from across the long, narrow bridge outside Mirus as the castle and the entire city burn and crumble into smoke to ash.

"We are in the thick of it now." Jonathan cannot hide the worry in his voice.

"Hardly," says March. "This adventure is only at its beginning."

Cheshire looks into their eyes with dark, unyielding resolve. "It's only the ending which concerns me."

EPILOGUE
PAT & BILL

Minor repairs to the southern buttress and the castle's main cistern took the majority of the day and night. After a long day of labors around the castle, Pat and Bill extinguish their work candles, slip their tools in their belts, and make their way out of the main gate as the moon crests overhead.

Their walk from the castle is quiet. More so than previous nights. But even through the silence, many of the citizens of Mirus are wide awake, even at this late hour. The buildings of the Crest and the Row are speckled with hints of glowing candles placed on the opposite side of their rooms. Shadowed figures block the dim light as they peer out of drawn shades or cracked shutters at the slightest noise. Pat and Bill labor throughout the castle and city daily, and no one pays them any mind, however, this night, they can feel every eye upon them, and their skin crawls, covered with a thousand tickling insects.

They do nothing different from their normal routine, but with the noticeable decline of soldiers and patrols within the city, the news regarding the defection of the Red Knight, and the warnings about the Queen Slayer's eminent return to Mirus, the citizens are restless. Unfortunate for them, Cheshire will soon make his presence known, causing all manner of chaos in the city. Pat and Bill can also sense their days and nights will be full of repairs because of him.

It has been four days since they last encountered Cheshire. His presence does not surprise them in the least. To them, it was never *if* he would return, but rather *when*. But his timing is impeccable. They cannot ignore the signs of a storm brewing, one which none may recover from. To have Cheshire, the Duchess, Jonathan and March, Lysander and Uriah, the Gryphon, and the new queen candidate, Mary Anne, in the capital all at once is unprecedented, volatile, and ominous. However, not all the players are accounted for as of yet. Word will spread of this gathering as well and they, too, will make themselves known, eventually. There are also others who Pat and Bill hope are never uncovered. Only time will tell.

As they exit the Great Gates to the city and walk down the wooden stairs to their cabin, Bill catches sight of one of the missing players. The moonlight reflects off something curved and metallic at the tree line on the opposite side of the ravine. Its shape is unmistakable—the Ace's ax.

He steps from the shadows of the canopy and stalks the cliff's edge like a wild cat on the hunt for his prey. In the pale moonlight, his glowing skin and the darkness of his hood make him appear to be a fearsome, headless apparition. But he is no specter. Far from it. And his presence promises much blood and death. He will skulk in the shadows around the perimeter of the city and wait for Cheshire to make the mistake of leaving Mirus.

Fortunately for Cheshire, he is safe within the castle walls. At least from the Ace. There are other pressing matters and threats he needs to concern himself with for the time being.

When Pat and Bill reach the cabin, they allow themselves to relax as they look at their home with grateful eyes. Every morning they leave, not knowing if they will ever see it again. It is a quaint and simple home. One large room without walls or dividers holds everything they would ever need. Their world.

Pat places their tool belts in their work area, where their tools are methodically arranged—wrenches, pliers, calipers, chisels, saws, drills, tongs, crosspeen and soft-faced hammers, scrapers, vice grips, and three dozen more assortments of tools, hand forged by her, hung from the wall on their assigned pegs.

They slip out of their clothing and Bill puts their trousers in a basin of soapy water to soak overnight and hangs their aprons in the hand-carved wardrobe next to their bed. Pat waits for him outside under the spigot, and once he joins her, she pulls the cord and wonderful cold water rains down on them both. They wipe away the dirt and sweat from each other's bodies and hair, as they do every night.

Pat steps closer to Bill and rests her head against his chest. He rests his chin on the top of her head and wraps his arms around her. They both share the same thought, as they do every night. No matter how many times they watch the dirt and filth slide down their legs and disappear through the wooden slats beneath their feet, they will never be clean, never feel clean.

Once the shivers from the night air have run up their body, and their fingers have wrinkled, Pat pulls the other cord to stop the water. Still dripping, they walk back into the cabin, his arms around her shoulder, and hers around his waist. They stop in the middle of the room and stare at the large flag hanging as a tapestry on the cliffside wall. The bottom and top are cut to fit the short height of their cabin, but the slightly jagged edge of the right bottom corner reveals the original tears. At its center, Queen Dinah's crest gazes back at them, unblinking—the infinite line creating six loops, with the chalice, the heart, the acorn, the sword, the coin, and the shield in them. Each represent the different regions of Wonderland united against King Muiread. They walk closer and the small unnoticeable drops of dried brown blood, forever fused with the woven cotton strands, become clear. At least to them. The stains serve as a reminder of how and where this twisted game began.

Bill pulls the flag to one side to reveal a wall of tally marks scratched into the wooden planks in clusters of five. He and Pat look from ceiling to floor at all the tallies, some fresh, some worn down and almost invisible within the grain, and the original mark carved deep into the wood for Queen Dinah. Perhaps if they started the tallies smaller, there would still be space, but there was no way of knowing how long this would carry on. They never meant to begin this morbid tradition, but someone needed to keep record, to keep the count.

"One hundred and thirty-eight," says Bill, running a finger

over Queen Dinah's notch. "Do you think Mary Anne will be the last?"

"No," says Pat. "She'll only be the next."

ACKNOWLEDGMENTS

An everlasting thank you to my friends who helped bring this story to life all those years ago. Dakota, Ryan, Ashton, Abigail, Julie, Lani, Karen, Kristie, and Rachel. This world would never have existed without you.

To Matte, Ismael, Seth, Stacey, Jessie, and Travis for continuing the journey with me and breathing new life into it.

And to Luke, Tommi, Brian, Bailey, Marisa, Katie, Ricardo, Jordan, Tari, and Kathy for making it real.

ABOUT THE AUTHOR

BRANDON T BERNARD is an international award winning playwright, and has been featured at the Edinburgh Fringe Festival. The works of Lewis Carroll have been his favorite literature since he was a boy, and cultivated his peculiar imagination. He has been a storyteller and artist from an early age, and worked behind the scenes in the film and theatre industry for almost twenty years. It's now time for him to tell his own stories. This is Brandon's debut novel.

instagram.com/authorBrandonTBernard
twitter.com/BrandonTBernard
facebook.com/AuthorBrandonTBernard

MAD WORLD BOOK 2

COMING 2022

For more information and exclusives,
Join the Madness at

www.BrandonTBernard.com

Printed in Great Britain
by Amazon

26318684R00256